Love and War
in California

Also by Oakley Hall

LOVE AND WAR
IN CALIFORNIA

Oakley Hall

THOMAS DUNNE BOOKS
St. Martin's Press 🛤 New York

THOMAS DUNNE BOOKS.
An imprint of St. Martin's Press.

LOVE AND WAR IN CALIFORNIA. Copyright © 2006 by Oakley Hall. All rights reserved. Printed in the United States of America. No part of this book may be used or reproduced in any manner whatsoever without written permission except in the case of brief quotations embodied in critical articles or reviews. For information, address St. Martin's Press, 175 Fifth Avenue, New York, N.Y. 10010.

www.thomasdunnebooks.com
www.stmartins.com

Design by Phil Mazzove

Two chapters from this book appeared, in different form, in *Cottonwood* and *The Santa Monica Review*.

ISBN-10: 0-312-35762-1
ISBN-13: 978-0-312-35762-7

First Edition: April 2007

10 9 8 7 6 5 4 3 2 1

This book is for Barbara.

BOOK ONE

Gates of Bone

Chapter 1

THE FIRST TIME I SAW BONNY, THE FIRST TIME I PAID AT-
tention to her, anyway, was December 8,1941. We were all in the Caff at
San Diego State College that Monday morning, listening to the terrible
news on the radio, the losses, the deaths, the Day of Infamy, the declaration
of war. The Japs! We drank coffee or Cokes and listened to the bad news.
No one knew then how much more bad news we were going to hear before some good news began to filter through.

The college junior I was then sat at a tile-topped table with some of
my fraternity brothers, including Pogey, my best friend, and Johnny Pierce,
a senior.

Barbara Bonington, his sophomore girlfriend, or "meat," as the cruder
of the brothers would put it, came to the table beside him, bobby socks and
saddle shoes, a blue sweater set with pearls around her neck, and his Alpha
Beta pin. She had thick blond hair, blue eyes, and a pretty face with a little
pad of baby fat beneath her chin, which vanished when she raised her face
to the radio on its shelf, pouring out its deep-voiced horrors. We hadn't had
the time and clues to figure how we were going to be affected by them
yet—although some guys were already blowing off about enlisting and
killing Japs. I'd been reading *A Farewell to Arms,* and I thought about what

Hemingway had said about guys dying in a war being like the stockyards in Chicago except nothing was done with the meat except to bury it, and about bullshit words like "in vain." Those poor guys at Pearl Harbor had surely died in vain.

Johnny didn't stand up, grinning as he raised a lazy hand to touch Bonny's pearl necklace, running the Add-A-Pearls through his fingers as he turned the necklace on her pretty neck. It was obvious she didn't like this from the indentations at the corners of her lips, but Johnny kept doing it as she gazed up at the radio. He thought of himself as a big-time cocksman. I considered him an asshole.

When I thought about it later, there was something in her stance of the slave girl, come to be fondled by her master, but I had liked her posture, straight-backed in her sweaters, the blunt tips of her breasts lifting the cashmere and the fraternity pin, and the dents at the corners of her lips.

Johnny Pierce enlisted in the Air Corps that week and was gone.

I was not a cocksman. When I was a junior in high school, my friend Harrison's sister beckoned me up to her room one afternoon after school, shucked off her dress, and stuck her meager bosom out at me. Under her direction I sat on the bed, and she straddled me with her hot crotch, grinning into my face with her cheeks squinched up until her eyes were slits, rocking up and down until I came. Later Harrison apologized for her; she did that because she wanted boys to like her. That summer his parents packed her off to a home in Northern California, and after that nobody had the nerve to ask Harrison about his sister.

The summer after I graduated from high school, my friend Tim Eaton set the two of us up with dates at Mission Beach with a pair of girls who were known to put out, and we ate hamburgers and bought some beer and took blankets out to the beach. I was doing pretty well on my blanket, with my hands on my date's breasts, which was what I was most interested in at the time, when she figured out from my name and something I'd said that I was Richie Daltrey's younger brother. This caused her to become hysterical because she had known Richie at San Diego High, and there was a lot of implied weighty stuff I didn't want to know about, and that was the end of that.

So I read *Sexology* magazine and jerked off. The last year or so I had gone out with different girls, most often with Martha Bailey, who was a necking fiend, but nothing below the neck, forget that. It was as though I were waiting for some big change in my life.

I danced with Bonny at the prom a week or so after Johnny Pierce enlisted, and asked her to a movie another time. I'd see her in the Caff, and we had Cokes together. She never talked about Johnny, but about Charley, her brother, who'd been flunking out of Stanford and had enlisted in the Coast Guard to beat the draft. Her criticism of her brother was a shock to me.

Then, in February, I invited her to come dancing at the Hotel del Coronado across the Bay on a Saturday night with me and my friend Bob-O, who was going off in the Marines, and his steady, Amy Perrine, who was Bonny's sorority sister. Then my brother, Richie, showed up from Pensacola. He and Liz Fletcher, to whom he was engaged, had to be included, so it was going to be a big evening.

It was going to be a lot bigger than I had bargained for.

Bonny lived in Mission Hills, not far from where I had lived before the Depression, in a white stucco and red tile Spanish-style house like my family's onetime house, but two stories. Inside were the thick, arched doorways out of my memory, the tan walls with broad plasterer's swirls. Bonny showed me into the living room, where Dr. Bonington sat by the fireplace with a kerosene heater and the shucked peels of an orange in an ashtray on the taboret beside his chair. He got up to shake my hand, a tall man with round shoulders.

"This is Payton Daltrey, Daddy," Bonny said. She wore a white formal, and she'd pinned the gardenia I'd brought into her hair.

There were bookcases on either side of the fireplace, with only four books on one shelf. I was introduced to Mrs. Bonington, who came out of the dark dining room just then. She looked like Bonny but with darker hair than Bonny's thick blond mane, and skinnier; good legs, though.

"Please sit down, Payton," she said.

"I'll just be a minute," Bonny said, and disappeared up the stairs.

When I sat down in a straight chair by the archway, Dr. and Mrs. Bonington looked at me as though I were a new gunfighter in town.

"Well, what do you think of this war we are in, Payton?" Dr. Bonington said.

I shook my head and clucked, so as not to say the wrong thing.

"I suppose you'll be in it soon."

"I'm in a midshipman's program. I go in after I graduate."

Mrs. Bonington looked as though that were a danger also. Johnny Pierce must have scared them. There was a skin-crawly silence.

"We used to live just up the street," I said, in case that would be reassuring. "On Presidio Drive."

"Oh, yes?"

"The house on the corner there."

"Oh, yes."

"And where do you live now, Payton?" Mrs. Bonington asked.

I rented a room in the cottage of an Indian barber and his redheaded wife in a part of town called Normal Heights, and I worked afternoons delivering groceries for Perry's Fine Foods, and weekends for a disreputable and aggressively lowercased weekly newspaper called *the brand,* which they'd think was Commie. They didn't need to know any of that.

"Out on Meade Street," I said.

"So you are going dancing at the Hotel del Coronado," Mrs. Bonington said. "It's very beautiful there."

"A friend of mine's leaving in the Marines tomorrow. His girlfriend's a friend of Bonny's."

That seemed to relieve them.

"My brother's coming along," I added. "He's a jg in Naval Air." Come on, Bonny!

"Our son's in the Coast Guard," Mrs. Bonington said. "He's stationed on North Island."

Bonny came downstairs in a fur coat, and we went out the door with the usual parental cautions about coming home early. The Boningtons were going sailing in the morning. Their Rhodes, the *Sun Bear,* was moored at the Yacht Club on Point Loma. Bonny's father drove a Packard. The Boningtons were richer than the Daltreys had been before my father went broke.

In Ol Paint, Bonny tucked her coat around her and sat over against the passenger door.

"I guess that's the way parents look at their daughter's date," I said, as I started down the hill.

The pale shape of her face turned toward me.

"Like a dog that might bite," I said.

"They didn't like Johnny," she said.

"Why not?"

"They didn't like it that he was two years older than I am."

"Well, I'm a year older."

"That's all right," Bonny said. She moved slightly closer on Ol Paint's seat as I headed down Coast Highway toward the Coronado ferry.

Now that we were months past Pearl Harbor, we were used to the bad headlines, and there was a phony kind of lightheartedness. There were almost as many men in uniform as civilians in the lobby of the Hotel del, the girls sleek in their formals with bright lipstick smiles. Bob-O and Amy Perrine stood by the antique openwork elevator, his arm around her. We hailed each other with raised hands and all moved toward the stairs that curved down to the ballroom on the floor below. As soon as we had located an empty table and ordered Tom Collinses and whiskey sours, the girls trooped off to the ladies' together.

"Hey!" Bob-O said.

"Off to the trenches tomorrow!"

"Shiiit!" Bob-O said.

"Amy's looking terrific."

Bob-O waggled his head on his thick football neck and leaned toward me. "She's really glad Bonny's going out with you. She said Johnny Pierce treated Bonny bad."

I didn't want to hear about it.

Just then I saw my brother Richie and Liz on the stairs, star-dusted like a couple of movie stars, Richie tall in his black uniform with the gold stripe and a half on the sleeve, his cap under his arm, Liz in a blue formal, with tan shoulders and her face turned up to Richie. She had always been Richie's San Diego girl, though he'd had a starlet girlfriend when he was at USC. Liz was a girl who hadn't even been pretty, with lips and eyes and nose that didn't fit together right, until all at once she switched on like an electric light and became beautiful. She was a dance senior at State.

Richie headed her toward us, a grin on his tan, narrow face with the heavy black eyebrows that almost met over his nose.

Richie put an arm around me and called me "Brud," and I felt a flash of that affection for my brother that even when I was mad at him would swamp the mad, so whenever I was around him I could feel myself grinning like a patted pup. Richie shook hands with Bob-O. Liz kissed me. She and I often saw each other after our nine o'clocks on campus. She smelled elegant.

Richie had always been a star, in basketball and track at San Diego High, and he could've played first or second singles on the tennis team if he'd even wanted to go out for tennis; he'd attended USC on a basketball scholarship. I had met his starlet up there once. Richie had drawn lines carefully, however, Val in LA and Liz in San Diego. When he graduated from SC he went to work in the movie industry for the director David Lubin, and he was friends with movie stars and involved in a picture or two, and then all of a sudden he threw that up and went into Naval Air. Now he was an instructor at Pensacola; no more Desmond's suits and shell cordovan loafers, no more coffin-hood Cord car.

A glass ball over the center of the dance floor sprayed specks of colored light on uniforms, sports jackets, and formals. At our table Richie went on about some flying business, using the palms of his hands as a couple of planes while the bits of colored light flicked over him. I saw that Bonny was interested, which I liked and at the same time didn't like.

"There I was, on my back at eight thousand feet," Richie said, laughing, which was some flyboy joke nobody else got.

I danced with Bonny. Her hand rested lightly on my shoulder. She moved nicely, and her flesh felt good beneath her formal. I disliked the stink of the gardenia I had given her.

"He's nice," Bonny said.

"He always was big-time."

She nodded as though she understood my situation as the younger brother of big-time. I bumped a Marine in the crush and excused myself. Richie and Liz swept by. It was as though no one could get close enough to them to bump.

"There's Errol Flynn!" Bonny said.

I steered her until we could both see the entrance to the pergola bar off the dance floor, where Flynn stood looking over the crop of San Diego girls in their formals. He wore a blue jacket with brass buttons and white trousers. His fuck-you jut-jaw and little mustache were unmistakable.

Flynn kept his yacht *Sirocco* in San Diego Bay and often came down from Hollywood. He had a Don Juan reputation, scary and charming at the same time. It was a legend that he invited girls out to the *Sirocco* and screwed them, and often his crew got sloppy seconds. Once he had invited the whole Beta Epsilon sorority from State out on the boat, and they had a fine time with no bad stuff. But there were rumors that a couple of girls had gone back later and paid the price, though no one seemed to know who those girls were.

Flynn turned to speak to a tall naval officer and a girl in a blue formal—Richie and Liz.

"Richie knows him from when he was working for a studio in Hollywood," I told Bonny. "He played tennis at Flynn's court up there."

"We saw Flynn on the *Sirocco* last weekend. He had his shirt off. I guess he's proud of his build."

Johnny Pierce had been proud of his build. He had liked to issue challenges to arm wrestle. You could hardly get out of it. He would place thumbtacks two forearm-lengths apart so when he pinned you you had a thumbtack stuck in the back of your hand. The more I got to know Bonny, the less I could understand her putting up with Johnny Pierce.

We'd probably seen the last of Richie and Liz for the evening, and that was typical. Richie had made a big deal out of joining our party at the Hotel del, and then a bigger-time party had turned up. I saw that Bob-O was pissed off, too. Everybody lost concentration craning their necks to see Richie and Liz with Flynn in the little bar, and conversation was jerky and off the point. It wasn't the first time Richie had screwed me up, nor probably the last time, either. I had had to follow his tire tracks through grammar school, junior high, and high school with more expected of me because I was Richie's brother than I could produce, or wanted to. So I would be picked first when captains were choosing up sides for softball, then disappoint by not starring as I was supposed to do. I'd gone out for football instead of basketball, which was his thing, and though I hadn't been first string at San Diego High, at least I'd thrown a pass that had won the big game with Hoover High. And I played tennis pretty well, though I'd never had the nerve to beat Richie.

I danced with Amy and Bob-O danced with Bonny, and then we switched back, and had another Tom Collins, and tried not to keep glancing toward the pergola bar where Richie and Liz had disappeared. We talked about Marine Corps boot camp, where Bob-O was headed. I had another year to go at State before I graduated and went off to Navy Mid-shipman School. My being an officer was important to my father.

A broad-shouldered guy in a checked jacket bellied up to our table, flecks of light chasing over his brown, broken-nosed face and cottony hair. He raised his arms as though including the four of us in something.

"Say, is one of you guys Richie Daltrey's brother?" He looked at me as he said it.

"I'm Wally Toland. I'm a friend of Errol's." He was a stuntman, he said. "Anybody see *They Died with Their Boots On*? Those Injun falling off their horse when the cavalry shot 'em was about half me and half Pancho Hagen. Errol's having a little weekend for bunged-up stuntmen.

"Errol and your brother and his lady have gone out to the *Sirocco* for champagne," he said to me. "I'm to ask you all to come out and join the party."

I had a glimpse of Bonny's big-eyed face, and Amy with the tip of her tongue pressed to her upper lip. "Sure," I said. For that was Richie, too; just when you thought he had let you down or forgotten about you, you'd find yourself included.

"Oh, no!" Amy whispered.

"It'll be all right," Bob-O said, maybe a little shaky. "If Richie's out there."

So before we knew it we had followed Toland out to the boat landing in the winter chill. Bonny stood close beside me in her fur coat, looking back at the Hotel del all lighted up with its high dome outlined with light-bulbs.

"Did you know it was the lights of the Hotel del at night that gave the guy that wrote the Oz books the idea for the Emerald City of Oz?" I said.

"L. Frank Baum," Bonny said.

"My father will just kill me," Amy Perrine whispered. "Amy" was short for America. Her father owned a couple of shoe repair shops.

"Yeah, maybe we got pimped," Bob-O said. We both had to pretend there was nothing scary about going out to Flynn's yacht.

A three-quarter moon threw down a freckled track on the choppy wa-ter. Somewhere out there, beyond the Bay, the broad Pacific heaved off to the distant horizons where the subs and battleships of the Japs prowled— who, since Pearl Harbor, had spread over Asia as though nothing could stop them. Only last year it had seemed that they could not even defeat the tat-tered armies of the Chinese.

Even with all the bad headlines, people were still saying the war would be over before 1942 was out. Day by day, especially at midterm time, more guys from State were disappearing from campus, as Bob-O was doing.

He offered his pack of Old Golds to the girls. A flame illuminated Amy's cheek.

"Stop that shivering!" Bob-O ordered.

"I'm just worried about Daddy," Amy whispered.

The water taxi slid up to the pier with a hoarse putting. Toland helped hand the girls onto the launch. The four of us sat knee to knee facing each other on slat benches. Bonny was probably shivering, too. The driver stood at the wheel with Toland beside him, pointing the way.

I thought about doped champagne. There was doped champagne in a *Black Mask* story I'd read. In some funny way, though, Flynn seemed like an antidote to Johnny Pierce.

The fact was that I had got myself into a kind of two-sided mental state over Bonny. On the one hand, you were supposed to be trying to get into girls' pants, but on the other, I didn't really want an involvement with that mess of hysteria and recriminations. It really did seem an unfair game as far as girls were concerned. I had gone through all the shit with Martha Bailey, playing the role of the desperate hard-on knowing she wasn't going to put out, which she never did. Which was a relief. Johnny Pierce had always thrown up a lot of implication about the tail he was getting, and though he had never mentioned Barbara Bonington by name, the fact was that she had worn his fraternity pin. She was called Bonny because there were four other Barbaras in her sorority.

I tried to work up a scene for a mystery story for *Black Mask,* private eye Jeff Dodge aboard a water taxi, with the collar of his trench coat turned up like Alan Ladd, snapping his cigaret, spinning sparks out into the black water (don't forget the smells!), stink of salt, tar, and diesel oil. Headed out to a yacht on the Bay where a beautiful redheaded woman—

We were headed for Errol Flynn's notorious *Sirocco*!

"I understand you lose your virginity just stepping aboard Flynn's boat," Bob-O said. "But you can get it back buying war bonds."

"Oh, shut up!" Amy said.

"Are you scared?" Bonny whispered in my ear.

"No."

"Will you take care of me?"

"Sure I will," I said, and she leaned against me.

11

The putting of the engine revved, then ceased as we slid alongside a long shape with the loom of masts disappearing into darkness, a leak of light past a curtained porthole, and moon gleams on polished woodwork. A figure crossed the deck with a scissoring of white trouser legs.

I sucked a deep breath to brace against my own shivering. "Tell him to come back for us in an hour," I said to Toland, who repeated the order to the driver. Bonny made an approving sound.

The band of water between us and the *Sirocco* narrowed. The deckhand reached out a hand to help us across. The taxi drifted away. Light splashed across the deck as a door was opened. Ducking under a low lintel, we passed down steps into a gleaming mahogany cabin, with chairs ranged around in it. As soon as I saw Richie lounging with his long, uniformed legs stretched out, I thought it would be all right. My brother looked at me, grin spreading on his tanned face with the black bar of eyebrows.

Flynn came forward to greet us, head ducked under the low ceiling.

"Payton's here!" Liz called out. She sat in a director's chair with a champagne glass in her hand, smiling at me, her silken ankles crossed, her dark hair piled up from the nape of her neck. She raised her bright face to Flynn as he moved past her. Liz's dark eyes reminded me of the "ox-eyed" goddess in *The Iliad*. At State she was only another dance major with good legs, but dolled up in a formal with her hair up she was beautiful.

Flynn pivoted like a swordsman helping Bonny and Amy off with their coats, repeating the names as Richie made introductions. He had a stuffed-nose British accent and a pleasant voice recognizable from his movies, and he smelled of some scented lotion. He drew a heavy green bottle from a silver bucket and wrapped it in a napkin.

Bob-O said it was nice of him to invite us out on his yacht.

"It is brave of you to come, my friends," Flynn said, easing the cork, and everyone laughed in relief.

The walls of the cabin reflected confused shards of light from the glass on the framed photographs there. I peered at one that showed Flynn bare-chested in a boxer's raised-fists stance. Others were of movie people. A photograph of Carole Lombard had a faded white blossom stuck in a corner of the frame.

Flynn poured the champagne, gimbaling right and left, putting everyone at ease with jokes and attentions. I didn't see how the champagne could have been doped. I thought about Flynn charming the crowd of Beta Eps from State.

"Here's champagne to our friends and pain to our sham friends," he said. His laughter made me grin. He aimed his glass at Liz, posed in a graceful *S* in her chair. "To Miss Fletcher, who gleams as lovely as the stone in the ring on her finger."

"Hear!" Toland said, lighting a cigarette.

Liz held up her hand to show off Richie's ring.

"And has the date been set?" Flynn wanted to know.

"Last week of June," Richie said. "Unless they ship me out first."

"Just as soon as the Senior Dance Performance is over," Liz said. She had a slight lisp, as though her Bette Davis mouth didn't work quite right. Her father was a Navy captain, a real bastard, Richie said. She was twenty-three, old for a senior, having been out of school sick for a year. She was supposed to receive an inheritance from her dead mother when she was twenty-five. Just as easy to fall in love with a rich girl, Richie had said, making a joke of it.

"Are you going to live in Pensacola?" Bonny asked, with her smile that was like opening a door on an illuminated room.

"Married Officers Quarters," Richie said, nodding.

Flynn pointed his glass again. "And here's to the fair Miss Bonington and the dark Miss Perrine. And Mr. O'Connor and the younger Mr. Daltrey."

I felt myself flush at the attention. On the wall beside me was a poem, glassed and framed:

> One ship sails east, the other west
> By the selfsame winds that blow.
> It's the set of the sails—and not the rules—
> That decides the way to go.

Then they talked about *They Died with Their Boots On*.

"I cried!" Amy said.

"They called Custer 'Old Iron-Bottom,' you know," Flynn said. "Ah, what a sore backside I had. We actors earn our pay! I've just signed to play James J. Corbett in a film. Rigorous training will be required."

Bonny asked who Corbett was.

I told her that he was called "Gentleman Jim," and he'd won the heavyweight boxing title from John L. Sullivan.

Richie squinted at me as though he'd caught me showing off.

"Bruiser versus artist," Flynn said, nodding. "It will be hard work playing Gentleman Jim, but it will be an adventure. And that is what we are here for, is it not? To make our sun run, rather than stand still, eh?"

Andrew Marvell! I thought I'd better not parade my English major or Richie would get the squints again.

Flynn turned his attention to Bob-O. "And you are off to a life of adventure in the Marine Corps, Mr. O'Connor?"

"Due at the Recruit Depot at two-oh-two tomorrow!" Bob-O said, flexing his shoulders in his glen plaid jacket. "How about you, Mr. Flynn? Does the draft board go after movie stars?"

"Does it not! Unfortunately—fortunately!—the physical examination disclosed some rather nasty spots on my lungs." Flynn stood with his head inclined under the low ceiling, one hand in his pocket, the other gripping his glass, always the center of attention.

"In all truth, this war is not an adventure in which I care to participate. Colonials have had enough of pulling Britain's chestnuts out of the fire."

"But aren't you English?" Amy asked in her small voice. She held her hands clasped together before her bosom, her shoulders in her pink formal as frail as bird wings.

"Ah, no, little one. I am Australian, a colonial, as you were once also in this great country. I'm o' Irish stock in addition, and you must know how the Irish feel about the Sassenach! I will tell you what true adventure is, my friends," he continued. "New Guinea! I worked in the goldfields there. Headhunters! Orchids! Creepers strangling trees a hundred feet high! Men were men in that place, and women stayed well away. I bought the first *Sirocco* there, transporting native labor. Someday I'll go back."

He lowered himself into a chair and set down his glass to light a cigaret. Bob-O had lit up also, and the cabin was layered with smoke. Richie looked amused, watching Flynn.

"First ran across Jack London's books in New Guinea," Flynn said. "No one reads Jack London anymore."

"I'll bet Brud has," Richie drawled. "My brother's read just about everything."

He had sounded proud of me! I said I'd read *Martin Eden*.

Flynn said to me, "That's the way to go, is it not? Off the taffrail when the voyage is over."

I explained the ending of *Martin Eden* to the others, Richie grinning.

Just then the deckhand in the white trousers came down into the cabin on squeaking rubber soles. Flynn introduced him as Pancho Hagen. Hagen nodded curtly to us and moved into the galley, where he seated himself on a stool and lit up, as though trying to conceal himself in a smoke screen. He was dark-complected, with a hard, lined face like a cigar-store Indian.

I remembered Toland saying Hagen was a stuntman, too, and Flynn their host aboard the *Sirocco*.

When Flynn went on to talk about a film project Richie had worked on with David Lubin at Fontainebleau Studios, I saw Hagen thrust his face forward as though his attention had been caught. Then it was withdrawn into the smoke and shadows again.

"I want to make films," Richie said. "Someday I'll make a film with Liz dancing."

"I'm a good dancer," Liz said in her husky voice.

"I'm sure you are, my dear," Flynn said, gazing at her with his head cocked admiringly. And I saw that Liz was aware of it.

The *Sirocco* rolled and pitched from something passing.

Flynn asked Bob-O what he intended to do after the war. Bob-O said he would go to law school and join his father's law firm. Amy wanted to be a schoolteacher. And the fair one?

Bonny said she would marry a doctor. "We'll have a boat. My family all have boats. It doesn't have to be a schooner, though," she said, to make a joke of it.

The men in the Bonington family were all doctors. Bonny's mother read novels like *The Forsyte Saga* and *The Sun Is My Undoing* and played bridge.

"Ah, a schooner is not so large a boat, my dear," Flynn said. "Especially when it is filled with lunks who have performed too many stunts without their helmets on."

Toland gave this the big laugh. Hagen lit another cigaret. Cocooned in smoke in the galley, he radiated that kind of anxiety you feel when some drunk seems primed to raise a ruckus.

Flynn raised an eyebrow at me. "Younger Brother Daltrey?"

It was queer that I had been ready for his question, and then was not ready when it came. I said I wanted to be a writer.

"A writer for your brother, the producer-to-be?"

"Well, a fiction writer." Like Raymond Chandler; I didn't say that.

Richie watched me, not quite squinting. Bonny glanced sideways at me. It was interesting that people seemed embarrassed when you said you wanted to be a writer. In fact I was already a writer, with five unpublished stories back from *Black Mask*.

Amy asked if Flynn had known Carole Lombard, pointing to the photograph with the faded flower. I saw Liz touch the flower in her own hair as she glanced at the photograph. Flynn rose to refill glasses.

"A lovely lady," he said, nodding. "The pilot lost the beam, I understand. Carrie and twenty others dead in an instant. Yours is a dangerous trade," he said to Richie.

Hagen was rocking on his stool with his shoulders hunched up around his neck.

"I had a student who ran into a gas storage tank two weeks ago," Richie said. "Killed himself and his instructor. It was just luck I wasn't his instructor that day."

"Talk about killers!" Hagen said in a sudden, growling voice that struck everyone silent.

"Please spare us your mutterings, Panch," Flynn said. "I'm afraid you are drunk."

Richie made a show of slipping his cuff to glance at his watch, and, like prayers answered, there was the slight jar of the water taxi returning.

"Does the young Martin Eden play tennis?" Flynn asked Richie.

Richie said I had a pretty good forehand if I'd just get the racket back early.

I had as good a forehand as he had.

"You are invited to visit me at Mulholland Farm!" Flynn said to me, then extended a hand in a large gesture to include everyone. "I'll give you good tennis! You'll meet my friend Jack Warner. He is always interested in young people he might turn into stars of the silver screen."

"And writers," Richie said.

Liz gazed at Flynn with a nakedness to her face that was embarrassing.

Richie helped her into her coat, shaking hands with Flynn with some dialog I didn't hear. Toland helped Amy up out of the cabin, following her and Bob-O.

In the galley, Hagen rose, shoulders hunched, dusting his hands on his trouser legs. He lurched toward Richie. "You throat-cutting studio cocksucker!" he growled, and surged inside Richie's arm, smashing Richie staggering back. Liz cried out. Then Flynn was in motion, and with a crack of sound Hagen stumbled back across the cabin floor, knocking over two chairs with a crash of glasses, to finish squatting on the floor back in the galley again, shaking his big head. Bonny caught hold of my arm as though to stop me from hitting someone. Who had promised her I'd take care of her.

"My apologies for my drunken friend," Flynn said, extending a hand to help Richie straighten. He wasn't even breathing hard. Richie's face was white as paper.

I helped Bonny up the steps and out of the cabin. Liz followed us, then Richie. I turned toward him, but he hissed, "Just forget it, Brud!" He put an arm around Liz, moving her toward the water taxi. Bonny held my arm.

Seeing my brother at a disadvantage had unstrung me with the kind of panic I remembered from when my father had announced that he had to sell the house on Presidio Drive.

When we were all aboard, the water taxi turned past the stern of the *Sirocco* toward the Emerald City lights of the Hotel del. Richie and Liz had their heads together. Bob-O offered his pack of Old Golds. No one spoke.

At the pier, Richie and Liz called out good night and good luck to Bob-O, then disappeared into the darkness, Richie's tall figure with the pale glow from a light standard kindling the white cover of his cap, Liz tucked against his arm.

Back in the ballroom, the four of us ordered another round of too-sweet drinks.

Bob-O and Amy didn't seem to have been aware of the fuss in the cabin of the *Sirocco*. After another dance set they left, mounting the stairs to the lobby in lockstep, as though they couldn't wait to be alone in Bob-O's V-8.

Bonny watched them with color in her cheeks, smiling with just her lips when I met her eyes. Maybe we were thinking the same thing. Bob-O's last night.

"Am I not supposed to ask what that was all about on *Sirocco*?" Bonny said, looking down at her hands on the table.

"I don't know what it was about."

"That scary guy! Did your brother knock him down?"

"It was Flynn." I got a laugh out and said, "I guess it should've been Richie."

Bonny nodded solemnly. "That's like my brother. He's always supposed to do the right thing."

We danced, cheek to cheek, flesh adhering to flesh in the body heat of the crowded dance floor with the flecks of colored light coursing over the uniforms and the formals and the bare skin. Bonny's body slumped against mine, sweet gardenia stink in my nostrils. She couldn't help but feel my hard-on. Maybe the pink flush on her cheeks was the feminine equivalent. From my researches in *Sexology* magazine I knew that girls had the same genital instincts as men, but with more inhibitions. Crouched in the tangled shadows of going all the way was that disaster beyond contemplation of getting pregnant. I understood all too well the female risks, all prospects destroyed in one moment of getting carried away.

"I don't want you to make me feel funny!" Martha Bailey had said in her fake frank way.

"Is that all you think about?" she had asked.

I'd already thought about Bonny coming to my hospital bed to cover me with the tent of her fair hair like Catherine Barkley in *A Farewell to Arms*.

We left after the "One O'Clock Jump." Bonny sat at a neutral remove in Ol Paint's front seat on the ferry ride back across the Bay, arms folded on her chest, while I contemplated whether to try to kiss her parked in front of her house, or before the front door, or not.

In front of her house, I didn't make a move and she didn't get out, though she sat with her back to the door and her arms still folded.

"What a funny night," she said. "It wasn't fun exactly, but it was something. That terrible stuntman guy!"

Hagen had made me wonder about Richie in Hollywood in a way I'd never wondered before. What did "throat-cutting" mean? Everybody knew that Los Angeles was a bad place, and Hollywood the worst of it.

"Payton," Bonny said, and didn't go on right away.

Then she said, "You have a job south of Broadway, don't you? That funny newspaper down there?"

"The brand," I said. Lowercase.

I couldn't see her features in the darkness under Ol Paint's top. "Do you know people down there?" she asked. "I mean, they're different people down there, aren't they? Closer to—things?"

I couldn't think what she was getting at.

"A friend of mine has to have an abortion," she said in a little burst. "I thought you might know of someone—down there."

I managed to say I'd ask around, very easy, although something swelled up in my chest to suffocate me, because sure as anything she was talking about her own self and Johnny Pierce.

So she'd had her reasons for going out with me, who had a job south of Broadway in San Diego.

"Could you find out about some doctor who does that? It's for a friend of mine."

"Sure," I said. "I'll see what I can find out."

"Thanks," she said, and opened the car door. She was hastening up the steps to the front door before I could get out to accompany her.

I waited until I saw the light come on in a second-story window, and then I started Ol Paint and drove home to my rented room in Normal Heights.

In the lighted window of the corner drugstore, as I turned into Meade Street, I could see the newspaper headlines: ROMMEL ESCAPES DESERT TRAP and MANPOWER GOAL 4 MILLION.

Chapter 2

1

NEXT MORNING, FIRST THING, I WENT TO SEE MY GRAND-
mother. She lived in a white clapboard bungalow on Albatross Street in a
neighborhood called Hillcrest, closer to downtown San Diego than Mission
Hills, smaller houses, older cars along the curbs. I parked Ol Paint and trotted up the twenty-two steps. White wooden columns supported the roof of
the little veranda, where two wicker chairs faced the street behind baskets
of ferns. It seemed to me now that I could have been happy living here
with my grandmother during my high school years if I hadn't been so intent on being the Dogfaced Boy—which was what Richie had called me
because of some long-suffering attitude of misery and loss.

Grandma Payton met me at the door, throwing up her arms in dramatic
surprise like a Chinese happy god, as though my arrival were a wonder. She
wore a shapeless flowered print dress, gray lisle stockings, and squashed-
looking bedroom slippers. With her white hair stacked into a bun and rimless glasses on her nose, she resembled a cartoon grandmother.

When I embraced her, the smell of potpourri brought a rush of emotions. She directed me to the easy chair with its antimacassars and the

scratchiness familiar to my bare elbows. She stood over me, hands clasped to her bosom, beaming. I wondered if Richie had been to see her.

"Shall I make a pot of tea, dear?"

"Great!"

She bustled into the kitchen while I sprawled in the chair with the pleasant guilt of being waited on. Over the fireplace was a murky painting of brown trees, an amber pond, and two brown and white deer, one drinking, one looking up startled. The glass-fronted bookcase was jammed with books in sets and single volumes: Kipling, Mark Twain, Richard Harding Davis, the American Winston Churchill, *Beau Geste* and *Beau Sabreur,* Alexandre Dumas, E. P. Roe, the Waverley novels.

On a card table beneath a floor lamp were my grandmother's plans for the braces that would save parachutists from breaking their legs, a neatly drawn and lettered arrangement of springs, clamps, and boots. I was ashamed of having made fun to fraternity brothers of my grandmother's contribution to the war effort.

When I left she would always tuck a dollar bill into my shirt pocket, which she referred to as "a picture of our first president"—a tip for coming by, like tips I sometimes received on my delivery route for Perry's Fine Foods. I would accept it with weak protests and guilt, for she lived on a pension.

"It was so nice seeing Richard!" she said, returning with a tray holding cups, saucers, a sugar bowl, a creamer, and a teapot. "He brought that pretty young lady with him. They only stayed a minute! It does seem, with the war, that time isn't what it used to be!"

"Don't I know it!"

"And how is Eddie?" She had always been fond of my father.

"I'm going over there later."

She poured the tea and settled into the chair facing me. Her husband had died in the Philippines, and she had sold the Payton farm in Indiana and brought my mother and Uncle Faye to San Diego, where my mother married a construction man named Edmund Daltrey.

From the stories she loved to tell, I was as familiar with the Richmond of her youth as I was with the San Diego of my own.

I took a deep breath and said, "Did girls who weren't married get pregnant in Richmond?"

She looked startled. "Why, yes, dear, of course they did."

"What did they do?"

"Why, sometimes there was a hurried wedding, and sometimes the young lady went to visit relatives in another part of the state." She gazed at me solemnly over her glasses.

"Did they have abortions?"

"Oh, dear, sometimes they would try to do that themselves, and terrible things would happen. I remember—" But she stopped herself there.

"It's a friend of mine's girlfriend," I said quickly. "I'm supposed to help find a doctor. I wonder if you could ask Dr. Bell what this girl should do."

Dr. Bell was a jaunty old fellow with yellowing white hair, a false-teeth smile, and lots of jokes. He couldn't drive anymore, so Grandma Payton would take him for rides in her chevy.

I knew I shouldn't have asked it when her face turned pink.

"I just can't do that, dear! I know he feels very strongly about the kind of doctors who do that."

"Sure. Okay. Sorry."

She sighed and said, "Faye and Ellen were so welcome when I found I was going to have them. And Ellen so much wanted you and Richard. But I don't think parents should have babies unless they are prepared to just love them."

Richie, as always, would know what to do, but I'd thought Dr. Bell might be a possibility.

Something had reminded my grandmother of her husband. "I wonder what you would have thought of Aaron, dear," she said. "He was tall, like you and Richard, but he was so impatient. Anxious to get on with things. There were so few careers for young men in those days, and he just didn't like farming. He'd want the corn to come up faster. Then the war with Spain came along, and he enlisted. Those poor boys died of diseases they know how to cure now."

"Well, you are taking care of this family's war effort," I said, gesturing toward the plans of her invention on the card table.

"I didn't tell you! An officer came to look at my braces, a Captain Jenkins, a very pleasant young man! He asked for a copy. I just sent it to him yesterday."

I gaped at her. Could the Army actually be interested? My father pulled strings to get into the Seabees while my grandmother pulled no strings at all and the Army took her invention seriously enough to ask for a copy of her plans.

"That's terrific!"

"He said they would have to be manufactured very small and light if they were to be useful."

She sipped her tea and remarked how much Liz Fletcher reminded her of my grandfather. "Her eyes are like his. Looking to see if something exciting isn't happening over *there*. He was never satisfied. There was always some wonderful thing that was going to happen if you were just over *there*."

"I've never heard you criticize him before, Grandma!" My throat thickened to recall that she had never criticized me, who must have been an impossible little shit in my dogfaced miseries.

"Well, he had responsibilities! He said we weighed him down so he couldn't make something of himself. So he went to be a soldier. He thought he would be a hero, and then everybody would pay attention."

"You think Liz is like that?"

"Richard says she wants to be a movie star."

"She's going to be rich. She doesn't need to be a movie star." But I remembered Liz's expression, aware of Errol Flynn's admiration aboard the *Sirocco*.

"I don't think being rich is what is important, dear. I think it's people paying attention to you." Her china-blue eyes blinked at me over her spectacles. "I do worry about Richard's interest in such a wealthy young lady. I don't like to see the wife holding the reins, you see."

I'd never heard her criticize Richie before, either. It was another jolt, like Hagen shouting "throat-cutting studio cocksucker" at him in the cabin of the *Sirocco*.

When I got up to leave, I told her I would mow her lawn the next time I came over.

"Oh, you're so busy, and I like to let the men who come by for a snack mow it. It makes them feel they haven't had to take a handout, you see."

"Listen, Grandma, I don't think you should be feeding those tramps. You know, they leave some mark on the house so others will know you're an easy touch."

Her lips tightened as she said, "Well, I am an easy touch! This country has been just terrible to those men. They are veterans! They served their country, but their country will not serve them!"

My grandmother was more involved with social issues than my boss at *the brand,* who liked to pat himself on the back for his sympathies and compassions.

When I went back down the steps to Ol Paint, I turned to survey the front of the house. Beneath an evergreen bush at the corner of the steep lawn were two bricks, one stacked crosswise on top of the other. I separated them before I got in the car to head for Mission Beach for lunch with my father, my stepmother, and my brother.

I drove out through Mission Hills and past Bonny's house on the way. The Boningtons' Packard was in the driveway, the chrome bumper and fittings gleaming in the sun.

2

I felt the slam of the surf on Mission Beach through the soles of my shoes as I stood on the porch of my father and Weezie's beach bungalow. Framed in the window beside the door was the big console radio with the black ceramic panther prowling on top. My father spent the war listening to the news on the radio.

Stretching a little I could see Richie, in faded blue trunks, sprawled in the wing chair with his bare ankles crossed. Our father was out of sight except for a spiral of gray smoke.

I could feel resonances of the past like the vibrations of the surf on the sand.

I remembered Richie in this same room years ago, before Weezie and our father got married. Our father had moved in with her, and Richie usually stayed with them when he came down from LA. This time Weezie and our father had gone off somewhere, and Richie and I were sitting on the couch in our swimming trunks, Richie wearing his USC jock T-shirt, humming along with the music from the radio. I was fourteen.

I told Richie I was thinking of running away.

That got his attention. "What's the matter, Brud?"

"Weezie doesn't like me much," I said.

"She's been damned good to Dad!"

"Well, she can't stand me! And Mom's got this cruddy little place in Logan Heights."

Once when I'd heard late-night sounds from the living room where my mother was entertaining Bill Hutchinson, who was a big shot in the Teamsters' Union, I sneaked into the kitchenette to crouch under the breakfast table and peer into the darkness. What I could see was my mother's electric pale flesh with Mr. Hutchinson's big belly looming over her, the motion, and her leg stretched up as though she were trying to touch the ceiling with her toes. I could hear her murmurs, as though she were quietly drowning.

I couldn't tell Richie that, because he took our father's side against our mother anyway. By being up at SC on a basketball scholarship, Richie had steered clear of the wreck the other Daltreys were mashed into.

"Mom ought to get a bigger place," Richie said.

"She hasn't got any money at all! Dad doesn't give her anything!"

"He hasn't got anything to give! You know that."

"Well, it's the cruds," I said. I scrubbed my hand over my eyes. "I just feel like I'm in the way all the time!" I could feel the tears dribbling from my chin.

"Let's give this some practical thought," my brother said. His black hair was cropped short, and his face was brown and solemn. "How about coming up to LA to stay with me?"

LA!

"Maybe Jack and I'll take an apartment up there instead of staying in the frat house. You can stay with us! Deliver papers or something. We'll have a real bachelor place."

"You can't do that," I said.

"Why not?" Richie put an arm around me, and it was as though some big warm animal were turning and stretching inside my chest.

"We'll do it! The Daltrey boys!"

Richie kept telling me we'd do it while I cried. I knew he didn't mean it, but that didn't matter. At least my brother cared about me when everybody else was too busy and worried and screwed up to bother.

I rapped and opened the front door. My father rose to greet me, with his anxious, lined face, a cigaret burning between his fingers, which were yellow from smoking. He was inches shorter than Richie, who didn't get out of the wing chair. Weezie appeared in an apron and a blue dress. Her glasses caused her brown eyes to enlarge spookily when she looked straight at you.

The routine was gone through: "Well, son . . . , How are you, Dad . . . , Hi, Weezie . . . ," with Richie watching, grinning, scratching his shoulder. Our father indicated the sofa, and I sat down, leaning uncomfortably forward. Weezie joined me at a one-cushion remove, bringing her bag of yarn and big needles like bayonets. She was knitting a gray sweater for our father.

Richie settled back into the best chair, stretching with his hands reached above his head. He was at ease here, where he'd always been welcome, while I had to be careful not to act like a jerk because of old wrongs.

"Now they're going to require a license to live on the coast," our father said, who lived only a hundred feet from the ocean. It must have been the continuation of a conversation he'd been having with Richie. "I suppose it's necessary. Aimed at enemy aliens. I see you are going to have to register for the draft, son," he went on, nodding to me. "Twenty to forty-four now. Just misses me!"

"You don't have to register if you're in an officer program."

He cocked his head judiciously. His whole stance was one of slants: the tilt of his head; his nose, broken in some construction accident, angling to one side; his habitual posture, one hand in his pocket and a lowered shoulder in an acceptance not so much of defeat as of more bad news received.

Tully, my boss at *the brand,* who had been one of my mother's boyfriends, said my father had been destroyed by the capitalist boom-and-bust economy, by which he meant the Great Depression.

I remembered the terrible months after my father lost his job: the schemes; the new hopes; the dashed hopes; the garage my father and a friend named Jake Katz had bought, which had gone broke; the quarrels with my mother; the announcement that the house would have to be sold. My father had moved in with Weezie, who had a job with the school district.

Now my father was hoping to get a commission in the Seabees.

"Your responsibility to the Navy is to make passing grades and maintain normal progress toward your degree, as I understand it," he said to me.

"Well, I've been thinking about enlisting,' I said. Why had I said that? I didn't mean that! Jerk!

"Oh, my goodness, Payton!" Weezie exclaimed, looking over at me with her eyes swimming behind her glasses.

"You're not serious about that, son?"

"I guess it's better for a writer to be an enlisted man." This was the opinion of Frank Tully, and I knew it was stupid. Why did I need to poke at my father's obsessions? Because he was always more concerned with Richie than with me?

"Where'd you get that idiot idea, Brud?" Richie drawled. His nostrils whitened as though he were trying to keep from laughing at me. "Throat-cutting studio cocksucker," Hagen had called him.

Our father lit another Lucky Strike, looking worried. "I can't urge you too strongly to get that commission, son. It's too simple to say that it is the difference between horsemen and foot soldiers, but when officers came home from France in the AEF they found positions, not jobs. They'd had experience handling men. Enlisted men came home to jobs."

Richie and I knew that our father had come home from France a lieutenant. He kept his gold bars in a decorative metal box that had squatted on his dresser in the house in Mission Hills, along with his service ribbons with their stars for battles—the Argonne and Belleau Wood. Maybe they had been chucked by now, along with the German helmet with the bullet hole in the exact center of the forehead and its acrid, medicinal smell, which had been stored in the hall closet. In Edmund Daltrey's long retreat from a position of Mission Hills affluence, so many of his possessions had been discarded or left behind.

"You went in a buck private, though, Dad," I said.

"I didn't have a college education like you and Rich. I was just a kid out of high school. Who wanted to help make the world safe for democracy." He chuckled.

I saw that he was preparing for a speech, tapping the ash from his cigaret, pushing the sleeves up on his thick, pale arms, leaning forward.

"The way this country works—every family sees its children have a better chance in the world. Everyone came over from some old country sometime, and they knew it was their duty to see their kids had a better chance than they had. Of course it's fine to be a writer," he said, head tilted at me. "It's an ability I never had. But you have to be able to make a living when times get tough! It was the people in the professions who were able to ride out the Depression."

Wasn't writing novels a profession? Didn't Raymond Chandler make a living? Didn't Hemingway? I said, "Well, Richie's got a good profession while there's a war on. And when he marries the richest girl in Point Loma he ought to be okay if times get tough."

"Go fry your head," Richie said, stretching again.

Our father was not to be deflected. "I would certainly take some courses at State that would help me in a profession like accounting, son."

He'd been impressed by an *A* in algebra in high school. Maybe I'd bragged about it, trying to make him proud of me.

Weezie glanced over at me again, with her enlarged eyes, keeping out of this father-and-son advice and evasion. She was a Jap-hater, a subject she and I had tangled on. Long before the war she had prophesied that the scrap metal shipped to Japan would be returned in the form of shells and bombs. I hated the fact that she had been right.

"I'm afraid you didn't raise your sons to be bookkeepers, Dad," Richie said, being a good guy. What did "throat-cutting" mean?

Lunch was toasted tuna sandwices, an apple-and-nut salad, and iced tea. My father got started on *the brand*.

"You mean 'that Commie rag'?" I said. Richie gave me a cool-down glance. "That's how I'm getting through college," I said. "Working there and at Perry's."

"Some people do look on it as a Commie rag," our father said, frowning with his head canted.

"It's Socialist-Labor," I said, forking up apple and walnut. Anything you had to defend too often could get you overwrought. Weezie was tight-lipped, afraid this would get out of hand. Tully had promised to let me do some writing, one of these days.

"I know some of the fellows at the post are upset about it," my father said. He belonged to an American Legion post downtown, which was bad, but he didn't attend much, which made it better.

"The Red Menace is everywhere," Richie said, straight-faced.

"This is a time when people feel especially tender about their country," our father went on. "Sometimes your paper seems to threaten things that are precious to them. You can understand that."

I could understand that, but I still felt ugly. My father hated Tully for having been one of my mother's boyfriends, as well as for being a Commie, which he wasn't.

"I just hope BuPers doesn't hear about this when I'm up for lieutenant," Richie said with a grin. "My brother a printer's devil for a Commie rag!"

———

After lunch, when our father was dialing the radio for news, Richie and I took an outing on the boardwalk, past the high white swoops of the winter-closed roller coaster, the boarded-up baseball throws, and hot dog and saltwater-taffy stands. The air felt soft, with an off-the-ocean nip to it.

Storm surf smacked the beach, gray-green glassy backs bending to the spangled shore water in furies of spume.

Richie walked with his head down, sneakers scuffling on the sandy concrete walkway behind the seawall. We both knew the subject of the stuntman Hagen had to come up.

I said, "If someone asked you to help find an abortion doctor, what would you do?"

His face swung toward me. "You?"

"Not me! A friend."

He shrugged elaborately. "I don't know this town anymore, Brud. You've got a job down south of Broadway. Don't you know any of the hookers down there?"

"Don't know any."

"They're not hard to get to know."

"I know a pimp, actually."

Richie made a that's-it gesture. He frowned at me and said, "Have you been doing your reading in the *Manual*?"

"Sometimes," I lied. A friend of Richie's in LA had introduced him to *The Pisan Manual,* which was something like Machiavelli, by another ancient Italian. Richie regarded it as a kind of Bible.

"Important if you're going to be a writer," Richie said. The tightening of his jaw meant I'd better pay attention. "You ought to read a chapter a night."

In fact, I considered the *Manual* Fascist bullshit. "'It is the talent of the Great to agree with the Great,'" I quoted. "'A Man of Insight and Judgment commands the World!' That's real Superman crap, Rich!"

"You can lead the kind of shit life Dad and Mom have lived," he said. "Or you can try to be Someone. That's what it's saying!"

Of course our father going broke in the Depression had affected Richie, too. It had seemed to me that Richie had escaped the shit-storm by going off to USC on a scholarship. He had been a poor boy at a rich-boy school, but he had solved any problems he might have had by turning himself into a rich boy. Why wouldn't my brother think himself a Superior Man, a Man of Insight and Judgment, when he had done everything right? I'd admired him tooling around San Diego in his slick Cord with the big chrome turbocharger pipes curving out of the coffin hood, with Liz—that year he was working in Hollywood.

Everything right but whatever it was Hagen had shouted at him.

"Listen, Brud," Richie said. "You keep saying you want to write private eye stuff like Raymond Chandler. You don't even know what you're talking about! Private detectives are whores! If you want something really rotten done, you hire a private detective. Chandler's just making those rotten whores romantic. I can tell you they're not!" He stopped to wipe the back of his hand over his mouth. "Private detectives are shit!" he said, showing his teeth.

"Listen, Rich," I said. "What was all that about on Flynn's yacht?"

I could see his chest rise as he took a breath. He laid a hand there. "Val killed herself," he said. "You remember Val."

When I'd met her she'd been in a bathing suit, and I'd tried not to look at her smooth legs. I couldn't even remember her face.

"Somebody hired a detective to find out about some bad stuff she had on her record, so she wrapped up some bricks in a kind of sweater thing and jumped into a swimming pool."

"Jesus!" I said. "Who hired him?"

"Never mind," he said. "People you don't know."

He leaned on the seawall, looking out at the ocean. "Some people blamed me, but that's BS," he said. "I guess Hagen knew her," he added.

"He called you a throat-cutter," I said.

"That's bullshit!"

"Everybody wondered why you went off and joined Naval Air," I said.

"I got sick of a lot of Hollywood shit that was going on. That was part of it. It was that December when I signed up," he added.

I'd never heard any of this before. He fished a pack of Chesterfields from his shirt pocket and shook a cigaret from the pack. It took him several tries to get a light. I could see the white scar on his thumb, from some fight with a tramp he'd been in at SC. I felt the trembling of the concrete under our feet, from the slamming of the waves marching in from Asia.

"Listen, Brud, don't fuss Liz about any of this, will you? She's rattled already, with her father, and Gilliam on her back for the spring dance thing."

"What's it about her father?"

"He might do something so we can't get married. It really gripes him that her mother left the estate to her, not to him."

"Jesus!" I wondered aloud why Liz didn't move out of her father's house.

"He's got control of the income till she's twenty-five, though she may be able to get some of it when she graduates. I guess she loves him. He's her father, after all."

I'd seen Captain Fletcher once, with Liz, a stout, erect, florid man in his Navy uniform, with a lot of gold striping and his hair brushed so close to the scalp his head looked too small. He'd had a hand under Liz's elbow as though supporting it, but holding it captive, too.

"She's afraid he'll rig it so I get sent out to the fleet," Richie said. "He and Admiral Swenson were buddies at Annapolis."

"Can I use that? It sounds like a terrific plot."

"Fry head," Richie said, grinning.

We started back. "Playing much tennis?" he asked.

"No time."

"You ought to keep your game up. It's a really great way to get to know people. You heard Flynn last night."

"Did he really mean it when he asked us up there?"

"Sure he did!"

So he had steered the conversation away from Hagen and had not told me much. He had always been good at that.

3

Calvin King had played left halfback on the San Diego High football team, in what the *San Diego Union* sports page called the "Tutti-frutti Backfield." The backfield had consisted of Calvin, Stan Takahashi, John Rodrigues, and Buddy Ruger. It wasn't so tutti after John broke his leg and Payton Daltrey substituted at right half, but the jokes had continued, and we all got tired of the "frutti" part. I had thrown a pass to Calvin that won the game with Hoover High. Calvin, who'd been knocked down, caught the ball lying flat on his back. Calvin had a lot of style.

I hadn't seen him since high school until a couple of months ago, when I'd encountered him zoot-suited on 3rd Street. "Workin for my Uncle

Red," he told me mysteriously. Next he cruised alongside me in a year-old Chrysler convertible with the top down. He wore a fuzzy stylish hat, and a cigar as pale brown as his face jutted from his jaw. He pulled over and directed me to the Fremont Bar, not far from the printshop, where we renewed acquaintance.

I was shocked when he told me he was a "player," by which he meant that he was a pimp, with a white girl working for him.

It had been well known at San Diego High that Coach Garland had warned Calvin about messing with white girls.

"Told me I'd better leave the white meat alone," Calvin had said, regaling the Tutti-fruttis. "Told him they wouldn't leave me alone!" He crowed with delight, grabbing his leg halfway to the knee.

Coach Garland also warned the team of the dangers of sex to athletes. Calvin's exchanges with him had become legends:

"How about just once on Friday night before the game, Coach?" Calvin asked, before his awed teammates.

"You heard me, Cal," the coach said, folding his fat arms over his belly. "A man cannot afford to lose his vital fluids before a demanding physical test."

"How about Thursday, Coach?" Calvin insisted, and it had become a password for the team.

After leaving Mission Beach, I drove downtown to 3rd Street to try to find Calvin King.

South of Broadway was the servicemen's bar-and-whorehouse part of San Diego, where I worked at the *brand* printshop two evenings a week and Saturday mornings. Six months ago there had been mostly a population of bums and drunks, but as the numbers of servicemen increased, the bums had vanished.

BRITISH RETREAT and SINGAPORE DOOMED? were the evening headlines on the newsstand on the corner, illuminated by the streetlight there, as though for my benefit. The war headlines made me short of breath.

I parked in front of the dark window of the printshop and started down to the Fremont Bar, where I thought I might find Calvin.

Five stories of the Benford Hotel gleamed with lights. On the big Saturday nights, women leaned out the windows calling to the servicemen in the street. I passed clumps of sailors, and Marines in greens, and MPs with white puttees and belts, carrying nightsticks. I felt like a civilian jerk among the uniforms.

I followed a platinum blonde, big-assed in her tight red dress, wobbling on high heels. I remembered encountering her in the White Castle hamburger stand and thought of asking if she knew Calvin. A pair of drunken swab-bies catcalled after her.

Coach Garland had often showed slides of the horrors of venereal dis-ease to the team, one of them a syphilis guy with his prick eaten away and a sickly grin. When I'd signed into the midshipman's program, a bunch of us had been taken for a tour of the Navy's San Diego Recruit Depot. In the men's john, half the stalls had carried the sign VD ONLY.

The Fremont was half filled, reeking of beer, the bar an expanse of uni-formed backs. Music from the jukebox pulsed through the clamor: "A-Tisket, A-Tasket," Ella Fitzgerald. A colored bartender with a face like a slab of brown beef slid beakers of beer along the counter to outstretched hands.

Calvin was at the far end of the bar, his pork-pie hat with its jaunty feather cocked back on his head. There was an empty stool beside him.

"Hello, child!" he said as I took the free stool.

"How about Thursday, Coach?" I said.

"How about a Cuba libre?" he asked, grinning, and signaled the bar-tender. I met sailor-glances. A colored man had been lynched only weeks ago in Missouri for an "attack" on a white woman. I squinted at Calvin's handsome tan profile.

"Dessy's out makin money," Calvin said. "She'll be along directly." He tossed out a crumpled bill when the bartender placed rum and Cokes be-fore us.

"If a fellow can get more'n one lady on the stroll, he is doin good," he went on expansively. "If I cop a couple more I am full-fledge. You know, these ladies can pull down a hundred bucks on a Saturday night."

I opened my mouth and closed it on air. A hundred dollars!

"Dessy's not pullin anything like that yet."

"What does she do, give you some?"

"Give me all. I give her back some. I take care of her, see?"

It was hot in the bar as well as noisy. Sweat tickled under my arms. "Don't you ever get in trouble in swabbie bars like this?" I asked him in a low voice.

He produced something from his pocket. There was a snick of metal. "Boy's best friend," Calvin said, exposing a bright blade.

I swung on my stool to conceal the knife between us. Calvin wore his habitual aloof expression as he pocketed it again.

"Do you know a doctor who'll do an abortion?" I asked.

Calvin's eyebrow hooked up. "You, child?"

"Friend of mine went in the service and left his girl knocked up."

"Tijuana, Child. Nothing in Dago."

I asked what it cost.

"Hundred and fifty ought to do it."

A girl had come up behind us, brown-haired, young. Calvin slid off his stool, establishing proprietorship with a long arm. I was shocked to see her tuck something into his jacket pocket. All of it!

"Child, this here's Dessy. This my old pal Payton Daltrey."

She offered her hand. When I pressed the limp bit of flesh, I couldn't take my eyes from her face. Long lashes framing sooty eyes like Ella Cinders's, pink mouth with the upper lip hiked up, a spit curl at her temple, a thin tender throat. Calvin's brown hand gripped the shoulder of her gray jacket.

"Ain't she a pretty thing, though?"

"I'll say!"

Dessy's upper lip tucked up into her tremulous smile. She leaned against Calvin.

"How about a drink, beauty?"

She made a wailing sound. "I just want to go home, honey!"

"Well, we'll just do that," Calvin said, and swigged long from his glass.

"Honey, there's some bad men down the bar. They kind of scare me."

"We'll just take care of that, too," Calvin said, and signaled to the bartender.

The bartender pushed my glass aside and raised a section of the bar on a hinge. "Shake it along."

Dessy slipped through the opening with Calvin behind her. I didn't know what to do but follow them, out a narrow doorway into an alley past ranked trash cans.

Dessy clasped Calvin's arm, hugging herself to him, checked skirt, silk-stockinged legs, high-heeled pumps.

"How about T-town tomorrow, child?" Calvin said, over the top of her brown head. "We'll take Chrysie-car, check some things out."

"Tomorrow afternoon," I said. I'd get one of the other drivers to take my Mission Hills route.

"Pick you up at the printshop at two!"

Dessy flipped a hand good-bye. I watched the two of them move away up the street, arms around each other, hips bumping. I had a mean guilt hard-on thinking of Calvin bringing Dessy home to take care of her. It seemed that I had moved into Calvin's sphere just by inquiring about an abortion doctor.

I called from the pay phone outside the White Castle. Mrs. Bonington answered, and I asked for Bonny.

"Listen," I said, talking fast. "There aren't any in San Diego. There're some in Tijuana. My friend's going to take me down there tomorrow afternoon, check them out."

I could hear her breathing.

"It costs about a hundred and fifty dollars. Has she got any money?"

"I've got money."

"I'd probably better take some tomorrow, if I'm going to make a date."

"Payton," she said, "it's me."

"Okay," I said, and told her I'd see her in the Quad at State tomorrow morning after our nine o'clocks.

Chapter 3

1

I USUALLY ENCOUNTERED LIZ FLETCHER COMING ACROSS the Quad from the Dance Department. We played a little game, she the vamp and I her goggling admirer—which wasn't all that far off, actually, but of course it was all covered because she was wearing Richie's engagement ring.

Liz would glance at me coyly, head tipped down, eyes cutting up at me, and say, "When are you going to take me away from all this, Payton?" And I would try to think of some snappy response.

Here she came today, raising a hand in greeting, striding toward the black Aztec statue in the center of the Quad. She wore a sweater and skirt like the other coeds, but silk stockings and high heels instead of bobby socks and saddle shoes—because she was a little older, or engaged.

She had a way of moving just a little closer to you when you were talking to her than was comfortable, as though she were near-sighted. As we walked together across the Quad toward the arcades, she matched my stride, her leg almost touching mine. She was wearing dark red lipstick that made her cheeks look pale.

Richie had caught a ride back to Pensacola this morning, she said, though he had another day's leave. "He has to take whatever transport he can find."

"That was some wild night on the *Sirocco,*" I said.

"Wasn't Errol wonderful? It was like a fight in a movie!"

"I was going to deck that guy, but Flynn beat me to it!" I was afraid that sounded like a reflection on Richie, who had not decked Hagen.

"My protector!" She was laughing when we stopped in the shade of the arcade, gazing at me in that way she had—as though regarding me totally. She had an appointment with her psych prof, she said.

I had an appointment with Bonny Bonington.

"When are you going to take me away from all this, Payton?" she asked.

"As soon as I get my schooner," I said. "We'll head for the goldfields."

When she strode off, laughing at that, I watched the swing of her neat hips in her plaid skirt.

Bonny stood in the shadows under the arcade, her gray notebook held to the breast of her blue sweater. "Hi," she said.

We headed for the Caff, where we sat at a table under the high amber-glass windows away from the others. When she put down her notebook, I checked her sweater where she'd once worn Johnny Pierce's fraternity pin. She had something else to remember him by. Her face was pink.

She took a wad of twenty-dollar bills from her wallet and pushed it at me. I started to count it. "It's two hunded dollars," she said. "Do you think that's enough?"

"My friend Calvin said about one fifty."

She made a releasing gesture with her hands.

"Do you want some coffee?"

"I'll get it," she said, starting to rise.

I said I'd get it, and left her sitting in the amber light while I brought back two cups of coffee. It seemed important not to spill any in the saucers.

"Thanks," Bonny said. Her fair hair was pinned back with a silver clip. She looked scrubbed clean, as though she'd just washed all over with Lifebuoy and a rough cloth.

"You're a friend of Johnny's," she said.

"No, I'm not."

"Well, a fraternity brother."

I shrugged. Whenever the subject of Johnny Pierce came up, I'd find myself pretending total disinterest.

Bonny looked down at her hand holding the cup. "Johnny told me he is going to get killed. He saw it in a dream. He saw the way it would happen."

"You don't have to tell me about it," I said.

I saw the muscle clench at the angle of her jaw. "In a ball of fire," she went on. "But he was going to enlist in the Air Corps anyway."

Fucking con artist. "Listen," I said.

"There isn't anybody else I can tell," she said.

"Sorry," I said. I meant I was sorry there was no one else but me she could tell. Didn't girls tell that sort of thing to each other, whispering on the way to the ladies' room? I gritted my teeth to think of Johnny Pierce conning her.

"Do you want me to make a date if one of these places looks okay? I guess they're kind of clinics."

She nodded.

"Some morning? Mornings are better for me." I could cut school easier than work.

"Are you going to take me?"

"If you want me to."

She raised the cup to her lips but didn't drink, and set it down in the saucer again. She was left-handed.

"Why are you doing this?" she asked.

I waited awhile for the anger to peak and start down. "Did you ever read *The Great Gatsby*?"

She shook her head.

"Somewhere there it says that there're people who make messes, and other people that clean up after them."

Her blue eyes flashed at me.

"You asked me to find out about this and I said I'd do it. Wouldn't you do that if somebody asked you?"

"Yes," Bonny said, ducking her head as though I'd rebuked her.

"Besides," I said, "on the way out to the *Sirocco*, you asked me if I'd take care of you, and I said I would. Got to go," I said, and rose and picked up my books and binder. Bonny watched me with her pink face. "I'll call you when I know something," I said, and left her there.

From the door I looked back at her, sitting in the long slant of amber light with her cup half raised, and wondered if I was punishing her.

Professor Chapman was reddish-haired, balding, maybe forty, wearing a thick tweed jacket. He looked as though he had never done anything athletic in his life, but he was a good teacher and he'd written books about writers. I'd come for his office hours. His office was small and cluttered, with metal bookshelves on three sides and a window on the parking lot.

Sitting at his messy desk, he held out my paper on *The Portrait of a Lady* with his face screwed up like a bad smell.

"You are capable of better work than this, Daltrey."

I knew it was a lousy paper. No time! "I hate all that jerk-American stuff. Henrietta Stackpole!"

"Why didn't you make such a case?" He removed his eyeglasses and polished the lenses with his handkerchief, brown eyes squinting up at me. "I want you to write me another paper."

"Yes, sir."

"I recognize that it is difficult to get one's mind on the England of seventy years ago when there is a war on, but James is instructing us in the regulation of our lives, and I believe that that is important in any era."

"Yes, sir," I said.

"You are an intelligent student, and you would not be satisfied with the grade I would give you on the basis of this paper."

"I like the ghost," I said. "The ghost of European evil. It's like the Nazis."

Mr. Chapman smiled with his thin lips. "Indeed, it is things like the ghost that make this a great novel, despite the jerk-American stuff. Why don't you write your paper on the ghost?"

I was feeling some enthusiasm despite myself. I said I liked the way James ran his dialogs. "Isabel says, 'Is there a ghost?' and Ralph says, 'What do you mean, a ghost?' She says, 'A ghost, a thing that appears.' Then they play Ping-Pong with some other word."

"That is interesting!" Mr. Chapman said, squinting at me with his glasses back on.

I said I'd been trying to write stories and was working on dialog. "Hemingway's supposed to be the best at dialog, but James is good, too."

"Ah, and so is Stephen Crane. Why don't you show me one of your stories, Daltrey?"

I felt myself flush, like Bonny in the Caff. I didn't think Professor Chapman was interested in pulp magazine fiction.

"Henry James would be pleased at your compliment to his dialog," he continued. "But pay him the further compliment of affording your examination of *The Portrait* sufficient time and effort."

I jammed the paper into my binder and left. Is there a ghost, a thing that appears? It seemed to me that a ghost of some old evil had appeared in my life, involving Richie's starlet girlfriend who had drowned herself in a swimming pool, and a crazy stuntman who called Richie a throat-cutter. Which might mean some kind of coup de grâce.

2

Top down on Chrysie-car, wind snapping at my hair, Calvin straight-arming the wheel, the Tijuana expedition sped south through the small towns between San Diego and the border. Calvin, his pork-pie jammed down on his head, fiddled with the radio knobs, fine-tuning Dinah Washington on a race station.

From the long curve through San Ysidro, the last town on the American side, the hills of Baja California were visible across the broad river bottom. At the border the two of us were looked over by a brown-uniformed Mexican officer in a salty cap. Calvin wore a fawn-colored suit with the collar of his black-and-white-checked shirt turned out over the lapels of the jacket, a St. Christopher medal on a silver chain around his neck. Beckoned on into Mexico, he accelerated past a trio of ancient trucks with SERVICIO PARTICULAR signs on them, whatever that meant.

"Looked us over pretty good," I said.

He brought a slim tan cigar from his pocket and clenched it tilted between his teeth, FDR style. "Wait'll we cross back into the U.S. of A. There's always some peckerwood likes to make trouble. I wouldn't come down here with Dessy, there'd be a mess gettin back."

"Rugged," I said.

"What's that, child?"

"Putting up with that crap."

"You ought to try gettin a haircut."

"You get mad a lot?"

Calvin waved a hand, dismissing the subject. "I'm supposed to see this Meskin friend of my Uncle Red's at the Molino Rojo while I'm down here. We'll go drop by there after."

I recalled the prom after San Diego High won the City Schools Football Championship. The Tutti-frutti Backfield sat at a table together, Peggy Fleming and I, Buddy Ruger and his cheerleader, and Stan Takahashi with a Japanese girl whose name I'd forgotten. Calvin had worn sweat socks with his tux and black shoes, on the theory, he had explained, that colored guys should wear white socks because white guys wore black. It had been a complicated evening.

"How'd you get into this racket?" I asked.

Calvin laughed fatly. "I was a player all my life. I was always playin doctor with the girls. Then at Coolidge I found out white girls liked me. How I ended up with Dessy!"

"I guess I don't understand what they need you for."

Calvin laughed again, steering the Chrysler along a potholed street past sheds stacked with terra-cotta pots. "I set Dessy up in a nice apartment. I bail her out of jail if she gets pulled in. I give her a foundation. You know? These ladies get very good at manipulatin men. Me, I don't manipulate."

"How did you meet her?"

"Met her at the bus depot. Knew her the minute I saw her. And she knew me! Hand in glove. If I just had me a couple more ladies like Dessy I'd be in business."

I asked how Dessy got to be a professional.

"She's from some little burg up north, and she'd gone to San Francisco to work in a office. Had to fuck her bosses to keep her job. She slipped into the life that way. She got hooked up with a player that told her he'd kill her if she tried to leave him. So she took the bus to Dago and there I was. She is delicate, though. She gets these headaches. She'll get so low sometimes I don't know if I can spring her out of it."

Had my mother had to fuck Mr. Perkins to keep her job? I had a kind of treaty with myself where I had declared myself neutral in anything to do with my mother and sex.

Calvin swung into the Avenida Revolución, broad and partially paved, cops directing traffic white-gloved at the intersections. Servicemen in civilian clothes, identifiable by their cropped hair, ambled along the sidewalks past shops and bars. We passed Caesar's Hotel and the Foreign Club.

Turning two more corners, Calvin drifted to a stop in front of a dingy row of shops. He pointed out a high sign: CLINICA OROZCO.

The clinic was up a flight of steps. A sour-faced Mexican woman wearing a nurse's cap let us in and seated herself behind a desk. She brought out an appointment book and a receipt pad from a drawer. The fee was two hundred dollars, one hundred necessitated now, the rest on the day of the procedure.

The clinic office was clean enough. The medical part must be through the door behind the desk. I peered at an official-looking document on the wall, framed and glassed. There was a green filing cabinet with a coffeepot on top. I didn't like the coffeepot, but it seemed a minor demerit.

With Calvin's help and a calendar, the date was set for Tuesday morning. I counted out Bonny's twenties, and the nurse wrote a receipt.

"*Cuanto tiempo?*" I asked, and she replied something that I took to mean half an hour. The realization of Bonny's predicament hit me suddenly like a cramp.

Back in Chrysie-car I asked Calvin what he'd thought of the Clínca Orozco.

"Seemed okay. She's probly tried jumpin off tables already. Runnin down the stadium steps."

I asked him why professional ladies didn't get pregnant.

"They don't get pregnant unless they come, and they only come with their boyfriend, and he wears a scumbag."

I knew that was bullshit.

"They douche," Calvin said, laughing. "Sometimes they get knocked up, too."

I asked what they did to keep from getting that other waiting-to-pounce horror.

"They check dicks. They better! They see the doc once a week, too."

"I'll never forget those slides Coach showed us."

"Fucken homo!"

We drank rum and Cokes and had a supper of tamales with Carta Blanca beer, afterward heading for the Molino Rojo, the huge Tijuana whorehouse where Calvin's uncle had connections. I'd been to Tijuana many times to buy six-dollar cashmere sweaters, but never to the infamous VD Park.

"Supposed to be fourteen-year-old virgins on hand for special guests," Calvin said, steering Chrysie-car out of the noisy glow of downtown into Mexican darkness. "And they've got a pony fucks women for a show."

I'd heard of the Shetland pony.

Groups of pedestrians were headed down the unpaved lane, and a pair of glaring headlights followed us. A taxi jounced toward us, how-do-you-do lights and a whiff of dust as it passed. The Chrysler nosed into a gully and swung in among parked cars. A taxi beside us disgorged men with harsh American voices. Calvin and I followed this group past a wire fence, stumbling on cracked paving. I gritted my teeth to keep from shivering. We were heading between two wings of a building whose eaves were decorated with electric bulbs. Music pulsed with whining strings.

We followed the music onto a terrace where two soldiers with rifles lounged, smoking. Beyond them a door was open onto a small theater with a floor and seats raked to a stage upon which stood a mariachi group in tight suits and broad-brimmed, braid-heavy sombreros. The place was jammed with gringos.

In front of the mariachi band was a naked woman. A dog stood on his hind legs behind her, bandaged paws resting on her shoulders. His pink tongue flopped out of his jaw, and his hindquarters humped in rapid motion. The woman interrupted the proceedings from time to time to swipe at her thighs with a towel. She had a dark round face.

"That hound's a real stayer," a man near us commented.

The woman threw the dog off, proffering her shaven crotch, which the dog licked eagerly. She pantomimed ecstacy.

When the woman and the dog had faded offstage, the mariachis played a brassy number. Then, to fanfare, a pony was led onto the stage. He was black-and-white spotted, with his mane parted and tied with blue ribbons. The pony reared to his back legs, displaying a cock like a length of black pipe.

I was sweating with tension and the body heat of the little theater, half-nauseated from rum and Coke and beer. Men yelled and catcalled. Another naked woman appeared, a girl, slim, young, smoky tan, with a kittenish face and her hair tied back with a blue ribbon that matched the pony's ribbons. She stepped up onto a box in her high-heeled pumps and offered her rump to the pony, which a white-clad attendant led toward her, staggering on his back legs with his awful hard-on.

"Let's get out of here," I murmured, but not loud enough for Calvin to hear. I was afraid I was going to puke.

With some steadying from the attendant, and snorts from the pony, the enormous cock was introduced into the girl's crotch as she grasped her buttocks in her hands and leaned forward, smiling. Men around us were yelling. I closed my eyes.

"Let's haul out of here, child," Calvin whispered.

Adjusting my own hard-on in my pants, I followed him outside. Another clamor followed us. The two soldiers still smoked at the top of the steps.

"Disgustin," Calvin said, flipping a hand like tossing something away. He inquired of one of the soldiers where he could find Señor Carlos Rodriguez, and the man indicated a sign with an arrow and the word DIREC-CION, and double doors.

"See if I can't procure us a couple of these virgins," Calvin said, as we entered a dim hallway.

"Well, I guess I won't," I said. "I'm not feeling so hot."

His yellowish eyes were sympathetic, "Yeah, bad stuff," he said. Ahead an older woman occupied a doorway, respectably dressed, smoking. Beside her was a sign as tall as she was, a hand, the palm numbered and labeled in Spanish: a palm reader. "I'll see you back outside," I said to Calvin, and ducked into the room past the woman.

She closed the door and indicated a table and chairs. In a shiny tin cage was a blue and yellow parrot. I was breathing as though I'd been running.

"Speak English?"

Nodding, she seated herself opposite me, smoke from her cigaret drifting past her face. She wore a blouse with red embroidery at the neck and sleeves. Her hair was graying. When whores like the kitten-faced girl with the pony got too old, did they become palmists? I didn't think anything anywhere near that good happened to them.

"One dollar, señor."

I gave her a bill from my wallet, and she placed it beneath the pack of Chesterfields on the table.

She pushed my right hand aside and beckoned for the left. She touched a pad of flesh, her head bent so that I could see the part of her hair, like a chalk line.

"The gender is very strong," she said. "You must take care that love does not triumph over wisdom." Her finger tickled my palm; smoke drifted into my eyes. I couldn't get the kitten-faced girl's visage out of my head. The woman spoke rapidly in English, but I only half listened as she touched different parts of my hand. The parrot sidled on his perch, watching me with one eye, then the other.

"Are you a college young man, my friend?"

I said I attended college in San Diego.

What did I study there?

I studied English literature.

"One must study philosophy in college."

I had studied philosophy last year. The idols of the cave!

"There is philosophy to be discovered in this place, my friend. Here is revealed the profound difference between the genders. Men are animals, and women the slaves of animals. It is only the wise who may transcend their gender!" She sounded like Richie's *Pisan Manual*.

She tucked my hand into a fist and pushed it back at me, and scrubbed out her cigaret in a copper ashtray.

Outside on the terrace, men were milling. Apparently the show was over. Calvin sauntered toward me. I inquired about his virgin.

"Wasn't any virgin and wasn't fourteen, either. I wasn't having any of that."

When we got back to 3rd Street, where I'd left Ol Paint, it was only ten to nine. I phoned Bonny from the pay phone at the White Castle.

I had to go through her mother again.

"It looked okay to me," I said, when she came on. "I made a deposit for next Tuesday at ten o'clock. It takes about half an hour, the nurse said."

"That sounds like fun!" Bonny said in a cheery voice, as though we were making a date.

I said I'd see her at school.

"Yes," she said. "Oh, yes. Thanks."

———

The lights were still on in the printshop, and through the window, past the lettering

THE BRAND
PRINTING

I could see Tully at his desk, suede shoes up on the metal wastebasket, reading the *Los Angeles Times*. The headlines were visible through the window: BALI BATTLE and COAST SPYING DISCLOSED.

He put down the paper when I came in. He wore his leather cap and ink-stained loafer jacket. Last Saturday's *brand* was spread out on the counter. On the beaverboard wall behind him were thumbtacked newspaper photographs and headlines: SACCO AND VANZETTI DIE! A photo showed Tom Mooney handcuffed to a policeman, another a Spanish Civil War soldier in a tasseled cap in the instant of dropping his rifle and falling. Still another was of John Reed, who looked a good deal like Tully. *The brand* had something to do with the SWP, the Socialist Workers Party, which had something to do with Trotsky, who had been murdered in Mexico City a year or so ago. I'd never heard Tully speak of any Russians but Stalin, whom he hated.

"Saw your car parked out front," he said.

I said I'd gone with a friend to Tijuana, to the Molino Rojo.

He looked alarmed. "You didn't dip your wick in that venereal snake pit!"

"Never fear."

On the front page of *the brand* the headlines were HUAC COUNSEL NAMED and TOTS MOLESTED IN QUARRY. Smaller heads were STRIKE DEADLOCK and OPA SCANDAL. The news stories, which Tully wrote, were boring. *The brand* was not interested in the war but in "social issues": the tuna cannery strike and the trial of some strikers up in Yolo County, wherever that was; the latest outrages of the House Un-American Activities Committee and its California offshoot, the Tenney Committee.

Tully perused the San Diego and Los Angeles papers daily and received others in the mail. He didn't subscribe to the *Daily Worker*.

On the other side of the counter was the door to the pressroom, domain of the Dutchman printer, Tee-John, where Charlotte, the cranky old press, hulked up in her concrete pit like a grizzly bear.

"If you want to do some writing, you might try your hand at this," Tully said. He folded the *Times* to an inner page. YOUTH MOLESTED, JUDGE NAMED. A judge in Altadena who had consulted in his chambers with the eleven-year-old son of a couple seeking a divorce was accused of inappropriate behavior with the boy.

As I scanned the text, the pretty kitten face of the girl at the Molino Rojo crowded my eyes.

The judge had been arraigned and released on a thousand dollars bail. The attorney representing the judge—neither of them named—maintained his client's innocence. The boy had been treated at a local hospital and released. I was interested that the *Times* writer had managed to produce outrage out of bare facts.

"What a shit," I said.

"Use short, declarative sentences, and don't offend Mrs. Grooms."

Mrs. Grooms was the widow of Erwin J. Grooms, the founder of *the brand*. The molested-tots right-hand column had been a feature of *the brand* as long as I'd known it, a come-on of the kind of underground evil sex news the *San Diego Union* never printed, so people would buy *the brand* to be shocked and scandalized by the political and social molestations with their SWP slant in the other columns of the paper.

Once I'd asked Tully what molestation meant exactly.

"Someone with power over someone else doing something humiliating to the party of the second part," he said. "Fondling, buggery, rape, incest, any kind of sexual abuse. It's not an exact term."

A fat envelope from the clipping service arrived every week, with clips from all over the country.

It was Tully's pronouncement that war was the ultimate molestation of the young. Only kids, he claimed, would fight a modern war, because they did not yet really believe that they could get killed.

"Pretty low on specifics," I said, handing back the paper. "Altadena. March second. A thousand dollars bail."

"You will have room to exercise your talents."

"I'll tell you where I'd like to exercise my talents. At the Molino Rojo there was this young girl, maybe she was eighteen. She was being fucked by a fucking Shetland pony. That's evil!"

"Someday, my boy, you will have to read *Das Kapital,*" Tully said. "Especially the terrible chapter entitled 'The Working Day.' Marx would point out that your Tijuana whores make their living under relatively pleasant circumstances."

"If I get hold of some Mexican tires that have been smuggled across the border by the people who run the Molino Rojo—have I contributed to evil?"

He leaned farther back in his chair with a creak of metal and beamed at me, revealing his gold tooth. "My boy, my boy—what gasoline do you use?"

"Whatever's cheap."

"If you fill up with Standard, you are contributing to a cartel that still maintains connections with Nazi Germany. That is evil."

"My mother says LA is evil," I said.

"Your mother is very often correct in her judgments," he said. "Los Angeles is the biggest Protestant city in the country, with the usual Protestant persecution of anybody with an irregular opinion. Now they are summoning their energies to put the coast Japanese into concentration camps." He blew out his breath in a hard sigh. "In addition there is Hollywood, operated by a pack of New York garment district parvenus, who are so overwhelmed by their money and power that the only outlet they know is an indulgence in sexual license."

That was too close to my brother and the dead Val. To change the subject, I said, "Yeah, well, my father says his American Legion buddies are pissed off at *the brand*."

"A paper that does not offend some people is not worth its ink," Tully said, pouting his fat lips, and I went home before he could lecture me any more.

Out of his bullshit lectures and the clipping service, however, I had been formulating a kind of theory connecting the abuse of the young by the old, the weak by the strong, the dumb by the cunning, Negroes by whites, and more specifically Bonny's seduction by Johnny Pierce and the fourteen-year-old virgins in Tijuana who ended up fucking dogs and ponies.

Chapter 4

1

I WAS A SPEEDY GROCERY DELIVERYMAN. I'D SET THE HAND brake just right so that when I stepped out of the blue and silver Perry's Fine Foods panel, the truck braked itself to a stop with the rear doors beside me. I'd wrench the right-hand door open, snatch the numbered box out of the stack within, and trot with it to the kitchen door or service entrance.

I'd convinced Lois Meador, the dispatcher, that I was a natural for the particular problems of delivering the Mission Hills route, since I had lived there as a boy. I could summon up heavy dogfaced ironies from the fact that I was delivering groceries in my khaki shirt, green twill pants, black leather clip-on bow tie, and twill cap to the back doors of houses I had once entered by the front.

Today my next-to-last stop was old Mrs. Blair's mansion on the Rim overlooking Mission Valley like a Spanish castle. Mrs. Blair usually left a tip thumbtacked with the next day's order to the cork bulletin board. I resented the tip—two dollars today—which turned me into a servant instead of a college boy delivering groceries. But I pocketed it.

Last stop was the Emmetts', a high pink stucco wall with a sign over a wrought-iron gate: SERVICE. As soon as I had let myself in, juggling two heavy boxes, the Emmetts' midget Hound of the Baskervilles was yipping and snarling at my pants cuffs, so I had to cross the service yard in a kind of dance, kicking at Bitsy as the mutt made dashes at my ankles.

"Don't you let him in here!" brayed Mrs. Sims, the cook, as I shouldered through the door, fending Bitsy off with my foot. She was seated at the zinc-topped table, glowering at me over the headline: JAPANESE CROSS SALWEEN RIVER.

I began unloading the boxes onto the counter.

"Can't you knock, boy?"

"Yes, ma'am."

"You did not knock!"

"No, ma'am."

"You knock next time, you hear me?"

"Yes, ma'am," I said, meaning I heard her. In fact, however, if I'd made two trips, so that I wasn't overloaded, I could have dealt with Bitsy and knocked as well.

When I started out with the empty boxes, Mrs. Sims raised her voice. "How many times have I told you to put the meat in the Frigidaire?"

Mind on the Japanese crossing the Salween River—where was the Salween River?—"Yes, ma'am." I stowed the white-wrapped packets in the refrigerator, backed out the door with the empty boxes, and danced and kicked across the service yard to the gate. There I raised a finger in salute to Mrs. Sims and clanged the gate shut so that Bitsy scurried away, yapping.

My friend Pogey Malcolm lived on Wisteria Street, just around the corner from the Emmetts. When I'd U-turned to park in front of his house, he appeared in his upstairs window, slight and neat in his blue cashmere and cords. He had a sunburned nose like a Koala bear from tennis at his father's club.

"Have you got time to come up?"

The front door was unlocked, and I knew the way, although, delivering groceries, I would have to go to the back door.

He was sitting at his blond wood desk. It was a terrific room, with a rag rug on the polished floor, bright impressionist prints on the wall, a bookcase, and a brand-new Royal portable on the desk. I sat on the bed.

"Where's the Salween River?" I asked.

"Down by Singapore, I think."

"The Japs just keep going and going," I said.

"It's bad."

"Pretty hard to maintain irony and pity delivering to that fat-ass cook at the Emmetts'." I motioned in their direction.

Lately we'd been talking like Hemingway characters.

"Something you don't feel good after," Pogey agreed.

Last summer the two of us had had fun trying to concoct the plot of a mystery novel like *The Big Sleep,* but for all his neat desk and new Royal typewriter, Pogey never seemed to get any writing done.

I said I'd sent my "On the Dodge" story off to *Black Mask.* "I'll get it back in about three weeks," I said.

"Maybe not, this time."

"Tell me something," I said. "What did you think of Johnny Pierce? As a guy, I mean."

"What do you mean, 'did'? Is he dead?"

"No, I mean—just gone in the Air Corps."

Pogey looked puzzled. He was very loyal to the tong and the brothers.

"I thought he was a real shit," I said. "I hate that kind of big jock guy. Whenever you start to say something, he raises his voice to talk over you. That kind of stuff. I mean, I've been taking Bonny out. I don't see how she could stand a guy like that."

"Well, he's a fraternity brother," Pogey said, about as close to arguing as he ever got. He had been my best friend since grammar school, but I couldn't tell him about Bonny Bonington and Johnny Pierce. I surely couldn't tell him about the Clínica Orozco.

There was a knock, Pogey called out a "Come in!" and his stepmother opened the door. She was a hippy, good-looking woman in a gray suit and silk stockings, with a helmet of crisp black hair like Louise Brooks.

I got to my feet. "Oh, hello, Payton," she said.

"Hello, Mrs. Malcolm." She seemed to me too young and pretty for Mr. Malcolm, a bald, wrinkled old gent who walked as though his feet hurt.

"Will you put the Packard in the garage for me, dear?" Mrs. Malcolm said to Pogey. "Your father has moved some of his things, and I'm afraid I can't get in past them."

"Sure, Beth," Pogey said.

"I'm just going," I said.

"No hurry, really!" Mrs. Malcolm said, and smiled brilliantly at me. Then she was gone.

"She's sure pretty," I said.

"She sure is no good at parking the car," Pogey said, grinning and scratching his sunburned nose. "Seems like when they get started they don't leave a guy nothing," he added.

"*Nada y pues nada,*" I said.

2

At home I tried to write something out of the *LA Times* clipping Tully had showed me. I was trying to grasp what had really happened and not just the kind of abstract pissed-offness that I usually felt from the clipping service items:

The husky bailiff led the boy along the tiled corridor to the judge's chambers.

"Here you go, sonny," he said. He knocked. The door opened eighteen inches. The boy slipped inside. The judge faced him in his black robe. He had fat red lips. The judge's eyes seemed to look right through him.

"So, little fellow," the judge said. "Come over here while I ask you some questions." He stepped toward the boy and grasped his wrist with a hand that felt like an ice tong—

How did you do it? Like Bonny telling me that Johnny Pierce had said he'd had dreams of himself dying in a ball of fire. Like Hemingway writing in *A Farewell to Arms* that the battery in the garden fired twice, which made the front of his pajamas flap. So you believed it. You could put the whole picture together from those few words. So she'd let him do it to her.

3

Parked in front of the Clínica Orozco pretending to read the *Black Mask* I had brought along, I didn't have to wait for anything like half an hour before Bonny was coming down the steps in her sweater set, skirt, bobby socks, and saddle shoes, with her shining hair caught in its silver clip. She gave me a flash of a smile as I hustled out of the car and around to where I could take her arm. I'd thought she might need some support, but she seemed fine.

"How was it?" I asked when we were inside the car.

"It wasn't so bad."

I started Ol Paint and pulled away from the curb.

"He was a nice man," Bonny said. "He spoke English." She giggled suddenly. "I'd thought of killing myself!" she said. "Like Connie Roberts's sister. Isn't that stupid? Oh, wonderful! Thank you, thank you!" she whispered.

I was trying to get out of Tijuana without getting lost.

"You're the only one who knows," she said.

I said, "Johnny—" before I could stop myself.

"He doesn't know."

"Don't you write him?"

"Oh, no!"

I didn't understand that. I got past four intersections and then turned onto the Avenida Revolución, which was the only way I knew to reach the border.

"Why wouldn't you write him?" I asked.

"I hate him."

"What?"

"He said he was going to die, and I had to. But it was just a trick to seduce a stupid—fool! And I even knew it was."

It was the style I'd been trying to understand, where she didn't have to say exactly what had happened, his pants and her slip and her garter belt or whatever girls wore, or any of that; because just the idea that it was all a trick, and she had known it was a trick, carried it along so that I could feel the outrage with an ironical twist to it. She'd had to live with thinking her life was ruined, wondering if she would have to kill herself like Connie Roberts's sister taking poison on the train down from LA, until she had got up the nerve to ask her date if he could find an abortionist.

"Does it ever seem to you that things get all hooked together sometimes?" she said. She was talking brightly and too fast.

It was just what I had been thinking, Bonny hooked together with the kitten-faced whore, and the kid and the Altadena judge.

"I didn't even like him," she went on. "He scared me, but my mother hated him, and she kept—you know. So I wore his pin. I was such a fool! Then when I thought I was pregnant I couldn't tell her. I couldn't tell anybody. I knew I didn't fool you when I said it was for a friend of mine."

"It's over now," I said. I slowed into the line of cars waiting to cross the border in a stink of exhausts.

The customs officer wanted to know where we were born. "San Diego," I said. "San Diego," Bonny said, and he waved us on. I drove on into the United States. Bonny locked her hands together in her lap, like some kind of gear made of white fingers, and bent her head over them so her hair parted over the back of her neck.

"I guess I'm not a girl anymore," she said in a shaky voice. But the nape of her neck was a girl's neck. She was crying, and I put my arm around her.

After that we were going steady, with nothing particular said about it. I just didn't date anyone else, and she didn't, though I was embarrassed to tell her I loved her, and I didn't tell her, and maybe she was the same.

4

Johnny Pierce was killed in April.

In the inky dome of starry night on Point Loma, parked on a slope at the end of a dirt track so if the radio ran the battery down Ol Paint could make a compression start, with Barbara Bonington in my arms, I gazed past her at the lights of the Bay and San Diego. I reached an arm around her to tune up the radio—Benny Goodman and "Sing! Sing! Sing!" I could feel the clasp of her bra against my arm, and I thought about unfastening it, but she had been quiet all evening, something bothering her: maybe her parents.

I tuned the radio down when the jock's voice came on, and I asked her what was wrong.

"Johnny's dead," she said.

"How do you know?"

"His mother phoned me."

I didn't know what to say. She would know I wasn't sorry, though maybe I was sorry for her. "What happened?"

"She only said it was a training accident." And she said, "In his dream it was in a ball of fire."

I guessed she was crying then. She said in a small voice, "His—you know—*fetus*, and now him."

I thought about that.

"I don't have to hate him anymore," Bonny said.

"No."

"Sometimes at night I'd hate him so much I'd almost throw up. Why did he have to do that? Why did I let him? It didn't feel good, it just hurt. Maybe he felt good, but I think he just felt good because he'd—you know, got me. What made me so mad was he probably bragged about it, like Charley bragging about his women. Did he brag about it?"

"No," I said.

"Like pilots shooting down enemy airplanes, like becoming aces. You're not like that," she said.

I wondered if I was.

She moved away from me to lean against the far door, a dim, pale-capped figure against the black window.

"Sure," I said. "If we were in some wonderful place. Where there were no obstructions. Where there wasn't any danger of you getting pregnant, or of getting emotionally—you know, screwed up. And nobody was going to find out about it, and think what they'd think about you, and about me. I mean, I don't want to be an ace, but if we could get together like that, and you were as willing as I was—boy!"

Bonny giggled, her arms wrapped around herself. "Girl!" she said. "It's just—it's not fair, for girls," she said. "Boys don't risk anything much, and girls risk everything."

"I know that."

"Will you still like me if I don't want to do it? I mean, I did it and it was—well, I told you, it was like an operation. I know you've done it. Haven't you?"

"Just somebody's sister."

"Was it wonderful?"

"Hemingway says somewhere that the good things are things where you feel good afterward. So it was bad."

"Well, I'm sorry Johnny's dead," Bonny said. "But I don't have to be grief-stricken."

"You are the thing in my life I feel good about," I said.

"Me, too," Bonny said.

It was a moment to say something more, but I let it go by.

"I want to have the best marriage I can!" she went on. "Someone I love. I don't want to live in some terrible place and be poor. With a baby. But you know, I don't want to just get married to somebody like Daddy and be like my mother, either. I mean, that's just what you're supposed to do if you're a girl. You're supposed to *want* that! Is that all there is?"

Was that what I wanted, only the male side of it? Be a successful guy with a Packard like Dr. Bonington? Since the Depression I hadn't known to what socioeconomic class—in Tully's terminology—I belonged, but I surely didn't want to go on being poor.

Bonny's head tipped forward so that her profile became indistinguishable against the window. Glenn Miller was playing "Moonlight Becomes You."

After a time she said, "Don't you ever get scared?"

"What?"

"The war! What if we lose? We keep losing and losing!"

"We'll start winning."

"What if it just goes on and on?"

"It won't!"

She flung herself back into my arms. We kissed and kissed.

5

I sat on the long counter in Perry's basement with Herb Brownell, Ted Sparks and Chuck-the-checker in his tan apron. The two other drivers were smoking after-work cigarets and commiserating with Chuck, who had received his draft notice.

"Everybody's going to have to get in it if we're going to beat the little bastards," Chuck said. He sat on an upended delivery box with his skinny legs stretched out. Smoke hung in a high pall against the ceiling. The drivers rarely hung around after work unless it was a special occasion, such as Chuck's induction orders, or Big Bill Hutchinson, the union steward and once my mother's boyfriend, come to establish the Teamsters' presence.

In her glass cage Lois cranked up the day's CODs on her adding machine.

"From the President of the United States, Greetings!" Herb said. "Greetings from Eleanor, too!" He and Ted were twenty-eight and twenty-nine, which seemed to me close to the end of acceptable life.

Ted said, "What do you do, College? Just stay in school till you finish, and then they hand you a commission?"

"Those snipers like to pick off the lieutenants first, I hear," Chuck said.

I should have hustled home to do homework, but I knew there should be some ceremony about Chuck's induction orders.

"I'm Navy," I said.

"Navy's not doing so good these days," Ted said.

"Hope to God my 4-F holds," Herb said. He coughed dramatically, hand to chest, and I remembered Errol Flynn talking about his lungs.

"I couldn't stand seeing all that good pussy going to waste," Herb went on. "This town's full of snatch, their husband's off in the fleet. It's a public service."

"How many you got out on your route now, Herb?" Ted inquired admiringly.

Herb held up three fingers, which he reduced to one, pumping it obscenely. I only half-believed his tales of conquests. His habitual stance was slightly bent forward at the waist, as though his back troubled him because of the demands made on him on his Park Boulevard route.

"Did you ever fuck a Jap, Herb?" Ted asked.

"Shit, yes!"

"Ted wants to ask the oldest question in the world," Chuck said.

"What's that?"

"Was it set sideways?"

Ted collapsed with delight. These were the workers Tully considered more virtuous than the bourgeoisie. These jerks made me feel like a Superior Man.

"I wouldn't fuck a Jap," Chuck said. "Probably keep a razor blade in there to slice your dick off."

"Treacherous bastards," Ted said.

I spoke up to say that one of my best friends was Japanese. "The best quarterback San Diego High ever had. He's in premed at UCLA." Why had I had to say that?

"Most of them traitors, it looks like," Herb said.

"Bullshit!" I said.

Chuck's brown eyes flashed at me.

Spraying spit in his vociferousness, Ted said, "Everybody knows they've got radio transmitters to call Tokyo."

"That's all bullshit," I said. "Why do you want to believe that bullshit you read in the papers? They're just trying to make you hate Japs." I knew I wasn't going to persuade anyone here by quoting editorials from *the brand*. And there was the chance I'd fallen for *the brand* bullshit just as they fell for the *San Diego Union* variety.

I'd had a letter from Stan Takahashi, with sarcastic jokes about his father out in the shed with the powerful transmitter and his mother planting the lettuces in rows that pointed at Consolidated Aircraft. He'd related a joke about the rabbis who were such expert circumcisors that with two more strokes they could rid Japanese of the epicanthic folds.

Not joking, Stan had written that his father was afraid to go out of the house, and his Uncle Jiro had had to sell his fishing trawler for nothing when the Japanese were evicted from Terminal Island. Now the assholes were trying to get them evacuated from the Coast. There were marches and rallies at UCLA, but it looked bad.

The outrage had come out in his letter.

"It's you college kids that'll believe anything the pinkos tell you," Chuck said, who had been good to me as a junior driver, and who knew I worked for *the brand*.

"They caught this Jap out in East San Diego sending radio signals," Herb said. "The FBI came and took him away. No shit, Payt."

I kept my mouth shut. Everywhere the Japanese were victorious, and their cruelties in their victories were appalling. How did you tell the good ones from the bad ones, my mother wanted to know, since they all possessed epicanthic folds? How did I know Stan was a loyal American, and how was I so sure that the diminutive Mr. Takahashi did not have a transmitter out in the shed, and that his truck gardens were not planted in treacherous patterns? Because people of whom I was contemptuous believed crap like that?

"I don't have to hate people Westbrook Pegler and Henry McLemore say I'm supposed to hate," I said.

"We're watching you, College," Herb said. "Hanging around with Jap quarterbacks and working for that Commie rag."

I managed to grin, but Ted and Chuck wouldn't look at me now, lighting fresh cigarets.

"What about pachucos?" Chuck said, blowing smoke. "You got a pachuco football buddy, too?"

I had a Negro football buddy, another Tutti-frutti.

"They sure beat the shit out of the pachooks up in LA," Ted said, sticking out his jaw. No doubt he wished he had been there, helping the sailors and Marines clobber the East LA zoot-suiters. Some sailors had been robbed, and mobs of servicemen had roamed the streets of LA, beating up any Mexican who had the temerity to show himself in a drape-shape.

It seemed to me I got mad too quickly these days.

I slid off the zinc counter and drifted toward the stairs. Lois had removed her Perry's apron and was applying lipstick, peering into her purse mirror. I leaned in the doorway, admiring the pretty half-rounds of her bosom in her tight blue suit. I had a daydream of asking her to have an after-work Cuba libre with me sometime when her husband was out of town.

"Going home?" I asked.

"Ray's picking me up." A flake of lipstick had stuck to her crooked tooth. She regarded me with an almost smile. "How's your love life?"

"Just fine!"

"That's good," Lois said. In a different voice she said, "Were you boys telling dirty jokes back there?"

"Talking politics. They think I'm a Red."

"I know they talk about me. I can't stand that Herb Brownell. All he can think about is one thing."

"All the women on his route are after him."

"Oh, I'll bet!" Lois said, and laid a hand on my chest.

Just then Herb mounted the steps past us, with a wolf whistle. Lois snatched her hand away, and I felt my face burn.

"Well, good night!" I said.

"Tell your girlfriend I'm jealous," Lois said, gazing straight into my eyes.

6

Over Cokes in the Caff, I showed Pogey my latest rejection from *Black Mask,* a slip of mimeographed paper, thanks but no thanks. This one was initialed, however: "PR." P. D. Ratner was the editor.

"The editor read it, at least," Pogey said. His white shirt was starched and crisp, his face earnest, his nose sunburned as always.

The fact that I received another rejection slip for my collection meant that I was at least writing stories and sending them out. I had finished three stories this school year, when I had no time.

No time meant I had gone to sleep necking with Bonny on Point Loma and had done badly on two midterms.

Last summer Pogey and I had had great fun planning our private eye novel, laughing as we thought up crazy plots with Dick Tracy villains, like a muscleman called Le Cric, from Jean Valjean the human jackscrew in *Les Misérables.*

We didn't seem to have that kind of fun anymore, no time for tennis or for sitting around talking books. It was Bonny, lately, but the war, too, and working two jobs, and Alpha Beta. I didn't know what Pogey would do if the brothers really got mad at me for not attending meetings. If they were pissed off enough they would vote a silence, all of them forbidden to speak to the offender.

Pogey handed me back the rejection slip, which I refolded into my wallet. "You and Bonny are kind of pretty serious," he said without looking at me. His ears had turned red.

I shrugged elaborately. "She's supposed to marry a doctor."

"That sounds like a bad novel I can't remember the name of," Pogey said.

"Never darken Lady Barbara's doorway again, young whelp of Daltrey!"

Pogey grinned and rubbed his nose. It was like cranking an engine that wouldn't catch. Rich-kid Pogey would never know what it was like to be disapproved of because he wasn't up to some mark. Poison frogs and stones, the bitter tea of General P.

Looking down, Pogey said, "You ought to come to tong meeting Monday night. You know it?"

"I don't think I can sit still for all the shit I'm going to have to take."

He nodded miserably.

"It just doesn't seem serious anymore," I said. "I mean, we're losing the war and all they talk about is beer busts and attitudes."

I didn't want to quarrel with Pogey over Alpha Beta. The tong had been important to me, too, once, but now I was impatient with oaths and the Greek alphabet and critiquing each other's attitude. Something had happened to mine.

Liz Fletcher threaded her way toward us between the tables, classy-pale face beneath her dark hair, red lips, slim and long-legged. We stood to greet her, and Pogey looked at his wristwatch and said he had to make a class. Liz slipped into his chair.

She'd heard from Richie. "He's hoping he'll get to fly some new kind of plane," she said with her soft lisp.

"SBDs?"

"Maybe that's it." Her eyes fixed on me in that way she had; she licked her lips. "The *Sirocco*'s back in the Bay," she said.

"I guess you can see it from your house."

"I know all those yachts. John Ford's *Araner* and James Cagney's *Martha* and Richard Arlen's *Joby B*. I forget the name of George Brent's."

I thought of Lana Turner, who had been discovered sitting at a drugstore counter on Hollywood Boulevard, and Rita Hayworth discovered dancing in the Foreign Club in Tijuana. Of course Flynn would seem a way for Liz to be discovered.

I asked what her father had thought of her going out on the *Sirocco*.

Little muscles tensed around her mouth as though she were trying to smile. "He thinks Errol is a Nazi sympathizer. He keeps a file on him."

Her father was in Naval Intelligence at the destroyer base, so he was a detective of some kind.

"I kind of liked Flynn," I said.

"He's wonderful!" She held out her hand to admire Richie's ring, which glittered in the lights. "Do you think Richie has another girlfriend back in Pensacola?"

I stammered that Richie wouldn't do that.

"He did before," she said, smiling and turning the ring on her finger.

That was the year after Richie graduated from SC, when he was working for the studio and had the famous Cord car. He was down from LA staying with my father and Weezie.

"It's tough being in love with two women, Brud," he had said, leaning on the seawall at Mission Beach. It was a brilliant blue summer day with a few white puffs of cloud, and rollers sliding in to the beach. Seagulls hovered, and people lay on blankets on the sand or sat beneath beach umbrellas. Some kids were playing touch football, and a black dog charged and snapped at the last gasp of a wave.

"Liz Fletcher and your starlet," I said.

Richie gave me a severe look. "She's a feature player!"

"Oh, yeah," I said.

"So you've got a girlfriend now," Richie said, squinting out to sea. Her name was Ellie Minton. "Well, we've gone to some movies."

"Are you getting into her pants?"

I felt myself flush all the way into my hair.

"Be careful," Richie said. "You may think, they let you do it, it's a real present all wrapped up in fancy ribbons. But you pay for what you get. The more you get, the more you owe."

One of the kids playing touch caught a pass and ran across the goal, which was a line scraped in the sand.

I said it all sounded too complicated for a simple country boy.

Now I thought that Richie had been bragging that day, the way Bonny was afraid Johnny Pierce had bragged about getting into her pants.

I asked Liz if she wanted a Coke, but she said she had to run. She patted my hand and with her thin smile started away, swinging her hips to sidestep the tables.

I had a flash of Bonny across the Caff and raised a hand to signal her, but she disappeared. I knew she didn't like my meeting Liz on campus, as though I had the hots for my brother's fiancée, as though I, too, were in love with two women.

7

This week's *brand* was on the counter at the printshop. The headlines were BIDDLE TESTIMONY REFUTED, OPA ISSUES NEW ALLOTMENTS, and MOLESTED TOT NAMES ASSAILANT.

Tully handed me an envelope. "Fan mail," he said.

The handwriting on lined paper torn from a tablet was shaky, maybe from age, or rage.

Dear Rats,

Why don't you rats go back to Russia. I know you rats "bore from within." You print filthy lies about decent American judges and evil lies about the govt. We are on to filthy rats like you kikes. I am warning you there are plenty of us onto your tricks, and if Rep. Dies don't know about you he is going to.

The signature was illegible, but legible beneath it was "American Legion Post 5."

I dropped the letter onto Tully's desk, the letter that was not merely from the American Legion but also HUAC, the Silver Shirts, Father Coughlin—the Jap- and Jew-hating shitty bottom layer of America.

"Hey, Commie rat!" I said to Tully, who gazed back at me with his arms folded on his chest and his jaw set like a Christian martyr with the lions snarling and pawing the sand.

My own anger leaked away at the realization that he was scared stiff of the threat of the House Un-American Activities Committee.

Tee-John stamped in from the pressroom to lean on the counter beside me, his jaw working like a camel's on his chaw of tobacco. Tee-John was an old IWW stiff.

"How about it, Tee-John?" I said. "What if the Legion sets up a picket line?"

"Break fockin arms!" Tee-John raised an arm-and-hammer fist.

"They'd smash Charlotte," Tully said.

"Bring gun," Tee-John said.

"That's not a good idea, Tee."

My father had warned me about feelings at his Legion post against *the brand,* and one of the reasons I didn't want to go to a tong meeting was that I didn't want to find out how my fraternity brothers felt about it. Irony and pity were called for.

"Well, it's good to know somebody reads the paper," I said.

They both frowned at me. Tully asked me to make a coffee run.

Heading out the door, I almost knocked down Calvin's Dessy.

"Sorry!"

In the streetlight-illuminated dark she didn't recognize me immediately. Then her hand flew up in greeting.

"It's Cal's friend! I'm going to the White Castle for something to eat."

"I'm going for coffee."

She started along with me. She wore silk stockings and high heels; she must be ready for an evening of tricks! But I found I was pleased to be walking beside her down 3rd Street; there was something exciting about her availability. A V-8 drifted past, a man whistling out the window. Dessy ignored him. When I thought of her having to screw her bosses in San Francisco, I felt a familiar gob of outrage in my throat again.

She wobbled along beside me on her heels. She smelled of concentrate of flowers.

"You look nice!" I said.

"Thank you!" She had a chirpy voice with a sexy catch to it.

She took my arm with a flick of her Ella Cinders eyes at me. Her business was manipulating. I didn't think Bonny even knew how to flirt.

In the steamy warmth of the White Castle, we sat in a booth with a freshly swabbed table. Dessy ordered a poached egg on toast and a Coke, and I three coffees to go. Cal was out of town, she said.

When she asked what my sign was, I didn't know what she meant.

"Your Zodiac sign!"

I didn't know.

"When's your birthday, silly?"

"July fifth."

"Cancer! I'm Aries, April eleventh. Don't you know astrology?"

When her eggs and coffee were delivered, I found myself insisting on paying. Manipulated! Dessy didn't seem like the other south-of-Broadway hookers except for her painted eyes.

"April eleventh of what year?" I asked.

"Nineteen twenty." She was older than the young whore in the donkey show at the Molino Rojo. "And you?" she asked.

"Nineteen twenty-one." I watched her ring-laden fingers tearing her toast into bite-sized segments. She popped a piece into her mouth, like a chipmunk with a nut.

"Tell me one of your dreams," she said.

I thought about it. "Well, I'm on a bike going up a long hill that keeps getting steeper until it finally goes convex, and I have to pump really hard to get over the hump. I can't remember what happens, so I guess I make it."

"I'll look it up. I'm sure it's meaningful. Fear of falling, maybe. My father died in a fall when he was out hunting," she said in a frail voice. "My mother died on my fifth birthday," she added.

"That's too bad," I managed. I couldn't bring myself to inquire about her dreams, and I had better hustle the coffee back to Tully and Tee-John before it got any colder. Dessy pouted down at her untouched egg.

"I get so lonely when Cal's away," she said.

I wondered if Calvin was helping his Uncle Red smuggle Mexican tires across the border with the connivance of someone in the *Direccion* of the Molino Rojo. How did Dessy feel about Calvin being a Negro? Maybe she had to pretend she loved him. Maybe she really loved him.

What would Marx think of her working conditions?

"I know it's silly," Dessy went on, "but I have to have a man to take care of me. I know it's because Daddy always took care of me, and he died."

I had the sensation of some sticky substance clinging to me.

"Cal wants to drive out on Sunday and see that big dirigible come to Camp Kearny Mesa," she said. She raised her arms to stretch, her breasts pressing the wool of her sweater into little peaks. "Would you and your girlfriend like to come along?"

I said that sounded like fun, but my girlfriend went sailing with her parents on Sundays.

8

Dr. and Mrs. Bonington were in the study listening to the evening news, so I didn't have to deal with Mrs. B.'s disapproval. Bonny wore tan shorts and a white shirt with the shirttail out, pacing barefoot as I perched on the arm of the sofa. She left to make us some cocoa.

Through the unlighted dining room with its thicket of chair and table legs, I could see her bare legs in the bright slice of kitchen doorway. I admired the perfect H's of the backs of her knees, and the ascent of her thighs into her shorts. I stretched and tried to feel a proprietorial ease, but there was something jagged in the air.

Bonny returned with cocoa mugs and a pot on a tray. Her face was pink from the heat of the stove, and cheek pieces of fair hair swung forward as she bent to pour the cocoa.

"Charley got orders to ship out," she said.

I whistled. "Where to?"

"He thinks Australia."

"I thought the Coast Guard—"

"God!" Bonny said. "I've been hearing that all day!" Her eyes were dark with resentment as she seated herself on the footstool.

"Sorry."

"Well, I'm sorry I'm in a bad mood. When we have kids, we're going to pretend each one is as important as the other."

It was a complaint I'd heard before.

"He was flunking out of Stanford and he was going to get drafted, so they talked him into enlisting in the Coast Guard. Now Daddy's trying to pull strings to get him out. God, they must get sick of people pulling strings for their precious sons!"

It did not seem a good time to mention an expedition with Calvin and Dessy to see the world's largest dirigible arrive at Camp Kearny Mesa.

"Mother and Daddy are listening to the news back in the study. Do you want to listen to the news?"

I had not come here for the news, which I hated. I had come for kisses. I didn't want her to know that I was a hypocrite when I pretended to comfort her when the news was bad.

I reached out for her, but she shook her head. "We can't tonight. I'm a mess tonight."

Chapter 5

1

THAT SUNDAY, WHEN BONNY WAS SAILING WITH HER PAR-
ents, I went along with Calvin King and Dessy to see the Navy dirigible
Canton put down at an airfield on Camp Kearny Mesa, north of San Diego.
The three of us rode in the front seat of Chrysie-car, top down and the
slipstream snapping in my hair, Calvin at the wheel wearing a checked cap,
and Dessy tucked between us with a scarf tied over her head. Calvin was in
semi-zoot and Dessy in a sleek pink dress and high heels. This was south-
of-Broadway highlife in the new-smelling car with its plaid upholstery.

I had been shocked to see Calvin's hand cup Dessy's breast as casually as
handing her into the car.

Crossing Mission Valley and climbing to the mesa, Calvin performed a
stylish double-clutch into second to slow into a line of cars.

I lounged against my door with a hand palm-planing in the wind.
Dessy's hip pressed against me. Sometimes she leaned her head on Calvin's
shoulder, sometimes on mine.

There had been headlines for days announcing the arrival of the *Canton,* and some morbid interest because of the fate of the *Hindenburg,* once

the world's greatest dirigible, which had blown up in New Jersey with a terrible loss of life. The *Canton* was guaranteed safe because it was filled with American helium instead of dangerous German hydrogen.

On the mesa, cars accelerated into a field where sailors directed them into rows facing a red dirt airstrip. Beyond it were huts with corrugated metal roofs, and a flagpole where a windsock flapped in a gust of wind that kicked up a swirl of red dust.

Calvin pulled up beside a Hudson, and a Model A turned in next to us, cars continuing to fill the third rank of parking. People wandered among the cars or seated themselves on running boards in the erratic winds, some with picnic hampers. The three of us sat on the back of the front seat with Calvin's silver flask of gin and orange juice.

I grimaced at myself for hesitating to lip the mouth of the flask after Dessy. Coach Garland's slides of syphilis victims! I was conscious of glances from the surrounding cars. Maybe they thought Calvin was the chauffeur.

I squinted north, over the glare of the sun off the metal roofs. Clusters of sailors were also peering north, their caps like popcorn.

"Aren't those sailor boys cute?" Dessy said, snuggling between us. Her silk-stockinged legs, thin as a child's, dangled down the back of the seat.

"You just think how cute we is," Calvin said. "That'll take care of that, beauty."

"You two are the cutest and you know it!"

I hated glancing around to see who was watching Dessy flirting with Calvin.

"It's too bad Bonny couldn't come with us," Dessy said. She turned her starry-eyelashed eyes toward me. I blew out my breath to think of Mrs. Bonington's reaction to Bonny going for a ride with a whore and her Negro pimp.

"Is she nice to you?" Dessy asked.

"What she means is does she put out," Calvin said.

"I'm afraid she wouldn't know what that means," I said. Dessy put a hand on my knee, perhaps to comfort me. Her hand on my leg and the pressure of her hip made me glance at Calvin, who was surveying the horizon.

"Sometimes it is possible for the wise to transcend their gender," I said.

"How's that again, child?"

Just then there was a disturbance of voices raised and people pointing. Dust whipped into a halfhearted funnel that skidded along the airstrip.

The ranks of sailors craned their necks. A high speck had risen above the horizon.

The *Canton* drifted toward us, somehow enlarging rather than approaching, a silver football with a gondola slung beneath its belly. Close and low it filled the sky, turning to circle the field.

Ropes drifted at a slant from narrow ports in the gondola. They trailed across the ground. Sailors scampered after them.

Another gust whipped up red dust, and the great shape lifted again to shouts of alarm. Two sailors still clung to the ropes, both capless, sailing twenty feet above the ground and swiftly rising. One dropped, waving his arms. The other still clung to the rope.

He soared over the ranked automobiles, legs trailing, white face peering down. Then he was falling, arms and legs flapping. Dessy screamed. There were other screams.

I put my arm around Dessy's straining back. Her hands covered her face.

The silent silver shape floated northward, dragging its shadow over the parked cars. People ran in different directions.

Dessy wailed.

Calvin slid down behind the wheel, and I piled into the backseat. In slow stop-and-go we rolled off the field and back onto the road, Dessy curled into a ball against her door. I felt a vast embarrassment for the United States, for its sailors, soldiers, and Marines, for its fliers like Johnny Pierce. How could incompetents hope to win the war?

Calvin was murmuring to Dessy, arm around her. Her father had been killed in a fall.

The Chrysler slowed and swung into a sandy lane lined with high brush. I glimpsed the *Canton* once more, in a stately turn over the rim of the mesa.

"I don't want to die!" Dessy whimpered.

"You are not gone die, beauty!"

Calvin stopped the car on the sandy track. "Child, will you take a little walk? I'll give you a toot."

I climbed out of the backseat and hurried ahead. Around a bend was a murky pool, fifty feet across. I stood at the edge, gazing up at the mesa for another glimpse of the dirigible. Death! We had become part of the war. Calvin would be employing whatever method he knew to calm Dessy down. Taking care of her. It was the complexity of the female genito-urinary system that made women prone to hysteria. Had I read that in *Sex-*

71

ology? Love and death were what novels were about, Mr. Chapman had said in a lecture.

It wasn't long before a horn tooted. Walking back, I tried to compose my face into an appropriate expression. Dessy was huddled against Calvin. I climbed into the backseat again. Sirens squalled on the Valley Road.

"You know what my stepmother said to me?" Dessy said in a normal voice, as Calvin backed out of the lane.

"What's that, hon?"

"Said Daddy was in the wrong place at the wrong time. That's exactly what she said."

"That's one cold bitch. We know that, don't we, beauty?"

"That poor sailor boy was in the wrong place at the wrong time."

"Hung on too long!" Calvin said. He rolled his eyes at me in the rearview mirror.

I thought Calvin really cared for her. He was gentle with her, he called her "beauty," he took care of her in every way, and he rented her out to sailors and Marines for whatever it was she charged. And what happened when she was no longer a beauty, no longer desirable, no longer exploitable? Did a descending progress take her to Tijuana, to fuck dogs and ponies?

I sprawled in the backseat watching Dessy's scarf-covered head leaning against Calvin's shoulder, with pity constricting my throat so that I could hardly swallow.

Is she nice to you? Dessy had asked, who had had to be nice to her bosses to keep her job in San Francisco, and had been better off then than now. Bonny didn't have to be nice to anyone. Her father was an ophthalmologist who lived in Mission Hills.

But she had been nice to Johnny Pierce. She would have to be nice to some doctor to make the marriage her mother wanted her to make.

Ol Paint was parked on Sunday-deserted 3rd Street. When I got out of Chrysie-car, Dessy sat up and beckoned to me. She put an arm around my neck, pulled my face down, and kissed me on the cheek.

"You are a nice sweet boy, Payton," she murmured.

Calvin got out to speak to me, and we halted together thirty feet from the Chrysler's grille. "Give her some pills, she'll sleep it off," Calvin said in a low voice. "She gets like that, her daddy dying the way he did and all."

I wondered how Calvin would react if I inquired about renting Dessy in a professional way—and became part of Dessy's exploitation-molestation fate. I wouldn't even know how to phrase the question.

I said, "I'm worried about us in this war. Those guys couldn't even tie that dirigible down without getting killed."

"Those are just stupid swabbies, child." Calvin's handsome milk-chocolate face gazed at me seriously. "You and me's got to get into this war if we're gone win it. Don't you know that?"

2

Tully, who often came in on Sundays, was visible through the printshop window, seated at his desk reading the funny papers.

I went inside, to lean on the counter and tell him what had happened on the mesa.

"Somebody's sons," Tully said. He wore a brown tweed jacket and a tie slipped loose at the throat. He had probably come to the printshop from church, maybe the only Commie SWP editor and Abraham Lincoln Brigade vet who attended the Episcopalian church up by the park.

"They ought to've known the wind was gusty! There was a windsock. We're never going to win this war if we keep getting fucked up like that!" I was talking too fast, almost spitting to get it out.

I was disgusted at the sear of tears in my eyes. Somebody's sons. "They died in vain!" I said.

"If this were a proper paper you would have a scoop," Tully said. "You could write an editorial on American unpreparedness, instead of the tots column."

I'd done several other right-hand columns since the Altadena judge.

Tully busied himself refolding the Sunday *Union*. "It's settled for the Coast Japs," he said. "The president's signed the evacuation order."

"Oh, shit!" I said.

3

Mr. Chapman handed the typescript of my story "Essential Parts" back to me. His office had a kind of Moorish window, looking out on the parking lot. Three walls were bookshelves, books stacked vertically and horizontally and at a slant. His desk was a big clutter of stacked books and papers.

"Very lively," he said. "*Black Mask* is your chosen venue, is it?"

"Yes, sir."

"Dashiell Hammett was published there."

"I like Raymond Chandler also," I said.

"The problem that I see," he said, "is if you have had none of these experiences of which you write, you are forced to remasticate the fiction of this kind that you have read. Thus a freshness is lost."

Shit. "But what do I know?" I said. "I know about parents getting divorced and the Depression and having to move out of Mission Hills to Normal Heights." Maybe something about love.

"Normal Heights!" Mr. Chapman said, gaping at me. "What an extraordinary stroke of luck for a writer—to live in Normal Heights! The possibilities for irony, and of course for heavyhanded symbolism."

"It's because the old normal school used to be there," I said.

"Ah, Daltrey, you must do something with Normal Heights!"

Where I lived with an Indian barber and his redheaded wife. There were many jokes about the name "Normal." I asked if he'd ever seen the weekly newspaper called *the brand*.

"Ah, yes, the lowercase radical sheet with the tots headlines."

"I write that column sometimes," I said. "Not that there's much writing involved."

"My goodness!" Mr. Chapman said. "Sit down, Daltrey, and tell me about writing about abused tots. Are your political beliefs congruent with those of your paper—a young man from Normal Heights? That is so un–San Diego!"

"Not really," I said. I didn't think Tully's were, either. Was that the way the world ran? You just did what you were paid to do, and never mind how you felt about anything?

I told him about putting the column together from the clippings with their little tags that identified what newspaper they had been taken from. I almost snickered at his expression of wonder.

"Think of it!" he said, his eyes squinting at me behind his glasses. "Normal Heights and molestations!"

I said, "You know what? It all seems to connect together. I know a girl who was seduced by her boyfriend going off in the service and had to go down to Tijuana for an abortion. And down in Tijuana, at the Molino Rojo—those Mexican girls doing it with ponies for a show. And those whores in those whorehouses south of Broadway, where I work at *the brand*.

And the Japanese evacuated from the Coast. And at the same time those Jap soldiers beheading British guys and using prisoners for bayonet practice. And those swabbies that got killed trying to bring the *Canton* in on Kearny Mesa. I mean, it's all—" I knew I was being a jerk, but I said, "The war's the greatest molestation of all!"

"That is very ambitious thinking, Daltrey."

"Yes, sir. But I keep at it."

"I will give you a hint as to what to do about it. Just start from Normal Heights."

At first I thought he was joking. When I realized he wasn't, I could feel my face burn.

"You mean a novel," I said.

"That's what I mean."

"I don't know enough to write a novel."

"But as you said, you know about parents divorcing, and the shocks of the Depression, and you will presently, no doubt, know about war."

I said I was only twenty.

"I believe you will be maturing very fast soon, Daltrey." And he said solemnly, "It is the talent it is death to hide."

I got to my feet. I felt as though I were watching myself from about ten feet off, a gawky college junior with a big head.

"I am very impressed with your ideas, Daltrey." Professor Chapman said. "I am also impressed that you are striving to perfect the writing skills that will be necessary to them. I only suggest that you widen your reading to discover what contemporary novelists are achieving. I will be very pleased to advise you on your reading."

No point in telling him I didn't have time to read anything but what I had to read, what with Perry's and *the brand* and school and Bonny.

"You've read Hemingway," he said.

"Yes, sir."

" 'Big Two-Hearted River'?"

"Yes, sir."

"It is a textbook of writing. I suggest you look at it again."

"Yes, sir," I said.

4

There was racketing in 3rd Street outside the window of the printshop, swabbies and gyrenes out in force, hurrying past the window. Los Angeles's riots had spread south.

"Noisy out," I said to Tully

"A good night for Mexicans to stay home," he commented.

A good night for civilians to stay home also. I'd had to ignore a couple of cracks about not being in uniform on my way to work, and I'd parked Ol Paint in the alley to keep out of trouble. The servicemen out tonight were not ones I wanted to quarrel with over the issue of the pachucos, nor the rights of the Coast Japanese, either.

10,000 JAPANESE TO BE EVACUATED IN 3 WEEKS. That meant Stan and his brother, Ben, in LA, and his sister and Mr. and Mrs. Takahashi in San Diego, and nine thousand and some others.

I didn't know what to do about outrages. I couldn't seem to get the essence to come out in the tots column, and I didn't know what to do with the idea of Normal Heights that Mr. Chapman had thought so important. I could always go out to Mission Beach and quarrel with Weezie about the Japs who were Americans and those who were the enemy, but my father would say something commonsensical and pompous that would infuriate me, and there was still that letter from the Post 5 asshole that I had to remind myself was not my father's fault.

Just now it seemed the better part of valor to be the spectator Tully thought writers ought to be.

Tully handed me the proofs, and I studied the right-hand column, with its head TEACHER EXPOSED. A third-grade teacher in Bakersfield had been arrested for "abusing" his students, boys. I was finding it more and more difficult to write the tots column. My brain shrank away from it; I could hardly make myself focus. I had managed to fill this particular column with almost nothing specific. I had looked up Bakersfield weather in the WPA guidebook and got a bullshit paragraph out of that.

From the pressroom came the sounds of Charlotte starting up and immediately stalling.

A gang of sailors surged past the window, looking like a crowd scene from a movie. Two Marines halted to light each others' cigarets, wearing green caps, their sharpshooter medals glinting on their chests. One of Bob-

O's letters had expressed satisfaction at his successes on the rifle range at Parris Island.

On Tully's desk was the *San Diego Union,* with an editorial on the front page:

ACT NOW—OR RESIGN AND COME HOME

The United States forces in the Pacific have participated in several engagements, bravely and courageously.

But they have lost each one, and along with the forces of the United Nations, they are retreating steadily . . .

"Rugged!" I said. I had a feverish feeling, like coming down with the flu. I hoped Bonny hadn't seen this paper.

Tully scrubbed his nose. A fringe of curls protruded beneath his leather cap. "Those poor devils in the Philippines are sunk, but once we get rid of some incompetent generals and admirals we'll win it." He looked at me anxiously, as though it were important that I believe that.

Maybe the anger of the servicemen in the streets was frustration at incompetence. Maybe because the war was being lost to Japs, they had to take it out on anyone with a different skin color.

Shouting revved up outside, and sailors hurried past the window again. The eagerness on their faces reminded me of a boys' game of Capture the Flag.

"Chasing some poor Mexican kid," Tully said. They'd beaten up on fourteen-year-olds in LA. What happened in LA was always worse than what happened in San Diego.

I went back to reading proof, dull stuff.

The door burst open and a man in a fawn-colored suit flung himself inside, panting like a locomotive. One of the lapels of his jacket was torn off, and a splash of blood stained his brown cheek. Calvin King.

"Need help, child!"

Two sailors crowded in the door after him, and Calvin spun away into the pressroom. Tully rose, white-faced, as more sailors jammed into the doorway. The door whacked against its stop.

I sprinted after Calvin, yanked the fire axe off the pressroom wall, and turned to face the sailors in the pressroom doorway.

I swung the axe in hard feints. More white caps and flushed faces congealed behind those in the doorway. If I let them past the opening, they'd surround me! I couldn't look to see where Calvin was. Tee-John gaped, inky-faced, from Charlotte's pit. I feinted with the axe, outrage surging in high-octane energy in my arms.

One of the sailors stared at me as though I were crazy.

"We want that fucken pachook back there!"

Milk-chocolate-brown Calvin in his zoot suit had been taken for a Mexican. I slashed out with the axe, panting like Calvin.

"Out of the way, punk! We're comin through!"

The swabbies crowding the doorway looked no older than I was, except for the leader, who was short and broad, with a mean squinting face. Beside him, another brandished a length of two-by-four. Outside a horn honked insistently. I couldn't see Tully past the crowd of black-and-white uniforms.

"Fuckin pachuco-lover!" one of them yelled.

"Four-F shit!"

The leader advanced half a step. I swung the axehead at his outstretched hand, which he snatched back with a yell. It shocked me almost into taking a step back that I had tried to hit his hand. All at once my arms were exhausted. Tee-John was beside me, black-stained face and glaring white-rimmed eyeballs. He held a big black revolver pointed.

"Get out of here you fockin pieces shit!" he shouted. He cocked the revolver noisily. Holding it in both hands, he jammed the muzzle at squinch-face. In a general retreat, Tee-John forced the door shut and jammed his shoulder against it. I threw the bolt.

Beyond the door a commanding voice was raised. "Out! Out of here! Move along, you people!" The Shore Patrol had arrived.

"Where's Calvin?" I panted.

Tee-John jerked his head toward the back door.

"Goal-line stand!" I said.

A flash of white split his stained face. *No pasarán!*

There was a single rap on the door, and Tee-John unbolted and opened it. Tully stood there pasty-faced in his leather cap, round-shouldered in his loafer jacket. I understood the contempt of the combatant for the noncombatant. Past him, through the window, the street was empty in the darkness.

Tully scowled at the revolver. "I told you not to bring that down here!"

Tee-John spun the gun by its trigger guard.

"Heard them telling the SPs you had a gun in here, and a German accent. The SPs will tell the cops. You'd better get going, Tee."

Tee-John spat. I glared at Tully. Just then the window behind him exploded. A length of two-by-four flopped onto the floor. Tee-John started for the door, but Tully caught his arm.

"Get going right now!"

While the printer changed his clothes, Tully and I carried half a sheet of beaverboard from the pressroom to cover the broken window, nailing it in place. If the sailors were coming back to beat us up, I didn't have the strength to pick up the fire axe again. Courage had swarmed through my veins in my outrage, but dribbled away when I had time to think.

"I told him not to bring that gun down here," Tully said. "He's got an indictment against him in Utah."

It occurred to me that Tee-John might have actually shot one of the sailors, as I had tried to hit one with the fire axe. Pale cast of thought!

"We'll have to do the pressrun by ourselves tonight," Tully grumbled.

I was trying to coax Charlotte into action when Tully called from the office that someone was here to see me. Dessy stood against the counter in a clinging brown dress and high heels, her mouth bloodred in her pasty face. Tully stood beside his desk.

"Can you come?" Dessy said in a low voice. "Cal's hurt."

My jacket hung on a hook behind the door, and I armed into it. I exchanged a glance of communication with Tully, who liked Calvin.

I followed Dessy out into the chilly night, clear black sky, pale stars, a salt breeze off the Bay. At the corners right and left, streetlights spread pale halos. Men lounged along the walls of the buildings down toward the White Castle and the Fremont Bar like fungus growing there. Nearer, a sailor leaned against a telephone pole. It was like a stage set. Dessy took my arm. I smelled her flower scent spiced with something bitter, maybe fear.

"Where is he?" I whispered.

"At the Benford. They beat him up."

I remembered the Hemingway story of the bullfighter whose legs refused to move him closer to the bull. I put one foot in front of the other, straight ahead, Dessy on my arm, hoping no one recognized me as the pachuco-loving 4-F from the printshop. We headed catercorner across toward the Benford with its high, suspended rectangles of windows. The pattern of light and dark was like some diagram signaling Japanese bombers.

In the next block were two MPs, white caps, belts, leggings, and nightsticks. I whispered to Dessy to ask how badly Calvin was hurt.

"He thinks broken ribs."

The watching sailors must think I was headed for the Benford to get laid. Dessy's beringed hand clutched my arm. The quiet was punctuated with the small clatter of her heels. In the Benford she led me down a corridor and opened a door on pit darkness. I trailed her down stairs. Another door opened on light. Calvin was spread-eagled on a cot, coatless, torn fawn trousers, ripped shirt, an adhesive pad on his cheek, the eye above it swollen shut.

"Can you take me up to LA, child? My Uncle Red's outta town, and I can't get to Chrysie-car."

A hundred and thirty-five miles and back on Ol Paint's two fair tires, two bald ones, and a terrible spare. And Tully counting on me for the pressrun.

Calvin struggled to raise himself on an elbow, wincing. "Got to get outta town, child. I knifed a swabbie."

"Is he dead?"

"He was sure as hell trying to kill me. Thought I was a fuckin pachook, for Christ sake!"

Standing beside the cot with one hand pressed to her breast, the other to her mouth, a scarf tied over her hair, Dessy looked like a tiny peasant woman.

"Can you make it upstairs if I go get my car?" I said to Calvin.

"Got to."

Outside a siren wailed, others joining it in a muffled swelling of sound. The light went out.

Calvin crowed. "My luck is holdin! It's a blackout."

5

The clusters of men were visible in the pale moonlight as I slanted Ol Paint to the curb by the side door of the hotel. Calvin groaned as he tucked himself inside, Dessy leaning in to kiss him while I searched the mirror for anyone coming up behind.

I drifted on down the street in the blackout with my list of worries:

Tully, who had an adversarial relationship with Charlotte, making the press run alone; driving in the blackout without an E gasoline sticker; tires.

I turned north on Coast Highway. Pencils of searchlight beams switched across the sky above the Bay.

"You said your uncle could get tires," I said.

"I'll give you his number and you call him up and tell him you're my pal." Calvin sounded as though he was hurting.

Lights were coming on. All clear! A false alarm as always. I switched on my headlights, to encounter oncoming beams. Soon we were heading up Rose Canyon, three and a half, four hours to Los Angeles: Del Mar, Solana Beach, Encinitas, Oceanside, San Clemente, Corona del Mar, Newport Beach, Huntington Beach, Long Beach, Signal Hill—

Calvin moved carefully to test one position after another, cursing. He smelled sour. Ol Paint's engine rumbled, quiet clinking of the key ring against the steering post.

"If that fucker croaks I'll probly have to enlist in their fucken war," Calvin said.

You joined up when it was too dangerous, or dull, or complicated, to remain a civilian; or because you wanted to go kill Japs or Germans. Why had Richie joined up when he had a terrific studio job, a Cord car, and two women? Because one of them had drowned herself?

"I thought you were 4-F."

"I got two names. I registered under Calvin Goodrich, and my momma sends back draft notices, she don't know any Calvin Goodrich. But if they start payin attention I'm up shit creek."

Headlights descended the canyon toward us. I turned on the radio, Billie Holliday singing: "But when he starts in to love me/ He's so fine and mellllow!"

Calvin said, "I'm not sayin Dessy can't take care of herself, but if you'd just be around for her? Case she gets down the way she does."

What if Dessy had to be bailed out of jail?

"Sure," I said.

Now he seemed to be dozing, sharp profile pressed against the window glass. Seal Beach, Long Beach, up Lakewood to Firestone, up Firestone into the heart of heartless LA; grainy-eyed, neck muscles aching, left foot tapping to the beat of the radio.

Calvin's destination was a two-story house off Central Avenue. He made a fuss of writing Red Goodrich's phone number on the inside of a matchbook cover and eased out of Ol Paint, stepping slowly up a walk with his elbow tucked against his side. He moved like he was seventy years old.

When he had disappeared inside the house, I made a U-turn and started back for San Diego.

6

When I came in, Mr. and Mrs. Button were eating breakfast in the sunny kitchen. I'd hoped to sneak into my room without any conversation, but Mrs. Button called to me: "Payton, you are to phone Bonny!"

She bounced out of her chair to pour me a cup of coffee. She was a plump, redhaired woman with big teeth, Mr. Button dark and dour. He was a different kind of dark than Calvin, with a grayer coloration beneath the skin and around his eyes. He was half Navajo.

I sat on the chair Mrs. Button indicated. My eyes felt like burnt holes and my shoulders ached. The coffee seared my mouth in a good way. Time to get down to *the brand* for the newsstand deliveries.

Mr. Button gazed at me solemnly through his rimless glasses. "Iris didn't tell her you were out all night, boy."

I said I'd had to take a friend to LA.

It seemed that Bonny had confided in Mrs. Button that her brother was shipping out.

Mrs. Button's gleaming teeth looked two sizes too large for her mouth. "I thought the Coast Guard was just for here!" she said.

"If I was a younger man I'd be out there," Mr. Button said. "But I did my duty last time."

Another hint that I ought to be in the service. I took my coffee into the living room to phone Bonny. It felt like a cat being stroked to know that someone was anxious about you. I promised to see her tonight.

In my room I trampled on the dirty laundry to sit at the typewriter and type out some dialog that had come to me on the long drive back down the Coast. I cranked a sheet of newsprint into the machine:

"I can get your legs broken for a hundred bucks," said the little man with the big nose.

"I can get yours broken for fifty," Dodge said.

7

From Point Loma the *Sirocco* must be one of the dark shapes out on the moonlit Bay. With Bonny in my arms, I was the recipient of bad news. She was going to be a nurse's aide two nights a week.

"I'll be helping at Mercy Hospital."

She would be doing something for the war effort, and I was jealous because there were two nights a week when I couldn't be kissing her.

"Your mother thinks we're seeing too much of each other," I said.

She buried her face in my neck. She had worn Johnny Pierce's pin because her mother hated him.

"It was Dr. Bailes," she said finally. "He asked me, and I said okay. It makes me feel better about me. You know, I do know some nursey things from Daddy." She laid her fingers against my neck. "That's your carotid artery."

I knew about carotid arteries. Jeff Dodge had stuck the muzzle of his automatic against Jake Gotch's neck and told him, "If you move I'll blow out your carotid artery and you'll strangle on your own blood!"

"I can feel your heart beat," Bonny said.

"Beats for you."

She asked me if Liz and Richie did it.

Of course they did it, they weren't kids like us.

Blues on the radio: "Hurry down sunshine/ See what tomorrow brings!"

"Liz was in some mess at State when I was at the Bishop School," Bonny said. "Do you remember that?"

I didn't.

"Daddy knows about it. That dance professor that was before Gilliam was fired."

"I guess Captain Fletcher's a real bastard."

"There was something about a private detective," Bonny said. "That's funny, isn't it? That's what you write about."

I didn't want to talk about Liz. I wanted to resume kissing and fondling.

She said intensely, "I just hate that!"

"What?"

"Saying mean things about Liz because I'm afraid you like her. That's so bad!" She tucked her knees up to her chest. "I don't want to be like that," she said. She sounded as though she were going to cry.

"You're the one I like," I said. "You're the one my heart beats for."

"My mother thinks I'm seeing too much of you," she said.

"She thinks you're precious and so do I."

I pulled her back into my embrace. We kissed and kissed, but there was that hollowness, an incompleteness that I did not want to feel. My crotch had turned to pure ache.

She told me she loved me.

Chapter 6

1

At my grandmother's I checked to make sure that the bricks remained as I had disposed them under the shrub at the corner of the front yard. I hated the idea of sneaky tramps receiving messages that my grandmother was alone in her little house.

She met me at the door with her arms-raised stance of delight. I hugged her and kissed her suede-soft cheek, sniffing the violet sachet.

I was tired of my detective Jeff Dodge, and I'd had the idea of using my grandmother's John Burgess in that role.

My story that had won the High Schools Fiction Contest in the *San Diego Union* had not been fiction, but one of my grandmother's tales hardly changed from her telling it. John Burgess was a character out of her youth, who, taken advantage of because of his credulity, would always by luck or pluck turn a situation to his benefit.

Locked in a cellar by mean kids, who seemed to have abounded in Richmond, John Burgess tried to dig his way out with a convenient spade and uncovered a Mason jar filled with double-eagle gold coins buried by a previous owner of the house. When he was driven away from the swimming hole by the town bully, John Burgess arrived at the turnpike just in time to save the daughter of the druggist in a runaway buggy. The grateful father gave him a job at the soda fountain, where he could drink his fill of sarsaparilla. Many of John Burgess's triumphs were over the bully Rupe Johnson.

I sprawled in the easy chair, smoothing the antimacassar over the worn place on the chair arm, while my grandmother bustled into the kitchen to make cocoa, which was presented, steaming, on the round lacquer tray. I remembered my years sequestered here, when no one else had wanted me. My grandmother stood before me, hands clasped in her apron, watching me burn my lips on hot chocolate.

"I forgot to get marshmallows at the store!"

"I'm too old for marshmallows," I said. Marshmallows were one of the uncomplicated pleasures of childhood, as were her custards, with their crinkled brown and yellow crusts. I remembered her reading Dickens to me when I was in bed with the mumps, Pip and J-O-Joe, and Lawyer Jaggers shooting his finger out accusingly, and Miss Havisham calling out, "Play!"

When she asked about my schoolwork, I told her I was writing a paper on *Huckleberry Finn* for Mr. Chapman. I said, "Huck reminds me of John Burgess. I was hoping you'd tell me a John Burgess and Rupe Johnson story."

Her pale blue eyes peered at me in surprise over her spectacles, but she seemed pleased. "Well, dear, Rupe was very jealous because John was Sophia Brinkerman's favorite boy at the Academy. Once Rupe was chasing John on his wheel. He'd let Rupe almost catch up, then he'd pedal faster. Until he came to a part of State Street where there were two potholes. John turned at the last minute and whizzed right between them, and Rupe hit one and just flew head over heels." She laughed in her tinkly way.

She continued with the familiar story of Rupe locking Sophia Brinkerman in the coat closet at the Academy, so as to capture John Burgess when he tried to set her free.

What a handy muse my grandmother was! I thought I might use the bicycle story, only with cars; John Burgess and the villain, a movie stuntman.

When I arrived at Perry's to check in, the evening papers were on the stands. RANGOON FALLS.

2

I phoned my mother from the pay phone at Perry's to say I had finished work early, and would she meet me for a drink at the bar around the corner from her real estate office?

"How wonderful! A date with my son!"

The RANGOON FALLS headline, illuminated by streetlights, snatched at my attention as I drove to the bar on 6th Street.

I ordered a Cuba libre and sat on the red leatherette stool waiting for my mother. I gazed at my image in the mirror behind the bar, in my deliveryman's khaki shirt and black leather bow tie, which I had donned for the evening check-in with Lois Meador. I unsnapped it and tucked it in my breast pocket.

My eyes seemed to me to be too close together under lesser eyebrows than my brother's. In fact, my face was a kind of twerp imitation of Richie's face. I needed a haircut.

The rap of heels signaled the arrival of Ellen Daltrey. She strode toward me, fresh lipstick, hennaed hair brushed out. In the mirror I saw two men at a table watching her.

"What's that?" she demanded. "I'll have one of those, too." She brushed my cheek with her lipstick and perched on the next stool, smiling sideways at me.

"Richie's coming out next week," she said. "He'll have more time this trip." She had been hurt because Richie had not visited her on his last leave.

"Liz told me."

She, too, examined her face in the mirror, sitting straight-backed, legs crossed, purse in her lap. The bartender brought her drink. I paid; that was new.

I whispered to her, "Those guys at the table back there keep checking you out. You look terrific!"

"Thanks!" she said with a dazzling smile. She cased the two men in the mirror. "Well, I do have to look my best these days."

What did that mean? I asked about her friend Mr. Levine, who lived with her—her Englishman lover. "The Jew-boy," my father called him. He ranted against all her men friends, her lovers. He called Bill Hutchinson a "labor goon," Tully a "Red" and a "Commie," Mr. Perkins "That rich son-of-a-bitch." It was as though my father had no capacity for understanding his own attitudes. I myself was all too often aware of doing something for a shitty reason, a conscience-imp on my shoulder to remind me.

"Gone back east!" my mother said. She produced a pack of Chesterfields from her purse, lipped a cigaret, and handed me the matchbook. I lit her cigaret, her eyes concentrating on the flame, lips pursed around the white cylinder.

"I've met such a nice commander," she said. "He's going to rent an apartment I showed him. He says the Naval Academy is mostly just engineering training. You're good at math, aren't you? Have you ever thought of applying to Annapolis?"

I said my father thought I should become an accountant, but I was going to be a writer.

My becoming a writer did not interest her, but the subject of my father did.

"Eddie thinks I ought to have entered a nunnery," she said, checking herself in the mirror again. "When I found out he was having other women, I was a mess! You remember. I screamed at him. I cried. I tried to make him feel sorry for me. I tried to punish him every way I could think of. It was like I was drowning, grabbing onto anything that would hold me up. I didn't realize that that was all he had then. He'd lost his job, but if he could still get women to come to bed with him he hadn't lost everything. It wasn't total."

"You figured that out," I said.

"And I realized I was all right. I had a job. Other people were laid off, but I wasn't. That was when? Thirty-four, thirty-five. Times were bad!"

Like something beating behind my eyes I could feel the recollection of it; hating Mr. Perkins, the strands of hair combed across his skull, his pink-rimmed eyes. My mother had left me with her mother while she jump-started her new life. If I'd understood, I'd've wanted her in a nunnery also.

"I never wanted to go through what I went through with your father again," she said. "I'm not saying it was all his fault! You know, I feel squeezed absolutely dry because Ben's gone. But I'll get over it. I mean, I know someday I'm not going to be attractive to men anymore, but right now I am. And it's exciting to look around at a party and think, *Let's see—*" She laughed her delighted laugh. "War times are good times for women, dear!"

One minute she was laughing about the good war times, and the next she lamented "this terrible war!"

I said carefully, "All the time I was living at Grandma's it was as though I wasn't paying attention to anything—"

"You were a sullen little twerp, dear. I know it was my fault for being a bad mother."

"Listen," I said. "You remember that year Richie was working for Mr. Lubin, and he had the Cord car and a lot of money. Then just like that he quit and went into Naval Air."

Her face took on an expression of dismay.

"I want to know what happened," I said.

"I don't know! Oh, God, I hate LA so much! I get upset every time I see that scar on Richie's knuckle."

The scar had come from a fight Richie had had with a tramp when he was at SC. "What about it?"

"You know, a parent just can't believe her child would have different politics than hers. You remember: He was a strikebreaker during the Okie troubles in the Valley. They hired those USC brutes, football players and fraternity boys, to go beat up on those poor farm people. It was just terrible!"

"I guess I didn't know about that," I said. Oh, shit, Richie! No wonder he had hated *The Grapes of Wrath*. We'd had spats about that. I hadn't understood why he'd got so down on the Okies. Tom Joad!

"Remember that LA girlfriend of Richie's?" I said. "Val something?"

She squinted at me with that almost cross-eyed intensity of attention she could turn on sometimes. She nodded.

"She killed herself."

"What's this about, Buddy?" my mother said.

"At a party last winter there was this guy that really went after Richie, yelling he was a throat-cutter. About that. It was scary."

She laid a hand to her cheek and gazed at me fearfully with her brown eyes.

"Remember that terrific Cord car? And he had really fancy shirts and sport jackets. He had Val up there and Liz down here."

In a mystery story the detective bored in until he found vital information, but I had the uncomfortable feeling that I was just talebearing on Richie and making my mother unhappy besides.

"I just know Mr. Lubin was going to help him be a movie producer," my mother said. "Then everything went up in smoke the way it does up there. Maybe because that girl did that. She was older than Richie, a cheap flashy girl with a pretty body."

"He was sure a big shot that year," I said.

"He wanted to be a big shot! That's what happens to people in LA. They get LA-ed! People catch something up there so they turn into toads."

"Maybe Richie joined Naval Air so he wouldn't turn into a toad."

We looked at each other. I stood up to embrace her, and she hugged me back.

3

On Friday when the American Legion made a call on *the brand,* I sat facing Tully at his desk with my own headline before me: TOTS MOLESTED IN VESTRY. This had happened in Cleveland. The guy was a vestryman, the girls aged five and six. Writing it had been wringing hard work, as though something heavy was seated on my shoulders as I typed. I wasn't even sure what a vestryman was.

Tully's editorial was on the news item: 9 ACCUSED CLEARED BY FBI.

Tully had hired a printer named Tex Boyle when Tee-John left town. Tex was so skinny inside Tee-John's overalls that it appeared to be draped on a hanger. We could hear him in the pressroom, cursing and banging metal.

A heavyset, sandy-haired man came inside. He looked like one of the salesmen of newsprint and printers' supplies who dropped in regularly. He wore a blue Legionnaire's cap.

"Post Five," he said in a tight voice. He glanced around the office with sharp eyes in a fat face. He scowled at me.

"Pardon?" Tully said.

"Name's Conley," the man said. "I'm with Brubaker Laundry and Cleaning over on Tenth. Some of us have been reading your paper." He jutted his jaw.

Tully rose, beer-bellied in his blue shirt and leather cap.

"We think you're a bunch of Commies," Conley said.

I rose, too, to lean on the counter staring at him. I felt light-headed.

"What is the purpose of this visit?" Tully said.

"Tell you we've got our eye on you."

"I will be aware of it," Tully said with dignity.

"Who're you, kid?" Conley said.

I felt as though I was coming down with the flu. I said I was the deliveryman.

"You a Commie, too?"

I took a deep breath. "Comsymp," I said, smart-ass.

"Is this an American Legion visit?" Tully said, folding his arms and swaying on his heels. "A Brubaker Laundry one? Or personal?"

"I'm telling you!"

"Telling me what, Mr. Conley?"

"Your paper is a piece of Commie asswipe!"

"I suggest that you not read our paper if it offends you."

"Tell you what we'll do if it offends us!" the Legionnaire from Post 5 said. "We'll throw a picket line around here so fast it'll make your head swim!" He scowled at me again. "You ought to be in uniform, kid!"

"I'll be in uniform soon enough. When I get out of it I won't spend the rest of my life wearing a stupid cap with tassels."

Tully gaped at me. Conley took a threatening step forward. I was shivering. My father's post!

"Let me tell you something," I said to Conley. "I belong to a fraternity out at State, a lot of football guys, basketball players. We hire out to bust picket lines. You throw a picket line around here, we will come down and bust it so fast it'll make your head swim!"

Conley said, "Oh, yeah!" I replied in kind, but it didn't seem to me I sounded convincing.

"Warning you we got our eye on you," Conley said to Tully, then glared at me and marched out. Another blue cap was waiting for him outside.

Tully blew his lips out in a whistle. "What got into you, my boy? They can cause us a great deal of trouble. Were you serious about your fraternity brothers?"

"They're probably going to give me the boot for working for *the brand*."

He plumped down in his chair and propped his suede shoes up on the desk. He looked scared. I was scared, too.

It was the fact that my father had warned me of this that had caused me to erupt in anger, and the knowledge that my brother had been hired to beat up on Okies in the Valley. I was coming out of my tantrum with a nauseated feeling and shaky knees, like after my defense of Calvin with the fire axe.

"Fascist sons of bitches," I said, wiping the back of my hand over my mouth.

"Just so," Tully said.

4

Richie had hitched a ride west on Navy transport. He was quartered at the JOQ on North Island and would come to the Navy dock in the whaleboat with his friend Will Gates. I was assigned to pick them up and bring them to Mission Beach for dinner. Richie would collect Liz from there.

The two jg's were already on the dock, two tall men in black uniforms and white caps, smoking and gesturing. They welcomed me noisily, Richie tapping the face of his wristwatch. Will Gates was as tall as Richie and broader, with a freckled midwestern face and a rock-crusher handshake.

"Give you a lesson in aircraft identification," Richie said, laying an arm over my shoulders and pointing. "What're those?" A flight had appeared over Point Loma, enlarging specks.

I didn't know.

Will squinted and grimaced as though he found Richie endlessly amusing. He had tricks of posture to try to make himself appear not so large. He didn't know, either.

"SNJs," Richie said. By now the flight was large enough for the planes to be recognizable. "What about that one settling down like a duck?"

"That's a PBY," I said, flustered with the Superior Man's arm on my shoulders.

"PB2Y," Richie corrected. "How about that one?"

"It's a B-24."

"Shall we pass this student, Lieutenant Gates?"

"Oh, I say, yes!" Will said in a phony British accent. "Especially since the lad will be giving us a lift. And what do you make of that aircrahft just coming into view, Leftenant Daltrey?"

"TBF, my dear Jellicoe."

There were many more flyboy jokes driving out to Mission Beach, slow going through the Consolidated Aircraft quitting-time traffic.

At our father and Weezie's, Richie borrowed Ol Paint to pick up Liz while we made conversation with Will, who had played football at Minnesota and admired Richie inordinately. Like everyone else.

Richie and Liz arrived with bright faces and laughter, Liz with a kiss for me. Richie was so loud the little room seemed too small, as San Diego had been too small to hold him. He sparkled most brilliantly surrounded by those who admired him: his father and stepmother, his fiancée, his sidekick from Pensacola, and his kid brother.

The six of us crowded around the table brought into the living room. Weezie fluttered back and forth from the kitchen with spaghetti and meat sauce, and a bottle of red wine, which my father measured into tiny glasses as though parceling out rubies. And why shouldn't he pour a little extra into Richie's glass, squeeze Richie's shoulder whenever it was within reach, laugh too loud and long at the Pensacola jokes? And why shouldn't Liz, who was engaged to marry Richie in June, hang on his arm and lean against him, and look into his face with her goddess eyes as though he was the only man in the world?

Our father was asking about preflight training.

"Rich brought me and a lot of others through with him," Will said. "He was four-oh on the exams. We all studied together. We only lost one out of Bunkroom B."

"Will and I were top of the class," Richie said. "That's why we're instructing instead of out with the fleet. 'That is the fourth crate you've cracked up this week, Officer!'" he said in one of the crazy accents he and Will bantered back and forth.

Head tilted, proud slant of smile, our father asked if many flunked out of flight training once they got as far as Pensacola.

"Not many," Richie said. "The Navy's got a lot of money riding on them by then. Some do what we call a 'technical flunk,' run into each other, run into the ground. Flying's easy and fun, but it can be unforgiving."

Will said, "I had to wash out that fellow Greenberg last week. He was never going to make his bird, and there was no point wasting any more instructor time."

Weezie asked what "his bird" meant.

"His wings," Liz said, leaning against Richie. She smiled at me with her vivid face, but I was anxious about my father picking up on a Jewish name like Greenberg.

"One of our aircrahft is missing, Air Vice Marshal, sir!" Richie said.

"Oh, I say, have you counted carefully, Leftenant?" Will said.

The fact that everyone seemed to think these exchanges funnier than I did warned me that I was wrestling with a sulk.

Richie asked if I could find a date for Will for Saturday night so we could all go dancing at the Hotel del Coronado. Maybe Amy Perrine?

"You mentioned a boy named Greenberg you had to flunk," our father said across the table to Will. "Are there many Jewish boys in flight training?"

It was like an engine revving up and gears engaging.

"Sure, there are some, Dad," Richie said, and smoothly changed the subject by starting another Limey dialog with Will. It seemed there had been a couple of RAF observers at Pensacola, with whom Richie and Will had partied.

When Weezie and Liz were clearing away the dishes, I was appalled to hear myself saying to Will, "A friend of my mother's is an Englishman like your RAF guys." I knew better than to mention Mr. Levine! It was as though I were so rattled in this place, in this company, that I blurted out the one subject I must stay away from.

"Are you talking about that kike Levine?" my father said, tight-lipped, head tilted.

"Eddie," Weezie said from the kitchen doorway.

Why did I have to defend Mr. Levine, who was not even my mother's boyfriend anymore? I reminded myself that I was always off balance with my father and Weezie, the more so when Richie was on hand. I didn't even know any Jews besides Mr. Levine, except for a guy named David Solomon in my French class.

"I hate that bigotry crap!" I said.

Richie glared at me, his long, heavy-eyebrows and face like our father's, only his head was set straight on his neck.

I watched our father's big construction-man's hands fold his napkin and place it on the tablecloth before him.

Everybody looked frozen, Weezie in the kitchen doorway with her eyes swimming big at me behind her glasses, Liz behind her, Will with the shit-eating grin of pretending it was all a joke. Was it what I'd wanted?

"I mean, how come this house is full of hating people that aren't named Daltrey?" I went on. "Jews and Commies. Kikes. Japs. I can't even mention my friend Stan Takahashi without getting into a beef! What're we fighting this war for, anyhow?"

"I don't see you fighting it, son," our father said.

"Never mind it, Brud," Richie warned me.

"I'd think you'd mind it. You're the one fighting for the Four Freedoms, or whatever it is we're fighting for!"

I was on my feet, shoving my chair out of the way, retreating to the door, to get the hell out of the mess I'd made of my brother's coming home. Richie caught me by the arm and swung me around.

"I can't stand that bigot talk!" I threw at him. Weezie glared at me. I stumbled outside, hastening away down the walk to the avenue, where Richie had parked Ol Paint.

Driving across the salt flats where once Mr. Takahashi had had his fruit and vegetable stand, I warned myself to slow down. All that was needed to make the evening perfect was a speeding ticket.

Where was I headed, anyway? Bust in on Bonny and tell her what a prick I'd been at my father's house? It was a nurse's aide night. I turned into the lighted sprawl of Kenny's big drive-in and went inside jingling the change in my pocket.

I gritted my teeth to think what they were saying about me back at Weezie's house, Liz hearing them talk about me. That line from *To Have and Have Not*, Morgan to his wife: "They aren't much good, are they, hon?" meaning their daughters.

I began sinking nickels into a pinball game, the shiny ball arcing over the top of the board, then dropping to bounce off the bumpers, numbers in satisfying thousands flashing on the display. I grasped the rails, urging the board right, jerking it left; TILT! I spent twenty minutes getting rid of my change before I went back outside.

Parked away from the service area, I leaned my head against the back of the seat and listened to the Ink Spots singing. I didn't need a chapter meeting of the Alpha Betas to advise me that my attitudes were faulty. I had manipulated my father into sounding like a bigot, and then jerked off into a phony fit of righteousness. We hadn't even been disputing over Jews, or about American Legion Post 5 and the First Amendment and Commie rags. No, we were talking about my father going broke in the Depression so that the house in Mission Hills was lost; we were talking about Richie Daltrey of the Great Expectations, the drowned suicide girlfriend and the scarred thumb. *I don't see you fighting it,* my father had said, meaning another disappointment in his younger son the slacker.

I started the car, turning off Cole Porter's cutesy rhymes, and drove out to Point Loma, and up of Rosecrans Boulevard to the Fletchers' house, halting below the grand picture window that surveyed the Bay and the yachts of the movie stars. The expanse of plate glass glittered darkly. It was more of a house than the Boningtons' in Mission Hills. A Navy captain more big-time than an ophthalmologist? Mrs. Fletcher had been rich.

I slumped in the seat, radio off to save the battery. I was wakened by a hand shaking my shoulder. "Brud!"

Behind Richie's white-capped head in the window, I could see Liz in silhouette against the light from the streetlamp. Richie would have borrowed our father's car.

"Sorry," I said.

"Come on inside. Liz will give us a beer."

The night seemed slow and mysterious as I followed my brother and Liz up brick steps in the slant of lawn beside the garage. Liz hurried past an ornamental lamppost with a skipping step, and it came to me that she must have skipped there just like that all her life.

Richie was two steps ahead of me, glints of white from his cap cover and his shirt cuffs swinging. I remembered so well Richie coming down from LA in his turbo-charged Cord, in his Desmond's tweed jacket and gray flannels and glossy wingtips, with his golden-edged style out of a Renaissance painting. I had wanted to be just like that!

The Fletchers' living room was dominated by the big window, muffled on this side by blackout curtains. There was a piano with a blue vase on top of it, overstuffed camelbacked furniture, green plants in pots, a blue and pink Oriental rug. Liz embraced me and brushed my cheek with her lips. I sat in a straight chair and accepted the cool cylinder of Coke she brought me. Richie faced me from the sofa, legs stretched out and a beer bottle in hand. A skinny white cat appeared to weave figure eights around Liz's ankles, with small ecstatic cries. Liz turned on the big console phonograph, something classical, with muted horns.

"'Bigot' is pretty rugged, Brud," Richie said in an earnest, big-brotherly voice.

"He sounds like Father Coughlin when he gets on the Jews! And Weezie really goes after the Japs!"

"Don't tell *me*! Ben Takahashi happens to be a friend of mine."

"She goes after the Japs the way you used to go after Okies."

Richie raised his hands as though surrendering. "Listen, Brud: You're the writer. You're supposed to understand people. Jake Katz ruined Dad in that partnership they had."

"Like Germans blaming Jews for losing the other war."

"Jesus, Brud!"

"Your father hated David Lubin," Liz said to Richie. She said to me, "David Lubin wanted Richie to be his son."

Richie's face reddened. "That was all really stupid."

I hadn't known about that. I gripped my glass, thinking of someone trying to take Richie away from our father.

"Dad's a good guy," Richie said. "He loves us. You know that."

"Sure, and you're a real satisfaction to him. He thinks about you a lot. When he sees me, he gets a kind of wrinkle between his eyes like trying to remember who I am."

"Cut it out!"

"I mean, you're four years older. He and Mom were still married when you were a kid. He wasn't chasing women yet. You didn't just get in the way."

The cat pounced light-footed into my lap and settled down, purring and making bread.

"Buffy likes Payton." Liz said. She was watching me sympathetically, she who had lost her mother when she was a child, lost only one of her parents. *Cut it out* was right.

I said to her, "Maybe that's the way it is in a divorce. One kid on the father's side, and one on the mother's. Richie thinks I'm hard on Dad, but he's hard on Mom."

"I know it," Liz said.

"Well, he's almost perfect."

"Oh, I know that, too."

"Fry head!" Richie said, grinning.

"Do you know what I thought after my mother died?" Liz said. "I thought they were just punishing me for being bad. For the longest time I thought she'd come back if I was just good enough."

Tears burned in my eyes. Liz got up to change the record on the console, the cat leaping out of my lap to twist around her feet.

Richie leaned toward me with the severe tightening of his features, his younger-brother-advising expression. "Don't your fraternity brothers object to your working for *the brand*?"

"That Commie rag?" I said. "Sure they do, but they're too polite to mention it." Like hell! It would be a major topic if I ever went to another tong meeting.

"Pays for my Desmond's jackets," I said.

"The local fraternities are pretty relaxed, I guess," Richie said, who had belonged to a national at SC.

"Payton and I would appreciate it if you wouldn't make snotty remarks about our alma mater," Liz said.

"A guy from a Legion post downtown came to tell us they were going to shut *the brand* down," I said. "He called Tully and me Commies."

"Isn't he?" Richie said, hands clasped behind his head, the Superior Man.

Captain Fletcher came into the living room. He was dressed like a movie gentleman, in a foulard dressing gown and fancy embroidered slippers. His skimpy gray hair was carefully brushed, and I had a flash of him before the mirror slicking away with two military brushes.

Richie was already standing at attention, heels together, when I got to my feet.

"Am I intruding?' Captain Fletcher asked.

"Of course not, sir."

No doubt junior officers had to suck up to senior ones. Richie introduced me, and the captain let me hold a slack hand. Then he dusted his palms together as though ridding them of Daltrey germs.

So maybe Richie was no more popular with Captain Fletcher than I was with Mrs. Bonington. Probably it wasn't Daltreys in particular but daughters' boyfriends in general.

"I believe I will join you in a little restorative," Captain Fletcher said.

I saw that Richie's ears reddened during a discussion as to whether Liz or her father would get his drink. Finally the captain slippered out to the kitchen, having won some kind of advantage. Liz rolled her eyes at Richie. She had a hard, pouty expression.

Captain Fletcher returned with a stem glass full of dark tan liquor. He seated himself on the piano bench, arranging his dressing gown over his knees.

"Payton had a quarrel with his father," Liz said, in a loaded sort of way.

"Ah, a Daltrey family crisis!" Captain Fletcher said. "Some children can be very severe when they discover evidence of human nature in their parents."

Richie laughed dutifully.

Captain Fletcher frowned at the cat, who had settled on Liz's lap. "Is it necessary that that smelly feline be included in this gathering?" He did not say it lightly.

"Not if she offends delicate nostrils," Liz said. She did not say it lightly, either. She thrust Buffy from her lap with what seemed an overdramatic gesture. When the cat passed her father, tail aloft, he caught the tail and jerked the animal, squawling and writhing, off her feet. I thought that the captain had started to do this in fun, but his mood had changed in the process. His face turned set and ruddy, and he held the cat off her feet too long. When he let her, go she galloped out of the room.

"That was mean!" Liz said.

Dusting his hands together again, the Captain rose and strolled the length of the room, his stance indicating that he was defusing a situation his daughter had irrationally intensified. He slid the curtain back to stand gazing out at the lights of the bay.

Did Richie have to endure a Fletcher family crisis like this every time he came here?

"Mean!" Liz said again. Captain Fletcher's shoulders twitched, but he didn't turn. It seemed to me that Liz had gained some sort of power out of the cat abuse to balance her father's advantage in getting his own drink. She was sitting up very straight.

"Can you see the *Sirocco*?" she asked.

"Impossible to make an identification at night, my dear."

"We'll probably see Errol at the Hotel del Saturday night. Richie wants to show his friend from Pensacola the San Diego sights."

Her father kept an intelligence file on Flynn in his office at the destroyer base. It seemed to me that Liz was as hard-nosed as he was. At least I hadn't mentioned Mr. Levine to my father on purpose.

"You are over twenty-one, my dear. I can hardly forbid you associations I think are pernicious. Only warn you."

"Oh, you've certainly warned me."

"It has been my experience that a man's reputation will usually catch up with him," Captain Fletcher said, still standing at the window.

Liz stared at his back, bright-eyed. She was a Liz I'd never seen before, and I thought she looked very beautiful with color in her cheeks, a set chin, and her sleek hair. Something passed between Richie and her, a sign to lay off, but she jerked her head in a negative.

Richie looked relieved when I said I had to be going.

Captain Fletcher turned with a saluting gesture. Liz sprang up to embrace me. Richie said he would walk me out to my car.

In the darkness between the porch light and the ivied lamppost at the corner of the garage, Richie halted to produce a cigaret and light it and wave out the match. I breathed an acrid sniff of smoke.

"What if that guy Hagen is at the Hotel del with Flynn Saturday night?" I said.

"Why would he be? Errol won't put up with stuff like he pulled on the *Sirocco* that night." Richie flipped up his hand with the cigaret in a good-night gesture and stood watching me as I stumbled on down the steps to Ol Paint.

5

Saturday night when I picked Bonny up for a triple date to the Hotel del Coronado, Mrs. Bonington invited me to come out with them on the *Sun Bear* the next day. It seemed a sign that they had decided to take me seriously as Bonny's suitor. Probably there would be familial disputes, as with the Daltreys and the Fletchers.

Rain pattered on Ol Paint's top, and the breath of the six of us jammed together steamed the inside of the windshield while the wipers scrubbed the outside. I had to keep clearing a patch of glass with the palm of my hand as I drove down to the ferry.

Will Gates was extravagantly courteous with Amy Perrine, handing her out of the backseat and, in the hotel, helping her off with her raincoat. Amy had taken some persuading to accept a date, but now she had a high, pretty flush to her cheeks as Will steered her down the red-carpet steps to the ball-room.

Bonny and I brought up the rear, Bonny in a new blue dress and her Add-A-Pearls. My brother preceded us with his quick-footed casual stride. Of course the guys in his frat house at SC had sucked him along with them, making it sound like a party to go beat up on striking fruit tramps.

The Grapes of Wrath was a book that still stirred strong feelings. It would be inappropriate to praise it to Dr. and Mrs. Bonington aboard *Sun Bear* tomorrow, for instance.

I found myself looking at Liz's bare shoulders in her white formal.

If we ran into Hagen tonight, it was Richie's problem.

The band played "Don't Sit Under the Apple Tree," which might be a reproach to Amy. "Don't sit under the apple tree with anyone else but me!" Couples revolved on the gleaming floor with flecks of colored light drifting over them. More and more uniforms.

"Pretty soon everybody's going to be in uniform," I said. Then the Legionnaire Conley would be satisfied.

Bonny was quiet tonight, preoccupied, no smiles. She'd said she'd had a bad night at the hospital but hadn't elaborated. Her mother was taking Charley's absence hard, she said.

I swung her out onto the dance floor, marveling at the lightness of her, the delicate bones beneath the silken sheath of flesh.

Amy and Will Gates circled past us, Amy with her bare arms raised to her tall partner, who danced with his shoulders rounded over her as though afraid of damaging her.

"He's nice," Bonny said.

"Good guy."

"I read your paper," she said, head down as I guided her through the other dancing couples. What paper? *Huckleberry Finn*? She meant *the brand*.

"There was a column about children in Modesto. A teacher."

"I wrote it."

"I thought it was terrible," Bonny said.

I suggest that you do not read it, if it offends you, Tully had said to Conley. I didn't know whether Bonny considered the piece or its subject matter terrible.

"It's supposed to be a come-on to get people interested in buying the paper," I said to the top of her head. "It was important to Mr. Grooms, who started *the brand*."

"My mother brought it home," Bonny said.

I saw a connection with the invitation to a Day on the Bay that didn't make me look forward to tomorrow.

"Why do you write things like that?" Bonny said.

I pushed her around the floor. "Because I want to make people feel outrage about things like that."

"I don't know how you can write those things. I don't know how you can know—"

"That's what writers do! Everything hasn't happened to them that they write about."

Bonny seemed heavy in my arms, as though I were supporting her full weight. "Mother was upset about it," she said.

"Upset about the children, or because I wrote it? What's she going to do, get me out on your boat and grill me?"

She kept her head down. "You make fun of it, though," she said. "You call it the tot molesteds."

"I don't make fun of it! There's other stuff like that, too, you know. There's old guys making sure young guys go off to get killed in the war. I mean, sure it's a good cause, sure we have to stop Hitler and Hirohito, but it's people with power over other people making them do things they don't want to do. Like you and—you know! There's a poem—" I stopped, trying to remember the lines.

Bonny raised her head to look at me with her blue eyes.

"It's 'Sailing to Byzantium,' " I said. "It's Yeats. I forget how it goes exactly. 'The salmon-falls, the mackerel-crowded seas, the young in one another's arms.' That's the way life ought to be, not guys marching off to be cannon fodder."

"It'll be another year before you have to go. You said it would be over by then!"

"Listen, what is this tomorrow? Some kind of interrogation thing? My attitude?"

"You have to do it for me," Bonny said.

"To win you."

"Yes, to win me!"

I saw Liz and Richie through the doorway of the bar, Richie's arm around her waist. Errol Flynn was greeting them, appearing out of shadow with his sharp, handsome profile and his fuck-you grin. I guided Bonny closer.

Another man, a balding civilian, was also on his feet. Two women were seated at a table, one with flaming red hair. Richie shook the bald man's hand. The neck of a champagne bottle slanted out of a silver bucket. No sign of Hagen.

"Isn't that the reddest hair?" Amy said, when the four of us were seated at our table. "That must be Lili Damita."

"Is he still married to her?" Bonny said. She was clasping my hand so tightly it hurt.

Will peered toward the bar, where Liz and Richie were now seated. "I've never seen a movie star before," he said. "You San Diego people sure are fortunate!"

Richie and Liz returned after the next set, Liz flushed and animated.

"We're going to LA tomorrow," Richie said. "Errol's having a tennis thing at Mulholland Farm. There'll be some good tennis, maybe Jack Kramer and Frank Kovacs. Jack Warner will be there."

"He's a terrible letch!" Liz said, bright-eyed.

"You're invited, Will," Richie went on. "And the little one," he said to Amy.

"Oh, I can't!" Amy said quickly.

"And young Martin Eden and the fair one."

Bonny said we had a date to go out on the *Sun Bear* tomorrow with her parents, cutting her eyes at me as though I might protest.

6

When I'd taken Amy and Liz home, and deposited Richie and Will at the Navy dock in time to catch the last whaleboat back to North Island, Bonny did not object to our going out to Point Loma to neck, but something was wrong.

On the radio Jimmy Rushing sang, "Sent for you yesterday, and here you come today!"

Bonny sat over against her door facing me. She had something to tell me, she said.

"They brought this sailor in," she started out. "He wasn't even as old as you are, he was a boy! He'd been scalded in an explosion and he was wrapped in bandages and doped up. He was in pain."

She paused while the disc jockey put on "Frenesi," with the exalted line of Artie Shaw's clarinet soaring. I could feel her intensity across two feet of seat between us.

"The nurse was down in the ward," she said. "It was late, and his light came on. His room was dark, but there's a light outside the window so you can see. All I could see of his face was some dirty hair and one eye. He was sitting up in bed—halfway sitting up—"

I didn't want to hear this. "You don't have to tell me this."

"I have to!" She sounded close to tears. "He'd uncovered himself there! And he was whimpering, 'Please, please, please—'" She kept on saying "please."

"Listen—"

"Just listen! I mean, he was all bandaged, his hands and arms and everything but his one eye. And I knew what he was saying 'please' about. I couldn't just run away! I told Jeanine, she's the head nurse in the ward nights. She said she'd had to do that, too!"

I leaned against the steering wheel. Shaw's clarinet swooped up and up.

"Last night when I went to work he was gone," Bonny said. "They'd moved him to Naval Hospital. I asked Jeanine to call and see how he was. They told her he'd died. He was dead!"

The poor swabbie had known he was dying, and that was all he was ever going to have.

"It was like he was in pain from that! Not just the burns, but there!"

I stretched my lips into a grin, glaring out the windshield at San Diego Bay. The sky had cleared; stars were out. Hillcrest loomed, light-speckled, beyond the long, low bulk of Consolidated Aircraft. Naval Hospital was nearer downtown, in the park. Poor dying bastard with his hands bandaged so he couldn't even jack off in the face of eternity.

"I thought I had to," she whispered.

"Sure you had to!"

She came into my arms, with her wet face thrust into my neck. She was breathing as though she'd been running. I stroked her hair and kissed her teary face and told her she'd done the right thing, she was just fine, she was a nurse. Saint Veronica would've done the same thing. The Virgin Mary would've done the same thing.

Finally she sat up. I had better take her home now. I was to be at her house at nine o'clock in the morning, and we would drive with her parents to the yacht club for our Day on the Bay.

7

It was a high-fog Sunday morning aboard the *Sun Bear,* with glints of sun breaking through. Seated at the tiller, Dr. Bonington wore his salty skipper's cap. Mrs. B. and Bonny lounged on blue and white pillows in the mahogany cockpit. My assigned post was beneath the boom, and I gazed up at the bellying triangle of sail above me and thought of Richie and Liz at Mulholland Farm, Richie playing doubles with Flynn, Jack Kramer and Frankie Kovacs, and Liz being letched by Jack Warner of Warner Brothers.

Bonny's legs were slick and brown beneath her white shorts. She caught my eye and tilted her head toward a big two-master anchored with her bowsprit pointed toward the *Sun Bear*. The *Sirocco*! No one was on deck.

Mrs. B. handed around photographs of Charley that had just arrived from Australia: Charley in uniform with some buddies; Charley with a big, blond Aussie girl, both on bicycles with their left legs braced to the ground; Charley in tennis shorts and a floppy hat, tennis racket in hand. Dr. Bonington came about again.

Bonny's mother studied the photographs with an indulgent smile before passing them along. Dr. Bonington laid each one on the varnished wood beside him, frowning down as though it contained a message to be deciphered.

Bonny would look like her mother someday: high forehead under a fringe of silvering blond hair, sharp-cut nostrils, brown-faced from weekends on the Bay, some wattling at her throat, where she wore ivory beads; golf and sailing and bridge parties and organizing events for Children's Hospital and the symphony. Bonny's grandfather had been a doctor in Pasadena, and Mrs. B. read the stock market quotations in the *Union* every morning. Primary accumulation!

I squinted up the slant of mast to where two seagulls circled. The *Sun Bear* sliced through the Bay with a long faucet sound and a steady slap. Gold flickers danced on the water. I could thank Charley's photographs that the grilling on my employment at the Commie rag hadn't begun yet.

"Looks like he's put on weight," Dr. Bonington said. Charley had the beginnings of a beer belly, all right, and that Charley Bonington doing-exactly-what-he-wanted-to-grin. I said I'd heard they drank a lot of beer in Australia.

"He says Down Under agrees with him," Mrs. B. said. Her smile was thinner than that opening-up smile of Bonny's. Her eyes were guarded by dark glasses. She said, "We thought we were so clever, Charley going into the Coast Guard. Which is supposed to guard our coast. He's been around boats all his life, of course. He says the Navy needs people who know how to operate small craft. Can you imagine a Navy where no one knows how to operate small craft?"

No need to defend the Navy in this instance.

"He just means the Coast Guard's loaned him to the Navy," Bonny said, as though this had already been explained.

"Anyway, I'm sure it was the right decision to put off medical school until after the war!"

"He is going to have to study harder, after the war," Dr. Bonington said.

"Well, it looks like he's having a fine time," Bonny said. "Bicycling with blondes and playing tennis."

I shifted position on the hard deck, wishing I were playing tennis.

"I just wish the Japs weren't so close down there," Mrs. B. said.

"Coming about," the skipper said.

I guarded my head with one hand as the boom passed over and cautiously moved across the cockpit. Rope rattled through pulleys as the *Sun Bear* heeled over on her new tack. I had cast off the lines from the dock and jumped aboard, thereafter trying to keep out of the way. No doubt Dr. Bonington would tell me if I was supposed to do anything.

Bonny slid across the shiny mahogany until she was seated next to me, which I guessed was a movement of support for what was coming up.

The image of the dying sailor sitting up in bed begging her for a hand job would not shake out of my head.

Dr. Bonington cruised the Bay on different tacks. Now the *Sirocco* was out of sight.

Mrs. B. handed around red-and-white-checked napkins, fried chicken, and tuna sandwiches on whole wheat bread. She drank out of a chrome shaker. There were bottles of Pepsi for Bonny and me and a beer for Dr. Bonington.

Bonny's father inserted his bottle into a hole in the mahogany shaped to fit it, the Navy blue brim of his cap tipped over his eyes. Maybe he imagined himself a skipper on the high seas; maybe he was thinking of sailing Down Under to rescue Charley from that man-eating blonde. Maybe he was sick of being an ophthalmologist in San Diego.

"What does your mother think of your working for a Communist newspaper?" Mrs. B. asked suddenly, dark glasses fixed on me like machine-gun muzzles.

"It's not Communist, it's Socialist Worker," I said.

"It is Marxist, however," Dr. Bonington said.

I shrugged. "I don't know much about Marx." I cautioned myself against smart-assery.

"My mother's a Democrat," I went on. "She's for Mrs. Roosevelt and the CIO and Dr. Rollo." Dr. Rollo was the minister of a downtown church who was accused of being Comsymp because of his pronouncements on racial matters.

I didn't think Bonny's parents would criticize my mother's politics. "My father's a Republican," I added, and felt a twist of anger at having produced that suck-up information.

"And what does he think of your employment, dear?"

"Payton supports himself!" Bonny said. "I guess his family can't complain about what he does for a living!" She sounded proud of me!

"Barbara," her father cautioned her.

Bonny moved her hip an inch, to press against me.

"He calls *the brand* a Commie rag, actually," I said, and managed a laugh. I went on to tell of the Legion's threat of a picket line. Even the Boningtons must consider the Legionnaires jerks!

"The Communists are our deadly, deadly enemies, you know, dear," Mrs. Bonington murmured.

It was the Fascists who were our deadly, deadly enemies!

"You can understand our concern if our daughter is dating a Young Communist," Dr. Bonington said in a gruff voice.

"Well, I'm sure not a Young Communist!" I said. Maybe your protests always sounded feeble responding to the accusations of HUAC, the Legion, or your girlfriend's father.

Mrs. B. went after her shaker again, and the skipper's attention was turned to tacking us out of the track of a gray ship with a bone in her teeth and tall white numbers on the prow.

"May we ask what your politics are, Payton?" Mrs. Bonington said.

This solemn ceremony now seemed funny. I'd told Bonny I was a Socialist, maybe to shock her, and Bonny might have relayed that to her mother, who would equate Socialism with Communism. I felt the pressure of Bonny's hip; important!

"I guess they are about halfway between my father's and *the brand*'s," I said. "I believe in liberty and justice for all." I laid a hand over my heart as though pledging allegiance to the flag, but an edge of anger was right there.

"But not just for people who can afford it," I went on. "Poor people, too. The tramps my grandmother feeds at her back door, too! I don't think people should lose their farms and houses and jobs in a depression. I don't think farmers ought to lose their farms in any Dust Bowl thing, and when they move to California get beaten up by SC football players for being strikers. I don't think Mexicans ought to get beaten up because they wear zoot suits. And I don't think people ought to be locked up in concentration camps because they are Japanese. They are citizens of this country! And I don't think colored guys ought to be lynched, and they ought to be able to ride in a taxi and get a haircut like anyone else." That was enough, I was sounding like a jerk, but I couldn't stop myself. "And I don't think the House Un-American Activities Committee ought to call everyone who doesn't agree with them Comsymps—" Enough!

And I didn't think girls like Dessy ought to have to fuck their bosses to keep their jobs, and be turned into whores with no future but the downward slide to the Molino Rojo.

My bottom ached from the hard boards, and my neck ached with strain that wasn't just from ducking the boom. I squinted up the mast.

"Bravo, Payton!" Dr. Bonington said in his gruff voice. Mrs. B. fiddled with the cap of the cocktail shaker.

"That's just what I think!" Bonny announced, and the mast and sail turned misty in my eyes.

"Well, did he pass?" she demanded. "We don't have to elope, do we?"

"Oh, darling, don't even joke about that!" her mother said.

My face felt on fire, and I jogged Bonny with my hip to shut her up.

"That's enough, Barbara," her father said. "Payton does not need this hysterical support."

"Hysterical—" Bonny started, but stopped when I muttered her name.

"Coming about!" Dr. Bonington said. This tack headed us toward Point Loma, the *Sun Bear*'s prow slipping through the spangled water. Bonny leaned against me.

"I can't help worrying about Charley and that brassy-looking young woman," Mrs. B. said.

"She's probably an Australian Young Communist!" Bonny said, glaring at her mother. "She's probably Harry Bridges's daughter!"

"Barbara!" her father said.

We walked in along the pier from the *Sun Bear*, carrying gear. The stunt-man Hagen was on the next pier over, with a stack of beer and soup car-tons on a hand truck. He halted and tipped the hand truck up straight when he saw me. His dark face was smiling under a beret, his chest and shoulders in a striped T-shirt looked as though he was wearing shoulder pads.

"Hey, brotherman!" he called to me.

I nodded to him. I saw that Dr. Bonington was looking at Hagen with interest, thinking him a friend of mine and a yacht club person.

"That's that guy from the *Sirocco*, isn't it?" Bonny whispered. I almost bumped into her, hurrying on.

I said it was.

I was going to take her home in Ol Paint, but she stopped at the ladies' room in the clubhouse while I went on out to my car in the parking lot. I didn't even see Hagen approach, fishing in my pocket for the key, but there he was, an unlit cigaret in his jaw.

He held up a hand as though to stop me from whatever I was thinking of doing, making a process of digging a matchbook out of his pocket and lighting his cigaret. He waved smoke away from his face.

"You know what your brother is?"

I didn't say anything.

"He's a prick," Hagen said.

I shook my head at him. "That's your opinion. He's my brother."

"There was a girl I knew when we were kids together in Hanford."

"Where's Hanford?"

He sighed and jammed his hands into the pockets of his jeans, where I could see the fists lumping. "Up in the Valley." The cigaret tilted at the cor-ner of his mouth when he spoke. "She was the prettiest girl in school. She was always in plays and stuff like that. She sang. You knew she was headed for Hollywood. So she went down there and they shit on her and cut her up in pieces and threw her in the dump. For not being pretty enough, or not fucking the right people. She fucked your brother instead of the right people, and he was the one who cut her throat."

"I thought she drowned," I said.

He made a face as though I were stupid. I figured he wore the beret be-cause he was bald.

"I thought it was David Lubin," I said.

"Sonny, your brother held Lubin's dick when he pissed. Sure it was Lubin, but it was your brother that did the dirty."

He squinted at me, waving smoke. "Here is this sweet, decent girl that everybody who knew her liked her because she had a way of making people feel good about themselves. And they fucked her over till there was nothing left of her. And it was your brother that was the chainpuller for the Jew cocksuckers that gave her the final fucking over. So she drowned herself."

"I'm sorry," I said.

His face twitched. "Well, maybe you are," he said. "Where's your brother?"

"Fighting the war."

"He's a flyboy, he'll get killed," he said. "That'll take care of that. What's his cunt's name?"

I didn't answer, and he shrugged and turned away. He was walking back toward the piers when Bonny came out of the clubhouse. She didn't see him this time.

Chapter 7

1

On Monday morning I found my brother sitting in the Caff waiting for Liz to come out of class. His cap was on the table before him, his legs stretched out. He looked as though Flynn's arrogant grin was catching. I felt a twinge of envy that I had gone sailing with the Boningtons instead of joining the LA expedition.

"You know who played doubles with us?" Richie said. "Flynn and Vinnie Richards played Fred Perry and me. I couldn't hit anything the first set. Then I got okay, but they beat us two out of three."

I didn't have to tell him I'd seen Hagen.

"Jack Warner was there," he went on. "He watched the girls swimming. You'd think someone like that wouldn't just ogle, but Lizzy sure got ogled.

"Errol took us for the big house tour. His bedspread has question marks all over it. He is something! He was a real adventurer before he got into the movies. He's got mementos, and guns—There's a cocktail bar with a mural of a bullfight. You push on the bull's balls to open it."

"Terrific," I said.

Richie squinted at me to see if I was being sarcastic. "You've got to make it up with Dad," he said. "He really feels bad about that night."

I watched his eyes turn to follow a girl's bottom. *He's really smooth,* Bonny had said of him, but not as though the word was a compliment. The flying ace was ashamed of something bad that had happened in LA, and he was sure not going to tell his brother about it. I cautioned myself not to get down on him.

"Jack Warner would give Liz a contract anytime, but she'd be just a contract player," he went on. "When she signs on in Hollywood, she's going to be a star!"

Liz was coming toward us with her dancer's walk, as though she were skating between the tables, binder clutched to her sweater. Richie and I rose to greet her. She flung herself into Richie's arms, bending back with an arm outstretched in a dancer's pose. Students around us stared.

"When are you Daltrey boys going to take me away from all this?" she said.

She kissed me on the cheek and seated herself with a flourish, She must've had a good time in LA, too.

I asked about Will Gates.

"He didn't come with us," Richie said. "He sneaked over to see Amy. He's never met a girl named America before."

"She's Bob-O's girl, and he'd better not forget it."

"Go Navy," Richie said, grinning.

Bonny joined us. She wore a blue sweater and blue skirt and saddle shoes. I had to recognize that Bonny was not beautiful, as the party-Liz was, but she was pretty and appealing with her fair hair, her illuminating smile, and that no-sweat, cellophane-wrapped look to her. And I knew there was some kind of filter on my eyes when I looked at her.

Bonny and I had to hear about the day at Mulholland Farm in detail, Richie and Liz talking excitedly.

Will Gates plodded toward us, his white-topped cap underarm, hunching a little as though trying not to look so big. He wore an unhappy expression, and I felt a chill of dread.

"Amy's friend Bob O'Connor got killed," he said, when he reached our table.

I felt a pressure like a giant paw on my chest.

Bonny's chair skidded back as she got to her feet.

"I guess a mortar blew up on him."

Bonny trotted away across the Caff, her hair bouncing; going to Amy.

"First blood?" Richie wanted to know, gazing at me.

I shook my head. Johnny Pierce. Now Bob-O. Nothing new to Richie, fellow cadets in technical flunks, students taking their instructors down with them, news through the Navy grapevine of friends in the fleet who crashed in carrier landings.

"There'll be more," Richie said.

2

Two men wearing Legionnaire caps stood outside the door of the printshop. One wore a blue serge suit and shiny, high-top shoes, the other a buttoned-up gray sweater. It was a moment before I realized what this was.

"That's a Commie outfit in there, friend," the Legionnaire in the gray sweater said. He had a mole on his cheek, a gray hair sprouting from it.

I was infuriated by the squeak in my voice when I said, "I'd like to see you try to stop me going in there!"

"Calm down, sonny," blue-suit said, and laid a hand on my arm.

I jerked away, and blue-suit took a backward step. He looked like an Okie, with an Adam's apple as sharp as an elbow. If they asked why I wasn't in uniform, should I say that one of my best friends had just been killed in a training accident?

"What's your name, lad?" buttoned-sweater asked.

"I'll tell you who my father is. E. B. Daltrey!"

"Eddie Daltrey?" buttoned-sweater said. He and blue-suit gazed at me expressionlessly. I noticed that their blue tassels hung on the right side of their caps.

I jammed the door open and went inside. Tully stood gray-faced at his desk in his loafer jacket. He smiled wanly at me.

"I've been watching the door for HUAC, and here comes the Legion in at the window."

"I see how you stay mad all the time," I said shakily.

"This is just a—flidget!" Tully said. He touched the brim of his leather cap. "Not even bad enough to fill a flea's navel. Room left over for a capitalist's heart."

He was writing an editorial against the Un-American Activities Committee, which was holding its noisy circus in Los Angeles. I picked up one of the typescript pages he was revising: "This is the age of the investigator. The prober into files and records has become the protagonist of our time, when the klieg lights of Rep. Dies's carnival are turned upon men's lives and no one is cleared until he has been flayed, and penance done by the betrayal of his friends—"

My private eyes, Jeff Dodge and now John Burgess, investigators!

Later, when I barged out past the pickets to head down to the White Castle for coffee takeouts, it worried me that I hadn't seen Dessy lately. Calvin had charged me with looking out for her, but I had no idea how to locate her.

On Saturday two men wearing fedoras instead of Legionnaire caps, in a black Buick sedan, followed me on my route delivering the bundles of *the brand* to the newsstands. I gave them the finger whenever the Buick came up close behind Ol Paint. I knew they had taken down my license number. That was what investigators did.

3

The pickets alternated, one pair in the morning, another afternoons. Usually they hung it up about five o'clock, but today when I came to the printshop after my Perry's route they remained at their posts even though it was almost dark.

I sat at the Remington on Tully's desk, staring at the clipping from the *Sacramento Union*. Two first-grade girls had been molested in a place called Elk Grove. The accused man was a farm laborer. He had invited the children into his "cottage" to play with his puppy.

I was disturbed that Bonny had said I didn't know what I was writing about. It was what Mr. Chapman had said also. I tried to put myself in Elk Grove with the puppy, the man nice and not scary, brown-faced from working in the sun, wearing overalls; a little house that somehow resembled my grandmother's. Inside the cottage, with the door closed, a dim room except for a line of sunlight under the door—

Straightening to glance up at one of the pickets framed in the window with his sign, Tully said, "I remember Franz saying that to understand Social Reality one must be inside it. Maybe there is no way these times can be understood unless you have been picketed by the American Legion."

Tex came in from the pressroom, wiping his hands on some waste. "Leakin oil," he said. He was not much good as a printer. He squinted at the pickets outside the window. "Probably takin down names out there," he said cheerfully.

"It was very bad at the end in Spain," Tully said. "If you surrendered, the Falange would shoot you. If your name came up on the wrong list, your comrades would." He spoke in the solemn manner he assumed whenever the agony of the Spanish Republic was the subject. It was a subject I knew better than to joke about, Tully's Social Reality.

"They took down names up in Washington State, I can promise you!" Tex said.

A figure in a blue suit appeared gesticulating outside the window, then pushed the door open and came inside. Calvin King tap-danced a few steps and stopped with a Bill Robinson flourish. His suit had mighty shoulders that tapered to pants cuffs so narrow it didn't seem possible that he could get his feet through them.

"Hi, Mr. Tully! Hiyuh, child! Good-lookin gents outside!"

Tex squinted at Calvin with disapproval and stepped aside so the two of us could pass into the pressroom to talk.

I was glad I could stop worrying about Dessy. Calvin looked just fine. I asked how business was.

"Copped a couple of gals in LA, brought 'em back down with me. Got Chrysie-car out of hock. Nothin now but rakin in the mah-zoola!"

"I haven't seen Dessy."

Calvin scowled. "Some problems with that little beauty. She has messed herself up. Got in a fuss with her landlady. Now she's moved in at the Benford. Ugly!"

Calvin swung the folding chair around and sat down facing me over the back, a man comfortable in Social Reality.

"I tell her my first job is girls," he went on. "If I don't have but one gal workin for me I am nobody, and she is workin for a nobody. She says she understand that, but right down to it she don't understand. A man has to be an explainin ace! I have to keep upgradin. It is up or down in this bidness."

"Like running an elevator."

"That's right!" Calvin said, laughing. "Fact is, she did ten days in the coop. Nobody to bail her out. And she is hittin the pills hard."

I said I was sorry, I hadn't known. What would I have done if I had known?

Tex came in to start up Charlotte, taking a swig from his pint of Old Crow first. The press's breathless whackety-whack began. Calvin raised his voice to say, "My Uncle Red say to ask you did you get those tires okay."

"I did! Thanks!"

When I left the printshop that night, the pickets had left one of their placards on its stick leaning against the wall.

DON'T PATRONIZE COMMIES AT BRAND PRTNG
AMERICAN LEGION POST 5

I broke the stick over my knee, ripped the placard in half, and the halves in half again. I stuffed the pieces into the trash can on the corner.

4

When I got home to Normal Heights, my "Blood Street" story was back from *Black Mask* with the familiar rejection slip. This one was clearly initialed "PR."

There was also a letter from Stanley Takahashi from "Manzanar Relocation Center."

Dear Frutti,

Thanks for the letter about Bob-O. The memorial service sounds really rugged. I guess you were saying I am better off than he is, and I guess that's right.

We're all here, all right, my mom and dad and Ben and my sister. Dad lost everything. I don't know if he thinks he's better off than Bob-O.

It's the shits here, but it's not really bad. There aren't packs of Dobermans or guards with submachine guns, and no sadistic shit. There is a lot of barbed wire, though, and guards with helmets, and one hell of a lot of Japs. It's better now, but we were some of the first ones here, and it was misery cold with the wind coming down off the mountains to freeze your nuts. Now we've got mud. But the accommodations are Grade-A for a concentration camp.

I read a lot. We have meetings. Ben and the other lawyers are trying to figure some way to shortcut this fucking outrage to the Supreme Court. There is trouble between the old people who aren't citizens and are only scared, and the younger guys who are citizens and are mad as hell. In a way it would be easier if they were shittier to us, but the fact is they are mostly trying to do their best. If they beat up on us, or shot some of the troublemakers like Ben, I could be purer mad.

Thanks for taking the trouble to find out where I am and write me. Say hello to the King of Kings for me, and drop by when you are up this way, which is two hundred miles from nowhere with a terrific Sierra view. It is nice sometimes when the wind lets up.

But when you tell me you stood up for us in some stupid argument you had, I give you the rigid digit. Don't use me as an example of loyalty to the good old USA. I hope the Axis wins and the Nips come over and take all your Ford cars away.

If you see Mrs. O'Connor, tell her what a good guy I thought Bob-O was, and all that stuff.

Tutti

I heard Mr. Button come in the front door. After a while he called to me from the living room. He was seated at a card table, making repairs on a fishing pole, winding fish line and pulling it taut. His glasses were propped on his nose. The floor lamp shone on his work.

"Your daddy phoned, wanted to know where you've got to. Hasn't seen you in a month of Sundays, he said."

I leaned on the back of the sofa as Mrs. Button appeared from the kitchen. Her face was pink from washing dishes, her orange hair wispy.

"He had the idea you might've gone off and enlisted, dear. Jim told him you were just working and playing hard as always."

Mrs. Button stood watching me, drying her hands on a dish towel. "You got your letters," she said.

117

"Letter from a Japanese friend of mine in Manzanar," I said. "They've got them locked up up there. You're Japanese if even one of your grand-parents is Japanese. Bad stuff."

Mr. Button was nodding as though he knew all about that. He didn't look up.

"They don't call it a concentration camp, they call it a relocation cen-ter." What was I trying to do, work up a quarrel with Mr. and Mrs. Button?

"My Jim's people would know about relocation centers," Mrs. Button said. "Wouldn't they, Jim?"

"Never mind it, Mama."

"They made peace with the Army," Mrs. Button went on, drawing her-self up in the way she always did whenever she got onto the subject of Mr. Button being an Indian. "But they were sent off to camps where there wasn't enough food!"

Mr. Button jerked his head in a brusque motion that stopped her.

I watched Mr. Button's black-haired head bent over his work. His brown, hairless hands moved deftly.

"Never had any trouble myself," he said, as though he knew exactly what the subject was. "Found if I was friendly most fellows was friendly back. 'Course a barber is usually a well-liked fellow. Barber Jim, they called me. Kept my outfit's hair cut in Alabama, France, and Coblenz in the Oc-cupation."

I'd never heard Mr. Button speak so many consecutive sentences be-fore. Mrs. Button's steamed face had turned from pink to red.

"It's not always that way," she said. "My Jim will come home some-times so mad he isn't worth living with. Isn't that so, Jim?"

Mr. Button nodded, cutting the line with the small blade of his pock-etknife.

"Do you cut colored men's hair?" I asked, shocked that I had enunci-ated it.

He shook his head hard. "They come in my shop, I just point a finger at the door and they go right out. Yes, sir!"

"His regular customers wouldn't stand for it," Mrs. Button said. This time she was the one who knew what I was talking about.

How about a Jap's hair? I didn't ask it.

"I'd be out of business in a week," Mr. Button said, holding up the fin-ished handle of his fishing pole for approval.

"How about the American Legion?" I asked. "Did you ever belong to the Legion?"

"Never did," he said. "I always thought somebody might ask me, but nobody ever did."

I said good night and went to my room to study French verbs for a midterm.

5

When I'd finished delivering *the brand* to the newsstands, no tail on me this time, and no pickets on Saturdays, pressure off. I sauntered along 3rd Street to sit in a booth in the White Castle. I was cramming down a hamburger when Dessy came in. She half-raised a hand in greeting and wandered down the aisle between the booths to seat herself opposite me. Her flowered dress was cut low over her flat bosom, and she wore a cloth coat with a fur collar. Her Ella Cinders eyelashes were gummy with mascara.

"They're picketing that place where you work," she said with a severe expression. The White Castle stank of frying grease, but I had a whiff of her flower perfume.

"They think we're enemies of the people." I asked if I could get her something to eat.

"Just some black coffee."

She was too thin; she ought to be eating something. Patches of delicate pimples at the corners of her mouth were imperfectly concealed by powder, and her hair was covered with a tan scarf. I went to get her coffee.

"That dream you told me about," she said, when I came back. "Come up to my room and I'll show you what the dream books say."

Come up and see me sometime! I protested that I was due at Perry's for my Saturday afternoon route, but she insisted it would not take long.

She linked her arm through mine as we walked up the street toward the Benford. We encountered a pair of sailors, and a man in a leather apron toting a carton from a Coast Cartage stake truck into Ace Products.

With a queer loosening in my knees it occurred to me that I was going to get laid.

At the desk in the Benford a fat woman with a shadowy mustache handed Dessy a key with a red numbered tag on it. We climbed stairs. "It's

119

on the fourth floor," she said over her shoulder. I was watching the motion of her hips ahead of me.

Her room looked down on 3rd Street. In it were a bed with a white coverlet, a dresser bearing a vase with a paper rose in it, a green upholstered chair, and a stack of magazines on a shiny maple table. On the pillow of the bed was seated a teddy bear with a red ribbon around his neck.

Dessy directed me to the chair while she removed her coat and hung it in the closet with a jingle of hangers. She selected two of the magazines to bring to me. *Mary Gorham's Dream Book #28* was the top one. She sat on the arm of my chair and turned pages.

"It's here somewhere."

She showed me an amateurish drawing of a young woman stretching out her hands into a spiderweb that covered the space before her. Her fingers made sharp dents in the web.

"You understand that dreams never say exactly what they mean," Dessy said. "Almost always it's love, but sometimes it's money. Sometimes it's death. The bicycle means something is going too slow. See?" She pointed to a paragraph in the text that did mention a bicycle, but which I couldn't focus on. There were rings on every finger on her hand holding the magazine, two on the index finger, one red stone and one blue.

"Are you in love, Payton?"

I cleared my throat to say I was.

She took the magazine from me and opened the second one, leafing through until she found a drawing of a girl in a windswept dress standing at the top of a precipice whose lower depths were lost in shadows.

"You said you had to pedal out over space to get to the top. That's a cliff, do you see? That means a difficult decision. An important decision."

It seemed that I had given Dessy some advantage when I had revealed my dream. Manipulators of men.

She went to sit on the bed, where she had to prop her bottom on the very edge so that her toes touched the floor. Where she carried on her profession.

"It might be money, say if you and Barbara couldn't get married until you had a lot of money. Is Barbara like that? Or danger? Dreading that something bad will happen?"

Too close for comfort.

"My dream has a cliff in it, too," she went on. "I'm way up on a height place. It's scary! Down below there's someone calling to me to jump, they'll catch me, they'll save me, but I don't trust them. They might be lying to me. You know, you have more dreams once you start keeping track."

I got up, hands in pockets, to look down out the window. A car cruised by on 3rd Street. I could see the glint of the window of the printshop. My throat was thick with pity for Dessy. I didn't think I should bring up the subject of Calvin.

I glanced at my watch ostentatiously. "Thanks for looking up my dream."

She slid to her feet. "Come again when you can stay longer."

"Well, we'll see each other at the White Castle," I said, and she stood on her tiptoes to kiss me on the cheek.

I made myself descend the stairs slowly, to walk slowly to the alley behind the printshop, where Ol Paint was parked. What was the matter with me? You had to take some chances if you were going to get laid; you couldn't worry all the time what others thought of you. What did Dessy think of me, after she had got me up to her room like that?

Maybe she just wanted to be friends.

At Perry's, when I looked into Lois's cubicle, she said, "You've got lipstick on your cheek there, loverboy."

6

Tully invited me to dinner with "a young friend" on the day the Americans on Bataan surrendered, thirty-six thousand of them, the size of a football crowd in a big stadium. The POWs were probably about my age, maybe a couple of years older; prisoners of the Japanese, who had been savage in China, and murderous with the British soldiers and Gurkhas they had captured at Singapore. Bonny would be in a state. She was working at the hospital two nights a week, and our necking sessions on Point Loma were not so frequent.

I was nervous about meeting Tully's young friend, another Spanish Civil War vet, for I suspected he might be a competitor for my job on *the brand*. Not that there was going to be a job much longer, if the picketing continued.

Tully lived on the top floor of a rickety white house with peeling paint that towered off the steep street with a lower flat beneath it. From the steps there was a grand view of the Bay, with the sun setting over Point Loma, the rows of gray ships of the destroyer base, and planes slanting in to North Island.

Inside, Tully's pride was a big record player, and a beat-up Spanish Colonial chair, his "throne." Beside it was a wall of records, opera and symphonic. Tully listened to music at night, unlike my father hunched before the radio pouring out its bad news. The Bataan surrender was the really bad news tonight.

Symphony boomed from the big Capehart. Standing looking down at it was a skinny fellow not much older than I was, with a pasty face and hair so yellow it looked dyed. He wore a white shirt with the sleeves rolled, and a knurled stump of wrist was braced on his hip. His left hand was gone. He had a bottle of beer in his right hand.

"Have a beer?" Tully said, coming out of the kitchen. He handed me a brown bottle and flourished a fat arm. "This is Winston Jones. Winny, Payton Daltrey, my assistant at *the brand*."

Jones locked his beer against his chest with his forearm and gave my hand a single pump. "Hiyuh."

Tully pointed to a wicker chair, and I sat down and sucked on my beer. The music was so loud it was hard to talk. I didn't like Jones's looks, and a picture had congealed in my head, of a stadium full of American boys lining up to have their hands chopped off by Japs with swords.

Everyone had known the Americans in the Philippines would have to surrender. The Allies just kept losing.

Finally Tully tuned the music down.

"Winny was with the Brigade at the end," he said.

Jones held up his stump. "Teruel! I'll tell you, kid, when you get caught between the Reds and the Fascists it's time to haul ass. Fucken Reds gettin rid of anybody didn't toe the Party line. I mean, linin 'em up and shootin 'em! We could've licked the Eye-ties if we hadn't been fucked over."

"Must've been rugged," I said.

"Fucken cold, I'll tell you."

"Winny's come out to the Coast looking for work," Tully said. He kept glancing at his friend as though he was half embarrassed, half proud of him. If Tully wanted his pal to write the tots column, that was just fine, but I didn't see how Jones could deliver the bundles of papers with only one hand, or help Tex with the rolls of newsprint. And what would Tully do for a delivery car?

"Fought in the wrong war," Jones said. His teeth were yellow, with dark interstices. "Blacklisted wherever you go. I hear they are decent to you down in Mexico. A lot of fellows have went down there. I heard from a nurse that tended me in Spain. She was blacklisted in the States, so she went to Cuernavaca."

"Winny was one of the youngest Americans in the Brigade," Tully said. "He went to Spain before he finished high school. I've been urging him to write down his experiences. The war, yes, but what has happened to him in the so-called Free World since. 'Report me and my cause aright!' I thought he could help Tex during the week and start collecting his notes."

There it was. "Good idea," I said. "I want to take some time off anyway. I'm going up to Manzanar and see a friend who's there."

"Payton's a writer," Tully said in a fruity voice, not interested in Manzanar. "He writes mystery tales. And I have some qualifications as an editor. We will be glad to offer advice and support, won't we, Payton?"

"Sure!" I said. Bullshit!

Tully had called to a Chinese takeout place for paper cartons of chow mein and other gooey mixtures, rice, and dark brown beetle juice. He produced a bottle of red wine, and we sat at a table in front of the window, watching the lights of the Bay. Jones gobbled chow mein and heaps of brown-stained rice as though it might be his last supper, Tully watching him in that fond way. They were talking about a fellow vet named Scotty.

"Helluva good hombre," Jones said, straightening from his feeding to blot his mouth with his paper napkin. "Took things serious. Always help out an amigo."

"He wrote me about the Durruti Columns," Tully said.

"What's that?"

"Changing the Social Structure of the villages."

"Shit, they'd just go in and shoot a bunch of peons for reactionaries. That was toward the end. I don't believe Scotty was in any of that shit."

I thought of the Reds in Spain shooting peons, and Japs cutting off American hands with their swords. I was feeling sick. I had been drinking wine along with Tully and Jones.

I said to Jones, "You mean some guys were more Red than others?"

Jones squawked with laughter. "Shit, most of us hated those Party-discipline turds. Frankie's a lot Redder than I ever was."

Tully poured wine, smiling foolishly. "We were all dedicated to Marxist goals, however."

It is Marxist, however, Dr. Bonington had said of *the brand*. I leaned back in my chair with my arms folded on my chest to squeeze out the sick feeling. Reds! Marxists! Young Communists! Comsymps! HUAC lists and Legion blacklists!

Jones started singing, banging the butt of his fork on the tabletop: "Arise ye prisoners of starvation." "The Internationale!" Tully joined in, but they soon quit, unable to remember the words.

"Viva la Quince Brigada," Jones began. They sang this one, in Spanish, all the way through. Tully's face was blotched with emotion.

Left out, I thought of starting "The Star-Spangled Banner," but I didn't know those words all the way through.

Tully said solemnly, "You have to understand, my boy, that Marxism is the only viable opposition to the Fascism that is taking over the world. It is a tragedy that it is in the hands of that monster Stalin! But Communists are the only ones who tried to stop Mussolini and Hitler. It is the only philosophy of hope in an increasingly hopeless universe."

I said I hoped there was some hope for those poor bastards in the Philippines. I opened one eyelid and then the other. "They were trying to stop Fascism," I said to Tully.

I asked Jones if he was a card-carrying Communist. That was a phrase HUAC employed. I realized with a shock that I was drunk.

Jones fumbled out his wallet, extracted a card and slapped it on the table. It was too dim to make out anything but his name. Jones had said that Tully was Redder than he was.

"Are you one, too?" I asked Tully, without looking at him.

"You don't want to know that, my boy." Meaning yes. It was as though the ground had become treacherous underfoot.

"Shit!" I heard myself say. Jones was finishing the last of the rice in the carton.

"There is simply no place else for people like Winny and me to be," Tully said. "There may be no place else for you, either."

"Well, I think the Russians are just about as bad as the Germans," I said.

"The Russkies are assholes, kid," Jones said. He watched Tully slosh more wine into the glasses. "They got their revolution, though."

The Communists are our deadly, deadly enemies, Mrs. Bonington had said. I sounded like her! Here was Tully, a card-carrying Commie, with a big window that looked over the shipping in the Bay, North Island, and the destroyer base. Captain Fletcher ought to be told about him. Captain Fletcher, who kept a file on Errol Flynn—who might be a German sympathizer, a Nazisymp. Investigators were either the heroes or the villains of our time.

But the Reds weren't the deadly enemy in this war, the Axis was, and Stan Takahashi claimed he hoped they would win and come over and take away our Ford cars.

I must have blanked out, and when I came to they were talking about me.

"He's in something called a midshipman's program," Tully was saying. "He finishes college and then goes into officer training in the Navy."

It was Tully's opinion that I would do better to go into the service as an enlisted man so as to have the proper point of view for my war novel.

"Fucken officers," Jones said. "At the end there, if you got called up for one of those autocriticism-piece-of-shits, you'd better tell the fuckers what they wanted to hear."

It sounded like an Alpha Beta session on attitude. What if the HUAC asked me under oath if Tully was a card-carrying Communist?

I listened, eyes closed, to them arguing, Jones saying, "Shit, there's nothing for me here. I better get my ass down to Mexico before the FBI finds out I'm in town."

The FBI!

Then he was saying, "My arm was so swole I thought they was going to have to take the whole thing off. And you back in Paree sitting around in cafés drinkin wine."

"I told you I intended to come back and enlist in the Brigade." Tully sounded like a little kid defending himself. "But I had to file my stories. And by that time it was over."

I felt like Jim Hawkins in the apple barrel. Tully hadn't fought in the Spanish Civil War, he had only been some kind of reporter. I tried to remember if he had actually claimed to have been in the Abraham Lincoln Brigade. He had certainly given me that impression. Shit!

Now it sounded like Jones was crying. "They cut off my fucken hand. And it wasn't worth it!"

"It was worth it, Winny," Tully said.

Next I woke to music, Tommy Dorsey, the brass section going at "Our Love Affair." Somehow I'd got onto the sofa across the room from the table where we'd eaten Chinese takeout. A couple was dancing, shadows moving against the wall of records, Tully and Winston Jones dancing together, a sedate fox-trot, the stump of Jones's left forearm on Tully's shoulder.

I managed to get up and sneak around the corner to the door without their noticing. I halted in the dark entry, gasping to keep from puking.

I eased out the front door and pulled it closed behind me, shutting off the music. I made my way down the steps clinging to the rail. In Ol Paint I rested and tried to sober up, leaning my head back against the seat and staring up at the dim stars over San Diego—the same stars they could see in the Philippines.

Tully had been one of my mother's boyfriends. And what was wrong with two guys dancing together? Maybe soldiers in Spain had danced together because there were no women to dance with. But Tully hadn't been a soldier. And he was a for-real Commie!

I turned the key in the ignition and cranked the engine to life, for the careful drive home to Normal Heights.

Chapter 8

1

I STUCK MY HEAD INSIDE LOIS MEADOR'S CAGE TO TELL
her I had to take Monday off. She swung around on her stool.

"Going up to Manzanar to see a friend in the camp there," I said.
"Back Monday night."

"Somebody has to take that Mission Hills route Monday!"

"Bruce will take it along with Hillcrest. I'll make it up to him." I didn't
think she would forbid it. I needed the job at Perry's, but with the manpower shortage they needed me, too.

Winny Jones would help Tully and Tex get out this week's *brand,* and
they would make the Saturday morning newsstand deliveries in a taxi.

"Going up to see your Jap buddy?" Lois said. The crooked tooth at the
corner of her mouth gave her smile a raffish quality that contrasted with
her neat hair, neat pancake makeup, neat bosom in her Perry's apron. "You
and your girlfriend?" she asked.

"Yep."

"You be here Tuesday!"

"I'll be here."

"The Emmetts' cook called me—Mrs. Sims. She says you slam the door."

"I hate her! And that rotten little dog."

She tapped her fingers lightly on my arm. "The Emmetts are friends of Mr. Perry's. Let's go upstairs and have a Coke."

My date with Lois. She took off her apron and hung it up. Beneath a blouse of some pearly material her breasts made interesting peaks and shadows.

I followed her upstairs, nice silk-stocking calves and the squeegee sound of the white nurse's shoes she wore.

We sat side by side at the cool marble counter of the soda fountain and sipped cherry Cokes. Across the store was the meat market, two white-capped butchers working behind the display case. Between were aisles of fruit and produce, canned and boxed goods, and clerks in Perry's aprons waiting on customers and arranging stock. The offices were on the balcony, Mr. Perry in his green eyeshade visible through glass. The pneumatic cash-carrier whooshed and rattled in its tube.

"How's school?" Lois asked.

I said I was writing papers and memorizing French verbs.

"You write those papers so you won't be delivering groceries to Mrs. Sims all your life."

"Never fear."

"Ray quit State after a year so we could get married. He thinks if he'd finished he wouldn't be selling restaurant equipment for a living." She gave me a flash of her smile again. "You and your sweetie wouldn't be considering something stupid, would you? On this trip."

"Never fear," I said again.

She bent her head to her straw and sucked Coke. "Just don't get married because certain feelings get too strong for you."

"You sound like my mother."

She shook her head. "I'm not your mother. Well, I think you're good-guys for going to see your Jap friend." Her fingers tapped my arm again.

It was true that I was going to Manzanar to see Stan Takahashi, but also Ben, who'd been Richie's friend in high school and at SC, and who might know something of Richie's feature player who had drowned herself.

And maybe we'd see Errol Flynn. I'd told Bonny to bring her tennis racket.

2

Dr. Bonington seemed to have become my ally since the Sunday aboard the *Sun Bear*. I thought he had interceded with Mrs. B. to allow Bonny to make the trip to Manzanar with me. Also, the Boningtons had been customers of the Takahashi Produce Stand at Four Corners, and before that of the truck Mr. Takahashi or Ben would drive through Mission Hills, the tinkling bell announcing its arrival with the good vegetables and lettuces you couldn't buy anymore now that the Japanese gardeners were locked up in relocation centers.

Dr. Bonington belonged to the Auto Club and had good maps. Manzanar wasn't on any of them but was known to be on Highway 395 in the Owens Valley south of Bishop. Bonny and I would spend Saturday night with her aunt Rhoda in Pasadena and drive to Manzanar the next day, returning to Pasadena that night. Monday we would hang around Los Angeles, and maybe there would be an opportunity for tennis at Mulholland Farm, where I hoped "young Martin Eden" and "the fair one" were welcome. I didn't know if I had the nerve to go through with that.

Monday night we would spend a couple of hours listening to Art Tatum, who was playing at a bar on the Hollywood Strip, before starting back to San Diego. We were only cutting one day of school.

Aunt Rhoda, her mother's sister, was Bonny's favorite relative. I heard all about her on the drive to Los Angeles. She had been married to Uncle Doug, who had run off with a young woman, whom Bonny described as "a floozie."

Mrs. Farr seemed to have a good deal of money. She lived in a mansion on a Pasadena street of mansions and palm trees. A colored woman in a black-and-white uniform opened the door when we arrived, about ten o'clock, and embraced Bonny with a yelp of welcome. Mrs. Farr looked like Bonny's mother except that she was hefty. She and Bonny talked excitedly about people I didn't know, and finally I excused myself as excess baggage and the maid showed me to my room upstairs.

I had a rubber tucked into the pocket of my wallet, and I lay awake in a big bedroom with windows that looked out on the trunks of palm trees, thinking about Bonny. The furniture, looming out of the shadows, seemed to have been made for giants. I lay with my eyes jammed open and a grip

129

on the joystick as though I was bringing an airplane coming in for a landing, praying that Bonny would come—

3

North of Los Angeles the highway slashed like a ruled line across the desert. Wildflowers were in bloom, glazes of yellow, red, and purple. Bonny kept exclaiming, "Isn't it beautiful!" and "Oh, they're so lovely!"

"It would have been lovely if you'd come in to see me last night."

"You were sawing wood." She punched me in the side. "Some Casanova!"

"Try me again tonight."

"Maybe I will," she said, her lips parting in her solar smile. She laid her head on my shoulder. The wind whipped her hair into tight blond curls.

She had brought her aunt's wicker hamper with a picnic the cook had provided and a thermos of coffee. She sat on her bobby-socked ankles in her gray pleated skirt and sweater and poured coffee for us to share out of the chrome cap of the thermos.

Ol Paint was stretching out on these no-traffic highways, but I kept the speed down to prolong this time with Bonny. Occasion for some poetry:

"My vegetable love should grow
Vaster than empires, and more slow;
An hundred years should go to praise
Thine eyes and on thy forehead gaze;
Two hundred to adore each breast—"

She punched me in the ribs again, and leaned against me to blow warm breath into my ear.

"'And thirty thousand for the rest,'" I said.

"Stop that sexy stuff," she said.

I kept an eye out for motorcycle cops, who were apt to stop you and demand the purpose of your trip, when rubber was being conserved. I blessed Calvin's uncle Red for the set of Mexican tires.

Mountains hulked up on either side, ranges left and right, snow peaks, green slopes, water flashing everywhere. A chilly breeze poured off the mountains, and I stopped to put up Ol Paint's top. Bonny pressed against me when I got back in. The radio station to which we were tuned crackled on and off, finally giving up.

The sign read:

MANZANAR

RELOCATION

CENTER

Low tar-paper barracks extended back up the slope of the foothill, so many of them! Whirls of dust slunk along the rows of buildings, subsiding and building again. Two soldiers wearing white helmets manned the gate, revolvers in buttoned-down holsters on their hips. They passed us through. Words like "Relocation Center" didn't mean much until you had seen the barracks, the soldiers in their white helmets, and the barbed wire.

The first of the structures bore the sign RECEPTION. Two cars and two pickups were nosed into a barrier of whitewashed rocks. I could see some of the Japanese now, two young women walking on either side of an old man with a cane, then a group of young people. Trailing along with them was a kid who couldn't have been more than four. A swirl of dust blew across the group, and the child began to run to catch up with the others. Two of the girls were laughing!

In front of the Reception Center, flowers bloomed in a ring of white-washed stones. I stopped Ol Paint and leaned my forehead against the steering wheel.

When I raised my head, Bonny looked round-eyed anxious. "It's awful!' she said.

"It's because you can't tell the bad ones from the good ones."

"It's just the war," Bonny said, as though I needed to be comforted.

"It's the LA Chamber of Commerce," I said. "And some stupid general." And Franklin D. Roosevelt had signed the order.

Bonny accompanied me inside the Reception Center, keeping close beside me. A balding sergeant sat at a desk with a phone. Three other Caucasian civilians occupied straight chairs along the wall. The sergeant looked up names on sheets of paper in a clipboard and nodded to us to sit down.

He spoke into the phone and said that Mr. Takahashi would be along directly.

Bonny sat with her saddle shoes placed precisely side by side. I had a sensation of having introduced her to a new side of life. Except for reading *Crime and Punishment* on my recommendation, she had never had any lowlife experience. Except for the Clínica Orozco. Except for the dying sailor.

And she whispered, "We're awfully lucky, aren't we?"

"We're not really involved," I said. "We can turn around and go out the gate any time we want to. The only way we're involved is that our government is doing this, and it's us."

Bonny tucked her chin down as though she'd been reprimanded.

Stan sauntered in wearing jeans, a jacket, penny loafers, and sweat socks.

I rose to introduce Bonny. Stan greeted her coolly. "Let's get out of here," he said.

"We've got a picnic in the car," Bonny said. She looked childish in her pleated skirt and bobby socks. She had brushed her hair until it gleamed.

"I already ate," Stan said. "I'm on the eleven-thirty shift. You have to eat with your shift."

He led us outside and past two of the buildings, to a bench braced against a west-facing wall, in a band of sun. We sat down together, Bonny between us with her arms wrapped around her knees.

"What do you do all day?" I asked.

"What you do in the pen," Stan said. "Eat, sleep, daub around. Have meetings."

"Where's Ben?"

"He's here. Where else would he be?" Brushing his fingers through his stiff hair, Stan said, "I appreciate your coming, Payt. Bonny." He had seemed no different from anyone else at San Diego High, but now he was inexplicably foreign, shorter than I had remembered, and it was as though the scallops of flesh at the corners of his eyes had become more prominent.

"Calvin wanted to come, too," I said. "He wanted to bring his girls. Three of them."

"Whoops!" Stan said. "Could've thrown the ball around. BS'd like old times."

"The Tutti-frutti Backfield," Bonny said, trying to enter in. I frowned at her.

"Pretty rugged about Bob-O," Stan said.

I nodded. I took a breath. "Listen: How *is* it?"

132

Stan considered. "It's really hard on the old people. They've lost everything, most of them. It's tough seeing your parents really broken down."

"Payton says you were in premed at UCLA," Bonny said. "My brother was in premed at Stanford."

"How do you mean was?"

"He went into the Coast Guard."

"Well, he's in for the duration, too."

I was feeling an ache of discomfort in my shoulders trying to keep the conversation going.

"The trouble is we keep telling each other how rotten it is," Stan said. "We have meetings a couple of times a week to tell each other it's unconstitutional. The trouble is you're PO'd all the time. It's all you think about."

He sat with his feet stretched out, hands jammed in his pockets. "The people in charge aren't so bad," he went on. " 'Cock-asians,' we call them." He gave Bonny an apologetic glance. "They didn't do this to us. The Army and the president did. General DeWitt says a Jap is a Jap and it doesn't matter whether he's American or not." He made a snarling sound.

Bonny asked if anyone was doing anything.

"Ben and some of the lawyers are trying to get something to the Supreme Court, but the government can do about anything it wants to in wartime. They even knocked out habeas corpus in the Civil War." He leaned stiffly forward, his hands still trapped in his pockets. He looked relieved when two other fellows happened by. Everybody stood around Bonny, huddled on the bench.

I said it was a beautiful valley.

"It was until LA Water and Power stole all the water," one of the others said.

"Looks like plenty of water coming off the mountains."

"Headed for LA toilets."

The two others moved on. Bonny hugged her knees.

"You still going to be a writer?" Stan wanted to know. "You ought to write about this place!" He swung his arm. "Except I guess you couldn't do it unless you'd really been inside."

"To understand Social Reality you have to be inside it," I said.

Bonny glanced at me with her lips parted and the tip of her tongue touching the upper one.

"Well, come on and I'll show you around," Stan said.

"I knew a girl at Bishop," Bonny said. "Mitzi Yamamoto."

"She's here. We'll go find her."

"I promised my brother I'd look up Ben," I lied.

I managed to see Ben Takahashi alone while Stan took Bonny off to find her high school friend. Ben had a corner in one of the barracks partitioned into an office with olive drab blankets hung from wires. An office type-writer sat on a desk, and an Army cot was covered with another blanket. Ben wore black-rimmed glasses.

"Richie told me to say hi."

Ben flipped a hand toward the cot in an invitation to sit down. His shoulders were slumped from bending over law books, and he was not very cordial. He had a trick of slipping his glasses half off, then back again.

On the cot was one of the satin-faced pillows you could buy in the crummy shops along lower Broadway in San Diego. Embroidered in different colored threads was the message:

THE AMERICAN BILL OF RIGHTS

FREEDOM OF SPEECH   FREEDOM OF RELIGION

FREEDOM OF THE PRESS   FREEDOM OF ASSEMBLY

WORTH FIGHTING FOR

In the center was a figure of a Minuteman with his musket, outlined in red, white, and blue.

I sat down and leaned on the pillow, trying to seem at ease. "Listen, Ben, I've got to find out about some things that happened to Richie in LA."

Ben turned his chair toward the cot with a jarring of legs. "We didn't run in the same crowd at SC, Payt."

"He had a girlfriend named Val. She was a starlet or a feature player or something."

His eyes blinked behind the lenses of his glasses. "Sure. Val Ferris. Richie was proud of her. She was in some movies. I remember one called *Castaways.*"

"Well, she killed herself. Maybe because she didn't get a part in a movie Richie had to do with when he was working for that studio."

Ben slipped his glasses on his nose. "Can't you ask Richie about this?"

"He just says it didn't have anything to do with him really, but some people thought it was his fault. There's this kind of crazy stuntman guy—"

"Probably there was somebody getting screwed over. Or maybe coke."

"Coke?"

"Cocaine," he said, and grinned in a queer squinty way. "In Hollywood there is always somebody getting screwed, literally and figuratively. And a lot of coke. That guy Richie worked for, David Lubin, was famous for all that."

I nodded, hoping he would keep going.

"Richie was always hooked in with Hollywood people. There were guys like that at SC, that you knew they would end up in the Industry. Val Ferris loaded herself with bricks and drowned herself in Lubin's swimming pool. It was one of those scandals the Industry is good at hushing up. David Lubin was Fontainebleau Films."

"So probably Val was getting screwed."

"You know what I mean, humiliated. Screwed out of something. I mean, there's that terrible line between being someone and no one."

Calvin had said something like that.

"How come people would think it was Richie's fault?"

"She'd been his girlfriend, though I think that was all over. But Richie was Lubin's yes-man. It might be that. Maybe Richie—" He shook his head. "Lubin died of cancer a year or so ago."

"Well, thanks," I said, rising.

"How is Richie, anyway?"

"He's instructing at Pensacola. He and Liz are getting married in June." I pointed down at the embroidered pillow. "Everybody should have one."

"Everybody should have four," Ben said.

4

The colored maid served dinner for Bonny and me and Mrs. Farr and her friend Colonel Bunker, a courtly old gent with a southern accent, and a tweed jacket with leather patches on the elbows. Colonel Bunker considered himself an expert at mimicking the president: "Mah waff Ellynore, and mah littul dawg Fala . . ."

After dinner we played mah-jong with a beautiful set of antique ivory tiles. I'd never played before, and my mind kept lurching off after Val Ferris and Hagen taking some kind of revenge on Liz, so I wasn't much good.

The colonel went home at nine thirty, and I excused myself also, leaving Bonny in conversation with her aunt over tiny cups of coffee. In bed I listened to the rattle of palm fronds in the wind and watched the massive shapes of the dressers and armoire afloat in darkness. For some reason I couldn't get my mind off Val Ferris being fucked by Richie's boss as well as my brother.

It seemed that half the night had passed when the door opened on a vertical of lighted hallway. I heard the pad of a foot on the parquet, and imagined it on the carpet. I tried to keep from panting.

Bonny fell onto the bed beside me, pinning me beneath the covers, her breath in my ear. She clove to me as I tried to struggle free.

"Just lie there!" she whispered.

I managed to half turn over, one arm around her; I felt as though I was lying on the keel of a China Clipper. I lay still even though my arm felt paralyzed. I could feel the warmth of Bonny's body through the sheets and quilt.

I tried to relax in her embrace, layers of fabric between us, electric prickle of her hair against my cheek.

"How did you know it was wrong for us to fence those people up in that terrible place?" she whispered.

Because my mother had brought *The Grapes of Wrath* home from the lending library when I was at an impressionable age? Because I'd been raised on the Knights of the Round Table, and Robin Hood? Because I'd played in the Tutti-frutti Backfield at San Diego High with Stan Takahashi? Because I worked at *the brand*?

"It makes me so mad!" she said.

"Lot of things to get mad about, once you start," I said. Maybe someday I could tell her about Dessy and her San Francisco bosses, and the Tijuana whores and the Shetland pony, and David Lubin and Val Ferris; but I didn't know enough about that yet.

"I really got mad when they picketed *the brand*," I said. "Maybe you don't really feel it till it happens to you."

"What you said about Social Reality."

"Sure."

"It's hard when a sweet old man like Colonel Bunker makes fun of good people."

"It's hard when good people sign orders to put the AJAs into a concentration camp."

She lay unreachably tight against me in her aunt's guest bedroom. Finally I determined from her regular breathing that she was asleep. There was no way to disentangle myself and go into the bathroom in my desperation. I snapped awake time and again in a rhythm of arousal and subsidence. When I waked to gray dawn she was gone.

5

Breakfast was grapefruit, muffins, and coffee. Mrs. Farr wore a crisply rustling dressing gown, Bonny a white blouse with a loopy blue tie. When we said good-bye her aunt kissed me on the cheek and told me that Barbara had brought a very nice young man to visit.

We drove to Hollywood and wandered along Hollywood Boulevard, looking in shoe store windows.

A storefront displayed a recruiting poster in the form of a blown-up newspaper item. AVIATION CADET TRAINING. 100,000 MEN TO BE RECRUITED. OFFICERS TRAINING PLAN. Under smaller heads were the figures: $75 per month during training, $183 per month for ground officers, $245 per month for flying officers.

Headlines blazed out of the racks of papers in a newsstand: STARVATION KILLING 1,200 GREEKS DAILY.

Bonny stood beside me with her blond locks curving along her cheeks, shaking her head, blue eyes shocked. "I just hate the numbers!"

Thirty-six thousand prisoners on Bataan.

I said I liked the idea of $245 a month. "We could get married and live on that."

"I don't want you to be a flier," Bonny said. Johnny Pierce had died in Air Corps training.

"Okay then."

"I mean it!" Today she was affectionate in public in a way she never was in San Diego, clinging to my arm and bumping hips as we wandered along the boulevard among sailors and soldiers and their girlfriends. We went to look at the tar pits and had lunch at Farmers Market.

"Let's go play some tennis," I said. I reminded her that we had a standing invitation from Errol Flynn. It seemed to me that Bonny would do just fine in treacherous Hollywood terrain simply because she had classy tennis ground strokes.

When we had located Flynn's place, we drove to the end of a nearby dirt track that looked out over the sprawl of the evil city. Bonny changed into her tennis dress inside Ol Paint while I paced outside the car. Then I changed. She was very quiet as I turned off Mulholland into Flynn's domain, sitting up straight with one hand braced on the dashboard. Six or seven other cars were nosed up to a tall hedge that blocked off the tennis court, across a paved area from the house. Chrome and bright enamel winked in the sun. Ol Paint looked old and shabby among the other cars.

Carrying rackets, Bonny and I moved along the walk to the court, where I could hear the plock of a ball and glimpse through foliage people sitting at white tables under striped beach umbrellas. If Bonny hadn't been with me, my courage would have gone down the drain.

A foursome was playing, two girls in white shorts, an older woman in an ankle-length skirt, and a blond young guy missing a shot right to him. Hackers.

Flynn came to greet us, wearing pleated shorts and a T-shirt, a visor accentuating his sharp features. I had practiced what I would say:

"Hi, Mr. Flynn. I'm Richie Daltrey's brother, and this is Barbara Bonington."

"Of course!" he said, breaking into a grin. "The fair one and young Martin Eden." He herded us toward the others, two older men at a table with a silver shaker. At another were a too-handsome guy and a starlet type.

The older men, rising big-bellied to be introduced, were Mr. Warner and Mr. Wald. Mr. Warner was deeply tanned, with sleek oiled hair, a pencil-line mustache like Flynn's, and a flash of a red stone in his cuff link. Wald was younger, with a dark frog face.

"Let's have some respectable tennis here!" Flynn said, clapping his hands together. He beckoned the hackers off the court. "Come on, Billie."

Bonny and I faced Flynn and Billie, whose last name I hadn't heard. She was pretty in such a blond, sunny way that Bonny seemed almost sultry by contrast. New sparkling-white Pennsylvania balls! We rallied in practice,

Flynn with a big forehand, Billie not so good, but fun, squealing when she had to run for wide ones, Bonny with her good lefty ground strokes.

In play Flynn covered three-quarters of the court, poaching and jamming, so that he and Billie won the first four games. Then Bonny began banging her beautiful down-the-line backhand, catching Flynn poaching. When I saw that he made a joke out of getting passed, I started keeping him honest also. We broke Billie's serve, won Bonny's, lost Flynn's, but won mine after about a dozen ads for the set. It was fun! Bonny's Helen Wills deadpan broke into her luminous smile when Flynn complimented her, and I was proud of her in a host of ways.

Flynn dismissed Billie and called to the older woman, Esther Carnes, to be his partner. She must've been forty, but she had good strokes and a way of disapproving when aced, as though it was unmannerly, that caused me to drop two service games. Bonny and I lost the set 6–2.

Afterward we sat at the table with Mr. Warner, Mr. Wald, and Mrs. Carnes and drank Cokes from the courtside refrigerator.

"That is a very competent backhand of yours, Miss Bonington," Mr. Warner said, leaning toward Bonny. *That letch,* Liz had said of him. Richie had implied that he could have any girl he wanted to give a contract to. Jack Warner was smoking a tan cigar. All these people must have known David Lubin.

"It cost my father a lot of money!" Bonny said, and blushed at her temerity.

Flynn had disappeared, but Billie joined us at what I had figured was the A table. She and Bonny had a conversation going, Bonny listening, nodding, joining in. A Filipino in a white uniform appeared to see if anyone wanted drinks and took the cocktail shaker away with him.

I felt paralyzed with old, dogfaced ineptitudes. It grated on me that Bonny would be at ease in social situations that seemed to me fraught with possibilities for jerkery.

"I know your brother," Mrs. Carnes said, smiling at me. "There is quite a family resemblance. I am very fond of Richard."

Her face was as neat as her strokes, narrow and rather haughty, with a nose she kept raised as though to look down it at you. I thought she must be someone important, and Mr. Wald, too: someone rather than no one, as Ben Takahashi had put it.

Wald asked if I was interested in movies.

"Well, in fiction!"

"And so are we!" Wald said, laughing. Mrs. Carnes held up her glass for the houseboy to replenish from the shaker.

Bonny announced that I wrote stories, and I felt my face catch fire.

"Any published?" Wald wanted to know.

"Not yet."

"Where are you sending them?"

"*Black Mask* mostly."

"I know Percy Ratner," Wald said. "I'll tell him to watch out for your stuff. Daltrey? Pat Daltrey?"

"Payton." PR! This was the way the system worked, that Richie knew, had learned at SC and from *The Pisan Manual*! Who you knew, not what you knew.

"He's good!" Bonny said. I gave her a warning glance. Mrs. Carnes looked amused.

"I'm going to be good," I said. "I don't know if I am yet."

"Never admit that in this town," Jack Warner said in his gravelly voice, and blew smoke.

"Esther wrote the screenplay for *Wild Fire*," Wald said.

I looked at Mrs. Carnes with interest; *Wild Fire* was supposed to be terrific.

"Anyone for a swim?" Flynn said, reappearing. He pointed to the pool, freckled with gold in the sun. No one seemed to be inclined to join him, so he set off by himself, broad-shouldered and narrow-hipped in his T-shirt and shorts, a towel over his shoulder.

I hurried to catch up with him. I said, "I have to talk to you about that guy Hagen."

He halted, frowning at me as I hurried on. "You remember that night on your boat when he went after Richie."

A redwood table and two chairs stood in a patch of shade, and Flynn pushed a chair aside for me and sprawled in the other in his long-legged abrupt way.

"I saw him at the Yacht Club the other day," I said. "He is kind of on Richie's case."

Flynn bared his teeth and blew his breath through them.

"Panch was drunk that night. He does seem to have a gripe against Richie for some nasty mess that I think should be charged against David Lubin."

"That actress who killed herself, Val Ferris."

He blinked in a way that reminded me of a camera shutter. "Panch had known her from some previous existence. It is a curious fact that one unbalanced human can so often find another in this world of ours. Val Ferris was very intense, very dramatic. Once at an occasion here there was a scene, and she bolted, shouting imprecations. A search party was instituted! She was found lying on the diving board mother naked, having flung all her clothing into the pool. A considerable amount of trouble for everyone!

"One might have imagined her as a prospective suicide. The usual reasons. Career failure, love failure, awareness of exploitation and lack of regard, and the vileness of human nature as it is regularly manifested in this place."

"Hagen blames Richie," I said. "He kind of threatened Richie. I'm worried about Liz."

Flynn gazed at me, hard-faced. "I will tell him," he said, "that if he causes that handsome young lady any disturbance I will detach his testicles and hang them in the doorway like mistletoe. For daws to pick at! Will that suffice you?"

"Well, thanks," I said. "I was just kind of worried. Maybe—" But he seemed no longer interested, his eyes slanting away from me, and I felt like a pushy jerk for bothering him. He scraped his chair back and went away, leaving me there.

The vileness of human nature as it is regularly manifested here, he had said.

When Bonny and I left, Jack Warner told her in an offhand way to let him know if she wanted a screen test, and Jerry Wald said he would mention Payton Daltrey the next time he talked to Perce Ratner. Mrs. Carnes gave me her card.

6

The streetlights were coming on as we drove along Sunset Boulevard looking for the bar where Art Tatum was playing. It was a dark little place that stank of beer. On top of the upright piano was a brandy snifter filled with green bills. We ordered Tom Collinses and sat at a tiny table waiting for Tatum to appear. Bonny leaned against me.

"I don't understand about this afternoon," she said. "We didn't go there just to play tennis, did we?"

"I had to ask Flynn something about Richie and that guy from the *Sirocco*. We saw him that day at the Yacht Club."

Her lips rounded into an O.

Tatum appeared, to seat himself at the piano in a scatter of applause. He looked like a fireplug on the bench, with his dark glasses and snap-brim hat. He struck a chord, full of promise, and bent to playing "Honeysuckle Rose."

As we joined in the clapping when he had finished, Bonny said in a casual voice, "My parents are talking about me transferring to Stanford next year."

There was no way in the world I could afford the tuition to transfer to Stanford with her—$225 a quarter! I felt nauseated by the sweet drink in my hand.

"Is this because of me?" I whispered.

"They can afford it with Charley out of school."

"I'm sorry I'm unsuitable."

"It's because of Charley," she said, tight-lipped. Then she said, "They're afraid I'll start going steady like I did with Johnny."

"And you have to marry a doctor."

"I told you, that's just the way Mother is! She and my aunts are like that because they worshipped Grandfather."

I watched Tatum's fingers spiking down from fat black hands. Bonny rested her cheek against my shoulder. I was trying to understand what I felt: like being left out choosing up for a team because you weren't good enough. Like not being counted among the people to be invited to the party. I knew that Bonny loved me, but her parents regarded me as a threat like Johnny Pierce. To her virginity, or anyway her reputation? To her marrying a proper doctor? So the Stanford prospect was why Mrs. B. had permitted this trip. Bonny hadn't told me earlier so as not to spoil our days together. Greeks were dying and tankers were burning and sinking and all those Americans were Jap POWs in a war that just went on and on. But this crazy weekend was ending. Four hours driving back to San Diego, taking it easy through the beach towns down the Coast in the night. Stanford University!

The fat black piano player turned corny songs into sparkling music, but it was time to go.

Bonny drove the first leg, southward bound down Firestone Boulevard, then down Lakewood into Long Beach. She had her glasses on, and she wore a solemn expression, which whitened in the glare of oncoming headlights. I thought of a series of bitter comments, but did not punish Bonny with them. In Corona del Mar we stopped for gas and coffee, and I took over the driving.

The highway in Leucadia was divided by a row of huge-boled eucalyptus, peeling tongues of bark hanging off trunks as pale as flesh. My eyelids were heavy.

Someone was sprawled on the asphalt. Bonny cried out. I tramped on the brakes and wrenched the wheel. A sailor, bareheaded in a black jumper, a white face turned toward us as the tires screamed. Too fast! Ol Paint tilted up with a sensation of lightness, then crunched to four wheels again as I fought the steering.

We skidded toward the barrier of trees. The peeling trunks hung before us like a solid wall, but Ol Paint slipped between two of them. Rubber squalled again as the car surged out into the empty northbound lane beyond the trees, headed back toward LA. The wheel finally responded, Ol Paint slowing, jerking in high gear. The engine died. Stopped, I slumped against the wheel while Bonny clung to me in an echoing stillness. The headlights splashed the pavement headed north.

When I started the engine, my left leg was so weak I could hardly depress the clutch. Ol Paint drifted along the trees until I found an opening through which I could turn back into the southbound lane. Then I drove slowly on the shoulder of the road looking for the sailor we had almost run over.

"Where'd he go?" Bonny cried, and, when I stopped again, "Don't get out!"

There was something spooky in the night, all right. The sailor must have crawled into the shadows beyond the shoulder. Fallen out of some carload of drunken swabbies? I could see Ol Paint's skid marks, black streaks of Uncle Red's Mexican tires left on the pavement. The space between the trees, where brush had been flattened by the car's passage, could not have been eight feet wide. I couldn't pretend that I had aimed Ol Paint through that space.

Bonny leaned on my leg to peer out my window. When I put an arm around her, she jammed her face into my neck. I drifted on along the highway in the black shadow of the eucalyptus row, and off the pavement with a jar. Close against the vine-covered fence I switched off the lights and ignition, turning and clasping Bonny, hard breathing, hand to her crotch and her crotch thrust back against my hand. I fumbled under her skirt, unlatching stockings and panty girdle, her hot sweet breath in my face. Our mouths sealed together. Her hips lifted off the seat as I wrenched the rubbery garment down. My fingers encountered damp and heat. I fumbled for my own zipper; my hard-on came out of my pants as though spring-actuated. I rolled on top of her in the grip of some kind of absolute hard-thrusting reprisal for being found wanting, for having been ejected from Mission Hills, for not having $225 a quarter tuition to attend Stanford.

Her body seemed to be fizzing like a shaken 7-Up, and something huge and brutal commanded mine.

"*Oh!*" she whispered. Then, "*No!*"

I jackknifed.

A car swept by, headlights dazzling in the mirror.

"You didn't get any in me?"

"No."

She mopped at her thigh with a Kleenex, muttering, "Oh! Oh! Oh!—" She leaned back against her door, pulling her panty girdle on with convulsive movements.

"I've got to find that goddam swabbie. Maybe he's hurt."

She continued to pull her clothing together as I backed up and swung the wheel to turn on the headlights toward the fence line. The sailor was sitting against the fence. He had a scraped place on his chin. He looked about sixteen. He'd fallen out the back of a pickup truck that had given him and three buddies a lift back from Oceanside.

Bonny did not speak on the last stretch of our trip back to San Diego. Sometimes she sat with the flat of her hands held to her cheeks. The sailor stank of puke. His name was Tim Rafferty. He was from western Pennsylvania. Making conversation with him was like pulling weeds. Sometimes Bonny laughed inappropriately.

We let him off across from the bright lights of the main gate of the Naval Recruit Depot.

"What a lovely trip!" Bonny murmured.

"Close call," I said. Two close calls.

"Dear God!" Bonny whispered, and made a breathy laughing sound.

Something had changed like an enormous gear groaning as it mightily turned to settle into a new notch. We drove on up off the flatlands the rest of the way to Mission Hills in silence.

Chapter 9

1

O<small>N</small> TUESDAY MORNING I SAT WITH LIZ FLETCHER ON A concrete bench in the shadow of the Ad Building, watching the students crossing the Quad heading for classes or the parking lot.

She had a cloth bag in her lap, hoops of wood for handles. Out of the bag she brought a doll with a china head and hands, in a long white dress. The doll's eyes rolled shut when it was turned on its back, open when held upright. The face was old-fashioned, with a rosebud mouth and blooming cheeks.

"Isn't she beautiful?" Liz said. "She's Emma. She was my mother's. She's going to be the Bombing Raid Baby." They were doing civil defense in her psych class. "She's going to be a famous actress when she grows up, aren't you, Em?" Liz went on. She contrived for the doll to nod like a puppet.

"Smart, too," I said.

Liz spoke in irritating baby talk, bending over the doll. "But her lover-boy's gone off to be a sailor!"

She said in her normal, lisping voice, "My father says I'm too old to play with dolls." She sat with her leg brushing mine, ankles in silk stockings crossed. She smelled of flowers, like Dessy. Her dark hair was gathered up to show the pink lobes of her ears. I was glad that Bonny didn't have a nine o'clock on Tuesdays.

"What did Errol say about me?" she said.

"He called you 'that lovely young woman.'"

She rocked the doll back and forth, so the doll's eyes opened and closed.

"What did Jack Warner say?"

"He offered Bonny a screen test."

"That letch," she said. "Do you think Richie has a girlfriend in Pensacola?"

It was as though her mind circled like a fly around the idea of Val Ferris but didn't quite want to land on it.

"It's airplanes he loves in Pensacola. You're his girl."

"He'd better marry me in June if he wants me to be his girl," Liz said. She held up her doll to touch my forehead with its china lips. She looked at her watch and said she had to hurry. I watched her striding across the Quad, carrying her doll in its bag.

2

Heading for Mr. Chapman's class, I passed my fraternity brothers Ernie Baker and Bill Holmes in the hall. When I said hi, both of them glanced away as though some sergeant had commanded "Right face!" then went on along away. I almost stumbled with a sudden weakening of my knees. I was being silenced! They must've decided it last night.

After class I met Bonny in the Caff. She looked tired, the flesh beneath her eyes transparent, her face thinner. It was as though she was suddenly older.

"Charley's marrying that girl in the photograph," she said. "Eunice Coster. He wrote my parents a really awful letter. He's never coming home. He loves Australia. He loves Eunice's whole family. Mr. Coster sells cars. After the war he's going to set Charley up selling boats. Of course Charley would be so happy if he never had to look at a med school textbook again, and he won't have to go into practice as junior Dr. Bonington. It was a really cruel letter. He sounded as though he's always hated them!"

I had no reason to like Charley, and I disliked Mrs. B. for what seemed sufficient reason.

"Daddy tried to phone, but you can't get through."

It occurred to me that I was treating my own father as Charley was treating his parents. As Alpha Beta was treating me, who probably deserved it, which I didn't need to mention to Bonny.

Her blue eyes flashed at me. "It's funny about the war, isn't it? People can do what they want, like it's a new kind of freedom."

It was strange and tense with her, as though we didn't know each other very well. As though we were embarrassed by Sunday night. When she had gone to class, I waited in the Caff to see if Pogey would show up after his chem lab. There he was, cutting between the tables, slight and neat in his cords and blue cashmere, glint of his glasses in the light. His face was stiff.

I stretched out in my chair and said, "They did it, huh?"

He nodded. Behind him the high windows cast long slants of sunlight across the half-occupied tables. "You can come and appeal next Monday night."

"I'd have to eat a lot of shit."

Muscles crimped along his jaw. "The guys think if you don't have time to spend with them you ought to turn in your bond."

"Can't you even sit down?"

He shook his head.

"I'll turn in my bond so I can talk to you. I don't care if I talk to any of the rest of them."

"They're your fraternity brothers!"

The whole fraternity-silencing jerkery seemed so utterly stupid to me I could hardly focus on it. Pogey was my best friend, but it was as though I'd taken a long step toward something that he hadn't taken yet. Nothing made you grow up so fast as giant women in your life.

My neck ached from squinting up at Pogey where he stood beside the table.

"It's just too much snotty attitudes and high school grab-ass," I said. "I hate the thing where you sit around and criticize each other! So you can be a better fraternity brother. That's what they do in Communist cells, for Christ sake! I'm working two jobs, and I really don't have time to hang around with the guys, except you. I'm not interested in beer busts and joint meetings with sororities and all that shit."

147

"Well, don't get igneous," Pogey said. "I told them I'd tell you you can appeal, if you want."

"I guess I don't want."

"Okay," Pogey said, and, with a saluting gesture, walked away through the rectangles of sunlight.

3

When I came down the stairs with a load of empty boxes from my Mission Hills route, Lois jerked her neat head toward the basement. "Mr. Union Bigshot is here."

Big Bill Hutchinson, once my mother's lover, and the Teamsters' steward, stopped in to chat with the Perry's drivers every couple of months, a big-bellied, big-shouldered man with a tough handsome face running to jowls. Except for Mr. Perkins, it was with Bill Hutchinson that I had had the most trouble maintaining my no-blame, limited-involvement policy concerning my mother and her love life.

I had not been required to join the Teamsters, like the other drivers, because I worked part-time. Big Bill had, in fact, got me the after-school job at Perry's because I was my mother's son.

A blue layer of cigar smoke floated in the basement. Big Bill, in a tan gabardine double-breasted suit, sat on the zinc-topped counter with drivers surrounding him, smoking the stogies he always passed out. Bruce, Herb, and Ted were in their deliveryman uniforms, and Len Upton, who had come from groceries upstairs to replace the drafted Chuck-the-checker, wore his Perry's apron. I had forgotten to snap my bow tie back on, but Lois hadn't noticed.

"Hey, kid!" Bill called to me, raising a massive gabardine arm. The others' heads turned toward me. "How's your lady mother?"

"Just fine, Bill!"

"Good! Cigar?" He proffered his silver case.

I said I was trying to quit.

This was considered a fine joke because Bill laughed at it. I stowed away my boxes and joined them, given the place of honor beside Mr. Union Bigshot. Bill shook hands with his left hand gripping my elbow.

"How's school? Lots of those coeds available, I bet. Boys all gone off to fight for Dugout Doug."

There was more laughter at the premise that all coeds were sex-crazed.

"Telling these fellows we're getting them a twelve-and-a-half percent raise in the new contract. How's that sound? Join up and I'll get you a raise, too."

I said I was probably going to have to go on full-time anyway. I explained that the Legion pickets were shutting down *the brand*'s job-printing business. Len and the other drivers watched Bill's face to see what attitude they should assume in the matter of the Legion versus *the brand*.

"You people got a lawyer?" Bill asked, squinting at me through the smoke. "First Amendment! This is supposed to be a free fucking country. Free speech, free press."

"That's right, Big Bill," said Ted, the worst suck-up.

"They can't do that," Bill said, ponderously shaking his big head.

I said they were sure doing it.

"Who in the fuck do they think they are, deciding who is going to print what?" Bill said. "I hate those Legion cocksuckers."

"I deliver the papers to the newsstands on Saturdays," I said. "A couple of them followed me around my route."

"Intimidation!" The cigar stuck out of Bill Hutchinson's jaw like the bowsprit of the *Sun Bear*. "Beating up tramps in Hoovervilles, intimidating college kids delivering papers, that's about all they're good for. Let's just see if we can't fuck those birds right in the ear."

"What're you going to do, Big Bill?" Herb asked.

"Andy Oates is commander of some Legion post. He owns Coast Cartage, runs about twenty trucks. His contract's on overtime. I'll tell him I'll pull his drivers if this shit don't cease and desist."

The drivers laughed and slapped their legs. "Terrific, Big Bill!"

"And I can do it!" Bill Hutchinson said, with a wink at me.

"Can you get them beat up, too?" I asked, to more laughter.

"Just tell your lady mother this one's for her," Bill said, grinning and waving smoke away from his face. He turned to address the others in a confidential tone. "Tell me, fellas, is anybody getting anything off little Miss Iron-face in her glass box?"

4

TOKYO BOMBED! was the headline. I stopped at the newsstand across from the Benford Hotel to read the front-page text. The Japanese capital had been bombed, presumably by U.S. planes. There was a mystery as to where the planes could have come from.

I felt as though I were breathing clearer air in great draughts as I trotted on down 3rd Street to the printshop.

No pickets!

Tully sat at his desk with his feet up. "Didn't show up this morning," he said. "I guess they got tired of it." He looked smug, as though he had managed this victory personally, and I was pleased with myself that I didn't have to tell him about Bill Hutchinson.

"Have you seen the headlines?" I asked. At last there was a banner head I could stand to look at.

"I saw them, yes."

"Well, come on! It's terrific!"

"They need something terrific just now. It seems more men were captured on Bataan than were originally announced."

"Shit!" I said. "How many?"

"Maybe twice as many."

I leaned on the counter.

"Winny has deserted us," he went on. "He is not much interested in work, I'm afraid." He had given Jones money to take the train to Mexico City, where he had friends. "I can't imagine what is to become of him," Tully said sadly.

"I guess if you're a vet it's best to have been on the winning side."

"We would have been the winning side if the Western democracies hadn't sold out to the Fascists!"

There it was, the "we" of the Abraham Lincoln Brigade. But Tully hadn't fought in Spain. He looked like a big Raggedy Andy doll with his fat lips, high-colored face, and curls showing under his leather cap. Who cared about the Spanish Civil War anyway.

"What if the FBI shadowed him to your house that night?" I said.

"You must discount a good deal of what you heard on that inebriate evening, my boy. Winny can be a fool when in his cups."

I said I'd drunk too much wine, too. "Passed out, in fact." The hollow of my head buzzed with the numbers that always frightened Bonny. More than seventy thousand men!

There was some disturbance on 3rd Street, sailors trotting past the printshop window. I went outside for a look. A crowd had collected in front of the Bedford, three sailors hurrying to join it. I took off after them. Something was covered with a gray blanket. I slipped between a Marine and the fat lady from Quality Cleaners. A small hand thick with rings extended from under the blanket, and a dark tongue of blood had leaked over the curb.

I stared at the many-ringed hand. *I don't want to die!* Dessy had cried to Calvin.

"Jumped!" the fat lady said, pitching her chin toward the high windows of the Benford. The late sun dazzled my eyes.

I backed out from among the spectators. I almost stumbled over a slipper, high-heeled and decorated with green lace.

At the far curb I bent as though I'd been punched in the belly and puked yellow bile. Scrubbing my mouth, I retreated to the printshop.

"Suicide at the Benford," I muttered to Tully, backing against the door to close it. "She jumped out a window." Like the sailor falling from the dirigible, like Val Ferris filling her pockets with stones and jumping into David Lubin's swimming pool. For the usual reasons: career failure, love failure, and the realization of the vileness of human nature.

"About three a year go out those windows," Tully said, shaking his head. Mr. Social Consciousness.

"It was Calvin's hooker."

He made a pained face. "This is not a society to let miscegenation go unpunished."

"Oh, miscegenation, bullshit!" I yelled at him. "American kids in Jap prison camps and AJA four-year-olds at Manzanar and fourteen-year-old Mexican girls—" I didn't even know what I was ranting about.

"You sound as though you have only now been faced with the facts of life," Tully said severely. "Everywhere the ceremony of innocence is drowned, my boy! Now why don't you get started packing those fliers into boxes?"

I went into the pressroom to start unfolding the cartons. When I bent over, my head swam as though I was going to faint. Dessy had wanted a friend and all I could think about was my hard-on.

Tully had already stacked the fliers on the Masonite-topped table. They advertised a sale of car batteries.

I needed a new battery, all right, mine run down from Manzanar, Mulholland Farm, a near accident, and a messy sex fracas in Leucadia, and now a suicide on 3rd Street. From 1,200 Greeks starving daily, and 70,000

Americans surrendered on Bataan, and how many tankers a week torpedoed off the East Coast? Dessy with her head smashed.

A siren sounded, winding down.

Tully appeared in the pressroom doorway, fat white ink-stained arms. He stepped down into Charlotte's pit to smack the Start button. With the intent whackety-whack, fliers began flopping into the wire basket.

"Keep an eye on her. I'm going for coffee."

I glared at him, who didn't give a shit what happened to pathetic hookers. His sympathy for the workers was all talk. I wasn't going to let that happen to me.

"Child!" Calvin trotted into the room, wearing a fancy gray-striped suit and a hat with a cute little feather in the band. His face was the color of dirty cement. He halted in a melodramatic pose, fingers spread against his chest and his mouth turned down into a tragic mask.

"Why'd she do it, child?"

"Why, shit, Calvin, she just figured out exploitation and lack of regard, that's all."

He stared at me openmouthed. "I loved that little girl, child!"

"You fucking pimp!" I said.

I recognized the whuffling sound of Charlotte on the fritz and jumped into the pit to shut her down. When I turned again Calvin was gone, leaving the door open. I cleaned up the mess of crumpled fliers and went into the washroom to wash my hands and face. I was sorry I had shouted at Calvin.

I went in to sit at Tully's desk beneath the FREE TOM MOONEY headline, with the black tulip of the telephone receiver jammed to my ear like an ace reporter. I dialed the Mercy Hospital number. After some waits and transfers Bonny's voice came on.

I told her that my friend Calvin's whore had killed herself.

There was an empty buzz on the line.

"Went out the window of the hotel." I didn't know why I had to be terse and Hemingway when I felt like crying.

"I'll be through by eleven," Bonny said.

So we made arrangements to meet and to go out to Point Loma to our necking spot; and that would make me feel better.

It seemed that we did not need to speak of the incident in Leucadia, but something was very different between us. It was as though when she kissed me Bonny was thinking of something else.

5

Pensacola, Fla.
April 30, 1942

Dear Brud,

Sorry I haven't written more, but I figure Liz keeps you posted. I know you don't see Dad because he keeps me posted. You promised you would get back together with him and make it up. He is a grand guy and you ought to know it. The fact is that a lot of people in this country are anti-Jewish. You just don't run into it growing up in San Diego.

I understand what you told me, how you became Mother's kid, or anyway Grandma's, after the divorce. You could put up with Mother sleeping with different guys, and I couldn't. I know I kind of took Dad's side, and you took Mom's. But we are not kids anymore, Brud.

"The Superior Man does at once what the Fool does at last."

Liz probably told you I'm training in TBFs. I put in for Wildcats but what I got was these clunkers. They make 135 knots if you are lucky, and the idea of running in on a Haruna class battleship with a torpedo that only goes off about half the time (thank you, war workers) with every gun on that battle wagon banging at you does not give you a helluva lot of hope of coming home much less chalking off one Haruna class.

The dropping procedure is you come in at two hundred feet. The closer you get the more chance the torpedo has and the less chance you have. We are sure looking forward to getting into action against the Nips.

Lizzy is having a hard time with her father. He is a hardnose SOB. He was damned good to her after her mother died and that year she was so sick. When they quarrel it is very uncomfortable for me. Sometimes he will do crazy things that make you think he is really nuts. He really hates Errol though he doesn't even know him. He hated it that Lizzy and I went up to see Errol. It is not a healthy place for Lizzy there because she gets to playing games with him like you saw that night. There was that Mrs. DeFriez that lived there for a long time, that maybe he was shacked up with, but she got pissed off and left and so it is a lot tougher on Lizzy.

She is going to come back here just as soon as she has graduated. She has to graduate before any of her inheritance comes to her. I just pray to God I don't get shipped out to the fleet before then. The commander says we ought to be here at least three more months unless something big happens.

Lizzy and I have big dreams that will come true still, because I have some good connections in the industry, and she is damned good-looking and a good dancer, too, and Elizabeth Fletcher is a good marquee name so she will not have to change it. But all that will have to wait until the war is over.

If anything happens to me I want you to look out for her. I know you will do that for me.

I don't want you worrying about that other business we talked about. That was in another country and besides the wench is dead. It was a stupid, tragic business, but it is the kind of thing that happens in Hollywood where people get their sights set on something that just evaporates. Of course David did some things you or I wouldn't have done, but he knew he was a dying man and I believe you have to give people some leeway in that position.

It was signed *"TBF Pilot Lt. Daltrey."*

The TBF pilot had given me one more ounce of information about himself and David Lubin, and Flynn had given me maybe a little more. I didn't like Richie saying "the wench is dead," which made him sound like a shit, and I didn't like him talking as though something might happen to him. I knew well enough that things happened to fliers. Which was what Hagen had said.

I had told Liz that Richie was in love with airplanes, but it didn't sound as though he were in love with TBFs.

6

Dr. Bonington was seated in the rust-colored easy chair peeling an orange. He stacked the peel in the ashtray on the taboret beside his chair. The collar of his shirt gaped at the neck, making him look as though he had shrunk. The Japs were bombing Port Moresby every day, just across the Coral Sea from Australia, where Charley Bonington was stationed.

He chewed and swallowed an orange segment and waved a hand at the evening paper, folded on the floor beside his chair. "I see they are thinking about prosecuting Father Coughlin. That ought to please you, Payton."

"Yes, sir."

Bonny appeared in the archway at the foot of the stairs, wearing a blue sweater set, blue skirt, silk stockings, and heels. Her eyes flashed at Mrs. B., who came in just then, one hand supporting the other wrist as though it were broken. Mrs. B. looked old.

"Don't be late, dear. It's a school night."

I said we were just going out for a hamburger and to see *Wild Fire*.

Bonny ignored her mother, looking at me now with a tight-faced, snotty expression. Dr. Bonington slipped another wedge of orange into his mouth. Bonny had said her father was convinced that eating plenty of oranges was the key to good health. Tonight Bonny's parents looked as though they'd lost the key.

I hated the disarray in the Bonington house.

When I opened Ol Paint's door for her, Bonny said, "She doesn't give a darn whether I'm late or not. She just says that because mothers are supposed to say that." She flung herself inside.

As Ol Paint rolled away from the curb, I raised my arm. Bonny didn't slide over against me. I made a U-turn.

But she said, "Can I wear your pin? Maybe she'd pay attention then."

It would not be the first Alpha Beta pin she had worn. My meat. "They're probably going to give me the boot," I said. "If I don't quit first. It would only be a hollow symbol of our great love."

Bonny said, "Their lives are over. Their son doesn't love them anymore. They might as well be dead."

I drove on up Presidio Drive past the Daltrey house above its slant of lawn. A kid's tricycle was perched on the high porch under the porchlight.

"Daddy always let Charley skipper the *Sun Bear*," Bonny went on. "But I'm as good a sailor as he is! He's really careless sometimes, and I'm just not. I'm good in school, and I'm not lazy, and I'm not lightweight. I wish I could go to med school, but it's really hard for girls."

I'd never heard her say that before.

"How did Charley ever get up the nerve to write that letter? That big girl must've made him do it. He was never going to be what Mother and Daddy wanted him to be. They keep blaming themselves. They go over it and over it. And it is their fault! They pushed him into the Coast Guard so he'd be safe. So he got shipped out to Australia and met this girl. They were always maneuvering him."

"Manipulating," I said. "Where do you want to eat?"

"I just had to get out of that morgue." We drove along Fort Stockton Drive under the streetlights that stained her face with light like milk.

In a back booth at Brady's, she sat gazing at her hamburger as though she didn't know what it was. She looked prim and pretty in her turquoise sweater that made the blue of her eyes leap out of her face when she glanced up.

"Daddy doesn't really care about his patients," she said. "He just wants to make money so we can live in Mission Hills and belong to the Yacht Club. I wouldn't be that kind of doctor."

I felt a chill of unease. I took a bite of my sandwich and mopped my lips with a paper napkin.

"In China the peasants drown the baby girls because only boys are important," Bonny observed.

"Aren't you going to eat your hamburger?"

She looked down and nibbled a pickle round. "It's so unfair," she said.

"'Had I been born crested, not cloven, my lords, you would not treat me so,'" I said.

Bonny stared at me with her mouth open.

"That's Queen Elizabeth talking to her advisers."

She laughed one loud "Ha!" and slapped her hand over her mouth.

I found myself telling her about Dessy. "Her mother died on her fifth birthday, and her father died in an accident. Her stepmother didn't like her, so she went to San Francisco to work in an office. She had to go to bed with her bosses to keep her job. So she got to be a prostitute. Tully says every year about three whores jump out the windows of that hotel down by the printshop."

"Oh, God!" Bonny whispered.

"I think my mother had to go to bed with her boss, too."

Bonny covered her face with her hands. "I only think about myself!" she said through her hands. "Other people have real trouble— But you know what it's like. When your parents are supposed to love you and they just don't."

"I love you," I said, and meant it.

She let her hands slip down her face. "It's all such a terrible sham!" she said. "Girls're supposed to be virgins. So you can marry the right person and live in some Mission Hills. I mean, if people knew you were used goods, or pregnant, your life would be over! But, you know, my body is ready to have babies. It tells me so! It's all such a big fake! I mean, I can tell that you want to do it with me, and I want to do it, too. That night coming back from LA, I wanted to, too. But we have to play this stupid game! I hate this stupid game!" she said, rising. She said in a low voice, "Let's go to a motel and do it. I'll get pregnant and we'll have to get married and live in some stupid Army camp somewhere."

"I'm Navy," I said.

We went to see *Wild Fire* at the Pantages Theater. It was a film about two men in love with the same woman, one of them a forester/firefighter and the other a writer who banged away at his typewriter a lot. It was a good film, with John Garfield, Tyrone Power, and Susan Hayward, and in the credits the screenplay was by Esther Carnes.

Parked on Point Loma looking at the moon over the Bay, I tried to joke Bonny out of her angry mood. "I just wish I knew what I am!" she said at one point. I took her home early.

7

I had been home about fifteen minutes when my mother phoned to say that my grandmother had had a stroke and was in the hospital. I got to Mercy Hospital in a hurry, where Bonny worked as a nurse's aide two nights a week.

My mother strode toward me in the waiting room, heels cracking on the tiles like revolver shots. She wore a navy blue suit and had her purse clasped in the crook of her arm like a football. She looked haggard.

"My poor mom!" she said, embracing me. She reeked of Tabu.

"What happened?"

"Her right side is paralyzed, and she can only make some sounds. She managed to get the phone off the hook and dial my number. She said, 'Pet—Pet—Pet—' That's what she called me when I was little. What if I hadn't been home?"

"Is she going to die?"

"I don't know, darling. Oh, I suppose she is!"

My eyes were leaking as soon as I got into the hospital room, where Grandma Payton looked like an ancient doll in her high white bed, white hair done in plaits with blue ribbons.

She was sweet-faced and unmoving, with her powdery cheeks, one side smiling, the other blank. When I saw the bandage on her temple, and some hair shaved for the adhesive tape, the backs of my legs crawled. The scene came to me, Grandma offering the tramp a plate with a sandwich on it at the back door, and the guy knocking her down and coming in to grab her purse—

My mother plumped down in the chair beside the bed, clutching my grandmother's hand. "How are you doing, Mom?"

I leaned on the chair back, feeling big and awkward.

My mother passed my grandmother's hand to me as though it was a thing. It gripped my hand with a queer soft strength.

My voice sounded too loud. "Hi, Grandma!"

Her bright left eye was fixed on my face. My mother burrowed in her purse to produce a handkerchief with which to dab at her eyes. I fixed on the plaster and the bandage on my grandmother's head. I had warned her not to give handouts to tramps.

"I hoped you'd tell me a John Burgess story," I said.

"What's that?" my mother said, swinging around.

"He was a guy that lived in Richmond when Grandma was a girl."

"John Burgess! So you've been telling Buddy John Burgess stories, Mom."

The plump soft hand squeezed mine, half my grandmother's face smiling, the other half dead and white. Shit, my throat had closed up. I was going to sob!

My mother had to leave, and I stood with her a minute outside the door of the hospital room.

"What happened to her head?"

"I suppose she hit it when she fell."

"Listen, maybe some tramp beat up on her and robbed her. She was always feeding the tramps." I sounded like my father ranting against Commies and Jews.

She looked surprised. The possibility, maybe the surety, kept nagging at me when I went back inside and settled into the chair beside the bed, holding my grandmother's hand. Some tramp who knew her for a soft touch because of the stacked-bricks sign left at her house, some IWW worker, someone inside Social Reality, someone dark-faced and foreign and poor, and she with her defenses turned the wrong way like the big guns at Singapore.

"I'll tell you a John Burgess story," I said, and told her the story I was working on. "He has to go to Manzanar to talk to this old Japanese woman that used to work cleaning house for this Hollywood producer. He's a guy who's worked with child stars, and he's really evil. He's called the Doctor. The Japanese woman is really afraid to tell John Burgess anything. Then, when John Burgess leaves, this big black car trails him, and they stop him, but he keeps a revolver in a clip behind the glove compartment of his car. There's this tough-talking dwarf in the car, and a big black-guy chauffeur. And the dwarf says to lay off if he knows what's good for him. And he asks if the dwarf works for the Doctor, and the dwarf says, yes, he works for Doctor Death."

I flinched when I said that, but the hand squeezed mine and I rushed on. "The dwarf says he can get John's leg broken for two hundred dollars, and John says—"

Just then the nurse came in to say it was time for Mrs. Payton's medication and rest.

I rose and bent to kiss my grandmother good night. Past a blur of tearing in her open eye, I saw terror shrill as a scream. I embraced her unresponding bulk and felt her good hand gently patting, patting, comforting me.

8

At school I saw Liz crossing the Quad and caught up with her on an intersecting path. I told her my grandmother had had a stroke.

"That sweet old lady!" Who didn't like Liz because her dissatisfied eyes reminded her of her husband's, because she thought Liz held the reins over Richie.

Heading for the Caff, Liz walked close beside me in that way she had, head down, books and binder clutched to her chest, steps matched to mine. Always she seemed to walk or stand an inch closer than another might do. *See how often she touches you,* Herb Brownell had said.

We settled at a table with mugs of coffee. Liz stirred sugar into hers. Her loosened hair showed off her cheekbones. She could look like a movie star, all right.

Emmett Buckley, Mark Davis, and Jimbo Martin sat at a table over by the windows. Buck glanced toward me and inclined his nose away. Fuck you! There were just too many things besides the tong for me to handle just now.

"Listen, Liz, what do you know about that girl who drowned herself?"

The dark discs of her eyes fixed on mine. Her face looked suddenly misshapen.

"We're rehearsing for the Senior Project!" she said. "I just want to dance!" she said petulantly. "I don't want to think about Val Ferris!" She wanted to be a star, whom people paid attention to, and Richie was supposed to help her with his connections in the industry. I remembered her body on the beach, not much on top, not even as much as Bonny had, but those long smooth legs you couldn't keep your eyes away from. She'd had Band-Aids on her toes from ballet.

My fraternity brothers were watching us. Bonny thought I was in love with Liz.

She rose and came around the table to press her lips to my forehead. "You're not supposed to worry me about anything. Richie said."

Buck Buckley was watching, one eyebrow raised, the three of them discussing us as Liz left the Caff. Fuck them.

9

It was a bad, no-concentration afternoon on the Mission Hills route. I mixed up two orders and had to go back and exchange them. I had changed my routing so the Emmetts were next to last, and everything was going badly today.

I cursed at Bitsy, kicking sideways as I guided two heavy Perry's boxes across the service yard. The little dog snarled with his usual nastiness.

I leaned the boxes against the door frame, rapped once, then opened the door and carried my load inside.

Mrs. Sims was on the phone, glowering at me. She held out the phone. "Here's your boss."

I set the boxes down. "What's the trouble?" Lois's cool voice inquired in my ear.

"I just got here," I panted.

"Late again!" Mrs. Sims said.

"She says I'm late," I told Lois. I cocked my wrist to look at my watch; almost four-thirty.

"You'll have to take the Emmetts earlier in your route," Lois said, and hung up.

"What's she say?" Mrs. Sims demanded, facing me with her fists on her hips like the Powerful Katrinka.

"Said I'd better take you earlier on my route."

"I want those groceries here by two thirty."

"Okay."

"Okay what, boy?"

"Okay you want your groceries by two thirty."

"You see that they are here then, hear?"

I didn't trust myself to respond, unloading onto the counter, one box emptied, and the bottom one up, meat packets in the refrigerator. I took up the boxes and started out. I slammed the door.

I kicked my way across the service yard, threatening Bitsy with the boxes. Outside the gate I looked up at the sign: SERVICE. The wealthy and powerful abusing those who had been less aggressive in primary accumulation.

Lois pointed her pencil at me. "Don't you slam the door on Mrs. Sims! I know she's a dragon, but Mrs. Emmett will go straight to Mr. Perry!"

The evening papers were on the stands when I left Perry's, banner headlines: BIG BATTLE LOOMS IN PACIFIC. I hurried up the hill to where I'd parked Ol Paint; it seemed that I was always on the run. It was as though I were holding on to some gigantic invisible dirigible that would jerk me off the ground at any moment.

Chapter 10

1

TEX HAD BEEN FIRED, AND I WAS SPENDING MORE TIME ministering to Charlotte's tempers.

I was sitting on the ledge of the pit extracting torn-up newsprint from the rollers when I looked up to see Calvin standing just inside the press-room door. He wore his hat tipped over one eye, and a cheesy loafer jacket.

"Hi, there, child!"

I climbed out of the pit. "How're things?"

He rolled his hands out in a massive shoulder shrug. "Got the hump just now," he said. "How about coming out for a Cuba libre?"

"How about in half an hour? I've got to clean up here first."

"See you down at the Fremont." The black pupils of his eyes danced away from meeting mine directly.

"How're your girls?"

"What girls is that?" Calvin said. He jacked up his pants with his wrists and high-stepped out.

When I had cleaned up Charlotte's mess, scrubbed my hands and face in the washroom, and stepped out of my overalls, I went into the office. Tully sat with his suede shoes propped on the wastebasket, reading the paper: CORAL SEA BATTLE CALLED TURNING POINT IN PACIFIC. If you could believe the papers, we had won this one, saving Australia and Charley Bonington. But I would never forget the original announcement of the number of men captured on Bataan, and the back-pages revision of that number.

I told Tully I was headed out for a drink with Calvin King.

"Did I detect a cloud over the glass of fashion?" Tully said, without looking up from his reading.

I halted to case the occupants of the Fremont Bar before entering, like Natty Bumppo eagle-eyeing for hostiles. Calvin was seated at the end of the bar, twenty feet from a trio of Marines. It was early yet, or the swabbies would've spilled out onto 3rd Street.

"How you doin, child? Gettin lots?"

"About the same," I said. One of the Marines scowled down at me. The bartender produced my Cuba libre.

"What did you mean, what girls?" I asked.

Calvin smoothed his hair with a tan hand. "All finished with that," he said. "Bad luck when one of your ladies goes out the window. G-men on my trail, too," he said. "Lookin for Calvin King. Just now I'm C. R. Goodrich."

"The draft?"

He made a motion of slitting his throat. "I'm in, child. Enlisted. Takin the train to Camp Roberts tomorrow."

It seemed that Calvin's mooring rope had snatched him off the ground before my own had. "Why the Army?" I asked.

"I don't like swabbies, and gyrenes don't like colored."

I thought of the humiliations awaiting the King of Kings. I wondered if this was some kind of memorial to Dessy.

I said I was sorry for what I'd said when Dessy died.

"Never mind it, child," he said, with his face turned away.

"Good luck in the service," I said.

"Thanks," Calvin said. We sipped our Cuba libres, not quite knowing how to say good-bye, when he was going into the Army and I remained a slacker.

2

My grandmother's good eye was fixed on me fondly as I sat beside her bedside, holding her hand. The doctor had not given much hope for her recovery. If she got better, she would get better; if not, not. Bonny had phoned to say she had looked in on her last night and had the same prognosis from the nurse.

I was feeling sympathy for Mrs. B. in her grief over her wayward son, and for my father waiting for his commission from the Seabees that never came through. And my grandmother waiting for what she was waiting for.

The bandage on her temple had been replaced by a smaller rectangle of adhesive. My mother had gone out to her house in Hillcrest and found her purse with some money in it, no signs of robbery. I was even going to have to forgive the tramps I had maligned.

Gripping the soft hand, I told my grandmother about the papers I had written for Mr. Chapman, Henry James last semester, and Mark Twain this. When I asked if she had read *The Portrait of a Lady,* there was a pressure from her hand. The bright eye was fixed on me.

"Remember what that first scene shows about Isabel Archer? It's the stuff a writer has to know how to do. This young woman in black comes out of the house, to where everybody's hanging around in the garden. Ralph Touchett's little dog barks at her until she snatches him up and holds him close to her face. That tells us a lot! She's impulsive, she's brave, she's not afraid of being bitten. That's what attracts Ralph Touchett to her! But she's too trusting, she can get hurt."

A tear ran down her pale cheek, and I blotted it with a Kleenex from the bedside stand.

"And remember in *Huckleberry Finn* when Huck and Jim have gone down the river together on the raft? They're friends, but Jim's an escaped slave, and it's against the law to help a slave escape. They are somebody's property. It's stealing! To be an abolitionist then was like being a Commie now. It's a crime and a sin for Huck to help Jim, but he is getting human feelings about somebody with different-colored skin. So he decides it's right to help Jim, and he says, 'All right, I'll go to hell then!'"

I went back to my John Burgess story, trying to push the plot along to entertain my grandmother in her hospital bed, and I could do it, unraveling it at the same time that I was patching it together, winging it.

———

Bonny told me on the phone that she and her mother were going to Stanford for the weekend, to stay with another sister of her mother's in Menlo Park. They would drive to Pasadena, as Bonny and I had done, and ride the Owl north. Back Tuesday night.

"See you when you get back," I said, as coolly as I could manage.

3

Coming in from the parking lot at school, I was cut by a pair of my fraternity brothers, but when I went into the lavatory Pogey Malcolm appeared immediately. He stood and unbuttoned at the next urinal. He wore his usual neat Joe College clothes, but he looked bad, a pimple on his chin and blue smudges under his eyes.

He said he was thinking about enlisting.

"What's the matter?"

It was pulling teeth for Pogey to speak of anything personal, but he said, "My father and Beth fight all the time. My father can be pretty mean."

I said it was a cliché thing, an older man married to a younger woman.

The corner of his mouth turned down as though that had been a stupid thing to say. "It's not that so much."

I shook and buttoned as he continued.

"She drinks sherry all afternoon, so she's stupid by dinnertime. She'll start crying and saying nothing's any good, she's no good. I guess the deal was there'd be no children. So my father shouts at her. Then she goes up to bed and takes sleeping pills to knock herself out. It's really the cruds!"

When I turned to wash my hands, I remembered the joke about the Stanford man rebuking the Cal man in the men's room, saying that Stanford men always washed their hands after they took a leak, and the Cal man replied that Cal men washed their hands before they took a leak. Bonny must be back from Stanford, and I ought to call her.

It was good that Pogey felt he could tell me his personal problems. I couldn't tell him mine.

He gloomily scratched the pimple on his chin. "It looks like the war's just going on and on. Everybody's going to have to get into it. I don't even believe we won the Coral Sea thing."

Reasons for enlisting. I said I'd thought his eyes weren't good enough for the Army.

"Anybody can get in the Army. Listen, wait a couple of minutes before you come out, will you?" He pushed out the swinging door.

4

When Weezie came to see me at *the brand*, I took her to the White Castle for coffee. She wore a gray suit and a blouse with a white collar. She didn't have her glasses on. I had hated her for a whole scale of reasons, and hated hard; now it surprised me that I didn't hate my stepmother anymore.

She had a dumpy figure but a sweet, worried face. She sipped her coffee and watched me with one open and one half-closed eye, as though sighting along a rifle.

"Your father's terribly worried," she said. She drew a pack of Chesterfields from her purse, extracted a cigaret from the pack, and fumbled for matches. I took the matchbook from her and applied flame to her cigaret, as my mother had instructed me to do.

"About Richie," she said.

That would be about right.

"He's afraid Richie's going to get shipped out."

I said Richie had told me he'd be at Pensacola until summer. A June wedding.

"I came about you and Eddie," Weezie said. "He was so pleased when you phoned the other night. We hadn't heard from you for so long."

I tried to look pleasant. Long ago the fact that my father had a young mistress had seemed big-time and exotic, even if I hated her. Weezie squinted at me through the smoke rising from her Chesterfield.

"You are a cold bastard, aren't you?" she said.

That shook me. Was that how I seemed? Was that how I was? Bonny had complained about somebody who was supposed to love you and just didn't.

"If you say so," I said.

"Do you think he doesn't care about you?"

"I'll bet he thinks he does." I tried to say it coldly.

"A lot of the trouble between you has been my fault," Weezie said. Her eyes looked suddenly swollen. "I was only twelve years older than you when I married your father. I didn't know how to handle a big boy."

"You didn't want a thirteen-year-old stepson, that was for sure."

She picked a curl of tobacco from her lips, started to speak but did not.

"It's okay, Weezie," I said. "It's over. I'm grown up now." I thought that I had not yet transcended my gender, however.

"I want to tell you I'm sorry, Payton. I was selfish. I was jealous. I'm grown up now, too."

"Okay well I'm sorry, too."

"You wrote Richie your side of it. Why did you have to come to Eddie to make it up? Why didn't he come to you?"

I had written that to my brother.

"It's because he knows he's in the wrong," Weezie said. She scrubbed out her cigaret and promptly produced another. I went through the lighting-up procedure again. Waving at the smoke, she said, "Do me a favor and come and see your dad."

"Okay."

"Come to dinner tonight! I'll get some steaks."

I couldn't face this without some days of dreading it. If you dreaded something enough, it would turn out to be not so bad. We could talk about Richie. I would reassure my father that Richie was not being shipped out. We could recall how good Richie had been at everything he tried, class president, basketball star, up-and-comer in the movie industry.

Strikebreaker. Throat-cutter.

We settled on Friday night.

"We'll celebrate Eddie's commission!" Weezie said.

"He got it!"

"Ninety percent certain, Captain Mahoney says."

"Terrific!"

"He's so excited about being in the Seabees! But of course he won't admit it. There've been so many disappointments."

That cut the cold bastard's heart like a knife.

Weezie stuffed her pack of Chesterfields back into her purse, straightened her jacket, and rose to leave. I realized that she was proud of her achievement of bringing father and errant son back together. Mission accomplished!

That evening the headline was NAZIS TAKE 100,000 RUSSIAN PRISONERS.

5

Wednesday evening I took Bonny to dinner at an Italian place in La Jolla so she could tell me about her trip, which I didn't want to hear about. She had loved the Stanford campus. It was old. She had talked to some students, and to a professor who was a neighbor of her aunt Honey.

I thought she was tuning down her excitement so as not to turn the knife in the wound.

When I brought her home, she neither moved close to me beneath the pale canopy of Ol Paint's top nor opened her door to get out. So there was more to be said. No doubt it was bad news. "Blue Champagne" played mutedly on the radio.

"Mother thinks I'm seeing too much of you," she said in a small voice.

Mrs. B., my enemy, was using Stanford to pry Bonny away from an unsuitable suitor.

"I have to stop seeing you, maybe just for a while. I have to do what she wants because of Charley. I just can't not!"

"Sure," I said in a rusty voice. "And they want you to go out with Brandon Porter." Brandon Porter was the son of a big-deal doctor friend of Dr. Bonington's. Probably Brandon Porter would be going up to Stanford, too.

"We had a big fight," Bonny went on. "I told her I'd do what she wants. I'll go to Stanford and pledge her sorority. And I'll get engaged to somebody she can brag about to the other ladies at the Yacht Club. She slapped me. And Daddy told me to shut my face. She's never slapped me before, and he's never told me to shut up like that. I must be grown up! I told them I'd do what they want, but I'd never come back to stupid San Diego."

"Just like Charley," I said.

"Don't you start in on me, too!" I could hear her breathing. "I'll marry someone really rich and live in Pasadena, and we'll have a better boat than a stupid Rhodes—" She sounded hysterical. And she said, "And I told them after you got to be a famous writer I'd divorce my husband and marry you!"

"The hell you will!" I said through my teeth.

There was a silence then, like cotton batting stuffing the car around us. In a calmer voice, Bonny said, "You have to try to understand. They are no different from Chinese peasants. I'm not worth as much as Charley because I don't have a penis. I can't take their money to go to Stanford and buy the clothes I need and join a sorority and live at a whole different level than I do here, then when I'm through tell them how much I hate them, what jerks they are, how I always hated them. Like Charley. They're my parents! I just can't break their hearts like Charley."

"You'd better watch out that you don't turn out just like your mother," I said.

I already wished I had not said that when she slugged me. Her fist glanced off my shoulder and cracked me above the eye. A mist of rage congealed in my head.

"Beat it!" I yelled at her. "Go have a great time at Stanford! To hell with you!"

She jammed open the door and slammed it behind her. She ran up the walk to the porch.

I guess I said, "Wait!"

She disappeared inside. The porch went dark.

I let Ol Paint drift down the hill. The engine caught and purred. I coasted on down to park under the trees in Presidio Park, where Bonny and I had often gone to neck when it was too late to drive out to Point Loma. With the ignition and the lights off, I sat gripping handfuls of my hair, my forehead pressed against the steering wheel. I touched the place above my eye where she had hit me.

A prowl car halted beside Ol Paint, and a blinding light was turned into my face. The cop asked what I was doing there and told me to go do my thinking somewhere else.

6

The papers were full of low-key bad news. A dim-out was ordered for the beaches of Southern California as a precaution against the submarine attacks on tankers silhouetted against city lights that were so devastating on the East Coast. Gasoline rationing was already in effect in the East and would extend to the Pacific Northwest on June 1, with California to follow.

What was I going to do about Bonny?

On the Mission Hills route I had been taking the Emmetts earlier. Today there were the usual two big grocery boxes. I guided them in under the SERVICE sign and made my balancing, skipping progress through the service yard with Bitsy worrying my ankles and, inside, Mrs. Sims waiting like a wounded water buffalo. Bitsy fled with a yelp when I kicked out. I knocked on the back door, waited a beat, called out, "Perry's!" and maneuvered my load inside.

Mrs. Sims glowered at me from the kitchen table, where she had a magazine open before her. I set the boxes down and swiftly stacked cans, bottles, cartons, and brown paper sacks of fruit and vegetables on the counter. I stored the meat in the Frigidaire and nested the boxes, preparatory to leaving.

"Mr. Perry used to have courteous drivers," Mrs. Sims observed. Her face was fat and unhealthy, high patches of color on her cheeks.

I said I'd got here by two thirty.

She stared at me with her mouth turned down. "If you were any kind of a man, you would be serving your country instead of delivering groceries," she said.

I felt my face contort into an expression similar to hers. I managed to keep my mouth shut, but I let the door slam when I went outside. Red-hot needles fastened onto my ankle.

I dropped my load of boxes.

Bitsy emitted about half a yelp, mashed under the boxes like the Wicked Witch of the West under Dorothy's Kansas house.

When I lifted the wooden containers, the shaggy little mutt lay motionless. I prodded him with the toe of my shoe.

I set the boxes down on the bottom step, knocked, called "Perry's!" and stuck my head inside. Mrs. Sims stood big-assed at the counter, scowling back over her shoulder.

"Your dog's dead," I said.

Back in my truck, I wheeled around the corner, light-headed.

After my last stop, my last Perry's stop for sure, I rolled on down Presidio Drive, swinging past the Daltreys' onetime house sitting up off the street, white walls, red tile roof, green lawn, that had no connection to me anymore. I dropped on past the Boningtons' two-story white-walls and red-tile house to see if Brandon Parker's convertible was parked there. Nope. I headed on down into Old Town, lowlife, poor people, Mexican town, where I remembered a bar with a beat-up wooden stoop and a neon sign for Budweiser. I sat alone drinking a beer I didn't want and trying to get my thoughts and my future together.

How now would I pay my rent, pay for meals, pay for books, pay for gas to take Bonny out? When I thought about Bonny it was as though I had a cold in my head.

Maybe I didn't even have to see Lois. Leave the truck in the loading zone with the keys in the ashtray. But there would still be a last paycheck to pick up.

There was no sign of Bitsy's bite on my ankle.

I nursed my beer to pass the time until everyone but Lois would have gone home.

She was waiting in her glass cubicle, her apron off. She shook her head at me as I passed her station carrying empties. When I leaned in her door, my grin felt as though it had been cut from sheet metal.

"Am I fired?"

"You're going to have to go out and explain to Mrs. Emmett about her dog."

"He bit me and I dropped my boxes on him." I bent to rub my ankle. "I'll probably get hydrophobia."

"Show them the bite."

I thought she looked very pretty and not angry at all, with her smooth makeup and her freshly brushed hair.

"I guess I don't want to go back out there," I said.

"I didn't think you would. You can pick up your check tomorrow."

She snapped off the light in her cage and came outside. I had forgotten how small she was. She reached up to unhook my bow tie and stuff it into my breast pocket. Her hand lingered on my chest for a moment.

"The only time you smile at me is when you fire me," I said.

"I've smiled at you plenty!"

"Would you come and have a drink with me?"

She cocked an eyebrow. "Why don't we have a drink at my house? Ray's in Bakersfield. Do you know where I live?"

She lived on 47th Street. I'd driven past her house several times months ago, when I'd had fantasies of her asking me over. Lois in the bedroom doorway in a black negligee. It was going to come true!

She preceded me up the steps to the street with what might be a little extra swing to her girdled bottom. Once she glanced over her shoulder at me, close behind her.

"In a hurry?" she asked.

It was not so steamy and exotic or even romantic as my Lois-fantasies had been, and I didn't think that, written as fiction, it would inform Mr. Chapman as to the Human Condition. Lois went right into the bathroom "to wash Perry's off," but instead of coming out in a negligee she called to me to ask if I wouldn't like to take a shower, too. At last I dug my condom out of its slot in my wallet. I joined Lois in the shower.

She said, "We don't need that!" stripped the rubber painfully off, and tossed it in the toilet.

My first uncomplicated copulation took place in Lois Meador's shower, with Lois straddling my hips and kissing my ear, and I came like my childhood gone in an ecstatic rush.

Afterward we drank rum and Cokes in the living room with the curtains drawn, I in my shorts and Lois wearing her peach-colored panties, surprising breasts with big aureolas like blossoms around the nipples. A kerosene heater stood before the blocked-off fireplace, an antique rocker that had belonged to Ray's grandmother, and the couch was covered by a black and chartreuse spread. Ray spent most of the time on the road, Lois said. She knew that he had girlfriends in Los Angeles, Santa Barbara, and Fresno.

We made love on the couch. After the first time I didn't prematurely ejaculate. Lois showed me positions she knew, very different from examining drawings in *Sexology*, and taught me how to please her. When I helped her along, she panted wildly and twisted her head from side to side in a violent way that half frightened me.

It seemed to me that I was being prepped for an examination I had already failed.

She cooked hamburgers and fried potatoes for dinner, and after dinner we went back into the bedroom. I didn't need to use a condom because she had her diaphragm in.

I was home by ten o'clock.

The Buttons were still up, listening to the radio. Mr. Button ignored me, but Mrs. Button greeted me with the elaborate surprise that she affected whenever I came home early.

I was sitting at my typewriter with a clean sheet of newsprint curling out of the platen when Mrs. Button knocked. I was afraid I smelled of

Lois. Standing in the doorway, she said in her overefflusive way that her Jim was making so much money at the shop cutting sailors' hair that they no longer needed to rent their spare room. Could I find another place to stay, say, next month?

I said I thought they felt I should be in the service.

Mrs. Button blushed violently. "Well, it is important to Jim, you see. Because he was in the other war."

How was I going to go on paying rent, anyway? I said I would miss them.

"Oh, Payton, how could you miss us when we never see you! Except this week when you've had a fuss with Bonny. Or else you are in here banging on that typewriter like killing snakes."

Guilt like a scratchy shirt had come on me for screwing Lois Meador when I loved Barbara Bonington. Who had kissed me off, however. Dates with Lois had been made.

"You know, Payton," Mrs. Button confided, "my Jim and I couldn't have any children, and Jim thought you might be a kind of son to him. We'd go to movies sometimes, and he'd take you fishing. But you're so busy."

A Jewish movie producer had wanted to think of Richie as his son, and an Indian barber had wanted to think of me that way. I told Mrs. Button I'd move out as soon as I could find another place.

7

At school no one was speaking to me. I had a glimpse of Bonny in the Caff, in conversation with Mike Phelps, blond and pretty, chin up, color in her cheeks, not even a glance in my direction. I couldn't seem to gather my thoughts about her.

Pogey and Jimbo cut me, though Pogey rolled his eyes.

I dropped by Mr. Chapman's office to be exhorted on the importance of reading important literature and trying to write it. He seemed to think, like Tully, that I should be getting into the service so I could write a novel about love and war.

I waited for Liz coming across the Quad from her ten o'clock. She looked wonderful in pink, her hair done up in a scarf.

"Richie phoned from San Francisco," she said, her big dark eyes fixed on my face. She laid her hand on my chest, like Lois. Her perfume reminded me of Dessy. "He must be on his way to the fleet. He couldn't say it right out."

The June wedding was screwed. Why was the wedding so important to me? Because there ought to be at least one happy ending, hero and heroine in one another's arms as the music came up.

I had begun reading *The Pisan Manual* again: "Know how to be all things to all men. A wise Proteus, he, who is learned with the learned, and with the pious, pious. It is the great way of winning all; for to be like is to be liked." Was that the way Richie regulated his life, in LA one way, in San Diego another, in Pensacola still another, so that everyone liked him?

Liz stood close to me, as though she was near-sighted.

"He'll be all right!" I said. How could Richie not be all right? But it appeared that another big naval battle was shaping up, and that was why he had been ordered to the fleet. Something hung in the air like static electricity that made my hair prickle. Richie had gone to the fleet with his slow TBF armed with a torpedo that only went off half the time.

"Come over Sunday, Payton," Liz said. "Please! We have to talk." She stared at me, lips parted, as though she were breathing hard. "I'm scared!" she said.

8

The Nazis were winning the war in Russia, and the Japanese claimed that the Battle of the Coral Sea had been their victory. Third Street was quiet, sailors and Marines sticking close to their bases, or being shipped out like Richie! Rumors congealed in the winds off the Pacific. Pearl Harbor had been bombed again, the bombing hushed up. Seattle had been bombed. The Japs were invading the Aleutian Islands. An impatient, jagged waiting-to-hear overloaded the air.

Something big was happening right now.

Out of a job at Perry's, I spent most afternoons at *the brand*, helping with the job printing. Tully had been unable to hire a printer to replace Tex. I tended Charlotte in my stiff-with-grease-and-ink overalls. It was as though my encounter with Lois had made me more comfortable with Charlotte, or the big old press easier with me. I had learned, if not how to please her, how not to displease her.

When I phoned Bonny from the office, she answered on the second ring. When I said, "Bonny—" she hung up.

9

On my way out to Mission Beach on Friday night, I drove along Coast Highway to see the new barrage balloons. The squashed-looking gray toys floated apparently unattached around the sawtoothed roof of the Convair plant, and Lindbergh Field. I supposed they implied that aeriel bombardment was to be expected.

My father's posture was that nothing unpleasant had happened between us. He asked if I would like a beer. I asked for a Coke instead.

"That's great about your commission, Dad!"

"Jock Mahoney says it's ninety-eight percent sure," he said, rubbing his big hands together. "It has been a long time coming!"

"They are a fine outfit!"

He was frowning as at a distant memory. "Heard your boss had a little go-round with Post Five."

"Well, you warned me." I didn't need to tell him that one of my mother's old boyfriends, the labor goon, had fixed the picket line.

"Bob Quinn is one of those fellows. His son was in the New Mexico National Guard that went to the Philippines a year or so ago."

Bataan!

"Bob hasn't heard anything since the surrender," my father said. But he wasn't really concerned about Bob Quinn's son, either. "Say, Richie sure doesn't like those torpedo bombers much."

"Too slow."

My father hadn't heard from Liz that Richie had phoned from San Francisco on his way out to the fleet, and I didn't tell him that. As I hadn't told Liz of my conversation with Hagen.

I didn't bring up losing my girlfriend, my job at Perry's, and my room at the Buttons house.

At dinner Weezie spoke of the son of a friend, seventeen years old, who had enlisted in the Marines.

I went home early, where I told Mr. and Mrs. Button that I was looking for a new place but hadn't found anything yet.

10

Liz lay in a canvas chaise beneath a sun umbrella in her backyard, a psych
text and her gray binder on the low table beside her. She was bare-legged,
wearing a long-sleeved blouse, her hair tucked back with a silver clasp.

Now I had to tell her of my conversation with Pancho Hagen, didn't I?

"I ran into Hagen out at the Yacht Club," I said. "He and Val Ferris
were friends when they were kids, up in the Valley."

Liz squeezed her eyes closed and drew one of her legs up. She didn't
say anything.

"He blames Richie for what happened to her."

"She thought Richie could tell David Lubin what to do." Liz said with
her eyes closed. "Nobody told David Lubin what to do! He was dying. He
did die! I don't see how she could think Richie could do anything for her."

I watched the rise and fall of her small bosom. *Just as easy to fall in love
with a rich girl as a poor one,* Richie had said. I found myself pitying Val Ferris, who had not been rich, who was from Hanford, who lived inside Social
Reality where Elizabeth Fletcher and Richie Daltrey had never lived. Or
maybe Richie did now, out with the fleet.

"She'd been David Lubin's mistress!" Liz said.

And she'd been Richie's mistress before that. I cleared my throat and
said, "She'd been Richie's LA girlfriend."

"He introduced them."

I gazed out at the blue sparkle of the Bay, with the gray toy balloons
rising around it. Liz laid a hand on my knee.

"She was crazy!" she said. "Richie said she'd taken pills a couple of
times, but she always let someone know in time to get pumped out. No one
has to feel responsible for a crazy person!"

She craned her neck to look past me, and I turned to see Captain
Fletcher coming around the corner of his house wearing his uniform with
its gold braid and his white-crowned cap. He walked stiffly, as though he
had a bad back, and he carried a folded newspaper.

I found myself rising to attention. He nodded to me. Frowning down
at Liz, he looked as though he were sucking in his gut.

"There's been a naval action near Midway Island," he announced. "It appears that a Jap carrier and a battleship have been sunk."

Haruna class?

"Richie's in it!" Liz said.

Her father showed us the headlines:

JAPANESE NAVAL FORCE FLEEING
PEARL HARBOR AVENGED, SAYS NIMITZ

HAWAII INVASION THREAT SMASHED

Good news!

Chapter 11

1

Aᴍʏ ᴘᴇʀʀɪɴᴇ's ᴠᴏɪᴄᴇ ᴏɴ ᴛʜᴇ ᴘʜᴏɴᴇ ᴡᴀs sᴏ sᴍᴀʟʟ ɪ could hardly make out the words:

"Will called me. A friend of his phoned him from Bremerton. He said Richie's in a torpedo plane squadron in the Fifth Fleet. Payton, he said the torpedo planes are all missing in action."

When she hung up, I went back to my room to sit on the unmade bed staring at my typewriter. I ought to be doing something. I ought to phone my father. And Liz! Of course fliers were shot down. That was what was so good about Naval Air. When they went down at sea, they floated in rubber rafts until the PB2Ys spotted them and picked them up.

I couldn't phone my father with information some guy in Bremerton had phoned to Will Gates, who had phoned Amy Perrine, who had phoned me. A TBF down in the Pacific Ocean, Richie on his life raft—Missing in action wasn't dead!

I went back into the Buttons' living room to sit on the arm of the sofa and dial Liz's number.

Her father's voice answered on the first ring. When I asked for Liz he said, "Lizzy is not here just now. Who is calling, please?"

I hung up as though the receiver had burned my hand. Back in my room I sat on the bed again. I had promised Mrs. Button I would be out by the fifteenth. I straightened the covers on the bed, kicked the pile of laundry into the corner, and straightened the few pages of manuscript beside the typewriter. I sat down at the table with my French vocabulary.

Maybe my father could find out about Richie through Captain Mahoney.

I gave up trying to study and left the house just as a gray Navy sedan swung around the corner and pulled up behind Ol Paint. A chauffeur wearing a sailor cap sat at the wheel. Captain Fletcher piled out of the rear door, grim-faced.

"Where's my daughter?"

I said I didn't know.

He thrust his face at me. The tough-looking sailor watched from the front seat. How did Captain Fletcher know where I lived? Intelligence!

"It was you who phoned just now?"

"Yes, sir."

"Why did you hang up like that?"

He pressed so close to me that I had to step back. "I didn't like the way you sounded," I said.

It was his turn to back off. "My daughter has learned that your brother is missing in action. She is very disturbed. I want to know where to find her."

I just shook my head, squinting up at the sun trying to break through the high fog; the same sky that hung over Richie on his raft.

This time I held my ground when Captain Fletcher pressed close to me, like Liz coming too close. Richie had said he was an SOB.

"Lizzy is unbalanced, you know," Captain Fletcher said, confiding suddenly. Everybody was unbalanced, crazy: Liz, Mrs. Malcolm, dead Dessy and dead Val Ferris.

"I am afraid this news has thrown her completely. She has disappeared. I am concerned that she will harm herself!"

I shook my head. What about my brother?

"She has had a nervous breakdown, you know. She may be having one again. Does the term 'manic-depressive' mean anything to you, young man?"

I knew who was unbalanced here.

"There is a real possibility that she will come to physical harm," Captain Fletcher said. "Her friends must help me see that she does not have to be put away."

I was to phone him if I heard anything from Liz.

When the Navy sedan had disappeared up Meade Street, I went back inside. Mrs. Button intercepted me in the living room. She wore her flowered dress and her big hat for shopping at the A&P. Her plain, pink, big-toothed face was anxious.

"Is something wrong, Payton?"

"My brother's missing in action."

She goggled dramatically.

"Got to phone—" I said, escaping. I sat on the arm of the sofa, gripping the hard black shaft of the phone.

My father was at Seabee headquarters, Weezie said.

"Listen, Weezie, it looks like Richie's missing in action. Maybe you'd better try to get word to Dad. Maybe Captain Mahoney can find out something."

"Oh, God!" Weezie said.

I had no sooner hung up than the phone rang, seeming to jump in my hand. It was Liz's careful, uninflected lisp. She sounded saner than anyone else I had talked to. "Payton, he's dead. He was in a torpedo squadron on the *Yorktown*, and they were all shot down."

You come in at two hundred feet. The closer you get the more chance the torpedo has and the less chance you have.

"Your father said he was only missing!"

"A friend of his phoned. They're all dead." It was better when her voice tore apart. Her father had said she was a manic-depressive, she'd had a nervous breakdown, her friends had to help to see she didn't have to be put away. Captain Fletcher was out of a British mystery novel.

"What about my father?" she said.

"He was here! He wanted to know where you are."

"What did you tell him?"

"That I didn't know."

"He killed Richie! He got him transferred to the fleet so we couldn't get married."

"How do you know?"

"He told me! He made me say I forgive him! When I could get away I came over here. I'm at Alice's."

181

Richie wasn't dead. He was floating around on his raft out in the Pacific. He'd always been lucky. I stared at my white knuckles holding the phone.

If anything happens to me I want you to look out for her, Richie had said.

"I have to see you," she said in the calm voice.

Her friend Alice Hoagland lived in East San Diego, near Lois Meador's little house. There was a movie theater nearby, on El Cajon Boulevard. "Can you get to the Cajon Theater from where you are? About ten o'clock? I've got to see my father; this is going to kill him."

"Yes," she said.

"I'll be about halfway down the aisle on the left side."

Indistinctly, as though she had moved away from the phone, I heard her say, "What am I going to do?"

When I had hung up I sat with my head in my hands thinking of Richie maybe dead and my grandmother dying, Liz and her father and Bonny who had to choose between me and her mother. Liz didn't know what she was going to do. I didn't know what I was going to do.

Mrs. Button stood just inside the front door with her big-brimmed hat shadowing her face. "This terrible war!" she said.

2

My father looked trim in his Seabees uniform, starched khaki, open collar showing a V of snowy T-shirt. A lieutenant's double silver bars gleamed on the shoulders of his shirt. His face looked old.

"Son."

I started to shake hands, but he raised his arms to embrace me. I hugged my father's starched, taut body, feeling a grimace like a vise on my face that was phony at first, and then was not. Weezie watched.

He released me.

He said, "I've been trying to telephone Elizabeth, but Captain Fletcher doesn't know where she is."

I said I'd talked to Liz. "Some friend of Richie's phoned her to tell her Richie'd been—shot down. She's run away. She says her father got Richie transferred to the fleet so they wouldn't get married when she graduated."

My father stared at me as though he couldn't take that in. Though his face was lined and his eyes red-rimmed, his head wasn't canted in the familiar way.

"I'm afraid I don't understand."

He seemed as shocked at the idea that someone might not like his son as by the fact that Richie had been shot down. Running in on a *Haruna* class battleship—

"Sit down, sit down, son." He waved me to a chair and sank into his own beside the radio. Weezie had disappeared into the kitchen. "I doubt that Captain Fletcher could have arranged such a thing," he said.

"Congratulations on the bars, Dad!"

His fingers rose to touch one of the bars, as though to reassure himself. "What a terrible price to pay," he said.

So he equated the granting of his commission with the loss of his commissioned son. His country had issued the silver bars of his rehabilitation, but his son had been taken in exchange.

I bent forward to reach a hand out to him. He grabbed it as though he were drowning.

"Does your mother know?"

"She was out when I phoned."

He slumped in his chair, grasping my hand. Weezie came out carrying drinks on a tray, ice cubes tinkling. My father cleared his throat and scraped his fingers through his cropped hair. "It was for his country," he said.

I lurched forward to kneel before his chair, and he hugged me to him, smelling of cigarets and aftershave. They were trying to force his shoulders to the mat again, killing his firstborn son! The firstborn was always the most important one. Surely I could understand that. Surely I could explain that to Bonny. I ought to understand that, who had read more novels than everybody else in my family and had learned from them how to connect.

"He was such a fine young man!" my father said. "He could've been anything in the world he wanted to be!"

"Sure he could!"

"He was there when his country needed him!"

"He didn't die in vain!" I said.

Where my father's grief had been low-key and devastating, my mother's was histrionic. She was grieving for her mother also, who had gone into a coma.

Her new boyfriend was on hand to comfort her, Commander Parker, a skinny, balding guy in starched khaki like my father, only with gold leaves on his shoulders.

I got away as soon as I could.

I had been seated in the Cajon Theater about five minutes, trying to pay attention to Gary Cooper killing Germans, when Liz slipped into the seat beside me with a scent of flowers and the electric touch of her fingers.

"Let's get out of here," I whispered. I was sick of seeing soldiers dying in World War I, advancing through barbed wire and bomb craters against machine guns. In Ol Paint, under the pale cover of the top, Liz sat an inch away from me. I turned a couple of corners and parked in the dense shadow of a pepper tree.

"What're you going to do?" I asked.

"I'm never going back!"

"He was pretty rugged. He said you were unbalanced, you'd had a nervous breakdown and might have one again." Maybe I shouldn't be saying this!

It was as though I could feel her determining not to become hysterical. She sat with her head bowed. Once she leaned against me, so that I didn't know whether I was supposed to put my arm around her or not. Then she straightened.

"Would he really try to put you—somewhere?"

"He talks like that sometimes. He can't do that. I'm twenty-three."

"My father thinks Richie must've been transferred to the fleet just because they were getting ready for a battle."

Her voice tightened a notch. "He told me he asked Uncle Harry to do it! He told me! He kept crying and holding me and saying how terrible he'd been. He's done things like that before. When I had a date he'd fix it so I had to break it some way, then he'd cry and say he was terrible. Did he say I'd refused to go to see Dr. Lasansky?"

"Who's that?"

"He's this creepy friend of Daddy's who told him I'm manic-depressive. I'd rather die than be alone with Victor Lasansky! He's not a doctor at all, he's only a psychologist. So they'd better not try anything."

Then she was whispering, "Damn him! Damn him! Damn him!" I

didn't know whether she meant her father or Dr. Lasansky. She searched in her purse for a handkerchief. "He was going to take care of me. He was going to take care of everything. He promised me. He promised he wouldn't get killed!"

She had been damning Richie.

Richie promising Liz he would not get killed seemed corny and pathetic. And Richie promising to make Liz a star seemed as jerk as Jack Warner offering Bonny a screen test. The Great Expectations! It was the Hollywood of Val Ferris drowning herself.

"I'm so scared!" Liz said, leaning against me. "I'm scared of Daddy, and I'm scared of not having Richie ——"

I put my arm around her, and she swung toward me and mashed her wet cheek against mine. I could feel her trembling. Her arms snaked around me, holding me so tightly it was as though she thought Richie's brother would now take care of her.

She murmured, "I have to go to LA. Will you take me?"

"Okay." She had to get away from Captain Fletcher.

She detached herself to sit with her face turned down and her hands in her lap. "I'm so worried about Buffy. My silly old cat! Could you go out to my house and get her and some things I need? I'll make a list.

"Daddy leaves for the base early every day," she went on. "Would you take Bonny? She'll know where to look for everything."

It seemed to me that Bonny would have to come with me because of Richie.

3

Bonny's voice said in my ear, "That's so terrible about Richie. I've been trying to call you."

It was as though I were getting some queer kind of credit for Richie dead. I explained Liz's situation into the telephone, Bonny listening in that kind of silence she drew around herself whenever Liz was mentioned. She would come to the Fletcher house with me.

I picked her up at eight thirty in the morning, and with Ol Paint's top down we drove out to Point Loma. Bonny was bare-legged in pedal-pushers and a sweater. She sat apart from me with her chin tucked down. I was sick that I could think of nothing to say when there was so much to be said.

I parked in the turnout in the alley behind the Fletchers' house, looking down on the tile roof and brick chimney. The sun glistened on the upstairs windows.

I led Bonny along the flagstone path around the side of the house. The key was under a flowerpot just beyond the front door. Bonny had Liz's list.

Trying to turn the key in the lock I muttered, "Shit! Shit! Shit!" It was the wrong key! I paused to glance out at the gray ships in the Bay as though swabbies might be spying through telescopes and phoning Destroyer Base Intelligence. Bonny's eyes flashed at me out of her stiff face.

The lock clicked finally, the door creaked open, and we slipped into the front hall. White balustered stairs rose to the right. Bonny followed me upstairs.

Liz's room faced on the alley, white net curtains on the windows, a bed with a frilly white coverlet, a white dresser, a dressing table with skinny bowed legs.

I opened the closet and found the suitcase Liz had said would be there.

"Look for the doll with the china head and a long white dress on," Bonny whispered.

Emma, who was going to be a movie star, was in the bed, her painted face showing against the pillow. On the bed was a note on beige stationery held down by a glass paperweight:

Daddy is glad his girl has come home. Phone me at the base. Honey, I had to have the kitty put away. She wouldn't stop yowling with you gone, and she made a mess on the stairs. Love, Daddy.

I replaced the note under the paperweight and took the doll to Bonny, who had the suitcase heaped with clothes. She tucked the doll inside.

"Let's go!" I said. Captain Fletcher's note had rattled me.

I closed the suitcase, and we hurried downstairs. I tossed the case into the back of Ol Paint and backed and filled to turn around. I killed the engine, started up again, and got out of there in a hurry.

"Amy's in love with Will Gates," Bonny said. "He wants to get married. I think she needs you to tell her it's all right."

Because I'd been Bob-O's friend.

I stopped at the curb before the Boningtons' house, and Bonny let herself out quickly. I got out to put the top back up. Stupid to have put it down in the first place as though Bonny and I were out for a last joyride before gas rationing clamped down.

She stood watching me, hands clasped together at her waist.

"I'm sorry I said that about you and your mother," I said.

She gave a nod of acknowledgment.

I was suddenly furious at the balky top, always a pain to put back up. When I gave the bows of the top a yank, the fabric ripped straight down the center, a foot of broken threads with an inch of right angle at one end. Shit!

Bonny looked comically concerned.

"Guess it's time for a new top," I managed. I shoved the contraption back into the well and got in behind the wheel.

It was as though I had to breathe deeply to keep from panting. "You thought it was terrible that I was writing those—tots columns. Because I didn't know what I was writing about. But the rest of the stuff in *the brand* is about molesteds, too. Strikebreakers, Okies and Japs, and bad judges, and money more important than people, and power used to make people miserable. AJAs in a concentration camp, women and children and kids four years old. Because they have epicanthic folds on their eyes! And what's going to happen to Calvin King in the Army because he's colored! And those fourteen-year-old girl prostitutes in Tijuana with syphilis. I mean, it's all connected!"

Her face had turned pink and her mouth made an O, but she didn't speak.

"You know what you ought to do?" I said. "You ought to go up to Stanford in premed. You'd be a doctor. That's what you ought to do."

"I know that," she said.

I mashed my foot on the accelerator, digging out of there before I said anything else stupid. In the mirror I could see her still standing at the curb.

4

I met Liz in the soda fountain of a drugstore next to the Cajon Theater. BATTERED JAP FLEET IN HIDING was the headline on the newspaper rack by the door. Liz wore a sweater set and a pleated skirt, with stockings and heels. She looked tired and not even pretty as she rose from her stool. She had a suitcase and a square toiletries case with her.

I had to tell her about her father's note. She cursed him so shockingly that I thought about the nervous breakdown he had mentioned. It wasn't grief about Richie, it was her cat!

She said more calmly, "Poor Buffy. God damn him!"

I led her outside to Ol Paint. I'd patched the top with strips of adhesive tape. It was not going to be like Liz and Richie driving around in the turbo-charged Cord.

In the car she opened her purse and her wallet and laid a ten-dollar bill on the dashboard, saying it was for gas. "You are finally taking me away from all this," she said.

Heading out of San Diego she sat erect on the edge of her seat, gazing at the road ahead. Driving north through the beach towns she settled down with her head against my shoulder. Gradually her head slipped down until it lay on my leg. When I realized what she was doing I panted suddenly, glancing down at the pale V of the nape of her neck. Outside the car the thick, peeling trunks of the Leucadia eucalyptus fled by.

When it was over Liz refastened the buttons, with a pat of finality there, and sat with her face averted.

I prayed she would not tell me that Richie had liked that. I didn't want to know that! Of course it was intended as a payment for my troubles in her behalf, but it had turned my nights with Lois Meador sour like milk left in the sun.

I'd thought I was taking Liz to her friend named Marjorie who lived in the San Fernando Valley, but she had changed her mind. In Hollywood, in the late afternoon, she directed me up into the hills and onto Mulholland Drive.

"You're not going to Flynn's!" I braked Ol Paint almost to a stop. A horn brayed and a Cadillac swung around me, a man with a plaid cap giving me the finger.

"Yes, I am!"

It was as though I'd been betrayed. And Richie. "I'm not going to take you there!"

"I'll phone him to come get me!"

It was like the ending of a good puzzle mystery, where you'd been given all the evidence and should have figured it out, but you'd been tricked into looking in the wrong direction.

"Listen, Liz—"

"He'll help me. He likes me!"

"Sure he does." At least Flynn would defend her from her father, who was crazy. They were all crazy!

"You don't know what it's like," she said. "Waiting until I graduate, and waiting for Richie to come home from the war. So we could—get started. Waiting and waiting. And now Richie's dead!"

There was the turn into Mulholland Farm. I swung the wheel, and the car drifted down toward the corner of the tennis court. The house lay across an expanse of asphalt paving in the late sunlight. A big red dog appeared, barking furiously.

"That's just Scout," Liz said. Her familiarity with the dog made me feel easier.

The dog braced his paws against Ol Paint's door and stuck his muzzle into the open window, mouth open and pink tongue lolling. Liz scratched his chin. "Dear old Scout!"

"I hope you have all the luck you need, Liz," I said.

She leaned over to brush my lips with hers. "Thanks," she lisped. She had to push the dog aside to open the door and get out with her makeup case. I wrestled the suitcase from the back and set it down outside the car just as Flynn appeared. He wore a long-sleeved polo shirt with a scarf looped at the neck, and white flannels. The famous seducer of women raised an arm in greeting to the young Martin Eden.

Liz ran toward him.

As I drove up out of Mulholland Farm, Elizabeth Fletcher shrank in the rearview mirror, standing beside her luggage with Errol Flynn's arm around her.

5

The address on the card Mrs. Carnes had given me was on Franklin Street in Hollywood. I parked in front of an apartment complex with two lofty evergreens on the front lawn, wondering what I wanted from her. It was almost dark, and I could see a lighted window of number 5 back at the base of the U. I walked in past an ornamental pool, my hand jingling the keys in my pocket.

Mrs. Carnes opened the door to my ring, frowning as though she thought I was selling magazine subscriptions. She wore a navy blue pants suit with silver jewelry on her wrists. Her thick, fair, center-parted hair reminded me of a thatched roof.

"It's Richard Daltrey's brother!" she exclaimed, and opened the door wider.

"He's dead," I said.

The flesh of her face seemed to droop. "Please come in."

On the walls were paintings of blocky shapes in bright colors. A sunrise-colored shawl was draped over the piano. She showed me to an easy chair near the fireplace and seated herself opposite me, her navy blue knees together and her hands, palms flattened against each other, placed beneath her chin. Her face was thin, classy rather than good-looking, her nose a high-bridged blade. I had a sense of big-time.

I told her all I knew to tell. I thought she had loved my brother in some way I didn't want to have to think about.

She went to make herself a martini and brought me back a glass of ginger ale. Her eyes were swollen.

"He was a hero, then," she said.

"I guess so." I was feeling teary also. I sipped the peppery liquid. She had a lot of books, two cases overflowing, books jammed horizontally on top of vertical ones, and piled on top of the case. I spotted *The Magic Mountain, Buddenbrooks,* and *A Farewell to Arms.*

By the window was a table with a neat little portable on it, and a half-inch stack of paper beside the typewriter. The paper was bond, not the newsprint I used. She was writing something that would be made into a movie, or published.

"You told me you were fond of him," I said.

"Yes, fond."

"There was a woman who killed herself."

"There was such a person," she said, nodding.

I took a breath. "It doesn't sound like Richie acted very well."

"Let me reassure you that Richie acted as well as he was permitted to act in perfectly rotten circumstances."

"It sounds like Richie kind of pimped her for that Lubin guy."

Mrs. Carnes frowned gently. "David Lubin had many sexual partners. When he knew he was dying, sex became even more important to him. Val Ferris wanted a part in a film David planned to make. Richie introduced Val to David. It was a favor to her, actually. By that time he himself was no longer involved with her, although she may have thought he was indebted to her."

"It sounds like Richie kind of—" I didn't know how to ask any of it.

"It was Richie's job to rid David of a nuisance. A considerable nuisance. A threat, really."

"What did he do?"

Her forehead was creased as though there were too much to explain in order to make things clear to me, or else she was thinking of a way not to tell me what had happened.

"He employed a private detective to investigate her past. She had a criminal record."

That was what private eyes really did, instead of investigating murder cases with sexy suspects.

"I don't know how much of Richie's situation you understand," Mrs. Carnes said. "David was his mentor. More than a mentor. Richie was David himself when young. Handsome, talented, full of promise. A kind of reinvigoration of the dying animal. Of course Richie was flattered by the role. When David was severely compromised, it was Richie's duty to come to his aid."

I felt numb.

"Suicide is often an act of aggression," Mrs. Carnes said.

"You blame Val Ferris?"

She shook her head with a swing of her thick hair. "I blame this cruel industry that is founded upon the exploitation of youth and beauty and talent. I blame David Lubin, who had become a monster. Val was able to punish everyone by drowning herself. Richie was devastated."

"So he joined up."

"He was David's heir apparent. He threw all that up. He has redeemed himself."

She set her glass down and knitted her long fingers together, gazing at me. Of course Richie had slept with her, with young starlets and not so young feature players and middle-aged screenwriters. Sophisticated LA blow-job sex.

Esther Carnes shimmered in my eyes. Shit, I was crying! She rose, her bracelets clacking, and came to put her arms around me.

I excused myself to go to the bathroom to take a leak and blow my nose and dry my wet face on a hard linen hand towel.

Mrs. Carnes stood by the piano holding a fat little book. "Let me read you something. 'The Sapient Man will not wait to be the sun in its setting. He will not wait until other men turn their backs on him to be buried, still alive, in their estimation. The man of Foresight puts his horse in the stable betimes and does not wait for it to fall in a race. The Beauty wisely cracks the mirror before it disillusions her.'"

She was reading from the *Manual*. When she glanced up at me her eyes glistened and some black stuff had made marks on either side of them, like untidy brackets. She must think that passage referred to Richie! Off the taffrail when the voyage is over! I preferred *Martin Eden* to *The Pisan Manual*.

"Did Richie give you that book?"

"David Lubin gave it to me. He had based his life upon it, and it was a considerable life. David Lubin produced five great motion pictures!"

"I hate those guys of Insight and Justice. Superior Men."

She put the book down on the piano.

"Well, thanks," I said. "I guess I could've figured it all out, but thanks."

"You must be proud of him. He was a part of the thin red line of young men who have sacrificed themselves to save their country from a ruthless evil!"

I didn't know whether she knew Liz, or knew of her, but I told her I had brought Richie's girlfriend to Los Angeles, to Mulholland Farm. "She wants to be a movie star," I said. "Richie was supposed to help her."

"Errol is certainly in a position to assist her career," she said. "If you feel the need to worry about her for Richie's sake, I advise you not to. She was to blame, too, you know."

I wanted to know why.

"Your brother's San Diego lady friend put enormous pressure on him. I believe some of the things we may decry would not have occurred if she had not always been urging Richie to forward his career. At every turn," she added, with an harsh edge to her voice.

Liz and Richie had ruined private eyes for me—Philip Marlowe turned into a HUAC investigator or a Hollywood dirt-digger, with Jeff Dodge and John Burgess only lousy imitations, copies of copies, as Mr. Chapman had pointed out. I could still think of Val Ferris as a victim.

When Mrs. Carnes asked if she could take me out to dinner, I said I had to go home to San Diego, though it seemed there was nothing there to go home to.

In Long Beach the adhesive tape broke loose from the rip in the top, and the canvas began to flap. I knew it was tearing further, but there was nothing to do but drive on.

6

All that was necessary was to write a letter resigning from the midshipman's program and enlist in the Army. Nothing to it. My father would think I had enlisted because my brother had been killed in action, which was probably no further from the truth than my own reason, which was because Ol Paint's top had ripped.

First I went to say good-bye to my grandmother. There seemed shockingly little bulk lumping up the bedclothes. Her face was slack and soft, with closed eyes and a shine of spittle at the corner of her mouth. I blotted it with my handkerchief before I went away.

I called Lois at Perry's from a phone booth in the lobby, to tell her I couldn't make it on Thursday. "Date with Uncle Sam."

"Uh-oh."

"I'll always remember you, Lois."

She wanted to know when the train left.

I called Pogey to tell him I had enlisted, but Mrs. Malcolm said he wasn't at home. I phoned Tully to ask if I could store my stuff in his basement, and if he could put me up for the little time I had left as a civilian.

I didn't know what to do about Bonny. It was as though if I kept moving I wouldn't have to think about her.

At the Buttons' I told Mrs. Button I'd found another place and began packing. I toted out to Ol Paint my suitcases, laundry bag, tennis racket in its press, typewriter, box of manuscript, carbon copies and paper, two cartons of books and *Black Mask* magazines, and three A&P grocery bags jammed with clothes and shoes, to store at Tully's.

Tully was sitting on his throne beside the wall of phonograph records, sucking on a Budweiser. On the table by the window was a sheaf of papers with a blue cardboard cover.

His feet in brown wing tips were crossed before him. His knit tie was slipped two inches down from his collar, and the cuffs of his white shirt were turned back on his plump forearms. He was dressed as though he'd just come from church.

I sat on the hassock by the big chair with my own bottle of beer.

"My subpoena," Tully said, indicating the papers on the table.

"The HUAC!"

"They are coming to San Diego. No doubt they have kept track of the complaints." He looked solemn, like someone listening to the National Anthem. It occurred to me that he was proud of the subpoena, a kind of Good Housekeeping Seal of disapproval.

I whistled.

"I will not be naming names," Tully said pompously. "That of course is the ritual of humiliation. For having possessed unacceptable ideas, one is required to betray one's friends in violation of Anglo-Saxon ethics."

"Will they send you to prison?"

"Have you read *Billy Budd,* my boy?"

So much to read yet!

"Billy kills the evil Claggart because he is tongue-tied when falsely accused. So he is hanged."

I tried to figure out what he meant.

"They will probably subpoena you also, my boy."

"Oh, no, they won't."

He gave me a pop-eyed glance.

I told him I'd enlisted.

"Oh, dear God," he groaned. "You haven't done this for me?"

I shook my head. Not for Tully.

I had to tell Bonny I was leaving for the war at two-oh-two on Tuesday. I called her from the phone in the kitchen.

"Bonny, I'm taking the train to Camp Roberts day after tomorrow."

"The war," she said.

"What I want," I said, "is for you to write me letters, and I'll write letters. Like soldiers and their girlfriends do. That's what I want."

There was a pause, before she said, "All right."

What was wrong?

She wanted to know when the train left, and said she'd be there.

When I came out of the kitchen, Tully was still sitting on his throne. He turned to gaze at me with his baloney solemnity.

"I know you haven't had time to read Proust yet, my boy. He points out that every love affair is a reflection of the first, poignant love affair, the one you will no doubt be writing about. Right?"

Shit.

7

I had lunch with my mother, and we arrived early at the depot. She wore black for Richie dead; she looked washed-out, her lipstick too dark red on her mouth. She was grieving for Richie and her dying mother, and she was frightened for her second son. She kept dabbing at her eyes with her handkerchief and squeezing my hand.

"I'm just sick you're going off to be a doughboy like this," she said.

"You don't say doughboy this war," I said. "You say GI. Or dogface." The Dogfaced Boy goes to war!

"Please don't get hurt, darling. I couldn't stand it if you got hurt."

I put an arm around her to hug her. Richie had promised Liz he would not get killed.

We strolled in the cool shed, along the olive-drab cars of the train aimed north. Like Manzanar, Camp Roberts was a couple of hundred miles north of LA, but off Highway 101, not 395.

Headlines on the stack of papers in the kiosk by the door to the waiting room were ALLIES PLAN SECOND FRONT IN EUROPE.

Another recruit, flanked by Mom and Pop, walked along beside the cars. We nodded to each other as I parked my blue bag beside the step of the car I was to board. Bonny ought to have been here by now.

My mother and I, arm in arm, turned and walked back toward the brightness of the sun pouring into the open south end of the depot. She gripped my arm as though she didn't intend to let me go. She was what she was. Everyone was what he or she was; we had all been made what we were. Richie and I and our father and the Depression, Bonny and her brother and her mother and father and their Rhodes. It seemed the kind of half-assed wisdom the *Manual* would make some smug point about.

"I'll write you," I said. I was looking forward to writing to my mother, as the way things ought to be conducted in wartime, and to Bonny, too.

"Of course you won't. Richie never did." She fished her handkerchief out of her purse again.

There was Bonny!

It wasn't Bonny, it was Lois Meador trotting toward us, trim figure in a blue dress, a black raffia hat on her head. She was smiling her tight smile that I had realized was contrived to conceal her crooked tooth. The way she was! I introduced my ex-boss to my mother.

Lois handed me a neatly wrapped packet, which I recognized as a product of Perry's candy department.

"Some chewy stuff for the train ride." She rose to her toes to brush my cheek with her lips. "Take care of yourself. We are all looking forward to reading your books."

I saw my mother draw herself up straighter as the present Mrs. Edmund Daltrey came out of the waiting room. Weezie also wore black, and the two of them kissed and made over each other with an exchange of 'haven't seen you for so long!'s. Lois was introduced.

"I talked to your father out on San Clemente Island by shortwave last night," Weezie said to me. "They're building an airfield there. He sends his love and best wishes. I'm to remind you that he started as a buck private in the last war and ended up a shavetail. He'll expect you to do better than that!"

To my mother and me, she said, "Captain Mahoney is certain Richie will be awarded the Navy Cross."

Posthumously. "Terrific!" I said. I couldn't keep my eyes away from the door to the waiting room.

It appeared certain that Midway had been a great American victory, the real turning point of the war in the Pacific. Those old, slow torpedo planes and defective torpedoes up against *Haruna* class battleships and the big Jap carriers. The whole squadron off the *Yorktown* had died, all the brave boys, beloved sons and brothers and lovers, the redeemed and the not. The dive bombers had sunk the Jap ships.

Frank Tully strode toward us from the sun-bright Broadway entrance. He wore a tweed jacket, his knit tie, and pressed gray flannels, very dapper and stately. Maybe it was his new outfit for the HUAC interrogation. He carried a book under his arm.

"Greetings, Ellen," he said with a bow. He bowed again when he was introduced to Weezie and managed to say some good things about Richie Daltrey. I could see that Lois was anxious to get away. Tully handed over the book: *Go Down, Moses.*

"Time you started reading Faulkner, my boy," he said. "This is his latest. There's a novelette in there, 'The Bear,' that will knock the private eyes right out of your head."

Richie and Liz Fletcher and Val Ferris had already done that. Thanking Tully, I tucked the book under my arm with Lois's box of candy. Lois said good-bye, touched my chest, and was gone. I felt a teary heating in my eyes as I handed over to Tully Ol Paint's keys in their worn leather case, and the ownership certificate in its envelope—like a balloonist dropping off another sandbag of ballast. Tully would sell Ol Paint or keep it for the Saturday deliveries.

More guys, with parents and girlfriends, were standing in groups along the platform. I checked on my blue bag, which looked small and deflated from here. Not much I needed to take into the Army with me!

Had I told Bonny the wrong time?

There came Pogey Malcolm in his blue blazer. He stuck his hand out, and I slapped mine into it. Old friend, tennis buddy, fellow writer, fraternity brother, and supporter. Thick and thin!

"Hey, have a good war, Payt!"

"You, too, Poge!" I had another rush of emotion with my brother in it, goggled and helmeted, gloved hand on the joystick as at two hundred feet and 135 knots the creaky old plane hurtled toward the vast gray flank of the *Haruna* class, with all those guns you saw in the newsreels banging away.

Where was Bonny?

Amy Perrine came out of the door of the waiting room. Bonny was with her, in her camel's hair coat. Bonny tilted her head at me and at Amy, so I knew I was supposed to speak to Amy about Will Gates.

We walked away from the others, Amy close beside me. I didn't want to walk along the cars with Amy Perrine!

"Listen, Amy," I said. "Bob-O would want you to fall in love with some good guy," I heard myself say. "Will Gates is a terrific guy."

She held up her hand to show me her ring. "I love him!" she squeaked, and I patted her shoulder.

So we started back. Bonny stood alone, staight-backed. She had on a blue beret that covered her hair. There was a funny tight look around her mouth.

Emmett Buckley and Mark Davis came at me, and I had to crack snappers with the brothers, who must have forgiven my trespasses because of my enlistment. Redeemed! It was some kind of awful retribution (for what?), my fraternity brothers come to see me off!

I managed to get over to Bonny. "I'll write you," she said.

"I'll be at Camp Roberts. Maybe we could meet in LA—"

"I don't think I can do that." She was looking at me as though she hardly knew me!

"Bonny—"

"I'm Barbara," she said.

Now there was a considerable crowd of young guys in their good-bye groups. It was clear I was not going to receive a good-bye kiss. Time to bail out of this shitpasture and climb aboard.

I mounted into the coach, found a seat, and chucked my bag into the overhead rack. I made desperate grinning faces out the window as the train lurched and moved. People on the platform began to slip away, waving. Bonny stood alone, facing toward me. She stood very straight, chin up; she looked proud, she looked fearless. In her camel's hair coat and her beret, for some reason I thought she looked like Joan of Arc.

How could she have known about Lois Meador? How could she have known what had happened in the car with Liz on the way to LA? She couldn't!

It was a judgment. It was punishment. Bonny had loved me and I had fucked Lois Meador. It was a betrayal. I had lost my beloved. I had done it to myself. My prick had done it to me. Alice Hoagland lived right around the corner from Lois. Somebody had seen me and told Bonny. That was the way girls looked after each other. I couldn't even weep.

The car shook as the train picked up speed, headed for their fucking war.

BOOK TWO

Staying Alive

Chapter 12

1

I WROTE BONNY FROM CAMP ROBERTS, FROM FORT JACK-
ass, and from England. She always wrote back, but it was as though someone were writing the letters for her, someone named Barbara. I began to
think that that new identity was what had happened to the Bonny Bonington I had been in love with and who I thought had been in love with me. I
didn't even know how to ask her what had gone wrong, though I was no
longer certain the problem had been Lois Meador. Bonny's letters were
impersonal about *us,* as though there had never been any *us,* as though I
were just some serviceman she wrote to dutifully.

That summer of 1942, she had gone to live with her aunt Honey in
Menlo Park, right next door to Palo Alto, where she was tutored in math
and science so she could go into premed at Stanford University.

She wrote of returning to San Diego at Christmastime. "San Diego
doesn't look very Christmassy, all palm trees and sunshine. Ginny Gormley
and I ventured out to Mission Beach, but it was lonely and a chilly breeze
blowing. We prowled through the shut-down shops and looked in at the
taffy machine, and up at the roller coaster, and drove home. Party at the

Hotel del, servicemen and local girls with gardenias in their hair. I notice I get a little more respect as a 'Stanford girl,' and I am careful not to make hurty comparisons to big-time San Francisco and this dreary burg where I have vowed my life will not be spent. Though I may confess that Marston's doesn't seem like much when one has gone shopping at the City of Paris. Aunt Honey took me on a clothes-buying spree! I am treated with more respect by my parents also. Imagine!"

In another letter she had responded to my questions about the Stanford campus. "It's like State only more so. Beautiful old buildings rather than fancied-up new buildings made to look like old buildings. When Leland Stanford Junior was dying he asked his father, the great railroad builder crook, to build a university where poor young men could get an education. This causes giggles when one thinks what one's parents are coughing up to keep us poor students here.

"After the boy died his parents went to Harvard to ask the president what it cost to build a university. The president of Harvard told them a university wasn't just buildings and faculty, it was traditions and history, library books and janitors, sports and all that. But Leland Stanford said he just wanted to know what it cost for the campus, and the president told him some millions of dollars; a figure. And Leland Stanford said to Mrs. Stanford, 'We can do it, Mama! We can do it!' Isn't that lovely?"

Bonny used "lovely" ironically a lot, also "dreary" and "putrid." "I think it's really putrid when rich people get together and talk about how to make poor people poorer!" She hadn't lost her democratic sympathies at a rich kids' school, at least.

She wrote that she and Aunt Honey had gone to see Macbeth in "the City," and I wrote back, "Blow wind, come wrack, at least we'll die with harness on our back!" Because it had been a kick to spout that in recruit training when we were suiting up for drill.

For my part I wrote her just what I was involved in, and I tried to write it as well as I could, to make her see, as an author is required to make the reader see, because I had it in my mind that my letters were a kind of journal I was keeping. I wrote to Pogey and to my father that way, too, typing with carbons when I could get access to a typewriter, or just writing by hand and thinking to remember it all. Maybe I fictionalized a little, going for what should have happened rather than what actually happened, and I left out the universal Army adjectives.

We crossed over the Channel shortly after D-day. We were held up for some weeks in the hedgerows, but with the St. Lo breakout we were off to the races.

2

Roaring across France in that August heat, six of us in a halftrack with a machine gun mounted on the cab, M-1s, carbines, captured machine pistols, grenades, and a case of calvados, we couldn't believe our good fortune. We had made no contact with Jerries, though we had heard gunfire off to the north a couple of times. We just kept going. It was like a rolling vacation.

We came into a little burg on a river beyond Orleans, maybe the Yonne, parked on a side street and jumped out under a sky as shiny blue as enamel. Cobbles slanted down to a colorless stretch of river, no one in evidence. We left Tallboy in the halftrack, and five of us trooped around the corner to a café-bar with a wooden sign showing a wine bottle and a bunch of purple grapes, and a locked door. Pappy Walton, called Pappy because he was thirty, banged on the door and hallooed in French until a wrinkled old lady with white hair twisted up into a topknot like Jiggs's Maggie opened up and bowed and muttered what we took to be welcome and stationed herself behind the bar. It was about three degrees cooler inside.

We knew well enough the word *bière,* and four of us ordered *bière* and Pappy *vin rouge.* We sat at a plank table in an alcove that had a view of the river through a window of small panes.

The old lady brought the beers and Pappy's wine, bowing as she set out the glasses. We raised toasts to her, to France, and to each other. Of course we knew it would not go on this easy, but easy it had been so far, wheeling into little *villes* like this one, making sure we kept a retreat line open, although speed was the order. We were proud of ourselves, as though this one halftrack were winning the war. We never saw any officers, communicating by radio, and the orders were to keep going. So we kept going, winning the war by ourselves, Pappy the first sergeant and I a buck sergeant second in command. Later on Pappy was killed in the Bulge.

We all stank of stale sweat, whiskered and dirty and feeling very tough.

It was as though the personal stink combined with the pleasant sour stench of the beer and Pappy's wine, and the whole wine-encrusted smell of the little bar aroused all the senses. The old woman behind the counter gazed at us anxiously.

Tallboy hustled in the door carrying one of the machine pistols. "There's a Jerry soldier down there!"

Standing beside our table, he craned his helmeted head at the window, pointing. We all rose, too. There he was, down by the river, just his helmet showing.

"Go shoot him," Pappy said to me.

"Hold on!" I said.

"Yeah," Ned said. "If there's one Jerry there's probably others. You don't want to get anything started."

"You'd better get back to the halftrack," Pappy said to Tallboy.

"Probly a fucking regiment just over there," Selden Orcutt said in South Carolinian.

"I don't think there's any fucking regiment over there," Pappy said. "I said go shoot him, Pat. That's an order."

A thin sun was coming through the high fog, glistening on the cobblestones. Sometimes the helmet moved, looking to one side, but it never turned back toward us. The German helmet wasn't all that different from the GI, but you immediately knew it.

"Better recon first," Rosy Rosenquist said.

I'd just as soon somebody else did any shooting, and Pappy knew that. He was looking pissed off, with his eyes jerking toward the window and back to me.

"Go shoot him yourself if you want him shot so much," I said. Tallboy had left the machine pistol on the table. Rosy and I had M-1s, Pappy a carbine. I drank some beer for my dry mouth.

"Take him prisoner," Ned said.

"What the fuck are we going to do with a prisoner?" Pappy said.

"Geneva Convention."

"Fuck the Geneva Convention!" Pappy leaned forward over the table, glowering and scratching his whiskered chin with a thumb. "Little moral dilemma, Pat? We don't shoot the sonofabitch and he hides out and snipes one of us. Where's your moral dilemma then?"

"Yeah," Rosy said. "And you shoot him and there's a fucking regiment just over the hill there and they come out and wipe us all out, where's your dilemma then?"

We watched the helmet through the streaky panes of glass of the alcove window. Sometimes he would turn to look upstream, then downstream, but mostly he just looked straight ahead.

"I'll do it," Selden Orcutt said. He took his wire-frame glasses out of his breast pocket and fitted them onto his face.

"I'll do it," I said.

I checked the clip on the M-1 and went outside. The sun was breaking through the clouds, and there was a glare off the damp cobbles. I moved along the side of the buildings until I had a clear view of the Jerry's helmet and back. I wasn't going to shoot him in the back, and I'd probably only have a second or two before he put up his hands.

"*Achtung!*" I yelled, the cold metal of the rifle breech against my cheek, and the front sight fixed on him.

The helmet turned toward me, framing a slice of white face. He rose, a boy in a gray shirt with white knees showing between his long stockings and short pants, wearing a German helmet. He was holding a fishing pole. He dropped it and raised both hands above the helmet.

I lowered the rifle and waved a dismissing hand at him. He stared back at me, slowly lowering his hands. I turned to see the faces crowding the window of the little café-bar underneath the wooden sign. Off to the west I could hear the low approaching roar of the heavy machinery of the 11th Armored.

From that nameless burg we headed on east. It was a long time before any mail caught up with us, a month-old cool and cheery letter from Bonny, Barbara, with her Stanford PO Box address. She was in med school.

"The teaching docs are all Johnny Pierce fascists," she complained. "and the male students treat Gloria and me like enemies." Gloria Nixon was the only other girl in her class. "They insult us all the time! They say we get better grades because the teaching docs hope to seduce us, and after our education we'll just quit medicine and have babies. I'd heard it was like this, but I didn't believe it. The men students are jerks, some of them are just stupid. One of them called me a San Diego bitch! The teaching docs are letches. I see how they make the girl students drop out.

"Where are you now?" she asked. "Can you tell?"

3

Late in November, we came into a settlement in the forest where a barn was burning. There was a terrific din of bellowing cattle in that barn that must've been hit by phosphorous shells. Fred Eichorn and I hustled inside, and I didn't think until we got into the shadows there that it might've been a trap. It wasn't a trap. There were about thirty cattle stalled inside, and they were on fire, too, for flaming timbers and hay dropped down from the roof and the haylofts, and the cattle pitched and bellowed in their stalls with their backs on fire, and at the same time they jerked hay from the trough and munched away.

"Christ almighty!" Fred Eichorn said, who was a farm boy.

He and I went crazy in that barn, shooting the burning cows and fighting off the burning hay that pitched down on us, in a terrific hurry before the whole roof fell in. I tried to fire just one round into an animal's head, but Fred went wild with his Kraut machine pistol. The bellowing got thinner but more hysterical, and chunks of wood and burning hay fell on us, with Fred hoarsely shouting. I had to reload and then jump at Fred to knock a big bunch of flaming hay off his back, switching and cutting around firing like western heroes gunning down bad guys in a hostile town, killing flaming cows. I remember that at the same time I was killing cattle I was trying to recall as if for some midterm exam who it was in mythology—was it Cuchulain?—who had gone mad killing cattle thinking he was killing his enemies.

The closest I came to cracking up in the war was killing flaming cows in a barn somewhere in Luxembourg.

4

It was the first clear November day for a week, sunny and cold, and already we could hear the planes out, bombers coming over high and once a P-51 whacking low across the clearing where we were, with that climax of sound like the sky falling in. There was a collection of stone buildings, chimneys with some smoke, pigstys and a cow in a yard, a cat sunning itself on a porch. Three of us gathered in the sun in a little yard enclosed by a fence of weathered palings, appreciating the warmth. A girl of about ten in a schoolgirl outfit came outside and shyly greeted us. She was delicately pretty with pale blue eyes and almost translucent skin, and fair hair in tight little braids on either side of her head. Tallboy gave her a Hershey bar, and I pulled at one of her braids while she grinned sunnily up at me showing pink gums, and there were *danke*s and *bitte*s.

We drifted on up toward tree line on the ridge, Tallboy with the Schmeisser, Ned with the BAR, and me with my M-1. We were on a patrol to make contact with Jerries and maybe not as regimental as we should have been. There was always the chance of the "million-dollar wound" which would take you home or at least out of the line without too much damage done.

Halfway up the hillside we sprawled out behind a down timber for a break. Tallboy, the last one standing, gave a "Psst!" and ducked down with the rest of us. A patrol of Krauts was coming up the clearing, maybe twelve of them slouching along together, not in any kind of order but more like a mob. The sun glinted on their helmets like so many black toadstools.

We crouched behind the down timbers watching this bunch as they halted by the little yard which we had just left, and the schoolgirl came outside to be made over by Krauts, who could speak her language at least but who probably didn't have any candy bars because things were getting very tough for Germans. It was an innocent scene of soldiers making over a pretty little girl in a sunny farmyard setting

There was flinching and ducking as another Mustang came over low with the disintegrating splintering of sound.

The schoolgirl looked up toward where we were, then she pointed, and we could see the faces of the Jerries like pale triangles under their helmets fixing on us.

I braced my M-1 over the log, whispered, "Shit!" and fired at the man who looked like the officer. Next to me Tallboy let loose with the Schmeisser like a deafening zipper punctuated by the timed whack-whack-whack of Ned's BAR. The Krauts went down like blocked defensive backs in some crazy football game, with shouts and screams and a few shots coming back. We wiped them out.

The schoolgirl lay facedown with her jacket turned to a bloody rag. I was afraid Tallboy was going to say something about his Hershey bar, but he didn't.

5

This was another farmhouse in an Ardennes clearing, stone like all of them, square, two-story, with a pig yard to one side and a stack of firewood on the other covered by a sheet of tar paper held down with stones. The firing off to the north sounded like the surf at Mission Beach, except that the individual sounds were more distinct: the cloth rip of a German machine gun, the flat whacks of artillery.

I stood in the shadow line of the pines, watching the house. A little smoke penciled up from the chimney. To my right Tallboy hunched on one knee behind a tree, the Schmeisser in his hands. Farther along was Rosy, his helmet like a brown potato. Ned was in the house. What was keeping him?

I knew what was keeping him. M-1 at the ready, I started down the slope. My boots crackled on a skim of ice. A trodden path picked up pretty soon, and I followed along six feet to one side of it. A big white pig watched between the bars of his pen. The door had an old-fashioned farm latch, and I thumbed it and threw the door open.

An old couple stood facing me, the woman with her hands in her apron, the man with his hands ready to rise if I said so. They both wore black clothing, muddy boots. Behind them was a green tile stove with a stovepipe.

"Where is he?" I said.

The man pointed to the stairs. I went on up, keeping my tread quiet. I could hear the bed. I pushed another door open. Ned's helmet was on the floor; his BAR leaned against the bedstead.

His pants were pulled down to show his white buttocks. One of her legs stretched off the bed, shoe half off, her arm over her face. His white butt worked up and down. He screamed when I whacked his tailbone with the butt of the rifle.

He tumbled off the bed pulling at his pants, his mouth open all over his face. The woman scrambled into a fetal position. She was not young, skinny, gray streaks in her hair.

"You shit," I said.

"Jesus, that hurt!"

"It's going to hurt when they shoot you."

"What the fuck're you talking about?" He scrambled to his feet, pulling his pants up over his swollen dick. I pointed the M-1 at him.

"You raped that girl back at l'Haute," I said.

"I didn't rape her! I gave her three packs of cigs!"

"You fucking rapist," I said. I could keep my voice level if I set my mind against it shaking.

The woman on the bed never moved, tucked into a bundle of black skirt and white blouse. One eye regarded me.

"Listen, Pat, for Christ sake—"

"Let's go," I said. I pushed the muzzle of the M-1 into his gut. His mouth ribboned all over his face again.

"Christ, Pat!"

"Put on your helmet."

He bent to pick it up. I took his BAR.

"Well, gimme my BAR!"

"You're under arrest."

"You can't arrest me!"

"We're going to act like it, though. Get going."

"Well, fuck you!" he said, and moved ahead faster than I liked. I cranked a round into the chamber, and he stopped. His whiskered, big-mouth face peered back at me.

"Just move along."

He slammed his boots going down the stairs. The old couple stared at us, standing his shoulder against hers. The man said something, cleared his throat and spoke louder, thanks or recriminations.

I marched Ned outside.

"You read that directive," I said. "They're going to shoot your dick off. That girl in l'Haute wasn't sixteen, and this—"

"These fuckers are Germans, for Christ sake, Pat!"

"What difference does that make? Anyway, they're Luxembourgers. They just *speak* German."

"You righteous bastard!"

I held the M-1 aimed at his crotch, wondering what I was going to do with him. We were supposed to be moving ahead to make contact all along this line.

Tallboy was loping down the slope toward us, with Rosy slanting over toward him and the two new guys, all of us whiskered and cold, all of us hating Germans.

"What're you going to do with him, Pat?" Tallboy said. His breath smoked. One of the repos, Roper, lit a cigaret and squinted at Ned.

"At it again, Ned?" Rosy said.

"Fuck you!" Ned said.

"Rosy's going to take him back to Battalion and they're going to court-martial him and shoot him," I said.

"Cut it out, now, Pat!"

The 88 rounds hit like the end of the world. Everybody ducked and shouted with that expulsion of breath from shock. The pig was screaming. Smoke drifted down the slope toward us.

Down on one knee with my shoulders hunched, I kept my M-1 pointed at Ned Macklin. He tried to stare me down with his red-rimmed eyes in his white face. Rosy and Tallboy got to their feet. The two repos had backed up against the wall of the house, rifles at port. The pig kept screaming.

"Take him back to Battalion," I said to Rosy. "Shoot him if he tries to fuck with you."

"Okay, Pat," Rosy said. He showed Ned his M-1. "Git along li'l dogie," he said.

Battalion HQ was about four miles back.

Ned and Rosy were halfway up the slope to the woods when another couple of rounds came in. I saw Ned's helmet fly off, and he went down with his arms stretched out before him like he was diving into a pool. Rosy had flattened himself on the frozen ground.

I ran heavy-legged up the hill to them. "Okay?" I said to Rosy.

He raised himself in a push-up. "Guess so."

The top of Ned's head had come off with his helmet. His brains looked like the pink and gray halves of a walnut. I sat down beside his body. Rosy took one look and then went back down the hill to where the repos waited, in the sunny spot in front of the house. They stared up at me when I got up to take Ned's dog tags off their cord around his neck.

6

"Tell me what happened, Sergeant," Major Dickhead said. I stood at attention. He sat at a table with a scarred wooden top in a big room at the *hôtel de ville*. His jeep, with its white star, was in the room past him, like his horse stalled there. He had a big, pale face, MacArthur combover hair on a bald head, and fat hands lying on stacks of papers on the table. There was always that distant racket of firing up to the northeast.

I told him what had happened.

"So you took time out from your mission to arrest this soldier for rape."

"Yes, sir."

"Would you say the rape was more important than the mission?"

I didn't answer.

He smoothed a hand back over his bald head. "I am asking, Sergeant, if you considered the rape more important than the mission to which your unit was assigned."

"What do you want me to say, sir?"

I remembered Lois telling me that I would have been the best driver Perry's had ever had if I had just put Perry's business ahead of my own.

He showed me his lower teeth. "I want you to tell me, Sergeant, whether you considered—the—rape—more—important—"

Fuck this. "Yes, sir," I said. "I guess you can say I did."

He leaned back in his chair with a sigh, took a pack of Old Golds from his breast pocket, tapped it against a finger, withdrew a cigaret, and lit it with his Zippo. He didn't offer me one.

"Very well, Sergeant, I consider you culpable in this situation. Your mission was your mission."

"If you say so, sir."

"Are you being impertinent, Sergeant?"

"I hope not, sir."

"Rape is an unfortunate concomitant of war, Sergeant. So are many other tragedies. Our mission is to get the war over with."

"Yes, sir, but it is this kind of thing I have assumed we are fighting against."

"Ah, it is a philosophical sergeant. I don't believe there is room in the TO for philosophical sergeants, soldier." He grinned at me, showing bad teeth, and I had the first sense that I might be losing my stripes.

"There was a directive, sir—" I started.

"I do not wish to hear of directives, Sergeant."

"Very good, sir."

Major Dickhead blew smoke. "Sergeant, I feel I am encountering a degree of stubbornness. I am trying to impress you with your error. It was not the time to arrest Corporal Macklin. It might be said that you are responsible for his death. Could not the arrest have waited until after the action?"

211

"Well, sir, all I can say is I didn't think so at the time."

"Do you think so now?"

"No, sir. When I entered the room he was raping the woman. I believed I was doing the right thing."

"And you still do?"

"Well, sir, I considered shooting him. I thought arresting him was the better course."

"Jesus Christ, Sergeant, that would have been murder!"

"Yes, sir." Many tragedies happen in war. At least I had the sense not to say it. It was as though I were coming off a drunk, suddenly sober and aware of screwing myself.

I said, "Sir, I came upon him raping her. He'd done the same thing to a young girl in l'Haute. I won't mention the directive again, sir. But I disapprove of rape."

He stared at me hard-faced. "I guess we are in a Mexican stand-off, Sergeant. And I have the rank to dissolve it. I want you to admit you made the wrong decision."

"No, sir."

"Very well, Sergeant, you give me no option. You are busted back to PFC. Now get out of here."

I saluted and left. Outside I stood taking in deep gulps of cold air. A couple of halftracks rattled past. A trio of planes hurtled over. I remembered Errol Flynn, grinning, jaw-jutted, saying, "Fuck 'em all, I say!"

At Fort Jackass we had prepared for a parade for a visiting major general, all equipment and clothing cleaned, pressed, spotless; heavy doses of close order drill. The general, when he came, was in a hurry, so we were ordered to run past him.

It was a defining moment for me. I had assumed that, like my father before me, I would somehow be commissioned in the process of the war. After the parade at Fort Jackass I no longer wished to be an officer because I disliked the whole corps of them as carrying along a principle of bullying and abuse. I hated the process of the more powerful bending the less powerful to their will. It was what I had supposed the war to be against, Hitler being the ultimate example of this power over powerlessness. But Allied forces had seized upon the excuse of having to defeat Hitler as their own means to the power of the stronger over the weaker. It was the Allied enlisted man in Europe who was being abused in the process. The generals never went anywhere near the front, unless it was to have their photographs made for newspapers, in effect astride their white horses with sabers pointed at the foe. Major Dickhead kept a careful couple of miles between himself and any action, so he had no idea what the dogfaced boys were going through up on the line, and Captain Shitface was only about a mile better, and was drunk a good part of the time to boot. Lieutenant Smith had been a decent soldier-caring officer until he cracked up.

Eisenhower was always calling home to the USA for bigger drafts.

I was on my way back to company to report to the captain that I'd been busted, when it began to snow.

The next day I didn't think I had the authority to order three repos not to sneak down to a big farmhouse to do some looting, and a German machine gun ripped them up, and ripped up my leg when I tried to drag Ernie Flores out. A Sherman tank came up to blast the farmhouse and the machine-gun nest to gravel.

Consequent to my session with the major and my million-dollar wound, I missed the first and worst part of the Battle of the Bulge.

I was taken out in a jeep and back to Paris to the American Hospital.

7

I sat outside a café in Montmartre, watching the rain slashing along the sidewalk four feet from my boots, and considered the depth of the shit I was in. My father had come home from World War I a horseman rather than a foot soldier, as he had repetitively put it, and his son was an AWOL jerk-off on the verge of desertion.

After three weeks the doctor had certified me as fit for combat, with orders back to my outfit. My million-dollar wound was not worth much on the present market. At the time Hemingway's "separate peace" sounded pretty good to me.

I had decided that my wound separated the men from the boys. Boys were those who were sure none of the 88 shells coming over had their names on them even when their buddies were getting blown apart. You were no longer a boy when you realized the truth of the situation, which was that your name was on a whole lot of different kinds of shells and bullets, and what you had instead of the courage of invulnerability was a pounding heart and shortness of breath, with a target affixed to your back and a terrific reluctance to expose yourself.

Except that as a man, "full-fledge" as Calvin had said once, I couldn't even go down on the Left Bank and sit around in the cafés where Hemingway had hung out because MPs would be there checking paper.

I sipped sour red wine with two saucers before me. The mustachioed waiter eyed me with a squint of anxiety. Rain blew in squalls along the street and among the bare black limbs of the trees in the little parc across the way. There were a few passersby between the showers, women in short black skirts (short, I was told, because of the lack of fabric), showing good legs. Whores gave me the questioning eye. Their rates were up because of the numbers of American soldiers in Paris, some on legitimate or medical leave, some AWOLs like me, some flat-out deserters, which I was sticking one toe into.

And here was my Company K pal Tallboy hustling up the sidewalk toward me, the shoulders of his GI overcoat and his cap dark with wet. He slammed into the chair beside me with a screech of jarred legs. "Pat!" he said.

"Tallboy!"

He fumbled in his pocket. His face was pale and long with a petulant lower lip. He was a better soldier than I was. He slapped on the table a packet of letters fastened together with string.

"Mail call," Tallboy said.

"Thanks." I beckoned to the waiter to bring wine.

Tallboy sneezed. "Fucken rain," he said. "We are moving back into the line Tuesday, Pat."

"Listen," I said. "I am a *blessé de guerre*. I am not recovered yet, whatever the doc says. I am not ready to go back there and get *blessé*d again, or dead. They are so fucking stupid I don't have to go along with their stupidity."

"Somebody has got to run the thing, Pat! They have got to have the authority to tell the soldiers what to do. They can see the big picture, we can't. You can't just have every sergeant deciding he would run the war a different way."

"This ex-sergeant has so decided," I said. I squinted at the packet of letters.

"At the Battle of Gettysburg," I went on, "Robert E. Lee sent I forget how many men of Pickett's Division up the hill in a stupid charge, and most of them got killed or *blessé*'d, and lost the war right then. They should not have gone up that hill into the Union guns. Just the way I'm not going back into direct frontal shit when we should be hitting flanks. You know why they are doing it this stupid way? They are just trying to impress Montgomery with Yankee guts. Doesn't matter if they get a few thousand GIs dead."

The waiter brought two more glasses of red on their little saucers.

"Pat, listen, with AWOL you'll have to take some shit, but if you desert you get the whole machinery after you. They'll put you in prison. They'll shoot you!" He stuck his lower lip out. "How's your leg?" he wanted to know.

"Almost okay. I can feel it, but it's okay. I'm not admitting it to anybody but you, though." I slapped my thigh, harder than I meant to.

Tallboy winced for me.

When the doctor told me he was sending me back to my outfit, I said, *What do you do, get a bonus for everyone you send back?*

They need you, he said. *They're taking a lot of casualties.*

I spread the letters in a fan. Letters from Bonny, from my stepmother, who wrote for my father, and Pogey in Kansas with an engineer outfit.

A squall marched down the street, sweeping leaves and a page of newspaper before it. Civilians hustled by, the men in dark ill-fitting suits and cloth caps, the women in their coats, short skirts, and bare white legs.

"That *poule*'s kind of giving me the eye," Tallboy said. The woman was waiting under a metal awning next to the café. She had a dark red mouth. Tallboy wanted to know if I'd be here for a while.

"I'll be here."

He loped along toward the woman, very American in his overcoat and cap. I saw her put her arm through his with a feminine motion that felt like a crimp in my chest. When they were out of sight I ripped one of Bonny's letters open.

More complaints about med school and men in general. I had begun to worry whether she was going to make it. I had come to a slow realization that her distancing from me was not because of any perceived betrayal with

Lois Meador she felt, but from a cast-iron determination to make a life she wanted, of which I was not a part. Where had she got that determination to be a doctor? What had caused that huge seachange in her?

Her aunt Honey had taken her and her friend Gloria to San Francisco to see Shaw's play *Man and Superman,* which I'd heard of but knew nothing about. Part of it, called "Don Juan in Hell," had the characters in Hell, discussing philosophical matters that had impressed Bonny. A week later she and her aunt and a professor couple, friends of her aunt's, had a play-reading evening reading the third act of *Man and Superman.* "They let me read the Dona Ana part! Jim was Don Juan and Maria the Devil, and Aunt Honey the Statue. There is an opera where the Statue appears and drags Don Juan off to Hell. We talked about the Life Force! Just ask me about the Life Force. I know the Life Force! It was a wonderful evening!

"Do you remember when I read *Crime and Punishment*? It obsessed me so, I could hardly think about anything else. Now it's like that with this 'Don Juan in Hell.' Shaw was so smart! Those lines itch in my head like hot wires. Gloria and I talked a lot about it, but she just doesn't feel the way I do."

Was that an implication that she wished I were there to discuss it with her?

I reread the *Man and Superman* paragraph again, feeling sour. I had urged her to read *Crime and Punishment.* I remembered her excitement, which I had been responsible for. I had been a year older than she was, I'd read a lot of books, I'd been a kind of tutor. Now she was excited about something I knew nothing about.

In another letter dated later in November, she had gone with her aunt to the opera in San Francisco. *Norma.* "It was simply divine! Do you know Bellini died when he was thirty-four? Those melodies! Norma and Adalgisa singing those long, sinuous duets!"

It seemed my education at San Diego State was not going to stand up to hers at Stanford.

8

In a sunny patch of sidewalk on the Champs, not far beyond the Arc de Triomphe, a Negro soldier sat at a little table with a blue cup and saucer before him, and the stub of a croissant on a plate. Calvin King's cap was tilted over one eye, and he wore a GI overcoat.

"Well, hiyuh, child!" he said, without apparent surprise. A young woman in a blue blouse and apron appeared. "You want a *café au lait,* child? Better than milk shakes."

"Sure," I said, but turned down a croissant. I grinned at Calvin. "Here we are in their war," I said.

Inside the café a machine was hissing steam. A pair of two-and-a-halfs rolled by on the Champs, followed by one of the Tinkertoy little French cars with corrugated sides, and a black gangster-style Citroën.

"Not me, bo," Calvin said. His face was leaner, finer-featured.

"AWOL?"

He shook his head. "All the way. They've got colored guys just driving trucks and carrying garbage cans for the white boys. Nuffa that."

I said there'd been a colored tank destroyer team near us in the Ardennes.

"That's new, then," Calvin said. He gazed at me not quite hostilely with his dark pupils in his yellowish eyeballs and sipped his coffee. "You know how many of us all-the-ways there's here in Paris, child? Some say fifteen thousand. On the loose."

"Doing what?" I said. I knew of the deserters, but his numbers were staggering if true.

"Makin money. Cigarets! You know what you can do with cigarets in this country? A couple of cartons of cigarets can get you blown by a duchess."

Calvin went through a complicated process of digging a pack of cigarets from his jacket pocket, English Players, shaking one out of the pack and offering it to me, lipping it himself, lighting it with a gold Zippo, squinting at me through the smoke.

"Colored guys don't have any stake in this war, child," he said. "You have any idea the shit a colored guy goes through in recruit training? That's just the beginning of the shit. No, sir, you fellows fight your own war."

I'd had an idea of the shit he was in for in recruit training.

"Well, that's great, Calvin," I said. "I always knew you'd do well." In the equation of Man vs. Superman, it seemed that Calvin was always over on the Super side. Maybe with a whiff of the Devil.

He grinned with a brilliant dental display. One of his front teeth was missing, with a wire remaining that must have been the pivot for a false tooth. It gave him an almost comical look of menace.

My leg had stiffened, and I stretched it out under the table. "How's your uncle Red?" I asked.

"Gone to a better world," Calvin said. "Heart attack. Damn, if I was there what I could do with his bidness!" He leaned toward me. "What do you hear from your lady friend, child?"

"Tough times in Stanford Med," I said.

When I left him I almost ran into a pair of MPs coming around the *Etoile.* I managed to head out of their way without breaking into a run, but barely; I was panting and pissed off when I had got a corner of a stone building between me and them. I didn't want to have to do that anymore. My money was going to run out in about four days anyway.

9

Corinne sat on the bed reading *Le Monde.* Fair cropped hair covered her head like pale flames. When they had shaved her head she had let it grow out this far, and now kept it cut short. Sometimes she wore a wig, but more often she faced down what she had to face down with her sleeping-with-the-Boche cropped head. She hadn't read *The Scarlet Letter,* and my little French had failed trying to explain it to her.

The old Royal portable with its French accents I'd bought at the *marché puce* rested on the little table.

"'Allo, Paht."

"'Allo, Corinne." I went over to the window to look out over the raked reefs of roofs, *les toits de Paris.* The twats of Paris. I said I was going to have to go back.

"Pourquoi?" she said.

"No money."

She said she could get money.

It was impossible to explain that I was not suited to a life that had seemed glamorous in theory, in rebellion against the stupidities of war. In fact, being an AWOL hiding out in a hole in the mansard in Montmartre with a girl who would go out and peddle pussy for money for you, like

Dessy and Calvin, where every time you passed an MP he would want to check your orders, as would the noncoms at transient messes and transient barracks, was simply too shitty.

I picked up the splayed-open paperback of *Swann's Way* and set it aside, to seat myself in the rickety chair facing Corinne. She had a pasty, sweet face with startlingly black eyebrows below her cropped head. When she got up to come to me, her breasts swung in her white blouse. She sat on my lap and traced a finger down my cheek and pressed her lips there with popping little kisses. She had been in love with a German lieutenant and did not apologize for it.

"You will leave me, Paht?" she said.

"Just for a while," I said.

I had thought I could be a writer on the outside looking in spectatorly on the bourgeois bullshit of Amurrucun life. But I would have to write about the bullshit from inside Social Reality, condemned to being just what I had hoped to rebel against. Write from Normal Heights, Professor Chapman at San Diego State College had advised me.

"My sweet boy," Corinne said. She smelled of soap and lavender. She propped my chin up to kiss me on the mouth, her narrow bottom squirming on my lap. She found the furrow of scar in my thigh beneath my pants and traced a finger along it; my wound fascinated her. It was her conviction that most sorrows could be solved in bed, and so we tried that.

10

So I went back to Company K in the town of X, and found myself curiously glad to be there, although there were not many comrades I even knew anymore. Because I was an old-timer I got my stripes back pretty quick.

The Battle of the Bulge ran from December 16, 1944, to mid-January 1945. There was no specific moment when it was over, as far as we were concerned, just one day an engineer outfit appeared with water trucks and showers, and we showered and were furnished with new uniforms to climb into, long johns, pants and blouses and overcoats, even caps. When I finally took my old clothes off I found that my hair had grown into the knit cap worn inside my helmet liner, it had not been taken off for so long.

We moved out of that sector west, through snow so deep the halftracks couldn't operate, so we were foot soldiers mushing through knee-deep snow, pushing and pushed, pushing bone tired toward a front where we could hear aircraft and firing of an intensity we'd never heard before, and P-51s banking low over us and cutting down over the ridge.

From the top of a ridge the river bottom spread out below us. It was a German river crossing in their retreat, four pontoon bridges across the river that snaked in broad curves down the valley where the snow was torn up with great muddy splashes, and what looked like the whole Kraut army milling, soldiers and machines and artillery, a lot of it horse drawn, and dead horses spotted in the snow, and the P-51s coming down along the river with all their guns firing at the poor bastards on the pontoon bridges, plane after plane, with a flourish of wings slanting up once almost lazily and then down-slanting and faster and totally intent on the strafing. One of them smoked and the wings flashed over and it crashed in a spurt of flame, but the flights of Mustangs and later Lightnings kept coming and coming. The Krauts died and you could feel sorry for them although you knew better, the planes coming and firing and you could see them shudder when their cannons went off, and bombs shot up water and men and pontoon planking, and still the Krauts would fix it up, and keep going across the river, so slowly, so intent and hopeless, and the bodies that you could not see floating down the river.

The order came for us to move on down the ridge toward where the Kraut killing was going on, but there was that terrific slowdown when every soldier was reluctant to move down that ridge, the noncoms like me as reluctant as anyone else, and the lieutenant ordering us on down reluctant, too, so the movement was so slow as to be hardly a movement at all, down toward where the Krauts were being slaughtered.

11

On July 23, 1944, the Russians freed the first German death camp at Majdanek. Although Western journalists and photographers were brought in, few accounts or photographs appeared in the Western press. Majdanek was dismissed as Soviet propaganda.

On January 27, 1945, the Soviet Army liberated Auschwitz.

On April 4, 1945, the American XX Corps liberated Ohrdruf. On April 11, the notorious Dora slave labor camp at Nordhausen in the Harz Mountains was overrun, and on the same day Americans liberated Buchenwald. On April 15, a British armored division entered Belsen.

On April 21, 1945, Americans freed the Frigga work camp, near Linz, in Austria, Sergeant Payton Daltrey among them.

Chapter 13

1

WE KNEW THE WAR WAS OVER. RUMOR HAD IT THAT A
white airplane would fly over the lines to notify us of Victory in Europe.
We were on the Danube then, with Russian troops on the other side of the
river. Sometimes Russians came over by boat, unkempt, enthusiastic guys in
partial uniforms and their Munchkin-looking caps. They kissed any Americans they could catch and stole the company radio. When Captain Shitface
complained to a Russian colonel, the colonel assured him that the culprits
would be found out and shot. After that there was not much commerce between the Russians on the east bank and us on the west. We moved on up
the river in our halftracks, watching for the white airplane, beautiful cool
and warm days with the fruit trees in flower and puffs of cloud, as though
this were a part of the world where nothing bad could ever happen.

Advance elements ran into a firefight, and we moved with glacial reluctance up into position. No one wanted to get killed in the last days of the
war. Tanks came up and fired some rounds, and we shut down for two days,
with a convoy of supply trucks coming up with food for the prisoners who
would be liberated, before we started on.

We could smell the camp before we reached it. At first no one identified the smell, like some kind of garbage dump. Then we came over a low ridge, and there was the barbed wire, an impressive-looking structure that must be a cell block, and ranks of low wooden buildings. Inside a gate were about a million people in black-and-white-striped pajamas, waving their arms, and over the gate was a banner with the message WELCOM AMERICANS.

Bunge, the driver, apparently didn't want to go down there, either, because he slowed going down the hill, and a couple of other halftracks hustled on ahead of us to liberate the Frigga work camp.

Inside the gate we were surrounded by the prisoners in their chain gang outfits, clogs on their filthy feet. They all looked like clothes on hangers, they were so skinny, with faces carved out of hard, grainy wood. They were happy enough to see us, cheering and waving with big rotten-teeth smiles. And the terrible stink. One of them climbed onto my halftrack and motioned to us to keep going, pushing on through the crowd of prisoners, "Come Amerikaner, see!" something like that, enough so I got the gist and told Bunge to keep going. One of the other halftracks fell in behind us, as though they had a guide also. We ran out of the crowd and along the wire on muddy ground. Ahead there were two of the gray Kraut bulldozers, not moving.

So we came to the pit where they had tried to bury the corpses. The firefight must've been to hold us up until the bulldozers had covered over the bodies. They hadn't got it done. More than 1,800 bodies were counted in that pit. They were stacked neatly in the Kraut way, naked men and a few women.

I looked from face to face in the halftrack, and I knew that no one else, like I myself, could think what expression to wear on his face. Our guide was grinning, grinning, pointing.

Later Colonel Grady assembled the men and women from the village, who of course maintained they'd had no idea that such things were going on, they'd just thought it was a camp where prisoners of war were making some airplane parts for the Wehrmacht, and there was a rock quarry. We herded the villagers down to the camp to dig up the corpses that had been covered over by the bulldozers, taking some pleasure in their weeping and puking and whining. Our own bulldozers dug new pits, and the villagers carried the bodies to them and laid them out. I guess it made us feel better. There was an awful kind of helplessness.

Some of the prisoners died from our feeding them. They had to be weaned back onto food, thin gruel to start with. Luckily Colonel Grady knew enough to lay that out early on.

There were some Pole prisoners who were as excited about kissing American soldiers as the Russians had been, but by now we knew enough to keep a hand on our wallets and an eye on the radio. The Poles were in the best shape of any of the prisoners, as a detachment of them had come in only two weeks ago.

Tallboy and Joe Pugh and I and some others talked with a Brit prisoner of war who was not in bad shape, as he'd bailed out of a fighter in March.

I asked him what had happened to the guards.

"Most of them they drowned in the river yesterday," he said. "They had a kind of bucket brigade, you know, and they'd pass the buggers along down to the river. The Poles held them under and then let them float on down.

"The commandant was a Colonel Bultman, who escaped over the river. The real sadist was Colonel Haupt, who also escaped, too bad about that. There was a major they tore apart. Guards and kapos, they killed them." The Limey leftenant discussed it calmly.

The camp was a work camp, slave labor, all nationalities but mostly Russian, French, Hungarian, and Polish, plus some Italian politicals and some Gypsies. The cell block was for important political prisoners. There had been a Rothschild there, and a member of the Polish nobility—but they were gone, flown out in a Junkers last month.

Outside the gate, the building a little way up the ridge was the officers' barracks. The officers had girl prisoners for sex. The attractive girls among the prisoners were assigned to the officers, and some of the officers kept their mistresses in rooms in the village, away from the stink of the camp.

The prisoners who had mechanical abilities were assigned to the aircraft factory nearer the village, marched there at five o'clock in the morning and back at five o'clock at night. Less fortunate prisoners, especially the Russians, worked in the quarry breaking rock. There were 186 steps down into the quarry, 186 back up. Prisoners did not make their twenty or thirty trips a day for many days.

Colonel Haupt liked to hang out on the rim of the quarry with his Luger and shoot anybody who halted to rest on the climb out. Others would be nailed to carry the bodies out, and they had better not pause to rest, either. Haupt had a number of other nifty tricks for Luger practice as well. He was the worst of the Krauts, the Limey said.

We took on what seemed our priority, which was feeding those poor people in their stripes and clogs, keeping order mostly. You had to hold them back from gorging on what bread and meat and carrot and turnip stew the cooks were able to jack up in quantity, so they wouldn't die in convulsions as we saw more than one of them do, feeding them in that terrible stink that only diminished when the bodies had been reburied in trenches, but many among them were too far gone, dying, and they had to be taken care of, too. It was both the worst time of the war, there at the very end of it, and the best; because the platoon, company, battalion were not just killing Krauts but trying to save lives, and we did try, and we did save lives, and we were better for it, though still that awful deep-running current of outrage for the deadly cocksuckers who would do a thing like this ran through and underneath everything.

For some reason the prisoners weren't crazy to break out and start walking home, wherever home was—as though they had to savor their liberation on the site, and the food furnished to them by us and later the Swedish Red Cross.

I remembered Stan Takahashi saying that Manzanar was not a real concentration camp. Little did he know.

The Limey took us through the cell block, which was empty now. The accommodations were not bad for a prison camp. The cells had writing tables; some of them had easy chairs, cots with white coverlets, a crucifix on a wall. The emptiness of the place, echoing with our boots, was spooky.

Later I went over for a look-see at the officers' quarters with Tallboy and Lieutenant Smithers. There was a big downstairs common room, with easy chairs and sofas and lamps, an office, and a window looking out on the barbed wire and the hovels of the prisoners behind the wire. There were women there, not bad-looking, either. Tallboy took upstairs a pretty Gypsy woman, who was willing enough, and came down with a case of crabs that hung on for a month.

Lieutenant Smithers, who prowled around in the office, called me over. He held a parchment lampshade out at a slant from the lamp, and he pointed at it with his other hand. I approached with that end-of-the-war reluctance, hoping this was not just one more thing I didn't want to have to know about, and it was that, all right, it was a tattoo on the lampshade, a heart with a double eagle head looking over the top, and in the heart some Cyrillic words, a tattoo that had belonged on somebody's body once.

2

About ten days after we'd liberated the camp, Lieutenant Smithers came off the phone with a finger pointed at me. We were in the commons of the officers' barracks.

"Daltrey, there's another report that bird Haupt's been seen in the village. Visiting some snatch there. Take a couple of guys and go take a look. Sometime it'll maybe not be a false alarm."

Robbie and Bunker and I took off in the company jeep, Robbie driving and Bunker in the back. I sat with a boot braced up on the dash and a .45 holstered on my belt. There'd been three reports of Colonel Haupt seen in town, from suck-up villagers.

Robbie drove up the dirt road to the village past the dump of rusting Kraut earthmoving equipment. Down in the next valley were the big hangar buildings of the closed-up aircraft factory, black humped roofs gleaming in the sun. From the ridge we could look back on the camp in its wire-enclosed spread backed up by the glistening ocher and shadowed rock face of the quarry, with its top fringe of grasses and black woods.

A Red Cross flag stirred in a little wind. The Swedish Red Cross had come in to take charge of the poor bastard inmates. They knew from other liberated camps how to bring these skeletons back from starvation. The war was definitely over, and rumors kept coming that we'd be moving on north along the river.

Robbie roared on into the town with its two-story tile-roofed houses like a toy village, where the good Austrians claimed they hadn't known of the camp five miles away, that you could smell when the wind was right, and even when it wasn't, and see the prisoners going in files to and from the aircraft parts factory. We knew the place where Haupt had been seen, and Robbie slammed the jeep to a halt before the building with a closed-up pharmacy on the ground floor. The door to the apartment upstairs was bolted, but Bunker shouldered it open, and I sprinted up the stairs with the other two behind me. Ahead I heard a woman's screeched warning.

I shoved open another door and followed the .45 in. A fat, blond young woman in a petticoat stood barefoot by the window as though thinking of jumping out. A man in a civilian jacket, corduroy pants, a blue shirt, and a striped tie faced me, smiling.

"Colonel Haupt?" I said, as the others came in behind me.

He made a shrugging motion of his upper body, still smiling. "Hi, fellows!" he said. "Any of you fellows from New Jersey?" he asked.

I felt silly holding the .45, so I holstered it. Robbie and Bunker carried M-1s.

"I spent seven years in Lakewood," Haupt said, no trace of a Kraut accent. "Seven good years," he said, smiling, nodding.

The woman sat down on a window seat, hands in her lap. She had a creamy pink-and-pale fat-girl complexion, and she stared anxiously at me.

Haupt had a dark, lined face with neatly brushed hair growing low on his forehead.

"There was a nice little bar there where you could get a good lager," he went on. "Or a nice bottle of Gerolsteiner if you were inclined."

"Pat!" Bunker said, and I put my hand on the butt of the .45 when the Kraut unbuttoned his jacket. He took the jacket off and laid it on the bed.

He made a gesture, asking permission, and stepped to the big armoire against the wall. I drew the .45 as he opened the door of the armoire. He took from a hanger a Kraut uniform blouse and armed into it. It had a colonel's insignia on the collar, and the black lapels of the SS.

The girl murmured in German.

"My uncle is American," the colonel went on. "He is a butcher there. A fine modern shop, very nice. All modern things. I worked for him."

"I understood you were a butcher here," I said.

His smile did not falter. "I kept company with a very nice girl there," he went on. "Her father was an automobile dealer. She was very nice. Sometimes we would go for picnics.

"Once I went with her to New York. We went to the Statue of Liberty, to a film also. We had supper there. We walked on Fifth Avenue among the rich people. It was very nice."

He made the permission gesture again and took a uniform cap from the shelf of the armoire and donned it. Now he wore a colonel's cap and blouse, with the brown corduroy trousers and the striped tie. He had straightened so he was standing at attention, his shiny shoes set at right angles to each other.

I told him he was under arrest.

He shook his head. I could see a gold-filled tooth at the corner of his lips. He had a little hairline mustache like Errol Flynn's, which you didn't notice right away because of the darkness of his face.

"Ah, no," he said. His voice had become deeper, that harsh Germanic bark. "I will only surrender to a person of proper rank," he said. "I will not surrender to a sergeant!"

"Yes, you will," I said.

He shook his head again. He made a military right face and started toward the door beyond the bed.

"Halt!" I said, cocking the .45.

He marched toward the door. I skipped after him and swatted him hard on the back of the head with the barrel of the .45. The woman screamed as Haupt went down on his face, the cap rolling free.

I bent over him as he laboriously turned on his back. He glared up at me, his mouth working. He spat in my face. I jerked upright, swiping at my cheek. Then I jammed the muzzle of the .45 into his mouth. My finger contracted on the trigger, but just then Bunker swung his combat boot and kicked the colonel in the head, putting out the lights.

There was no point killing him if he didn't know I was killing him.

"Get him out of here," I said, boosting myself off him.

3

Another sergeant, Tom Dowling, and I were sent to translators' school at the University of Grenoble in May of 1945. We came up to Paris whenever we could get away, and one night we were eating dinner in a hot little café on the Left Bank when somebody started throwing torn-off bits of breadstick. Tom and I scowled at each other over our bottle of *rouge*. From time to time bits of crusted bread bounced off us or the table. I finally figured that I was the target.

It was Americans mostly, some uniformed, some not. Just about everybody in the place had girls but Tom and me. It was one big party in Paris at that time, and we felt very out of it down in Grenoble. I had never looked up Corinne.

Finally I approached the table by the window where a major was sitting alone over a demitasse. The glass that had held the breadsticks was depleted from his games. He grinned drunkenly at me. He was Mr. Chapman from San Diego State College.

"Hullo there, Daltrey!"

"Hello, Mr. Chapman!" I said, making about a third of a salute.

"Major," he slurred, pointing to his shoulder pip. His eyeballs looked as though they'd been soaked in olive oil, his forehead was slick with sweat, and his tie was loose.

"What are you doing here, Major?"

"Enjoying life," he said and huff-huffed a laugh. "And what are you doing, Sergeant?"

I told him, standing uncomfortably beside his table while the couple at the next table tried to ignore us. Major Chapman's eyes didn't focus when he regarded me, as though he were fixed on somebody over my right shoulder. Major Shitface.

"Daltrey," he said in a low voice. "I have managed to imbibe more alcohol than my system seems able to process. May I ask you to help me home? I have been sending signals your way for the last twenty minutes."

Tom had paid our *addition,* and he and I helped Major Chapman, hard-breathing, out of the restaurant to the cooler air of the street, where Chapman took some deep sucks of breath. He stank of smoke and red wine. It turned out he was quartered at a narrow little hotel down the street, and we got him into an ancient elevator from which he waved a feeble good night as he was borne upward.

"Come see me tomorrow, Daltrey!" he called, just as he ascended out of sight.

4

He was not all that sober the next morning, either, but we went along to the café on the corner and had coffee and croissants.

"Daltrey," Major Chapman said with his jaw gritted as though he were trying to keep his face from falling apart. "What has happened to your determination to become a writer?"

"I got a letter from the editor of *Black Mask* saying he would help me get published there if I wanted to work with him."

"Ah!" the major said, sipping coffee. He squinted at me with what he must have thought was a steely gaze. "And have you in fact been published in *Black Mask*? I am interested, of course, in the literary progress of my former students."

"Well, sir, just about that time I got the letter from this editor, I'd started reading Faulkner. 'The Bear' in particular."

"Ha!" he said, rubbing his hands together and grinning. "Oh, my goodness, yes! 'The Bear!' So that was the end of your private eye ambitions?"

"Well, I've been busy fighting a war."

"And have you been provided with material for a war novel?"

"The liberation of the Frigga work camp, for one."

"Ah? And what of your theories of molestation?"

"I saw one of the lampshades."

"Really!"

He asked me to accompany him that night to a performance of *Ubu Roi* at a smelly little theater on the Left Bank. The performance in French was deeper water than my immersion in Langue et Littérature, and halfway through I was pretty much out of it, but Major Chapman was having a high time, drinking brandy out of a flask and ready for another merry night of breadstick throwing. I got him into his wrought-iron and brass-curlicued elevator again and was ordered to meet him at his office at *Stars and Stripes* the next day.

There it turned out that he was the editor of a magazine called *Soldiers' Monthly,* and I could consider myself detached to *Stars and Stripes,* with the assignment to write a piece on the liberation of the Frigga camp for the magazine.

In Paris I received a letter from Pogey. He had seen in the *San Diego Union* that Barbara Bonington was engaged to Daniel Rothenberg, a medical intern at Stanford, wedding in June. By this time Bonny and I hadn't corresponded for months.

Long ago she had warned me she would marry a doctor.

Only three days later, Tom Dowling came up to Paris from *Langue et Littérature* in Grenoble, with a battered yellow telegram that had been forwarded to me all over France.

It had been sent by Barbara Bonington on January 2, 1944. The address should have brought it to me, except that I had moved along a couple of times. It had taken five months to reach me.

PAYTON I AM SURE YOU ARE IN THIS TERRIBLE BATTLE AND I PRAY AND PRAY YOU ARE NOT HURT STOP PLEASE COME BACK TO ME.

Shit!

BOOK THREE

Love and War
in California

Chapter 14

1

IN NOVEMBER OF 1945, ATTACHED TO *STARS AND STRIPES*, I was sent by *Soldiers' Monthly* to report on the War Crimes Trials in Nuremberg and attended the execution of Colonel Haupt.

When *Soldiers' Monthly* folded, about Christmastime, I received my discharge. In New York City, I enrolled at Columbia University for two semesters on the GI Bill to get my B.A.

Tully lived in New York City, in the Village, and wrote for the *Village Voice* and a number of small, lefty political journals. He and I had several barroom evenings in Manhattan. He did love to regale an audience with his testimony, or the lack of it, before the House Un-American Activities Committee. He had not had to go to jail.

At Columbia I began working on a novel, for which my carefully preserved carbons and recollected letters to Bonny and others were a great aid. B.A. in hand, I enrolled as a graduate student in the Writers' Workshop at the University of Iowa, along with a regiment of World War II former soldiers, sailors, and fliers working on war novels. With a contract and an advance from Random House, I married a young woman, Norma Stowe, from my agent's office and spent a year in Cuernavaca (cheaper living in Mexico) finishing revisions.

Publishing wisdom in the late forties held that novels of World War II would not be acceptable by the public until at least ten years after the conclusion of the war, as per the huge success of Erich Maria Remarque's *All Quiet on the Western Front* after World War I. My novel, *Staying Alive*, was published in 1954, the wartime romance of an idealistic American soldier and a young Frenchwoman, whose head had been shaved by partisans for her affair with a German officer, against a background of the Battle of the Bulge.

The novel's sales were disappointing, and I came to look upon it as a sentimental melodramatization and a canard upon a young Frenchwoman who had treated me better than I deserved and been lied about and insulted for her pains.

2

In 1958, when my second novel, my San Diego novel, my big novel, *Gates of Bone,* was in press at Random House, Norma and I were living in San Francisco. I knew from sources that Bonny was a doctor in ob-gyn practice nearby in Palo Alto. She and her husband, a surgeon, had a kid. So did Norma and I, a boy named Jonathan.

Pogey, married, no children, was an executive of a huge construction corporation in Dallas. We exchanged Christmas cards, with brief annual notes.

Stan Takahashi had enlisted in the Army when the Nisei in the Relocation Centers had been allowed to do so. He lost an arm in Italy and became a medical researcher for one of the big drug outfits in Buffalo, New York. I never saw him again, after Bonny's and my visit to him in his concentration camp.

I had also lost track of Calvin King.

Elizabeth Fletcher was often in the news. As a protégée of Errol Flynn's, she danced in three successful motion pictures. She married a studio executive, Martin Ayoob, had a child by him and divorced him, married a hotel heir, Nicky Billings, and divorced him to marry an actor named Brian Forman, whom she divorced under messy circumstances.

Errol Flynn died in 1959 at the age of 50. The death certificate indicated as the causes of death myocardial infarction, coronary thrombosis, coronary atherosclerosis, and liver degeneration and sclerosis, although it was widely believed he had killed himself overdosing with morphine— gone off the taffrail like Martin Eden. The rumors that he had been a Nazi spy followed him to the grave.

In 1957, I had returned to San Diego for my father's funeral, thankful that he had not lived to see how I had mistreated him in *Gates of Bone.*

Nor would Bonny, Pogey, or Liz be pleased by characters in *Gates.*

The novel was what is called a bildungsroman, a narrative of a young man's youth and education. No doubt it melodramatized my youth, as my first novel had melodramatized my war experiences. In the ending Lyn and Jack were reunited, their misunderstandings on hold in a grand, and for that time shocking, sex scene. "Marred by the creak of bedsprings," the *New Yorker* reviewer was to cluck, although the sex scene took place in a car, not on a bed. The final scene had the lovers parted by the war, with a good hope that they would be reunited.

There were some good reviews, and the novel spent ten weeks on the the *New York Times* best-seller list. It was nominated for, but did not receive, a Pulitzer. There was a film option. *Gates of Bone* didn't make me rich, however—nor famous, except in San Diego, where I would never live again. There were controversies over it in the San Diego newspapers and letters to the editor, and it was denounced from the pulpit in my hometown as "a libel on San Diego's youth." (Nothing quite so bracing to an author as a denunciation from the pulpit!) I received some fan mail, assured by correspondents that "That's the story of my life!" enough times to make me think I had indeed brushed universal themes of the Depression and the war. The novel stayed in press for many years. As the British critic Cyril Connolly was to insist, a novel still in print ten years after its publication had become a classic. *Gates* was to become a classic.

It had not yet been published, however, when I saw Bonny again.

Chapter 15

1

1958

I SAT AT THE BAR OF THE PACIFIC TENNIS CLUB IN SAN Francisco on a Saturday morning, listening to the plock of tennis balls outside the floor-to-ceiling windows and regarding my sweaty countenance in the mirror behind the bar, where Joe the barman polished a glass. My singles opponent, a younger-than-I lawyer, had headed for the dressing room, having whipped me in straight sets.

I rubbed the scar just above my knee, amused at my tendency to limp when losing at tennis.

The women's foursome from Court Three, part of a member-guest tournament, surged into the bar from the stairs, young women with trim legs, three of them with real estate hairdos, the fourth with blond hair in a bun and wisps webbing over her forehead, whose backhands-down-the-line I had been admiring, and who was Bonny Bonington aka Barbara Rothenberg, M.D.

Mutual glances followed by cool smiles of greeting.

"Hello, Bonny," I said.

Nodding, smiling, she passed on along with her group. Glancing back at me, she said, without inflection, "Hello, Payton."

She'd be thirty-five. How well I remembered that left-handed backhand that had cost her father a lot of money.

She was in that position I remembered from wartime girlseeking, the targeted one surrounded by a defensive cordon of other females, so you had to figure a way to flush her out of the pocket.

My wife was still in action on Court Five, identifiable by her long-brimmed white cap.

One of Bonny's foursome was Betty Warloe, with whom I had some acquaintance. Bonny gave me an arched-eyebrow glance when I came over. Slick of perspiration on her chest, breasts poking at her white shirt, fine down of blond hairs on her tanned arm.

"Betty," I said, "could I have a few words with this lady? We are old friends from San Diego."

Bonny rose and waited to be directed. I was acutely conscious of the memory of her with Johnny Pierce in the Caff at San Diego State on the morning after Pearl Harbor.

With a slight pressure on her damp back, I pointed her to the second table down.

Seated opposite her, I searched her face for signs and portents.

"What happened?" I said.

"Pardon me?"

"Still wondering what it was all about."

"Oh, Payton; after all these years?"

"Still wondering after all these years. I was grateful for your letters, but I must say that they were not your letters."

She looked into my eyes. "They were always merry and bright, were they not?" she said.

"I didn't get the telegram you sent in January until five months later. In April."

She tipped her head to one side. "I apologize for that moment of panic," she said. "I was sure you were in the Battle of the Bulge. Were you wounded? I thought you must've been wounded."

"I was. Nothing to brag about."

Her partners at the other table were regarding us with interest. Some of the ladies at the Pacific Tennis Club had read my novel.

"But what changed you?" I said. "You had some kind of experience or epiphany that changed you into an absolute tower of determination to get your medical degree and to be Barbara, and to hell with old boyfriends. What happened?"

She gazed into my eyes, frowning delicately.

"I had a date with someone out in East San Diego," I went on doggedly. "I believe I parked my car near Alice Hoagland's house, where Liz was staying. Where some observer must have reported it to you."

Bonny shook her head. The corners of her lips tucked in, as though she were going to smile. But she didn't smile.

"All I did with Liz was drive her to LA and deliver her to Errol Flynn's."

"Liz the movie star."

"Yes."

Bonny gave a crisp shake of her blond head. "Congratulations on your novel, Payton. I'd read some of the early parts in your good letters."

I could feel my face heat up at the thought of her reading *Gates of Bone* when it was published, in October.

"Your husband's a doctor, too?" I asked, though I already knew that.

"He's an orthopedic surgeon."

"You live in Palo Alto?"

"Down the Peninsula."

"Kids?"

"Two girls. And you?"

"A boy, and one on the way."

"Congratulations, Payton," she said again.

"Tell me, was it your mother?"

"I think I must get back to my ladies. It was nice to see you, Payton."

So she left. Nice legs, slim hips. I had learned nothing.

My wife glanced appraisingly at my first love when I pointed her out, at lunch with her foursome. Norma's long-billed cap lay on the table before us. Her face was slick and whitish with sunscreen.

"Good hair," Norma said.

241

She patted my arm. She was two months along on a second child.

I phoned Betty, whose guest Bonny had been. Bonny was a friend of a friend. She and her husband were both in practice in Palo Alto. They were both graduates of Stanford Med. I still had found out nothing.

I had been happy to settle anywhere but San Diego, and San Francisco was Norma's hometown. Weezie had moved to Hawaii. My mother lived in Palm Springs with her husband, a retired Army colonel with some family bucks. I drove an MG, Norma a Mercury station wagon. We frequently visited Norma's parents in Marin County, who loved their bright grandson Jon. We were a happy, bourgeois family, living on my advance on *Gates*.

May 18, 1958

Dear Bonny,

Proust (the author of Remembrance of Things Past*) says that one's every love affair is a reflection of his first one. You were my first real love affair, but I can't say that my other love affairs (not so many as all that) have been such a reflection. However, the characters of my new novel, coming out in the fall, reflect Proust's dictum.*

I wonder what you will think of Gates of Bone. *There are characters you will recognize: Lyn and Jack, Virginia and Dakin and Eve. Parents.*

*If you have read Fenimore Cooper's Leatherstocking Tales (*The Last of the Mohicans, *etc.) you will have noticed that Cooper's "good" girls are fair, his "bad" girls dark. I have followed his formula. In* Gates, *Lyn is fair, consequently "good." Virginia is dark, hence "bad," i.e., at least more free and easy morally than my "good" girl, although not so free and easy as Eve Corey, who is meant to be the shocking far-out frontier-marker. These characters are based upon people you will recognize, including yourself. They are deeply involved in the theme, which is an obsession of mine you will remember.*

Flannery O'Connor, referring to a writer's available material, says that any writer who has made his way through childhood has material enough to last his lifetime.

So in Gates *you will see not only character but plot derived from our relationship.*

This letter is my apology for the big sex scene. Your mother will find it shocking. Maybe you will, too. I apologize for the Abba-Zabba Bar sequence. There will also be friends and acquaintances who are going to choose to think it really happened. Of course it did not, and all I can do is rationalize it as a literary necessity.

Thanks to you for the material upon which my forthcoming novel has been nourished. I will write no more fiction. I am embarrassed that my fiction has been dependent upon the exploitation of my friends and lovers: on a Frenchwoman with whom I had the affair described in Staying Alive; *upon a romanticization of our affair in* Gates. *Indeed, upon my friend Pogey Malcolm, who must recognize himself as Chad in* Gates. *Upon my father, whom I abused unforgivably. Indeed, this all must be looked upon as a betrayal of personal ties, as the sin of turning human beings into things. As I say, I will write no more lies, and, since as you may remember it has been my desire to make the world a better place, I will from now on turn what talents I have to nonfiction. You may take this as a compliment, and as an apology.*

Regards,
Payton

That letter was never sent.

1965

That year my little family was facing the shorts, so I took a job teaching a writing seminar at UCLA. *Gates of Bone* still had a cult following in Southern California, and I fitted right in to a comfortable slot as a visiting writer. I commuted home to San Francisco on weekends to be with my family, for Norma didn't want the children's schooling disarrayed by a move to LA.

A writer knows that if he goes to New York something advantageous may happen to him just because the local powers become aware of his existence. So is it also with Hollywood, where the fact that I was in LA caused my agent to make some phone calls. Presently he was dickering for a film option on *Gates of Bone*. I had a meeting with the prospective producer, who was not a fountain of enthusiasm for the novel, but who told me Elizabeth Fletcher was hoping to see me while I was in Los Angeles.

And so it was that I called upon Liz in her Italianate mansion in Bel Air.

Drinks were served by a pretty young maid in a proper maid's costume with a lacy apron. Liz and I drank mimosas. She finished hers in two gulps and ordered another. She was between husbands and didn't wish to talk about any of them. Dinner was served by a young Mexican waiter who bowed a lot. With dinner Liz drank kir royales. She was a champagne girl, and why not? After dinner we went for a swim, Liz naked and sleek, what I could see of her by moonlight, as though she were still in her twenties, and then to bed in the pool house. The bed was occupied by ghosts, Liz's, mine, and others'. Between bouts she directed me to open a bottle of champagne from a little refrigerator set into the wall. I wondered whether the pop of the cork marked the start of a race or an execution.

I supposed it was some sign of consequence that I could enjoy the favors of a major motion picture star in her boudoir, but none of the pleasures of my life had ever turned to shit so fast.

It came to seem to me that Liz, and not Liz so much as some complicated image of Liz in my mind, a stew of emotion, sensation, visual erotics, remembrance, willfulness, and sibling rivalry, had hung over my life like a dark angel. Dark! Liz dark and Bonny fair, the dark and the light. I had never understood my obsession with her, which Bonny must have realized. Certainly I had attended all her films, the dancing ones when she had partnered Harrison Kelly, the dramatic ones, and now the coasting ones of the height of her reputation. I had long realized that, as a writer, I was a finishing-freak; a writer, like a lexicographer working his way from *A* to *Z,* had to be such a completion-nut. So my affair with Liz was finally rounded off, as it seemed my affair with Bonny would never be.

The pool house was furnished with living, sleeping, eating, cooking, and bathroom accommodations. In the morning I sat across from Liz sipping mimosas at a marble-topped table set in a window that looked out through diaphanous curtains that stirred in a little wind off the ocean, over the swimming pool to the greenish sea of smog that was the LA Basin.

Liz had bathed and wore a white terrycloth robe and a towel wrapped like a turban over her hair. Her face was luminously pale, rather small-eyed without makeup, but her sculptured cheekbones and the sweet folds of her lips were classically beautiful.

I felt scruffy and unshaven in my gray flannels and limp white shirt. I had had from her information that confirmed what Esther Carnes had implied, that it was Liz who had insisted that Richie hire the private detective to investigate Val's past.

"I didn't think he was going to do anything about her! He just dithered. I was so mad at him! And David was mad at him. David depended on him!"

She had never seen Pancho Hagen again.

This was Hollywood, where sex as well as lunch is only a prelude to talking about properties, roles, and money. She was interested in the role of Eve in *Gates of Bone*. United Artists would option the film rights for her.

"Payton," she said firmly, "you have to change some of the Eve scenes. You know, she's very hard, she's self-centered, she's had to be! But you will change her, won't you?"

Some abysses were deep and some were shallow, and in Hollywood shallow abysses were followed by deeper and deeper ones.

"That's a different book from mine, Liz," I said.

"But I want to make *Gates!*"

"Eve as the bad girl is the key to the story!"

"She can think she's been so bad, she can say so—Jack can think so, too! But we have to know she hasn't been. That she did it all for Christy."

That wasn't the Eve of *Gates* that I had conceived, and Liz was too old for the role, twice as old as Eve would have been, twice as beautiful also, and too important. But if I signed an option with United Artists and the studio exercised it, Eve was not my property anymore. I knew that a film often required a stronger and simpler dramatic line than that of the novel from which it was adapted, as well as the support of a bankable star, and of course if Liz were to star in *Gates,* she had to be the heroine.

"I can't do it, Liz."

"Toby thinks we should hire an experienced dramatist, Payton. I so hoped you could do it."

I shook my head. Payment for first draft screenplay was about fifty thousand dollars, which I might be blasé about, but the actual sale of the screen rights, if they decided to make the film, was big, big bucks.

I snapped my fingers beneath the tabletop, smiling at Liz. The spectacles of the producer, Toby Schlicter, sported individual dark wings of glass that folded down over the lenses, turning them into dark glasses, or that could be raised into a kind of shelf that made him look like a Nazi interrogator.

He had announced that he had little faith in the ability of novelists to "lick" the film adaptations of their novels.

A breath of breeze rippled the swimming pool and blew the curtains in soft insistent folds.

Liz's smile had a sweet/sad good-bye quality to it. When I rose, she offered her makeupless cheek for me to kiss.

"Please call me next time you're in town, Payton," she said. "We can drink some more Veuve Clicquot!"

"Sounds great!" I said.

It may be that the reappearance of Liz Fletcher in my life wrecked my marriage, for it was as though Norma knew intuitively of my disloyalty, and nothing between us seemed to work after that.

I had rather willfully rejected a lot of money on the film United Artists might have made of *Gates of Bone,* about which there were to be some bitter recriminations. Norma wanted more money than I provided, and she found a job at the University of California Press. She went to live in Berkeley with our children, whom she was to retain as the "nurturer." Divorced, I left the left coast for New York and some publisher negotiations, then went to Northern Ireland to accumulate the facts and wisdom to write a book about the Troubles. Wasn't it my ambition to try to make the world a better place? At least I had not contributed to the delinquency of *Gates of Bone,* which, if it was not the Great American Novel, was at least the Great San Diego Novel.

2

1971

When my second wife, Gretchen Fairchild, and I returned from Indonesia, she spent most of a month in the darkroom working on the photographs for the book on East Timor. When she was done, and the text and photographs sent off to Viking, we flew off to Paris on a vacation and a whim of mine.

We prowled Montmartre, heading down from Sacre Coeur on the

steep, narrow streets. I assured myself that I was not looking for Corinne exactly, but there seemed a possibility that I would run into her, on the streets or in some bistro, and she would (I knew she wouldn't) look exactly the same. Ever since the war, maybe once a month I had experienced a little cold shot of shame for my casual mistreatment of her.

Montmartre had the feel of a village: open-air markets, blue-collar people, a general workaday bustle. In the Place des Abbesses, Gretchen and I drank vermouth in a brasserie, with advertisements for Corsican wine on the walls and that exhalation of *vin ordinaire* that Dos Passos had likened to the smell of sawdust. I remembered the brasserie but could not connect it to Corinne's *parc* in the tangle of cobbled streets.

Outside, the Parisian spring was not warm enough for the bright silk dress Gretchen was wearing—goose bumps noticeable on her arms, white beret on her red hair, her Hasselblad hanging like a sawed-off bazooka under her arm. Parisians, who were sick of tourists with their cameras, took her seriously because she carried a serious camera. She was not, however, photographically impressed with Sacre Coeur or Montmartre in general, except for the tangle of stone of the cemetery.

"So you can't locate your wartime love nest, *mon vieux*?" she said.

"She had a room in the attic of a building across from a little *parc*. I have the unlikely thought that I'll meet her on the street and ask her to forgive me, and she will. And I can forget about her."

I had explained to my wife what there was to forgive. There had been a tincture of *A Farewell to Arms* in my relationship with Corinne. I had given her the expectation that I was going to desert the war for love of her. Instead I had deserted her to return to the Battle of the Bulge. It was as though the war had provided me with an opportunity to be a shit, like the officers of whom I disapproved, and I had taken it.

She may have thought I had been killed in the Ardennes. After the war, when I was in Paris writing for *Soldiers' Monthly*, I had never tried to find her.

"There are many excuses in wartime," Gretchen said. "*Sacre bleu!*" She was having fun with French expletives.

We trod the narrow sidewalks. An old gent in a kind of frock coat, with a voluminous bow tie, raised his hat to Gretchen, who rewarded him with her lovely smile.

"I remember that place," I said, pointing to a corner café. "They used to sing *'Quatre-vingt Chasseurs'* in there. Just roaring out the verses. Night after night, as I recall it."

"I heard it sung by a gang of Frenchmen at Namche Bazar on the route up to Everest Base Camp," Gretchen said. "Yes, all its verses."

"Perhaps it sounded better in the thin air of the Himalayas."

"I believe it did not!" She laughed her joyful laugh.

"She was no more a professional prostitute than I was a professional soldier," I said.

"You have been to Paris several times," Gretchen said. "Why this now, *parbleu?*"

The recollection of having acted badly pestered me like the mouse behind the headboard.

"My thing," I said.

"Surely it is a stretch for even your so-expansible complaint, *mon ami*," Gretchen said. She unshipped her camera and went into photographer mode, long-legged, gawky, and very deft. Across the street in a second-story window, a girl child with an unkempt pouf of black hair was revealed with her doll held against her breast, three electric or telephone wires paralleling across the window in front of her. Before Gretchen could snap her picture, the girl had vanished.

"*Merde alors!*" Gretchen said, reassembling herself.

At that time of our happiness together, she must have already harbored the evil cells that were to molest her to death.

She and I collaborated on two books of photographs by her and text by me, including a high degree of social conscience on Tibet and East Timor, books that were popular enough to sell well, and make me proud besides.

Chapter 16

1985

Elizabeth fletcher's funeral was, of course, at Forest Lawn, a rolling green campus, with views out over Glendale, and black-clad ranks of Hollywood elderly attending the services for one of their own.

Across a crowded room, in a fume of calla lilies and expensive perfume, I glimpsed Dr. Barbara Rothenberg. She wore a long-sleeved black dress and raised a gloved hand to lift a fringe of veil on her black velvet crush hat. Her face was appropriately pale.

This was December 1985. As we listened to the eulogies, Bonny shifted her weight from one black nylon leg to the other, slim if not as slender as she was as the eighteen-year-old flame of my life. Errol Flynn had called her "the fair one," as I had been "the young Martin Eden." Under the expensive hat a lock of silver hair slid back like a curtain as she smiled stiffly at me, pink-faced with the recognition of the old boyfriend.

She was a divorcée, I knew. She had served on the board of Stanford Hospital. She had been an important figure in Planned Parenthood, perhaps a director. Once I had glimpsed her on CNN amid a squad of stern-looking women, with a banner overhead.

The drill now was to file past the casket where Liz Fletcher lay in beige silk upholstery, powdered, rouged, long-lashed old eyes closed. The pink lips of that famous pouty mouth gave me my first blow job. I followed a skinny lady with a cane, following an aged gent in an Armani suit.

Bonny was somewhere behind me.

I had had occasion to compare memorial services. This did not seem as classy as Liz deserved. She was a considerable star, briefly of the brightest luminosity. For a time she had the power to induce United Artists to contract for films she might star in, such as *Gates of Bone.*

Alzheimer's struck her down at what seemed a young age by my sexagenarian standard. She spent her last years diapered and wheelchaired in a home, her medication-swollen face with an eternal blank and pouty smile. When I visited her I had been able to rouse her interest by speaking of my brother, Richard, but the interest had faded quickly.

Bonny and I faced each other again as I started out the door, and I blessed the fact that I did not have a substantial gut and did possess a good proportion of my hair as well as a soon-to-be-surgically-corrected limp. I waited for her outside, feeling superior to the frailer elderly passing out of the mortuary. Below us lay miles of suburban Glendale, preternaturally clear in the smog-controlled and winter air.

Bonny appeared out of the farther doorway, donning dark glasses. I hastened to join her in the general exodus. There was a moment of indecision as both of us wondered whether or not to brush lips. She extended a gloved hand. "Hello, Payton."

"Can I bear you away from here?"

"I have a car. I'm staying with my daughter in Santa Monica."

We moved together onto the asphalt expanse of the parking lot, behind a man in a wheelchair pushed by a Filipino attendant.

When Bonny took my arm I felt a laughable electric chill.

"What a sad occasion for us to meet again," she said. "Your old flame."

"No, Bonny, you were my flame. She was my brother's fiancée."

She tossed her head in a recollecting way. "Those old ambiguities."

I prayed that she would not utter some cliché that would turn me off like a cold shower. Holding my arm, she stretched her legs to keep pace, her black-stockinged calf a precise distance from my gray flannel, not too close nor too far, either.

Once I had shouted at her that she would end up like her mother.

"That first time I met your mother," I said, "she looked at me as though I was Jack the Ripper."

"She's still alive," Bonny said. "Still playing bridge."

I directed her toward my car and opened the door for her. LA sunshine darted along the fenders.

"What about my car?"

"We'll come back for it later."

She slipped inside, tucking the seat of her skirt beneath her with a grace I admired. She sat with her handbag in her lap, hands clasped on top of it. Around us people slammed car doors; a black Chrysler headed past. The Jag's engine hummed to life.

Where were we headed? Down into LA. In my youth Los Angeles had been the City of Evil.

"So famous authors drive Jaguars," Bonny says.

"It was Gretchen's."

"I heard she died of cancer," she murmured.

"A folly of the Lord's." I could hear the clutch in my voice that I had meant to be light. "She was one of the good ones," I added.

"I'm sorry."

"Me, too."

"Two wives?" Bonny asked.

I nodded. "And you are divorced?"

"Dan wanted a younger wife." She laid her hands to her cheeks.

"I'm sorry," I said.

"I'm not," Bonny said.

"Are you still in practice?"

"Mostly retired. I don't take on new patients. I do some tours with DWW."

"What's DWW?"

"Doctors with Wings. It's an American version of Doctors Without Borders."

"Good for you."

"And you?" Bonny said.

"Researching a book on California water."

"Good for you. Where are we going?"

"To have a drink. Then dinner."

"I'm having dinner with my daughter and her family."

"Call her and call it off. Surely you knew you'd see me at Liz's funeral, and surely you knew I'd invite you for a drink and dinner."

Her blue eye flashed at me.

"Pick up where we left off," I said.

"That's so romantic!" she said, but not as though she really thought so.

It seemed that everything I said was off target, and maybe Bonny was feeling the same thing.

"You ruined my reputation with *Gates of Bone,*" she said cheerfully. "I can never go back to San Diego. I'm so grateful!"

"The writer contrives character and situation from primary felt experience," I said. "I apologized lengthily in a letter I never sent you."

Her eye flicked at me again, and away.

"Call your daughter and tell her you are having dinner with an old, old boyfriend."

"All right," she said.

We ate dinner in a shadowy Los Angeles clip joint called the San Andreas Fault, at a corner table with a bottle of forty-two-dollar cabernet before us, discussing our families. I had two children whom I did not know very well because they had been raised by their mother after the divorce: Jonathan, who taught English lit at the University of Wisconsin, and Diane, who lived in Denver with her stock-salesman husband and two children and who had a good backhand.

Bonny had two children also, both girls; grandchildren also. I lived in San Francisco, on Telegraph Hill, mostly alone. She had a condo in Palo Alto, a condo on the island of Hawaii, and a shared apartment in Paris. She had taken up golf. There were hints of men in her life. In politics we were both old-fashioned tax-and-spend liberals. Her Santa Monica daughter was a Republican, which was lamented. I pointed out that I disapproved of golf. I recalled having seen her in a newspaper photograph of Planned Parenthood brass.

"I held opinions that were not always popular with those good people," she said. "I held that the right or wrong of abortion is not the issue. A girl's body is her own, not government property. She makes her decision, right or wrong. Period."

And, as the waiter poured the last of the wine, she said, "What happened to your—social interests? You were so earnest about them."

"You may have seen my books on Tibet and East Timor, with my wife's photographs. I'm proud of those. I'm on some boards. Trying to do something about land mines, for one."

There was a fine pink glow to her cheeks from the wine. She said, "You know, I worry about sin. What is it that such a religious fuss is made over it? That Jesus died to save us from? Sleeping with someone whose divorce is not yet final? Coveting a friend's fancy car? I think sin is land mines. This nation has been at war almost continually since World War II, and everywhere we've fought we've left land mines to blow the feet and legs off children. I remember once you said Manzanar was our fault. Land mines are our fault! We will be punished for them!"

I said I agreed, and she nodded with a sharp dip of her chin.

"May I inquire what caused the change in you?" I asked. "Bonny to Barbara."

"Let's just have a pleasant time denouncing land mines, shall we?"

She sat with her face turned down in the candlelight. She said, "What did you want of me back then? Just—physical? I thought there was something else."

"You were Mission Hills, and the Daltreys had been ejected from that promised land, so to speak. Well, and I thought you were beautiful. If not beautiful, infinitely attractive. It had something to do with my exposure to those tot molestation clippings at *the brand*. That obsessed me then. You seemed to me to be some kind of armored rebuke to any such disasters. You were a symbol for the way things ought to be."

Bonny laid her hands to her cheeks again, as though to conceal her face from me. "Can I see you up north?" I asked.

"Of course." She smiled with a queer stiffness of her cheek muscles, rose, put down her napkin, and took up her purse. Dinner was over.

I parked beside her rental Ford, but she made no move to open the door. We sat in the Jag looking out over the lights of Glendale as we had spent a host of nights, aroused and unsatisfied in each other's arms, looking from Point Loma to the lights of San Diego.

"I was pregnant," she said.

I understood, like a roof falling in. "Coming down from LA?"

"Yes."

Premature ejaculation is the curse of the American male. I thought it best not to enunciate that. "Sorry," I said.

"I was very angry," Bonny said. "I was angry at you, at the whole trap of women, gender, God, San Diego, Johnny Pierce, my mother, myself getting pregnant at the drop of a sperm, the games you and I played that of course I should have known were Russian roulette. Mostly you. You told me you hadn't—connected. But a sperm had crash-landed in the *Zona Pellucida*."

"Sorry."

"Wasn't there a way of fizzing a Coke bottle—?" She made a sound like a laugh, not as though she thought anything was funny.

"Back to Tijuana?"

"I wasn't going to do that. I finished the year at State, then I went up to Menlo Park to my aunt Honey. I stayed with her till I had it. The baby. A girl."

"Sorry," I said again.

"They took her away immediately. I hardly saw her. That was the way you did things then. Gone. Out of my life. I was furious all over again. I was a furious girl. I got straight *A*'s in premed in my fury. I tried to write you letters as though nothing had happened."

"By the time I got the telegram you were engaged."

"I thought you should come home and marry me," she said. "But you didn't respond. Let me tell you," she went on. "That first year of medical school. There were two women. Gloria and me. The demands for sexual favors were—just intolerable. It was what you would have called molestation. You know, it still goes on. I was on the ethics committee for two years—" She blew her breath out in a hard sigh.

"Gloria and I decided if we were married they couldn't hit on us so. I'd read a book about the female prisoners on the convict ships sent to Australia. They had to take on one crewman, or all. I sent the telegram to you. I don't know how I thought you could have flown home from Europe just because I needed you. I guess I thought you'd be wounded, and I'd nurse you and they wouldn't keep after me because I was the wife of a wounded hero. But you didn't answer, and there was a nice young intern named Dan I liked. He and I and Gloria and Jim Higgins were married. It was supposed to be temporary. Gloria and Jim divorced right after med school, but Dan and I just went along." She said bitterly, "Until a young bimbo with a cute bottom and a talent for oral sex got after him."

"I understood that med school was an ordeal."

"A terrible hostility from the men students. The old complaint that women wouldn't stay the course, they'd just get married and become housewives, so their medical education was wasted. You know, it was so bad I just *wouldn't* quit!"

Sorry. I didn't enunciate it this time.

"I'm so apologetic about the letters. I knew they must have been infuriating. But I was so intent on my ordeal and my goal, and we were supposed to write cheerfully to our men abroad. Someday. Someday I'll tell all."

"Now."

"I'm going now," she said, still leaning forward with her face in shadow. "This has been an emotionally exhausting evening. Please let me go. I shouldn't have said that about Dan's new wife," she said. "I'm sure she is a perfectly nice young woman."

I went around to open the door for her.

"Haven't you tried to contact your daughter?"

"Why, are you interested?"

"Of course."

"I guess I thought it was her part to try to contact me!" She touched my arm, said, "Good night!" and hurried to her own car. The lights jumped out ahead; the motor roared. She was gone. I sat behind the wheel with a hand on my chest.

Back in San Francisco, I felt a curiosity about my new daughter that came in waves almost like the grief I had felt when Gretchen died. After some days I called Bonny in Palo Alto. The number did not answer, and there was no message. After a week I became concerned. I knew her Santa Monica daughter's name was Pearsall. It took some detective work to acquire her telephone number.

Ellen Pearsall had a cool voice. Her mother had flown to Paris.

When I mentioned my name she warmed a little. "Of course I know of you, Mr. Daltrey. She belongs to a medical group called Doctors with Wings. There's a group of them going to Africa. The Sudan! She volunteered as the Gynecologist. She's too old to still be doing that, Mr. Daltrey!"

"A good cause," I said.

"Oh, yes."

What would I have done if Bonny's telegram had arrived promptly, deserted?

A phone call from Bonny, back from the Sudan, on my answering machine: "Payton, it's Barbara. One of the other docs on this trip I'm just back from has an assistant who used to work in a private detective's office. She says she can find anyone who is not actually trying to hide in four phone calls. I gave her what information I have, and we'll see what she comes up with."

I called back to leave a message on Bonny's machine. *Good for you.*

Chapter 17

1986

Water in the west was a huge factor of man's abuse of his planet—from the hydraulic miners washing the Sierra down to clog the rivers and the Bay, to Powell's disregarded warnings on the poorly watered West, to the rape of the Owens Valley, to the San Joaquin Valley water wars. I had notebooks full of notes on a water-in-the-West project, sheafs of xerox copies, two shelves of books with bookmarks marking pertinent chapters. But I lacked the push to get started. Against my will a novel was stirring in my mind.

The shock of a daughter of whose existence I had not known, coming into my life. Coming into a protagonist's life.

It was like some shaggy shy beast nine-tenths concealed from me, but whose existence I could not ignore. A French son? Or a daughter? Conceived during the war and bursting into a middle-aged man's settled life, with what? Reproaches? Condemnations? Happy celebrations? Recriminations? Realizations of blinding joy? Retaliations? Epiphanies of longing?

Not French. Not gay. Straight American. It began to seem, as this presence reluctantly, hugely, dragged itself a little further out of its concealment, that it was the story of a life not my life but close to it, of which San Diego before the call to war was the beginning, the war itself the brief middle, the after-war stretching out into—what? Ending—how? Certainly a change of course with the arrival of the by-blow offspring. And they were *all* in it, whom I had vowed I would never molest again!

It was as though I were waiting for something to occur before I faced this intrusion into my life.

And here it was, a week after Bonny's communication, a phone call from my agent in New York. *American Literature,* a prestigious literary journal, was publishing a series of "classic" American novels. *Gates of Bone,* cited by them as such a book, was just out of print from a university press and so available. This publication was a signal honor for my old novel. I was designated a novelist again.

The phone call was followed by a letter informing me that I had been chosen by the San Diego Historical Society to receive its 1986 award for local writers and artists, specifically for my acclaimed 1958 San Diego novel *Gates of Bone.* Signed Marian Wright, President. I was to be honored at a dinner and presentation at the Hotel del Coronado on October 17. It was hoped that I would give a reading from *Gates,* or from other work that might pertain to San Diego, the next afternoon at the Historical Society's headquarters in Balboa Park. There would be copies of my books for sale at that event.

Gates was still remembered locally, apparently, and was to be republished nationally. It was time for me to go home to San Diego to be celebrated.

There had been no more communications from Palo Alto on the subject of our daughter, but the assumption was that Bonny was working on it.

Along the interstate on the outskirts of San Diego, vast housing developments had blossomed, congealing around the east shore of Mission Bay. I angled off the freeway in Old Town and climbed into Mission Hills, checking to see if my pulse had quickened. The Boningtons' house was as I remembered it, home of the golden girl of my youth.

On up Presidio Drive to the Daltrey house, heart beating faster here, all right; smaller than recollection, front lawn less steep, the big plate-glass west window curtained. I remembered my father's announcement that the house would have to be sold, because he had lost his job, because of the Depression; he had stood in the kitchen, with that slant of his shoulders in his checked shirt and necktie. I remembered the burn of outraged tears. (Or did I only remember the scene as I had fictionalized it, my father standing against the kitchen window with a kind of halo around his head and shoulders from the morning sun?) But surely I remembered the real estate man with his clipboard and snippy remarks. The sunroom, or son room, at the back of the house had been mine, where I'd learned to type copying out fight scenes from novels I'd read, for a one-of-a-kind anthology of heroic fights. Where was that historical document now?

The trees along the streets were already in blossom, in February. I remembered the San Diego early bloom, the soft air, the spring high fogs my mother had hated.

I drove on out of Mission Hills into Hillcrest, past the site of my grandmother's bungalow, which had been replaced by a pinkish, Moorish apartment building; on past Grant School. Once a cemetery had adjoined it, where boys had gathered for fights. In some connection I couldn't remember, the cemetery was called "the burying ground."

Confused trying to make my way back to the interstate from Hillcrest, I continued on downtown by routes engraved in the creases of my brain from my college after-school delivery job—elbow out the window, cap on the back of my head, patent leather bow tie stuffed in my breast pocket, headed back to Perry's Fine Foods to unload empty grocery boxes and flirt with Lois Meador, the dispatcher. My spirits lightened as I cruised on down the long grade along the park as though finished with an afternoon's deliveries.

Downtown San Diego had been much redeveloped, the south-of-Broadway bar-and-whorehouse part of town of my other job, at "that Commie rag," was now the scene of vast new constructions amid a flattened wasteland. San Diego had become a big renewing-itself city.

A high swoop of bridge crossed San Diego Bay to Coronado, from which the red roofs, cupolas, and turrets of the Hotel del Coronado were visible, another great intact pastness, whose lights at night, we had been told, had caused L. Frank Baum to dream of the Emerald City of Oz.

The Hotel del had been the scene of Saturday night dances, of friends and girlfriends and the increasing preponderance of uniforms in those days, of my brother and the future movie goddess Liz Fletcher, and Errol Flynn and the yacht *Sirocco*; all changed, enlarged, new and disorienting now. I was delivered to a third-floor room with windows that gave a glimpse of tennis courts, a slice of bay, a tacking sailboat. I ordered a whiskey from room service to quiet my nerves.

The steps down into the ballroom were like a descent into memory, the space smaller than remembered, and no central reflecting globe sent flecks of colored light coursing over uniforms and bright formal gowns. Tables were set up for the banquet, and early guests milled around a wine bar. Approaching them, I limped slightly, as I was aware I did under stress. There was Pogey Malcolm threading the crowd toward me, lean as a marathon runner, brown visage creased with age and sun. We clasped hands and grinned at each other. My oldest friend.

"Poge!"

"Payt!"

Men in dark suits and women in party dresses collected around us. Someone I recognized but couldn't identify patted my shoulder. I was the center of attention of this clutch of locals, beaming at me, shaking my hand. Fraternity brothers from State! San Diego people!

"Time to fess up, Payton Daltrey!" a heavyset fellow with a chin beard boomed at me. "Who is she?"

"We've been speculating all these years. Who was she, Payton?"

"Who?" I said.

"Eve Corey!"

"Emma Bovary, actually," I said.

This produced merriment. I was feeling light-headed, as though some blood-pressure medication side effect had kicked in.

"We figured out who Lyn was!" a lady with an exposure of pale bosom advised me. "You gave it away when you mentioned that her older sister had taken arsenic on the train down from SC. That had to be the older Roberts girl, right? So Lyn was Connie Roberts, right?"

They hadn't recognized Barbara Bonington! I cleared my throat and said, "My lips are sealed!"

More merriment, more people.

It had been decided who Jack was; not me, but Russell Ford, whom I'd known slightly. There were good reasons for Jack to be identified as Russell Ford. Of course Pogey, standing half behind some others, knew who the real characters were. And Bonny knew, who wasn't here! I'd done better than I thought concealing the real in the fictional. Why did I feel disoriented and embarrassed?

A glass of white wine was pressed on me.

"Here's to the famous author!" someone said.

A plump lady from the Historical Society staff who had visited Tibet had read my Tibet book and wanted to compare notes.

A humpbacked old gent with a head of white hair as fine as silk sidled up to me. "My name's Meador," he said. "You'll remember Lois. She was sure proud of you, Mr. Daltrey. Bought your books. Lois passed away last year."

I remembered Lois with some damp and heat in the eyeballs. Lois! "Glad to meet you, Mr. Meador," I said to the man I had cuckolded.

"Ray," he said, smiling, and moved away.

"Glad to see you all!" I muttered.

My son, Jon, the professor, appeared, a broad-shouldered young man in a blue blazer, hair rather long, pale Wisconsin face, Uncle Richie bar of eyebrows, straight-lipped mouth with deep-set corners of humor. We high-fived, which was the greeting he seemed to have decided to be proper for a father and son both in the literature racket. I must excuse Nora for not having come to San Diego for the festivities; parental duties in Madison. Sister Dinny also sent love and congratulations.

Jon was thirteen, Diane eleven when their mother and I divorced. She had custody, and I had made myself too busy to play much of a role in their growing-up lives.

Marian Wright was a gray-haired lady in teal blue with a short jacket. She named names, so that I began to connect faces. There was name-dropping and name-remembering. I didn't mention Bonny but did inquire of the girlfriend before her, Martha Bailey.

"Marty has not aged well," Marian Wright said with a tight smile.

Drugs? A sherry drunk?

Pogey asked how the writing was going.

"Between books," I said.

He flourished a hand at the scene around us. "Well, you are historical, that's for sure."

"It seems a lot of people have been figuring out who everybody was, mostly wrong."

"Not all," he said.

"Sorry," I said, and added quickly, "Actually I've been thinking about another novel."

He gave way to a dignified old fellow who had been a neighbor of the Daltreys on Presidio Drive and wanted me to know he collected my books. When could I inscribe them for him?

"I'll be glad to tomorrow," I said. "At the reading at the Historical Society."

We were seated; wine was poured and soup served in a pleasant clamor of San Diego voices. At my table were Marian Wright and her husband, a husky chap with a toothbrush mustache; Pogey and Mrs. Pogey, who eyed me brightly; a fraternity brother and his wife; and my son, Jon, who offered a toast.

Over dessert and coffee, Marian Wright proceeded to the podium and welcomed me back to San Diego. I was presented with a crystal slate engraved with my name, the name of my novel, and "First San Diego Writers and Artists Award, San Diego Historical Society, 1986."

I addressed in colloquial style the faces gazing up at me (I'd done this kind of thing before), easy but slightly diffident. I reminded them of Grant School in Hillcrest, the principal, Mr. Cable, with his hard right paw, the cemetery behind the school, where boys' fights took place, and where I'd thought someone's euphemism "burying ground" referred to the blackberry bushes that grew there, and where, during the war, one of the barrage balloons had been anchored.

And there at a table in the back of the room, back from delivering babies in the Sudan, was Dr. Barbara Rothenberg, displaying a flash of gleaming silver hair. In a clamor of recollected emotions I thought her classy and handsome.

After the festivities, I sat with Pogey in the bar off the lobby, pink tile floor beneath our feet, marble-topped table shaded by a rubber plant with narrow dark green leaves like spear points. Glancing toward the main lobby for a glimpse of Bonny, I had to recall that that had been an element of my friendship with Pogey—my not quite paying attention to the conversation because I hoped to see my girlfriend.

The crystal plaque of my San Diego reknown rested on the table on its T-shaped foot.

Pogey wore a starched white shirt, a Thai silk tie, and a thornproof tweed jacket too orange for my taste. A rich boy, he had always worn expensive clothes.

He was stirring sugar into his coffee. His complexion was the result of time in the sun. His company took on projects all over the world.

He said, "We were going to be writers together once, if you remember. I know writers write what you have to write. How did Bonny like the Abba-Zabba Bar?"

"It has not been mentioned."

He grinned at me.

"*Epater les bourgeois,*" I said.

"What's your new novel about, besides love and war?" he asked.

"Generations."

He sat gazing at me with his brown eyes in his brown, creased patient face. "I suppose this one will also have your old left-liberal stance," he said. "Do I remember Sam Goldwyn saying, 'If you want to send a message, call Western Union?'"

I said, "I remember what Handel said when someone congratulated him on the *Messiah* entertaining a vast audience. 'I didn't mean to entertain them, I meant to make them better!'"

He chuckled and said, "Long time between novels!"

"I was feeling bad about turning people I loved into characters."

"I was okay with it," Pogey said. "Maybe it was tougher for Bonny."

"It was toughest on my father, but he was dead by then."

Pogey's chair scraped back as he stood to greet his wife, and there was Bonny approaching. She looked just the way I wanted her to look in beige silk. Jon showed up also, who didn't resemble me particularly.

Bonny's face looked younger now that she had let her hair go silver. She had a way of raising her chin, which I realized was to minimize the loose flesh of her throat.

A big black man with a formidable corporation and grizzled curly hair, wearing a five-hundred-dollar tan suit, approached me closer to me than was comfortable and said, "San Diego's own prideful boy!"

"Calvin!"

"Congratulations, child!"

I hesitated, but he did not; we embraced. There was a lot of him, solid meat and bone. He smelled good, too: He grinned at me out of his dark face, gold in his smile, saggy bags beneath his eyes.

I introduced him to the assembled as Calvin King.

"Goodrich," he corrected me, shaking hands around. "Mayor sends his regards," he said to me.

Everyone was struck silent by this presence. I would never have recognized him as the slim, handsome young athlete who had been Calvin King. Many pounds, a darker face, and a great deal of dignity had been accumulated. Pogey would remember him; to Bonny he would only be someone I had talked about.

"These folks in your book, too, child?" Calvin asked, cutting his baggy eyes from one to another. He seated himself with some fuss because of his bulk.

"Not I," Jon said, who looked at ease in this difficult company.

"Nor I," Mrs. Pogey said.

Calvin said to Bonny, "You were the girlfriend, right?"

"I'm afraid so, Mr. Goodrich," Bonny said. She seated herself with her fingertips propped together.

"Cal," Calvin advised her. He said to Pogey, "I remember you."

"You were the football player," Pogey said.

"Handle minority contracts and such out of the mayor's office," Calvin said. "Child here had the usual whitey-fiction minority problem. Black sidekick stuck in his book to show what a fine no-prejudice fellow the hero is."

I grinned at him. He didn't grin back. I hoped he was joking. My character Jack with his black friend, and his gay friend; to show he was a good guy? I hardly remembered how I had thought about the lineup of characters.

Finally Calvin winked.

"It was just such politically correct characterizations of fifties fiction that helped this country move along politically," Jon said.

Defended by an English lit Ph.D.! Drinks arrived and were distributed. Calvin signed the tab.

I was oddly gratified to be among the characters of my last novel.

A young man appeared out of the shadows of the corridor, approaching me. He looked Hollywood, a shock of black hair over an old-young face modishly decorated with a growth of whiskers, a black suit over a black T-shirt.

"Payton Daltrey? Congratulations on your novel being republished! A lot of us always knew it was a classic."

I thanked him.

"I'm Jamey Fletcher." The name meant nothing to me. A slim blonde beautiful as a candle flame had appeared behind him.

"I'm Elizabeth Fletcher's son. This is Maria Pemberton. Payton Daltrey, Maria."

Hers was a name, face, and figure one might have run across in a *People* magazine in the barbershop.

"Liz's son!" I said, and wrung his hand. Introductions were made, chairs arranged. Everyone seemed to be watching me, not Liz's son.

"Liz's son by whom?" I asked.

"Martin Ayoob. I prefer to use my mother's name. He was a studio exec at Twentieth Century. I'm Fletcher Properties. We option film rights and provide a script and maybe a star, and offer the package to a studio. Guess what I'm interested in, Payton!" He glanced around him with a bright expression. Miss Pemberton slumped languidly in her chair.

"Your mother was interested in it also."

He barked a laugh. "She was way too old for Eve!"

The waitress returned, and he ordered Pellegrino water for himself, a fancy vodka for the blonde. Mrs. Pogey was leaning forward, watching him intently.

"It's historical, but historical's okay just now," Jamey said.

Bonny said to me, "Did Liz approach you about making a film of your novel?"

"She did."

Jamey was nodding vigorously.

"And you turned her down?" Bonny said.

"I did. She wanted Eve to be the main character."

"San Diego's proud of that lady!" Calvin said, hands spreadfingered over his considerable belly. "Who was it called her Miss Lovely Lips?"

"Louella Parsons, surely," Mrs. Pogey said.

"We're concentrating on Jack and Lyn," Jamey said. "Milly Grover's available for Lyn."

"Oh, my goodness!" Mrs. Pogey said, impressed.

I warned myself against thinking of Jamey Fletcher as a character in my new novel, who was thinking of my old novel as a film.

He said to me, "I have a fellow working on a treatment. Do you want to see it before we talk?"

I shook my head. "Just talk to my agent. It sounds fine to me. He's Bernie Oster."

"I know Bernie!" Jamey said. Drinks came. Miss Pemberton sipped hers. She and Jamey spoke admiringly of the young star Millicent Grover. I was trying to recall the emotions I had felt against Liz making over the character of Eve.

"These all friends of my mother's, Payton?" Jamey asked, smiling around at the assembled. Pogey raised a finger. After a moment Bonny did also.

"Miss Lovely Lips helped put San Diego on the map!" Calvin said. "Her and the child here. She'd hang out with Errol Flynn on his yacht!"

Jamey had a way of nodding as though to some interior monolog.

"Your mother was a protegée of Errol Flynn's," Mrs Pogey said.

"She loved him! You know, he made her get out and meet other men in order to marry someone who could hustle her career along better than he could. That was my father. Lucky for me! But Flynn was always part of her life! She took me along to his memorial service. I was thirteen, fourteen. She wept!"

I said, "She was surely a bankable star when she was interested in *Gates of Bone*."

"She knew how to be a star!" Jamey said.

"Jamey's proud of his mom," Miss Pemberton said, holding her glass of vodka up before her face as if in a toast.

"Proud of my mom!" Jamey said, nodding.

Bonny and I escaped to my room for a highball. She stood facing me, glass in hand, her face tight.

"Her name is Laura Mason," she said. "She is in the state prison at Corcoran."

Dear God! "Drugs?" I asked.

"Marijuana." She paced, halting to gaze out the window at night and palm trees. "Eighty percent of the women in prison in this country were convicted on drug charges," she went on. "In this country with five per-cent of the world's population and twenty-five percent of its convicts. Women are punished with longer terms because the men often have infor-mation they can exchange for reduced sentences. The drug war!"

"What can we do?"

"Nothing for her, I don't think. But there's a child. Gabriella."

I sat perched watching her, highball in hand. She gestured with her free hand to some thought she did not speak aloud, holding the highball glass to her chest.

"Did you see Laura?" I asked.

"I went to see her."

"Is she ours?"

"She surely is. She had found out who I was before she went to prison but hadn't acted upon it. Her adoptive mother had died, so she went look-ing for her birth mother."

"What's she like?"

"I liked her, though maybe that is only nature at work. She claims she is not guilty. Her lover, her child's father, is an American-born Mexican named Rodolfo Herrera. She was working as a clerk in a sports shop helping him to earn a degree in accounting at Orange Coast College in Costa Mesa. She didn't know he was dealing marijuana. The police raided their apartment and found the stash in his car. He'd been out in *her* car with the child in the car seat, and he came back, saw the police cruisers, and fled to Mexico. The child is now with his sister in Tijuana. Laura is afraid the sister's brute of a husband is abusing the child. I said we'd rescue her. Will you come with me?"

"Sure."

Bonny blew out her breath with a sigh. She sat down. "When will you be finished being famous?"

"Tomorrow afternoon."

"We'll go down Monday. That's what I told the lawyer in Tijuana, any-way. Payton, I have no idea what she's like. She was just a pathetic female in prison garb. She has blue eyes. She is slightly plump. She seemed intelli-gent. She's forty-four. Her child is three. I thought she was telling the truth. She cosigned for a loan with Rodolfo to pay for his tuition and books at the college, and he used that money to buy pot instead. To deal. Those terrible Rockefeller mandatory sentencing laws have put her in prison for twelve years for cosigning that note."

"What do we do about the child?"

"Through Chuck Hennings in Palo Alto, I contacted a law firm in Tijuana that deals with things like this. They will take care of getting the child away from the sister. We'll have to pay her two thousand dollars. There will be the lawyer's fees and some expenses. Up for it?"

"Up for it."

She rose to pace again. I admired her competence. I wondered what it would be like to live with it. She sipped her highball as she paced, halting again to gaze out the window south toward Mexico.

"What was it like in the Sudan?" I asked.

"It was an absolute horror with a few bright spots. One must cling to the bright spots."

"I suspect you were one," I said.

She sighed again. "I'm not sure of that, I have a difficult time with male managers. I heard the chief of the mission say, 'Just what we need, an effing female gynecologist!' We were in a Moslem country where a female's private parts range from her neck to her instep. A hundred women had been raped by the Arabs. What could a *male* gynecologist have done? I'm afraid I railed at him."

She turned. Her face was tight and tragic. "Payton, I'm sorry I have no better news about our daughter."

"What will we do with the child if we bring her back?"

"My second daughter might take her."

Or my daughter, Dinny.

Bonny said, "Did you really turn Liz down when she wanted to make a movie of your book?"

"I did."

She stood looking down at me. I knew what she was thinking because it was what I was thinking. But she said, "I'm going to leave now. You know, I've never forgotten what you said once, 'If there wasn't any danger of pregnancy, or anybody getting screwed up, or people finding out—Then!' But I'm a troubled mother. Do you understand?"

I said I understood. Tomorrow, as Scarlett O'Hara said at the end of *Gone with the Wind,* was another day.

Bonny slipped out the door.

The next afternoon I drove with Jon back over the high bridge across the Bay to San Diego, to the Historical Society headquarters in Balboa Park, for my reading.

Jonathan Daltrey's stance with me was, I had always thought, one of veiled condescension. As a professor of English, he was used to dealing with authors of considerably more stature than his father.

"What's a MacGuffin?" he asked. "It's a word you used in your last note."

"It's a Hollywood term. Hitchcock, I think. It's the thing everybody is looking for. The good guys and bad guys. Like the Maltese falcon."

"It is not listed in my dictionary of rhetorical devices."

"I'll bet it isn't," I said. "It's the Holy Grail. It's the White Whale. It's your old true love whom, because of some dramatic, romantic, or symbolic events, you are unable to forget."

His eyes bugged a little. "I understand that Dr. Rothenberg is related to your Lyn Burton."

"That's right."

"I always assumed the book was a reflection of your own early life. I read it again, Dad. It's good! But tell me; why did you back off from the happy ending?"

"Maybe I was trying not to be commercial," I said. "Maybe I didn't want a happy-ending novel. Maybe I didn't really know what I was doing."

"Seemed to me you knew what you were doing," Jon said.

"I was no genius, you see," I rattled on. "I was a quarter genius, like a quarter horse. Good for short sprints but not a long haul."

"You were a genius to Dinny and me. Are."

"Thank you," I said.

"Mother said it was tough having a genius around the house. She had to explain to Dinny and me that you were actually working when you were lying on the couch reading *Time* magazine."

"And just how is your mother these days?"

He took a deep breath. "Dad, I am trying to tell you that Dinny and I are proud of you and your career, and you change the subject!"

"Sorry," I said, hot mist in my eyes. "Thanks," I said.

―――――――

There was a lecture room containing about forty people on clinky metal folding chairs. There was Pogey and his wife, who had come from Dallas; there was my son from Madison; there were three Alpha Betas from my years at State; there were other familiar faces. And there was Dr. Barbara Rothenberg with her head of shining hair, in a blue jacket and skirt, in the second row.

Some had brought books for me to sign, among them a number of battered copies of *Gates of Bone* breaking loose from the boards. I signed a lot of books. There was a new edition in press!

A young San Diego novelist with a gold ring in his ear begged me to read his novel in galleys, so as to give him a blurb. He had caught me at a vulnerable time.

I stood at the podium, gave a humorous, phony little preamble to show I was one of the folks, and began to read from the first chapter of *Gates*:

"The first time I saw Lyn Burton, the young woman with whom I have been concerned for much of my long life, the first time I paid attention to her, anyway, was December 8, 1941. We were all in the Caff at San Diego State College that Monday morning, listening to the terrible news on the radio, the losses, the deaths, the Day of Infamy, the declaration of war. The Japs! We drank coffee or Cokes and listened to the bad news. No one knew then how much more bad news we were going to hear before some good news began to filter through—"

Back at the Hotel del Coronado, Jon departed for the airport. I had a drink with Pogey and Mrs. Pogey before they, too, departed.

Bonny and I had dinner alone together, with a bottle of Montrachet. There was some strain, which I counted on the wine to dispel: Bonny uptight about tomorrow, as I was also. Time for some poetry:

> "We shall not cease from exploration
> And the end of all our exploring
> Will be to arrive where we started
> And know the place for the first time."

"What's that, Payton?"
"It's T. S. Eliot. Referring to Tijuana, our destination tomorrow."

Female faces are enhanced by candlelight, as is well known. I didn't know how to tell Bonny I liked her sexagenarian looks. Her bosom might once have ridden some inches higher on her chest, and the hand she laid there from time to time was not the hand of a young woman. I remembered once observing that hand half-cupped before her on a table. The neat perfection of it had made the backs of my legs curdle. Her head was a helmet of sleek silver hair that had once been a golden helmet, and the pad of flesh beneath her chin was not the baby fat I had observed the first time I had taken notice of her, but a reminder that the skull shrinks with age. Her face had always had that golden glow of youth, health, sun, orange juice, and Mission Hills, and if that glow did not emanate from it now it was still locked in my eyes.

There was a flick of blue behind her glasses as she glanced back to meet my gaze.

"I used to rant about molestations," I said. "Maybe you remember."

"Indeed I do remember!"

"When I went to Tijuana with Calvin to look for an abortionist, we dropped in at the huge Tijuana brothel. At that time young girls from the interior were sent up to the Molino Rojo to make money to send home. Some of them had to commit sex acts with animals for a show."

"I don't remember you ranting about that."

"Times have changed, you see. Now the young girls from the interior are sent up to the border to work in the *maquiladoras.* Do you know what they are?"

"I've heard of them."

"Many are owned by Americans. As we know, the only thing wrong with capitalism is the greed of capitalists. There's no minimum wage in the *maquiladoras;* there's no OSHA. They are horrible sweatshops, and their effluent has poisoned the Tijuana River to a dangerous degree—and the Tijuana air. Not to speak of the workers. It is known that the girls in these sweatshops have to show their foreman their Tampax every month to prove they are not pregnant. Now, is that progress over having to screw dogs and ponies, or not?"

"Yes, Payton," Bonny said. "I suppose it is." Her face was creased with unhappiness, I thought for me rather than for the girls from the interior. I hadn't wanted to make her unhappy with my heavy-handed ironies.

"I see you are still a little nutty about molestation," she said lightly.

"Oh, I am!" I said. "Let me tell you another one. This concerns the

Maharishi University in Fairfield, Iowa. Do you know of the Maharishi? Meditation, the Beatles, all that?"

"Yes, Payton, I do," she said, watching me anxiously over her pressed-together fingertips.

"They practice levitation there," I went on. "It takes some intense meditation, as you can imagine. The men practice levitation under the Golden Dome. But the women have to levitate in the women's gym!"

Her face convulsed in laughter.

"Tell me, what could be wrong with mixed levitation?"

She continued laughing. It was as though she were getting over something.

She sobered to say, "In the Sudan, the Arabs murdered the men and raped the women separately." She leaned toward me. "But let me tell you about med school forty years ago. The teaching docs set up a seminar for just Gloria and me. The subject was something to do with male sexuality. We were told it was not proper for a mixed group of students to discuss the subject."

We laughed together, and finished the wine, and everything was just fine. In the elevator Bonny said, "Why me?"

"It was always you," I said.

Epilogue

"COULD THIS BE A TOT WE ARE GOING TO RESCUE?" I ASKED Bonny, as we sailed south on the freeway toward the border.

Her face inclined toward me.

"An abused tot," I said.

"I hated it when you were writing those pieces," she said.

"I went from writing about molested tots to writing about molested nations. I was trying to save nations when I should have been trying to save tots."

"Well, that is what we are doing," Bonny said. "Surely we can make her world a better place. Is that what you mean?"

In Tijuana a palmist had warned me to take care that love did not triumph over wisdom, and said that only the wise could transcend their gender.

"Try not to do any harm, anyway," I said.

At the border we were waved through by a stout, brown-uniformed Mexican in a salty brown cap. I felt a crunch of guilt at our conspiracy as soon as we were across the border in heavy traffic. I could see that Bonny's fingers were white clutching her handbag to her lap.

"Were you happily married?" she asked.

"The second time."

"What's it like?"

"If you don't know, I can't explain it to you. So you were not?"

She shook her head. "My fault. Well, circumstance. Did you sleep in the same bed?"

"Yes."

"We rarely did. Dan would be on call, or I would. We went to bed at different times."

"Too bad," I said.

Tijuana, the tourist section anyway, was not much changed from the Tijuana I remembered, no signs of *maquiladora* evils. Some bigger, more garish signs, traffic lights. I parked the Jag in a lot and with Bonny walked along past tourist shops, some touts beckoning, windows of silver, of leather jackets, of curios, tourists in twos and threes, shoeshine and chewing-gum salesboys, Mexican girls in jeans, on a corner a photographer with a cart hitched to a donkey painted with zebra stripes. The poisonous air smelled only of car exhaust.

We were to meet Miss Muñoz at Caesar's. I recalled that it was at the old Caesar's Hotel that Caesar salad had been invented. Rita Hayworth had been discovered dancing at the Foreign Club here. Bonny and I had come down to the Clínica Orozco on gynecology business in 1942.

Miss Muñoz wore jeans and a leather jacket. She had short black hair and a round face. She knew who we were on sight.

"Señora Rothenberg?"

Bonny introduced me.

"Señor Daltrey," Miss Muñoz said, shaking hands with a firm grip. "Come, we will have a margarita and speak on this matter. You have brought money?"

"I have brought money," I said. I did not wholly believe in my granddaughter yet, nor did I feel any real connection, except fictional, with the pathetic convict Laura Mason, my new daughter.

We were seated in a semicircular brown leather booth, margaritas ordered. Miss Muñoz addressed herself to me, more comfortable speaking to the male than the female in the case, although it was Bonny who had engaged her.

"You see, Señor Daltrey, Señor Serrato must be satisfied that this child is an American child, not a Mexican child."

She proffered her card to me. The law firm was Serrato Hnos.

Bonny snapped opened her purse, brought out a folded square of paper, and handed it to Miss Muñoz.

"What is that?" I asked.

"Birth certificate. The father is an American citizen," she said to Miss Muñoz. "Of Mexican heritage."

Miss Muñoz glanced briefly at the birth certificate, refolded it, and handed it back. "That is very well, Señora Rothenberg. And the father, you say, is in Mexico?"

"In Oaxaca, we believe," Bonny said. She was sitting up very straight, her lips tucked in severely at the corners. There was considerable street noise from Avenida Independencia outside, a couple of drunk Americans in Hawaiian shirts in noisy conversation at the bar.

Miss Muñoz looked pleased when our margaritas arrived.

"It has been arranged," she said. "Señor Alberto Chaves is in *policía* custody for a day or two. This required a bit *moneda*, you understand, which has been entered on the *cuenta*."

"That is fine," Bonny said.

"He is a bad actor?" I said.

This had to be explained. "Yes, bad!" Miss Munoz said. "Señor Serrato thought he might find himself unsatisfied with the *moneda* agreed upon."

"I see," I said.

"I have survey the *casa*," Miss Munoz went on. "It is in very ugly part of town. It is not agreeable part of town for gringos. It is part of Tijuana where gringos may be exposed to unpleasantness. I say this because if it is wished I will perform the payment and bring the child."

I didn't look at Bonny. "I would like to come along," I said.

"I will also," Bonny said. "Have you seen the child?" she said to Miss Muñoz.

"Yes, I did, señora. She is a pretty child, but of little energy. I think this must be because of the bites."

"The bites?" I said.

"How do you say—*picaduras de pulgas*."

"Fleabites," I said.

"Good God!" Bonny said.

There was a reflective moment of sucking margaritas through the furnished straws.

"And tell me, please," Miss Muñoz said. "What is to become of the child when you have taken her to Estados Unidos?"

Bonny said firmly, "Mr. Daltrey and I will see that she is cared for. I have a daughter who may take her."

"And I," I said.

Miss Muñoz nodded as though crossing an item off on a list. "You have American car?" she wanted to know.

"English," I said.

"It will be best if we use Mexico car. I have *policía* to drive."

It was indeed a part of Tijuana not agreeable to gringos, very Social Reality. Winding rutted streets curving uphill in long swoops with sharp junctions, down into a populous gully, then up again, alongside stripped cars, trash along the cutbanks, shacks, Mexican music squawking from ghetto blasters, young men in groups on street corners, smoking, watching us, women hurrying, always carrying something.

Our *policía* was a heavyset fellow in a blue Yale sweatshirt and a cloth cap. He stopped before a shack with a rusting corrugated iron roof, a veranda stacked with collapsed cardboard boxes, windows with shades drawn like closed eyes.

Bonny blew her breath out in a sigh.

I have knee trouble detaching myself from a tight-quarters car. Taking Bonny's arm, I straightened my shoulders and tried to walk, looking respectable, if not formidable, under the gaze of a pair of young men who had appeared on the other side of the street, one in a hooded sweatshirt. Our *policía* sauntered over to them. Miss Muñoz led us to the veranda.

A woman with a bruised swollen face and frightened eyes opened the door a slice. Miss Muñoz spoke peremptory Spanish. I didn't understand her words or the reply, but Miss Muñoz turned to me with a finger raised. I handed her the wad of bills in the Hotel del Coronado envelope.

Behind us more men had assembled. The sun beat down under the roof of the veranda with a kind of coppery resonance.

The woman took the envelope from Miss Muñoz and tried to close the door again, saying, "*Momento,*" but Miss Muñoz inserted herself inside, again with the monitory finger raised to Bonny and me. Someone called out from the assembly across the street. I was sweating in the sun.

"What did he say?" Bonny wanted to know, clinging to her handbag like a life preserver.

"Don't know."

Then Miss Muñoz was back with a child in a complicated white dress and shiny black shoes, a child who looked up at me with astonishing blue eyes in a small beautiful tan face. Her forehead was sprinkled with scabs under brushed and bowed brown hair. Her eyes were so full of intelligence I almost staggered.

She murmured something.

"What does she say?" I asked Miss Muñoz.

"*Dice*, 'Are you my daddy now?'"

It seemed crucial not to lie. I bent to take her little paw and pat it between my two hands.

Bonny took her other hand, and we walked her back to the car under the gaze of the assembly across the street, which now included two women. Our *policía* stalked before them, hustling back as we loaded into the backseat. Miss Muñoz sat shotgun, head up, grim-faced.

"*Vamos!*" she said. The young man in the hooded sweatshirt lumbered closer to glare in the car window as we passed him.

Bonny blew out her breath. The child sat between us with her elbows drawn in, smoothing at the lap of her dress. I could smell her.

"Eaten alive," Bonny said in a stifled voice. "Fleas. Lice. Scabies," she whispered as though to herself. "I left my bag at the hotel!" she complained.

We were delivered back to Caesar's, where Bonny leaned over the hood writing a check to Miss Muñoz. Holding the child's hand, I started back toward the Jaguar in its parking lot.

"Go to my momma?" the child said.

I could feel the prickle of tears; how to respond to that? "Honey, we are surely going in her direction."

"But we—" The words trailed off.

"We are going to the United States," I said, and prayed that would suffice.

She pulled a little at my hand.

"Listen, tot," I said, "I am your grandfather. The lady is your grandmother. Your mother's mother and father. We love you very much. We have come to bring you back to the United States, where you will be safe and happy."

The intelligent eyes gleamed doubtfully up at me.

Bonny caught up with us, striding, swinging her purse. We loaded into the Jaguar, the child between us sharing Bonny's seat. I headed for the border, into the line of waiting cars glacially moving toward customs and immigration. Bonny gave our grandaughter her bracelet to hold.

"Pretty," the child whispered.

When we were four cars away from the gate, Bonny said casually, "Little one, will you sit here on the floor for a while so we can play hide-and-seek?"

She helped our child to seat herself on the floor mat in front of her seat, then extended her legs and spread her skirt to hide her, in high smuggler mode.

The immigration officer, with his bristly little mustache, looked in my window. "Where were you born?" he asked.

"San Diego," I said.

"San Diego," Bonny said.

We were waved on through.

Back in the USA our granddaughter was raised to share Bonny's seat again, with a seat belt around the two of them.

"Are you comfortable, honey?" I said.

"I not Honey, I Gaby!" the child said. "Go to my momma now?"

"First we're going to a hotel and take a bath, Gaby," I said.

Bonny sat with her hands pressed to her cheeks.

I knew what had shaken her. *I'm not Bonny, I'm Barbara.* Only connect, said E. M. Forster.

"It was when you changed," I said. "When you said you weren't Bonny."

"I was pregnant. It was the end of the world!"

"Mine, too," I said.

"When I realized the trap had snapped closed the scales fell from my eyes—whatever scales are—I saw woman's estate so clearly. My mother in her misery was able to make everyone around her miserable. Because she was only meat. That was Johnny's ugly word—meat. A girlfriend was the boy's meat. Gloria and I were meat to those docs at Stanford Med. Well, I was never going to be anyone's meat! I was never going to be Bonny again. I elbowed my way through life! I had put on the red shoes, and I couldn't stop dancing. They were so glad to get this female meat cleaver off their ethics committee! But in fact pregnant meant I *had* to get out of San Diego!" she said.

I nodded.

"Last night you said you were starting another novel. Am I to be in it?" Gaby was craning her neck to look up at her.

"Afraid so," I said.

"Do you take me seriously, Payton? I have some accomplishments also, you know. I sit on ob-gyn committees at Stanford and UC Medical. I was cited on the Peninsula 'Best Doctors' list. I have been an associate in Doctors with Wings for eleven years. Do you know that this country has the highest infant mortality rates of any industrialized country in the world except China? Due to the lack of prenatal and postnatal care. I chair a Planned Parenthood committee working with Senator Findley trying to get legislation—" She grinned suddenly. "In the Sudan they had a name for me that translates as Madam Doctor Good Person!"

I said, "Madam Doctor Good Person, I will tell you the accomplishments that please me most. We've hardly seen each other for forty-five years, and yet we are parents, and grandparents of a beautiful little fleabitten granddaughter."

"With so little effort!" Bonny said, laughing.

"Would a family dinner with a bottle of Montrachet be out of order?"

"First I must go after these bites with Neosporin. Then!"

"We're all going to a nice place and take a bath and have dinner, Gaby," I said.

Gaby seemed to be humming. She was singing in a small, secret voice, hunched into a ball on Bonny's seat between us, twisting the bracelet between her grubby hands.

"That is such a pretty song, little cupid girl," Bonny said.

"I Gaby!" our tot corrected her.

"Insistence on her identity may mean her identity's been threatened," I said. "We don't know what went on in Tijuana." I tried not to sound pompous. "There is a famous case, a fellow who could fend off a bout of insanity by saying his name over and over. You would know about that, I guess."

"I Gaby!" Gaby insisted, her face raised tight-lipped to me.

"I guess I'm Bonny," Bonny said.

I wondered how rough it was going to be.

Last night nothing significant as to the future had been enunciated, but everything had been significant. Personal relations: good. Long-postponed sex relations: good. Conversation: wide-ranging between bouts of lovemaking. Past: deplored, subject of laughter. Politics: okay. Religion: not discussed. Social responsibilities: agreement. Environment: ditto. Some feminist paranoia. I could discuss suffragist history intelligently, but perhaps with not enough partisan heat. Tacit disagreement on the literary quality of *The Golden Notebook,* enthusiastic agreement on *One Hundred Years of Solitude.* Agreement on opera. Could theater vs. the symphony be an issue? Golf vs. tennis? When her mother died, she intended to dedicate her inheritance to establishing a prenatal clinic for unmarried young women, mainly black or Latino, on an already selected site in East Palo Alto. My own future was concerned with a novel for which I had no title, no plot, some preused characters, a handful of scenes, and considerable dread.

In the end, happy-ever-after was surely not going to be as simple as golf vs. tennis.

I was amused at retracing a route we had taken forty years ago to rid Bonny's womb of a trespasser. Maybe but for the war there might have been another gynecology trip in Ol Paint, with a bundle in a bassinet. Instead we had Gabriella.

I laid my open hand on the leather seat in front of Gaby. Bonny guided her hand around the child's back to slip it into mine.

It was growing dark as we freewayed on up into San Diego, lights on and a flood of beams coming toward us, banks of red taillights ahead. We arched over the high bridge toward Coronado, heading to the Hotel del Coronado with its big bathtub in my bathroom, those lights sparkling and gleaming in the oncoming darkness like the Emerald City of Oz.